INHERITORS
OF CHAOS

What Reviewers Say About
Barbara Ann Wright's Work

The Tattered Lands

"Wright's postapocalyptic romance is a fast-paced journey through devastation. ...Plenty of action, surprises, and magic will keep readers turning the pages."—*Publishers Weekly*

The Pyradisté Adventures

"...a healthy dose of a very creative, yet believable, world into which the reader will step to find enjoyment and heart-thumping action. It's a fiendishly delightful tale."—*Lambda Literary*

"Barbara Ann Wright is a master when it comes to crafting a solid and entertaining fantasy novel. ...The world of lesbian literature has a small handful of high-quality fantasy authors, and Barbara Ann Wright is well on her way to joining the likes of Jane Fletcher, Cate Culpepper, and Andi Marquette. ...Lovers of the fantasy and futuristic genre will likely adore this novel, and adventurous romance fans should find plenty to sink their teeth into."—*The Rainbow Reader*

"*The Pyramid Waltz* has had me smiling for three days. ...I also haven't actually read...a world that is entirely unfazed by homosexuality or female power before. I think I love it. I'm just delighted this book exists. ...If you enjoyed The Pyramid Waltz, For Want of a Fiend is the perfect next step...you'd be embarking on a joyous, funny, sweet and madcap ride around very dark things lovingly told, with characters who will stay with you for months after."—*The Lesbrary*

"This book will keep you turning the page to find out the answers. ...Fans of the fantasy genre will really enjoy this installment of the story. We can't wait for the next book."—*Curve Magazine*

"There is only one other time in my life I have uncontrollably shouted out in cheer while reading a book. [*A Kingdom Lost*] made the second. ...Over the course of these three books all the characters have blossomed and developed so eloquently. ...I simply just thought this whole novel was brilliant."—*The Lesbian Review*

"Chock full of familiar elements that avid fantasy readers will adore…
[*The Pyramid Waltz*] adds in a compelling and slowly evolving romance.
…Set against a backdrop of political intrigue with the possibility of
monsters and mystery at every turn, the two women slowly learn each
other, sharing secrets and longing, until a fragile love blossoms between
them…"—*USA Today Happily Ever After*

Thrall: Beyond Gold and Glory

"Once more Barbara has outdone herself in her penmanship. I
cannot sing enough praises. A little *Vikings*, a dash of *The Witcher*,
peppered with *The Game of Thrones*, and a pinch of *Lord of The Rings*.
Mesmerizing…I was ecstatic to read this book. It did not disappoint.
Barbara pours life into her characters with sarcasm, wit and surreal
imagery, they leap from the page and stand before you in all their
glory. I am left satisfied and starving for more, the clashing of swords,
whistling of arrows still ringing in my ears."—*Lunar Rainbow Reviews*

"In their adventures, the women must wrestle with issues of freedom,
loyalty, and justice. The characters were likable, the issues complex,
and the battles were exciting. I really enjoyed this book and I highly
recommend it."—*All Our Worlds: Diverse Fantastic Fiction*

"This was the first Barbara Ann Wright novel I've read, and I doubt
it will be the last. Her dialogue was concise and natural, and she built
a fantastical world that I easily imagined from one scene to the next.
Lovers of Vikings, monsters and magic won't be disappointed by this
one."—*Curve Magazine*

Paladins of the Storm Lord

"This was a truly enjoyable read…I would definitely pick up the next
book. …The mad dash at the end kept me riveted. I would definitely
recommend this book for anyone who has a love of sci-fi. …An intricate
novel…one that can be appreciated at many levels, adventurous sci fi
or one that is politically motivated with a very astute look at present
day human behavior. …There are many levels to this extraordinary and
well written book…overall a fascinating and intriguing book."—*Inked
Rainbow Reads*

"I loved this. …The world that the Paladins inhabited was fascinating… didn't want to put this down until I knew what happened. I'll be looking for more of Barbara Ann Wright's books."—*Lesbian Romance Reviews*

"*Paladins of the Storm Lord* by Barbara Ann Wright was like an orchestra with all of its pieces creating a symphony. I really truly loved it. I love the intricacy and wide variety of character types…I just loved practically every character! …Of course my fellow adventure lovers should read Paladins of the Storm Lord!"—*The Lesbian Review*

Coils

"…Greek myths, gods and monsters and a trip to the Underworld. Sign me up. …This one springs straight into action…a good start, great Greek myth action and a late blooming romance that flowers in the end…"—*Dear Author*

"A unique take on the Greek gods and the afterlife make this a memorable book. The story is fun with just the right amount of camp. Medusa is a hot, if unexpected, love interest. …A truly unexpected ending has us hoping for more stories from this world."—*RT Book Reviews*

"The gods and monsters of ancient Greek mythology are living, breathing entities, something Cressida didn't expect and is amazed as well as terrified to discover. …Cressida soon realizes being in the underworld is no different than being among the living. The heart still feels and love can bloom, even in the world of Myth. …The characters are well developed and their wit will elicit more than a few chuckles. A joy to read."—*Lunar Rainbow Reviewz*

House of Fate

"…fast, fun…entertaining…*House of Fate* delivers on adventure." —*Tor.com*

Visit us at www.boldstrokesbooks.com

By the Author

The Pyradisté Adventures

The Pyramid Waltz

For Want of a Fiend

A Kingdom Lost

The Fiend Queen

The Godfall Novels

Paladins of the Storm Lord

Widows of the Sun-Moon

Children of the Healer

Inheritors of Chaos

Thrall: Beyond Gold and Glory

Coils

House of Fate

The Tattered Lands

Inheritors of Chaos

by
Barbara Ann Wright

2019

INHERITORS OF CHAOS

ISBN 13: 978-1-63555-294-2

This Trade Paperback Original Is Published By
Bold Strokes Books, Inc.
P.O. Box 249
Valley Falls, NY 12185

First Edition: March 2019

Credits
Editor: Cindy Cresap
Production Design: Susan Ramundo
Cover Design By Sheri (hindsightgraphics@gmail.com)

Acknowledgments

As always, this book wouldn't be possible without my writing groups: Angela, Deb, Erin, Matt, Natsu, Pattie, Sarah, and Trakena. Y'all only get better.

A continuing thank you to Bold Strokes Books and all its authors. When I'm with you, I'm home.

Thanks to all the readers who've loved this series. Let's geek out sometime.

I love you, Mom. You made it all possible.

Dedication

For David

CHAPTER ONE

Patricia Dué had to admit that Dillon seemed to know what he was doing. Even after their former ship, the *Atlas*, had crashed in the mountains to the north and Patricia's newly conquered mine had collapsed, Dillon looked confident. He marched toward the shattered tunnel, barking orders before the dust had a chance to clear.

Even Patricia responded to his commands, using her macro-psychokinetic power to lift rubble clear of the mine shaft while her follower Raquel used a mix of macro- and micro-psychokinesis to drill a hole so those trapped in the tunnels could climb out. The other members of Raquel's group—like Patricia, former inhabitants of the *Atlas*—used their powers to direct Raquel's drilling.

Patricia could sense the trapped people, too. With her myriad powers, she could help them stay alive until they were rescued. And she could heal them after that, but she could do nothing about the dead. The miners lifted the bodies free anyway, so many corpses, and Patricia thought again of Naos, of the hundreds of years she'd spent as a prisoner in a mind that used to be her own.

Patricia's terror at seeing the *Atlas* blaze overhead had faded a little. She had time to escape. Even with all her power, Naos couldn't teleport or fly. On the ground of the planet of Calamity, she'd have to walk like everyone else.

Patricia turned back to the corpses, determined that no one else would die. These were her people, now, even if telepathy had initially made them that way. She couldn't help a jolt of guilt; she'd brought them to this disaster when she'd taken over the small community. Naos wouldn't have come here if Patricia hadn't escaped from their shared mind.

Every other part of Patricia rebelled against that thought. She'd treated these people well, brought them together, brought them peace with their plains and hill dwelling neighbors. So what if she'd had to use telepathy to do so? In the end, they'd been happy to be convinced. At least she wasn't like Naos who seemed on a quest to turn everyone into clones of herself.

Patricia paused and waited for Dillon's snide voice to disagree, to call her a coward or some other vile name, but of course, he wasn't a guest in her mind anymore. She'd found a place to put him: in the body of Gale's mayor, the former Liam Carmichael.

Between the power users and Dillon's efficient orders, many of the miners made it out of the tunnels alive. Patricia watched as they hugged their comrades or wept over the dead. Some seemed to be weeping in relief that they still lived, but they didn't know how bad things were about to get.

First of the many problems she'd have to deal with: Dillon. Dillon's new body walked toward her with a confident stride, cockier than the mayor's steps had been. The mayor's body was handsome, fit, and in its twenties or early thirties. He had a brown ponytail and startling green eyes. Combined with Dillon's cocksure swagger, it was a very attractive package, even if looking at him also made her want to smack him. She was just glad he wasn't in her head anymore to read her attraction.

He nodded to the house where she'd put him inside his current body scant hours ago. She followed without a word, leaving Jonah, her servant inside Dillon's *old* body, in charge of the miners.

The mayor's two escorts were lying right where Patricia had left them when she'd knocked them unconscious. A young woman in leather armor and a slightly older man wearing metal; they weren't going anywhere unless Patricia's power let them.

"What are we going to do with them?" Dillon asked.

It was a test. Did he want her to suggest killing them so he could accuse her of being bloodthirsty, or should she say to spare them so he could call her weak?

Unless… "Nothing," she said. She wanted to say they were his problem and leave him to it, but with Naos on Calamity, she needed allies. "With a little prompting, they'll get used to you as the new mayor of Gale."

He rubbed his chin, then looked at his hand in surprise as if just recognizing his new body. Her powered senses detected a wave of happiness rolling off him. "I'll need you to pull some details from them if I'm going to pull off that charade."

"If either of them knew the mayor well, I can." She wished she'd paid more attention to the personality she'd pulled out of the mayor, but in her haste to bring Dillon out, she'd scattered Liam's thoughts in her own mind, and there was no putting his memories back together again. "When did you want...I mean, are you going to Gale now, or..."

"Don't worry, sweets." He lifted a hand before she could protest the nickname. "Patricia. I'll help you out with Naos, the big bad wolf." He looked at his new body as if admiring it.

She turned away, sickened. She'd stolen yet another body, something Dillon had chastised her for, but she hadn't had a choice. When she'd claimed his old body, it *had* been out of a selfish need for companionship, but now she had to stop whatever Naos had planned, both for her sake and everyone else's.

When she looked back, she caught Dillon glancing down the front of his trousers. "Ugh, grow up," she said.

"Just getting the lay of the land, sweetheart." He gave her a wink.

She rolled her eyes. "I only hope you approve."

He gave her a calculating look, then smiled, and she knew what he was thinking without reading him. He feared her powers now that he wasn't lodged in her mind like a tick. Good, that corrected their imbalance of power a little. If he became too cocksure, she could take what she needed about combat and defense from his memory and leave him to rot, even if that left her without his forceful personality. It was good to know she had options, even if they all seemed shitty.

The sight of the *Atlas* flying overhead had made Cordelia's belly go cold. She'd seen the ship before on two out-of-body experiences, and she'd never forget that sleek hull, the acres of rare metal that would drive any Galean wild.

And she'd also never forget the madwoman in charge of it.

"Fuck, fuck, fuck," Cordelia muttered as she'd watched the ship rattle and boom overhead, headed for the mountains in the north before its crash echoed across the plains. It would be causing havoc at the mine, shaking the mountains down around them, around Liam.

She was still staring, worry after worry piling in her mind until she realized Nettle and Horace were talking with the others, asking her what in the world was going on.

"It's the *Atlas*," she said. No one on the planet had seen it except for her and the people who'd been alive two hundred and fifty years in the past when the *Atlas* had first come to this planet and launched Cordelia's ancestors to the surface to be their worshipers. Now the truth was out, and people knew that the original *Atlas* inhabitants who'd remained in space so long ago weren't gods. They were all on the planet, revealing themselves as human, but they still had powers that put everyone else to shame.

And the greatest of them just joined the party. "Naos is on board, has to be."

"Why would she come here?" Nettle asked, sucking her sharp teeth.

"Are you sure?" Horace said at the same time.

"Can you reach Liam?" Cordelia asked Horace, hoping his telepathic abilities could stretch that far.

He frowned and shook his head. "Finding one mind among so many would be difficult, and with that Patricia woman around…"

Cordelia nodded. Patricia had easily subdued him when they'd visited the mine. But with Naos around, maybe Patricia would let down her guard or turn the mine back over to Gale in order to have some allies. No matter what, she had to see that working with someone was better than facing Naos alone.

"Can you astral project that far?" Horace asked.

Cordelia shook her head. The ability to leave her body was quite handy in many cases, but her range wasn't that far. That fact comforted her most of the time. Remembering when Naos had separated her mind and body still gave her nightmares.

"Do we go back?" Nettle asked, her head swinging between the mine in the distance and the long road back to Gale. In the swamp where her kind, the drushka, lived, the whorls and marks on Nettle's dark brown skin would have camouflaged her against the surrounding trees, but here on the plains, where the only colors were the green of the grass and the white of stone, she stood out starkly.

As for her question, Cordelia had no answer. Part of her wanted to run back to Liam at the mine, but if Patricia didn't want to let him go, there was little Cordelia could do. She needed Simon Lazlo, and he was in Gale. He was the linchpin who could combine enough power to bring someone like Naos down.

The sun was setting. Cordelia needed to decide. She wanted to hurry back to Gale so she could collect Simon, then take him to the mine to free Liam. But the track leading from the mine to Gale meandered between hillocks and ravines that cut through the plains. With lanterns, her party of paladins and scouts could stumble off the track and get lost, eating up more time.

"We set up camp."

By the time they unpacked, it was already dark, and everyone fumbled through setting up tents. Cordelia didn't feel like sleeping. She stripped her armor off and sat outside, staring at the blackness to the north. No giant balls of fire were consuming the mountains; she supposed that was a good sign. She didn't like the idea of leaving Liam to deal with Naos's shit, but he was already dealing with Patricia's. He'd been a fine soldier—better at taking a punch than giving one, but still—and now that he'd been living outside his hard-ass mother's influence for nearly a year, he'd come into his own as a leader.

She clenched her fists, fighting the urge to run to him through the dark, and trusting that he could handle Patricia, make an alliance with her.

But he couldn't handle a fight with the biggest, baddest power user in the universe. By the time Cordelia gathered Simon and got back to the mine, Naos could burn it all to the ground.

Horace sat beside her, and she expected a lecture about going to sleep, but he only said, "Why would Naos come here now?"

"To fuck with us," Cordelia said, certain of it.

"But she can fuck with us from space."

"Simon cut her a bit last time they fought, made it so she can't possess people."

"So?" He tossed a clump of grass into the fire, looking pissed. "She can still harass people telepathically. She could grab an asteroid out of the sky and throw it at us. Why put her body in jeopardy?"

"Maybe she likes the thrill." She remembered their last encounter, how tired Naos had seemed after tangling with every other power user on the planet, but she'd been determined as well, angry. "Maybe she thought of a plan."

Horace sighed, a big sound she could relate to, the sound of someone who was tired of being fucked with.

Cordelia nudged him and smiled. "You ready to kick her ass?"

He nodded, his dark eyes fixed on the fire. He pushed his brown hair off his forehead and rested his narrow chin in one hand. "But then we get left alone for a while, right? With nothing to worry about except sleeping?"

She thought about it and shrugged. "I could do without the mad, power-hungry gods, but if regular people didn't try to kill me now and again, I don't know what I'd do."

Instead of laughing, he seemed thoughtful, opened and closed his mouth several times.

"Out with it," she said, thinking of a recent conversation she'd had with his lover, Simon, about how their lives had changed. When he stayed silent, she remembered how quickly he'd volunteered to come on this mission when he could have stayed home and worried about nothing much.

"I get it," he said at last. "When we were living out on the plains for months, there was always something to do, mostly minor emergencies, but *something*. When we got back to Gale…" He hung his head. "I'm afraid I've become addicted to adrenaline."

"Happens to the best of us."

"Not to me," He put his head in his hands, and the firelight brought out gold highlights in his hair. "I've always wanted to be content."

She put an arm around his narrow shoulders. "You can be content and not be standing still. And once we sort Naos out, there'll always be more to do in Gale."

"I want to learn how to defend myself," he said. "Without powers."

She thought of how easily Patricia had thrown them around. "Being able to fight didn't save me from Patricia, either."

"Even so." His eyes seemed haunted for a moment. "With my power to regenerate my own cells, I could live…a really long time."

She nodded slowly. She supposed the idea of living longer than everyone else was a daunting thought. At least he'd have Simon to never grow old with. And he could regenerate anyone else he really wanted. She shivered at the thought. The threat of dying had been part of her life so long, she couldn't handle the idea that it wasn't in her future. "When we have a moment, I'll show you a few things."

He gave her a grateful smile. She returned it, then yawned, the stress of this whole situation getting to her. Her back felt like a bag of sand.

"May I?" he asked, his hand hovering.

"Please." She was so glad he now asked instead of just helping. Most people didn't mind the occasional jolt of healing. She probably hadn't minded in the past, but with all the various powers flying around lately...

His power flowed over her like a warm bath, soothing her muscles. She hesitated a moment, afraid not only of *looking* weak but of *feeling* weak. He probably already knew what she had in mind, being a telepath and all. She trusted him not to dig in her thoughts, but she was probably projecting for miles. "I, um, could use a good night's sleep if you've got one handy."

He grinned. "My pleasure."

He didn't follow her into her tent, but he didn't have to. As soon as her eyes shut, she fell into a deep sleep, not even waking when Nettle crawled in beside her.

When they reached Gale the next day, Cordelia found it quieter than usual. People hurried through the streets rather than congregating and sharing news. She hoped it was only the arrival of the *Atlas* that had everyone spooked, but she knew they couldn't be so fortunate as to have only one crisis at a time.

She dodged the questions of those who tried to stop her and went to the Paladin Keep first. Private Jacobs informed her that Simon Lazlo had been attacked twice, once when he was almost burned to death in a warehouse, then his home was raided by a group of kidnappers trying to steal the Storm Lord's children. And the paladins hadn't been fast enough to save one of them.

Face flushed and angry, blue eyes flashing, Jacobs reported that Miriam, one of the telepathic yafanai, had been left for dead outside Gale, her newborn stolen from her, but Simon had saved her life and wanted to go after the kidnappers.

Cordelia was torn. She'd rather march on the mine and use Simon's power to bash Patricia into acquiescence. Then they had to prepare for Naos. On the other hand, a kidnapped baby needed her help. That was a problem she could put her blade to, not one that would be solved with mind-fuckery.

Before Cordelia could speak, the ground in front of the keep churned, and several brown roots burst into the light, bringing with them Pool, the tall, lean, green-haired drushkan queen. Her long brown face seemed grim, narrow mouth turned down, green eyes hard and unblinking.

"I have heard of the baby being taken, Sa," she said before Cordelia could greet her.

Cordelia nodded. The drushka hated the idea of anyone attacking children. As nasty as relations had gotten between Pool's drushka and the drushka from the swamp, they'd never involved children in their fights.

"My scouts tell me these cowards have fled Gale," Pool said. "Their trail leads into the plains."

"Going where?" Cordelia asked. "Jacobs said they used powers, so they're yafanai, not plains dwellers. Pakesh is the only plains dweller with powers, and he was attacked along with Jacobs and Simon."

"Perhaps they have struck some bargain with another clan," Pool said, lifting her hands and dropping them. The stern look on her face said she wasn't interested in what the kidnappers might now be doing or their motives. She only wanted them dealt with, and Cordelia was inclined to agree, though they had to decide which problem to deal with first: a stolen child or the madness of Naos.

It was time for a council of war.

CHAPTER TWO

S imon sat among the branches of Pool's large tree, communing with Pakesh, the only plains dweller known to have yafanai powers after his people had stolen some of the drug that made those powers possible.

Only he'd eaten the drug instead of injecting it, and it made his telepathy and macro-psychokinesis fluctuate wildly, enough for him to need a babysitter for his power.

"Relax," Simon said, sensing Pakesh's tension.

Pakesh sighed and drew his legs up. He ran his hands through his dark hair, then rested his face in his palms. The drushka had left them alone for this practice, and nothing but the wind sighing through the leaves surrounded them.

Despite the comforting surroundings, Simon could relate to Pakesh's discomfort. He'd had many problems to frustrate him lately: people trying to kill him, caring for Dillon's children and their mothers. And he still hadn't shaken the guilt for Gale being sacked by the boggins, never mind that he'd only augmented their intelligence under Dillon's orders.

Still, Simon had helped. He'd loved Dillon. He couldn't help carrying a little blame for everything Dillon did because he hadn't *stopped* Dillon.

He'd made up for it since then by healing Gale's population after they'd been poisoned by the drushka and bolstering their crops so no one would go hungry. He couldn't blame Pakesh for letting something weigh on his mind.

But Pakesh wasn't even trying.

"Pakesh—"

"I don't want this anymore," Pakesh said, voice muffled by his hands. "I couldn't stop the people who tried to kill you, who took Miriam's baby."

A series of images flashed across Simon's mind's eye: going through the warehouse, something being dropped on his head, the sight of Miriam falling under an attack, the screams as Pakesh's power broke loose. If Simon hadn't recovered, Pakesh would have torn the building down around their ears, maybe even the whole of Gale.

"That wasn't your fault."

Pakesh gave him a look that was far too astute for a fifteen-year-old. "That doesn't matter."

"You can learn to control—"

"I don't want to learn!" The anger in his voice was enough to rattle the windows. "I want to go home." His voice broke on the last word. Before he'd gotten his power, he'd been part of a large family, comfortable with children, beloved by everyone. With the power had become unpredictability and ostracization. His journey with Simon had started out a grand adventure, but after all that had happened...

"You can't go home yet," Simon said softly, soothing the boy with power. "Not until you learn—"

"Take it away," Pakesh said, not looking at him, cheeks burning in shame. "Take the power away as you once took Horace's and your own."

Simon took a deep breath, trying to hide his shock and think of something to say. He'd stripped away his own power and that of Horace so no one could use them to gain immortality, but their powers had come back.

Because they were micro-psychokinetics. Healers. With Pakesh, the power might stay gone.

"You should think about this. I don't know if I could ever bring it back for you."

"I have thought. I don't want it back."

Simon sensed his pain, his regret. He'd been so proud when he could use his powers to help people, but he was also right in that he'd ended up hurting someone more often than not. And Simon didn't sense any doubt.

"All right," Simon said.

"Now?"

"So soon?" Even after what Pakesh had said, Simon still expected him to think about it, to use his powers one last time, to dwell on what might have been, but his face held nothing but anguish, and from what Simon could sense, he seemed to be straining to stay away from his powers, if such a thing could be said about part of one's own brain.

Pakesh nodded, and Simon nodded back. Without ceremony, he fell into his own power, closing his eyes to concentrate. When he'd done this to himself and Horace, he'd been in a hurry, hurting both of them. Now he went carefully, cell by cell, rearranging Pakesh's brain until the power centers had been eliminated. Horace had always been afraid of doing this, afraid of causing Pakesh brain damage, but Simon couldn't deny him.

Simon checked him one last time, making sure everything was in place before he withdrew his power. When he opened his eyes, Pakesh was beaming. Well, Simon hadn't accidently wiped out his ability to be happy.

"I can't feel it," Pakesh said. Then he frowned. "I can't quite remember what happened at the warehouse, but..." He shook his head, and his smile was back.

Well, a little damage had been inevitable. "No other gaps?" When Pakesh shook his head, Simon nodded, happy for him.

Pakesh stood. "Will you tell Horace I said thank you?"

"You're going now?" Simon asked, gawking.

"I meant it when I said I want to go home." He stood and reached for Simon's hand. "I'll go to Wuran's clan just east. I'm sure they can tell me where my people are."

It wasn't a far walk to where the Uri usually camped, but Pakesh would still need some supplies. He waited just long enough for Simon to get a few things together for him from the drushka, and then they had Pool hand them down to the ground where they walked to Gale's eastern gate. Simon watched the boy walk into the distance with hardly a backward look.

And he'd barely had time to feel any loss from the boy's absence before he heard Cordelia and Horace were back through the northern gate and wanted to meet with him in the Paladin Keep. They'd heard about Miriam and her baby, and he had no doubt they wanted to talk about Naos going overhead in the *Atlas*, too.

Even after Simon had healed Miriam, he hadn't been able to face her. When he got to the meeting room in the keep, he couldn't look at her because he hadn't been able to prevent her child being taken. He distracted himself by hugging Horace hello and holding his hand, wishing they could be alone for their reunion. He greeted Reach and Nettle as well, who explained they were only waiting for Cordelia.

Simon led Horace to a corner where a pitcher of water waited. After pouring a drink, he told Horace about Pakesh while Miriam sat at the table alone, and Nettle and Reach spoke quietly in drushkan.

"You did the right thing," Horace said quietly. "We should have seen it coming that he'd want his power gone." His power flowed over Simon, not just soothing but reassuring, loving. "Maybe we should have offered it from the first."

When Simon nodded, Horace glanced at Miriam before his voice spoke in Simon's mind. "How is Evan?"

Simon sighed, wishing there wasn't a need for Horace to ask about the baby telepathically, but he clearly didn't want to mention another child in front of Miriam. Of course, she was a telepath, too, but Simon trusted that Horace's shields were tight enough to block his signal from going anywhere but between the two of them.

"Fine," he whispered. "We're all living in the tree."

Besides Miriam, the other mothers of Dillon's children had been moved to Pool's tree for their protection. It was safe enough.

Unless Naos killed them all.

"I heard that," Horace said, adding a glower.

"I hoped we were done with Naos," Simon said.

"We wounded her. We didn't kill her."

"She can't possess people. I'm certain we hurt her telepathy in other ways."

Horace shrugged. "It's hard to predict what someone with brain damage will do. And we've already seen what such massive power can do to a human mind." He shuddered, no doubt remembering his friend Natalya. But Naos had helped her even though she had a fragmented personality. Now she was split in two, with Patricia Dué taking over Gale's mine and Naos coming from heaven to screw with them all.

"I felt something," Simon said. "When we struck at Naos that last time, I felt part of her…leave. I thought it was just her power dimming, but I guess that was Patricia."

Horace winced. "I helped treat a mind fracture years ago. It's rare, but it happens. Abuse caused that one, not an influx of power." He tilted his head. "I wonder if one of my patient's personalities would have taken a new body if there'd been one available."

Simon shuddered. "Maybe the woman calling herself Patricia is all that's left of Naos, and the *Atlas* just fell out of the sky."

"Is that possible?"

"No. Its manual systems were designed to prevent orbital decay."
He sighed. "But we can dream."

Cordelia strode through the door at last with Pool behind her.
"Sorry we're late. There was some problem with the wells, and Pool—"

Miriam stood, her black eyes hard as obsidian. "I'm going after
the bastards who kidnapped my son. Are you coming or not?"

Cordelia lifted an eyebrow as she sat, but she was smart enough
not to snap back. "Pool talked me into it, yes."

"We will take the tree and the children and mothers," Pool said.
"All children are welcome in my branches." Her bright green eyes were
kind. Taller than other drushka, she loomed even when seated. Her skin
was nearly the same color as the wooden table, with more lines and
whorls. Dark as tattoos, all drushka had them. But unlike most drushka,
Pool's hair was a peculiar green tint shared only with other queens.

"But won't you be taking the children to them?" Simon asked.

Pool wrinkled her nose. "Only if they can find them, which they
will not."

Simon shook his head. "I don't know if I can leave Gale right
now."

"You will be safe in the branches, too, shawness," Reach said.

No doubt the paladins agreed. And Gale might even be safer
without him. The remaining Storm Lord worshipers had burned down
the Yafanai Temple to get to him, after all.

"And Naos?" he asked, hating to throw a wrench in the works, but
a kidnapped child wasn't the only problem they had to consider.

Cordelia sighed loudly and leaned back in her chair. Tall and
muscular, she was imposing, but she seemed world weary now, different
from the firebrand who'd once punched him for lying to her. "We can
plan as we go," she said. "We'll need all the info you can remember."

He nodded and knew that had to be good enough. If they acted
fast, they could catch the kidnappers before Naos had a chance to do
anything. And if she made it to Gale while they were gone, maybe
she'd follow them rather than flatten the city.

On the planet, she'd be as slow as everyone else. The *Atlas* wasn't
made to fly or land inside an atmosphere. If she'd managed to put it
down without killing herself, she'd still crashed. It wouldn't be going
anywhere again.

"When do we leave?"

"Now," Miriam said with a scowl.

Cordelia's mouth twisted, but she nodded, too.

❖

Lydia watched the battle and wished she could help. She didn't have any combat skills besides a few wrestling moves she'd learned from the plains dwelling Engali. She wasn't a tactician. With her prophetic powers, she could venture into the future and see how this battle turned out, but that wouldn't help anything in the present.

And if she saw something bad, she'd have to watch it twice.

On a rock-strewn stretch of plains, Mamet wielded her sword against an opponent who had a red eye painted on his leather shirt. If it wasn't for the odd symbol, he could have been Mamet's kin. He probably was in some distant fashion, but he'd been tainted by the power of the mad goddess, Naos, and now all of her old followers seemed determined to murder everyone they met.

Samira and Mamet stood back-to-back, their dark hair mingling, though Samira's long locks fluttered in the wind, while Mamet's short hair stuck to her forehead with sweat. They both frowned in concentration. Mamet fought well, but she could only handle one opponent at a time. Samira flexed her macro-psychokinetic power, throwing enemies across the field or bashing them into rocks. Like Mamet, she tried to wound since these enemies could be brainwashed innocents. Neither of them relished a fight.

Lydia stood in the stirrups of her ossor. She kept their small herd of the large insects well back from the fight, ready to ride in for a rescue should anyone need it. She could just see Fajir behind a clump of rocks. Unlike Samira and Mamet, her face was as serene as someone in deep meditation. Her long dark hair flowed around her shoulders as she whirled and danced across the field, her bone sword moving like an extension of her arm. She reaped the Naos worshipers like vengeance come to life.

Lydia wanted to believe Fajir was simply enjoying her brief bout of freedom. As soon as the fight was over, Samira would knock her around until she submitted to be tied up again. Fajir had almost strangled Lydia on a battlefield much like this one, and part of Lydia's job was to watch her during combat to make sure she didn't try to kill Samira or Mamet while they were fighting the Naos worshipers.

Lydia felt a tempting pull inside. She could easily see how this fight would end and know just when Fajir would be subdued. But if her power to see the future showed her something awful, there'd be no stopping it.

Plus, she couldn't help a nagging feeling that looking into the future somehow set it, making her personally responsible for any bad outcome. That guilt had led her out here to begin with; she'd dreamed that Fajir would save the plains from a coming catastrophe, a huge fire. So, she'd known Fajir would get loose from the Engali, and Lydia had felt obligated to follow her and make sure she didn't kill anyone else while she was saving the world.

How to stop her, though, was a different story.

"Samira, now!" Lydia called as Fajir slayed the last of her opponents.

Fajir glared, the large teardrop tattoos on her cheeks looking like holes in her face, but she didn't have long to sneer before Samira's power sent her rolling across the landscape.

"Stop!" Fajir cried. When she came to a rest, she held up her hands. "I submit, curse you!"

Mamet sent the last of their opponents running, though they'd no doubt return, compelled by their goddess. Mamet sheathed her sword and retrieved a coil of rope from her pack, following Samira toward Fajir.

Fajir stood and held her hands out, swinging her glare between Lydia and Samira. She saved a smirk for Mamet, the woman she'd once tortured.

Mamet didn't look her in the eye, scowling as she tied Fajir's hands and jerking the rope tighter than was necessary. If Fajir felt any pain, she didn't show it, only smiling harder. Samira and Mamet mounted their ossors, letting Fajir march in front of them. The large insects shied from the bodies in the field.

Leaving Samira to watch Fajir, Lydia guided her ossor close to Mamet. "Are you all right?"

Mamet frowned hard, her dark eyes locked on Fajir's back. She seemed so much older than her twenty years. "I don't know how much longer I can stand being near her."

Lydia nodded. Samira had told her about the torture Mamet had suffered, all because someone in Mamet's clan had killed Fajir's partner. Lydia wouldn't have wanted to spend time around her torturer either, if she had one. And Mamet had a kind heart. She couldn't just strike someone down, no matter what they'd done. The kindness might have seemed foolish to some, but it had won Mamet Lydia's friendship and Samira's love.

"You can go back home to the Engali," Lydia said. "Both of you. I'll watch her."

Mamet gave her a kindly but condescending smile.

Lydia rolled her eyes. "Just because she was killing me when you found us doesn't mean she'll catch me off guard again."

Mamet shook her head and gripped the reins so hard, her knuckles went white. "I won't take chances with your life."

"Seconded," Samira called.

Lydia stood in the stirrups and grinned. "Stop butting in on private conversations."

"Stop having private conversations where anyone can listen."

"All of you should shut your mouths," Fajir said over her shoulder.

Mamet bared her teeth, and Fajir laughed. She seemed to feed on Mamet's hatred, unapologetic for her past deeds.

"I'd say let's take her back to the Engali," Samira said, "but you'd just argue."

Lydia sighed from her toes. She didn't need to argue. She'd seen Fajir loose in the future, so Fajir would be loose. It didn't matter what any of them wanted, but she couldn't explain it yet again, tired of wasting her breath. "Try it if you want."

Samira rolled her eyes. "No, no. These Naos fanatics are out here killing people, and my conscience won't let them run amok any more than yours will."

The day before, a group of Sun-Moon worshipers whom Fajir had saved had returned to thank them. When Samira asked where the regular patrols from Celeste were, the worshipers told them that the Sun-Moon had pulled in their soldiers to guard the wounded city of Celeste, leaving the outer villages to fend for themselves.

Lydia wondered if their faith was wavering. She'd heard that the Sun-Moon listened to their worshipers' thoughts; they had to hear the suffering and were ignoring it.

The encounter had quieted Fajir for a time. While they were hunting Naos fanatics and protecting Fajir's people, she didn't complain as much. And she'd found new delight in tormenting Mamet.

As she marched, Fajir turned her head side to side as if stretching. "You can release me, Nemesis," she said to Lydia, a nickname that Lydia loved then hated from one moment to the next. "I'll continue to kill these plains vermin. In your name, if you like."

And once she was done with the fanatics, she'd kill any other plains dwellers she happened across. Lydia rolled her eyes. This was her first time trying to control the future in any way since she'd realized it couldn't be changed. She'd tried when she was younger, but what she saw always came to pass. At least this time she could make sure Fajir only killed those who were out to commit murder.

She thought of the fiery winds from her vision, of Fajir striding toward danger, the only one brave enough to stop the architects of the inferno. Lydia didn't have the courage to follow her own future and see if it all worked out.

"Do you know who killed your partner?" she asked, wanting to piss Fajir off as much as Fajir angered everyone else. "Did you kill that person already, or do you enjoy wasting time killing others?"

Fajir's expression turned to stone before she looked ahead again. Lydia glanced at Samira, who shrugged. Mamet sneered. At last, Lydia had hit one of Fajir's nerves. She didn't press, keeping further attacks in reserve for when she needed to shut Fajir up again.

Nemesis's words rang in Fajir's skull. Scant days ago, she'd had a chance to kill the vermin who'd murdered her beloved Halaan. The Galean Cordelia had offered to help her hunt that one vermin down in exchange for Mamet's life, and Fajir had agreed.

On the cusp of the moment, when she'd imagined her future stretching ahead with no purpose, she'd changed her target to the vermin's baby daughter. Cordelia had spoiled her shot, but Fajir still carried the vision of a glorious circle of violence that ended with Halaan's killer surrounded by a mountain of dead: family, friends, everyone he knew. Then and only then would he know her pain.

Then Nico, her stalwart supporter, had abandoned her. He was a fellow widow whose own partner had been his true love. He'd admitted his feelings for Fajir, then said that if she wouldn't truly avenge her partner's death, she didn't want to move on with her life. If she wanted the violence to continue, there was no help for her.

As if she needed help. She'd seen her true purpose: to kill and kill and kill until either she died, or all the vermin were dead. All widows were supposed to do whatever they could to prevent others from dying as their partners had. Nico kept a house in the wilderness as a sanctuary for those who lost their way. Others became doctors or cared for the elderly, smoothing the transition to death as best they could. Fajir was supposed to protect her people from the occasional plains dwelling vermin who tried to kill them, but if all the vermin were dead, none of her people would ever be murdered by one again.

Simple.

Then Nemesis had come into her life and told her she would live to save the plains from some inferno, that only she would have the courage to challenge whoever created that chaos. It was probably just another vermin, but Nemesis seemed determined to keep her in bondage until it happened. Whenever Fajir had tried to kill her, Nemesis used her power of future sight to anticipate Fajir's moves, or her friends saved her. It wouldn't always be so, but Fajir grew tired of waiting.

She thought again of the goddess Naos, who had appeared to her in the guise of Halaan, offering to free her if she would go west and kill someone specific. Fajir had agreed, thinking she would get to this person after carrying out her own plans, but Naos had sensed her thoughts and rescinded her offer. That was fine. Fajir was tired of gods anyway. Hers had refused to free her from these three, citing their fear of Simon Lazlo.

Pitiful. Gods weren't supposed to fear anything, not even each other. Not only did her Lords leave her in bondage, they abandoned their people to a horde whose goddess didn't even walk among them. Nico was probably fuming, desperate to protect those who might lose their partners.

At least she was doing what he could not. And if she submitted to the wishes of her captors enough, they would let down their guard and become fodder for her sword.

The day grew long, and her captors made camp. Fajir grimaced as they tied her hands behind her back, trusting her less in the darkness. Wise, but she wished they were just a little stupider.

They chattered as they prepared their evening meal. Fajir leaned against a boulder and watched the stars appear, wondering if Halaan was watching, wondering if he was proud. Nico had said that by leaving Halaan's killer alive, she was denying Halaan rest. Fajir thought he would be happy to forgo rest if all the vermin died, and no one would have to suffer as she'd suffered. Surely that would make him happy.

She searched her memory for any sign that it would, finding nothing in their life to compare. Instead, she found as she did every day that she saw his smile less clearly, could not quite remember his laugh or which ear he kissed first when trying to get her to forgive him. *Was* this the course he'd want for her?

She gritted her teeth. Such thoughts were for weaklings. The fastest way to find out what he wished was to ask him, and to do that, she needed a vermin to kill her. And that could only happen after she'd slaughtered as many as she could. She supposed she should feel grateful that she was doing so now while also protecting her people.

A shout echoed through the darkness, a cry for help. Fajir rolled onto her feet, fighting for balance. "Let me loose!"

"That might not be one of your—" Samira started.

Fajir rushed forward, bowling Samira over with one shoulder. Samira fell with a cry, and Mamet leaped to help her as Nemesis gawked. Fajir ran toward the noise. Even with her hands bound, she could help some poor villager in need.

And if some vermin managed to plunge a sword through her chest, so be it.

Her captors cried out, but no invisible hand swatted her down. The light was fading; she could see enough to run and follow the shouts. In a hollow beyond a line of rocks, two groups faced off, some bearing the Naos eye and others in clothing like Cordelia had worn, the trappings of Gale. A piercing cry carried on the wind, an infant's voice.

Fajir stumbled to a halt. Neither of these were her people, but she'd never pass up the chance to kill some vermin. She took a step when a pull from behind stopped her. Nemesis stood there, yanking at the rope, Fajir's sword tucked under her arm. In a moment, Fajir was free. She reached for the sword, but Nemesis hopped back and threw the sword over Fajir's head to land in the grass.

Fajir had to chuckle. She could grab the sword and attack Nemesis in a moment, but Mamet and Samira were running up behind. Better to do what she'd wanted in the first place.

Fajir scooped up her sword and ran into the fray, pausing only when one of the vermin flew away from the Galeans as if pushed with an invisible hand. So, they had power users among them. That was good. After she finished the vermin, perhaps she could convince the Galeans to free her.

She put that thought away as she tore into the vermin. Some were skilled, but none could match her; they crumpled like paper. Her sword twisted through them, scattering blood to the wind. Soon, all the vermin were dead. She turned to find the Galeans staring and her captors approaching from the side, a torch bobbing between them.

"Don't move, Fajir," Samira said.

Fajir breathed hard and tensed. Now, with the gratitude shining on the Galeans' faces, she could confront Samira and hope these Galeans fought her power with their own.

But by their stares, she knew some feared her, too. "I am Fajir," she said in their language, hoping that would put them at ease. "Who are you?"

Five of them gathered around a sixth holding the infant. "Sebastian," one said. "We're from Gale." He turned toward Fajir's captors. "Samira?"

She gawked. "Sebastian! What are you doing out here?"

"Gale's become...dangerous." He glanced at Mamet and Lydia, then his mouth fell open. "Aren't you the prophet?"

Lydia waved slightly, so awkward. "Not anymore."

One of the others mumbled something about betraying the Storm Lord. Samira frowned hard, but Lydia shrugged. Ah, a schism.

"The Storm Lord is dead," Samira said.

"He will return!" one of the Galeans yelled.

Fajir smiled. Any moment now. It was dark enough; they might not catch her movements.

"Everyone, be calm," Mamet said, holding up her hands.

She would die first.

The Galeans grouped tightly together, the one with the infant fading to the back. Samira put her hands on her hips and seemed ready to yell when Nemesis stepped into the middle, all of her shyness gone.

"We are not going to stand out here in the dark and fight about the freaking Storm Lord," she said. "It doesn't matter what any of us believes; there are dangerous people out here. That's one of them." She jabbed a finger in Fajir's direction, drawing all eyes to her, and Fajir wished she could leap the distance and throttle her.

"Let's go back to our camp with its nice campfire and talk. And if you don't mind, we're going to tie up our personal Naos-fanatic-killer first, or she will murder all of us."

The Galeans muttered, but several took a step away from Fajir. She only had time to renew her vow to kill Nemesis when Samira's force wave blew her over, sending her sword bouncing from her hand. She spat when Mamet tied her up and promised that even if Halaan did not require it, she would kill these three several times over!

CHAPTER THREE

L ydia didn't care for the visiting Galeans, not at all. She hadn't been close with any of them, and they spoke with too much reverence for the Storm Lord. They also cast a lot of hateful glances toward Samira and Lydia, pissed that not every yafanai had been in the Storm Lord's pocket.

At least Fajir was tied up, or she'd have found a way to use the newcomers to her advantage. The malice glittering in her eyes would have frozen Lydia to the spot a few weeks ago, but she'd grown used to it.

At camp, the Galeans stayed on one side of the fire, leaving Lydia, Samira, Mamet, and Fajir on the other.

"Why did you leave Gale?" Samira asked.

They'd probably been thrown out now that the Storm Lord was dead, but Lydia said nothing. The Galeans' whispered conversation cut off as suddenly as if someone gagged them.

"It's safer out here," Sebastian said.

"Why?" Samira asked. "What happened?"

Sebastian began a story about the drushka poisoning Gale and abducting everyone who didn't succumb. Lydia's mouth dropped open, but she breathed a sigh of relief when someone added that Simon Lazlo and Horace Adair had healed the victims and few had died.

Another Galean spat to the side. "If the Storm Lord hadn't been distracted by people like them in the first place, the chaos with the drushka never would have happened."

"People like them?" Lydia asked, clenching her fists.

"Troublemakers. Renegades."

Lydia sneered. Zealotry was just one of the many reasons she'd never socialized with other yafanai even though she'd worked and lived in the temple. Before she could fire back, Samira touched her arm.

"What happened to the people who were abducted?" Samira asked.

"Rescued by the paladins," Sebastian said.

The man who'd grumbled stood up this time. "The drushka never would have attacked us if the paladins had stayed in Gale where they belong!"

Lydia snorted. "Armor and guns wouldn't have done anything against poison."

"What would you know, traitor?"

Lydia shot to her feet, sick and tired of people who didn't know her passing judgment on her. "I lost the love of my life in that boggin fight, the one the Storm Lord started!"

Now the Galeans were on their feet, too, yelling, pointing fingers. All of Lydia's anger and grief for Freddie came rushing out of her. Now that the shouting had started, Samira was on her feet, too. It wouldn't be long until they were throwing power around. Lydia felt a tingle pass over her scalp, meaning someone was using powers already, most likely a telepath.

"Who the fuck was that?" Samira yelled. A wave of force came off her, guttering the campfire. "One of you just used telepathy. Where the fuck do you get off reading minds uninvited?"

"Things have changed," Sebastian said. "We're bringing worship of the Storm Lord back, starting with his children."

Lydia frowned. What children? The only child here was the infant. She stared. Could that be the Storm Lord's child?

The tingle fluttered over her scalp again, this time carrying a noise like droning insects. Lydia tried to cry a warning, but the sound overwhelmed her, cutting off her voice. She fell to her knees as she tried to think through the power assaulting her. It hammered at her mind, tossing away who she was and what she was doing.

Someone was yelling. Fajir. Lydia struggled to focus. Fajir's foot jolted through her bleary vision and connected sharply with her thigh; Lydia's mind came back with a snap.

"Rise, Nemesis!" Fajir screamed. "Or they will kill us where we sit!"

Lydia stumbled to her feet. Several Galeans were on the ground, no doubt thrown by Samira, who knelt in the dirt, head in her hands.

Mamet grappled with someone, but another crept up behind her and cracked her across the back with a wooden staff.

Lydia grabbed Fajir's sword, but one of the Galeans rushed her. The skin of her arms tickled before burning, the pain building as if she was covered in stinging insects. It had to be the work of micro-psychokinesis, but he didn't have a fraction of Horace's or Simon's strength. She fought the feeling, swinging the sword to drive him away. He darted around her clumsy swing.

Lydia fell into her power and saw his future self grab at her from the left. In the present, she dodged, keeping Fajir between them. Fajir reared up and bashed her head into his nose. He yelped and scrambled back, hands on his bleeding face. Lydia fumbled with Fajir's bonds.

"I don't know why you're helping," Lydia shouted, "but I'll take it."

"Worry not, Nemesis," Fajir said with a cackle. "No one will kill you but me."

"How comforting." Her hands went numb as the buzzing assailed her brain again. She stumbled and dropped Fajir's sword, fighting to tell up from down. "Shit!"

The feeling passed as if dismissed by her swear. Nearby, Samira stumbled, and Sebastian yelled, "I can't keep both of them down at once!"

Her and Samira. He was only attacking those with power, and he couldn't do both. Samira must have acted every time Lydia went down. Mamet was still fighting weakly, trying to hold off the rest, and several more Galeans had been hurled into the grass. If Lydia could distract Sebastian, that would give Samira a chance to end this fight. She left Fajir and hurled herself in Sebastian's direction.

Dizziness crippled her, but her momentum propelled her forward. She could barely see Sebastian through the vertigo, and he sidestepped her easily.

Someone shrieked, "The baby!"

Lydia's senses came back as Sebastian whirled around. He was thrown in the air by an invisible shove before Lydia could try to tackle him. She made it upright in time to see everyone standing still.

"The fighting will now cease," Fajir said in the sudden quiet. She knelt behind the woman who held the squirming baby against her chest. Fajir had one arm locked around the woman's throat. "Surrender, or I will kill this woman, and perhaps her falling body will kill the babe. Perhaps not."

The Galeans shuddered as if someone had thrown cold water on them. Only Sebastian could have stopped her in time, and he lay still at the foot of a nearby boulder. Lydia didn't know whether to be chilled or relieved as Samira and Mamet went to stand behind Fajir.

Lydia hurried over and held out her arms. "Give the baby to me."

The woman glared, then grunted as Fajir tightened her grip. She passed the child over.

Fajir smirked. "The baby is leverage, Nemesis."

"No, it isn't," Lydia whispered back. She turned and pointed at the micro cradling his nose. "You, fix her." She nodded toward Mamet.

He glared, but he must have thought she was as heartless as Fajir because he did as instructed. He could only make Mamet well enough to stand again, not heal her as Horace or Simon could. For the moment, it was enough.

Fajir hadn't let go of her captive. Samira and Mamet saddled the ossors. "Is this your baby?" Lydia asked the woman Fajir held.

She glared and said nothing. Lydia hadn't known many parents, but she guessed that a mother would claim a child. They'd said the Storm Lord was the father, so what had happened to the mother? Was she one of these "traitors" they mentioned? If so, had they murdered her and taken her child? A horrid thought.

"Give us the child and go," one of the Galeans said.

Fajir tightened her hold, making her captive croak. The others glanced at one another, but Lydia saw fire in their eyes. They weren't going to give up, and Lydia didn't want them dead. They were misguided, but anyone could change.

"Stand away from her, Fajir," Samira said.

To Lydia's surprise, Fajir obeyed, shoving her captive toward the others. Samira then shoved them all into the night with a great gust of force.

Lydia, Samira, and Mamet mounted their ossors. Lydia watched Fajir closely, but all she did was glance away as if thinking about escape.

"Mamet," Samira said. "Grab Fajir." She and Mamet grabbed Fajir's arms, and she dangled between them as they rode into the night. They went carefully, taking no light and with Fajir spitting and swearing, but the slowest ossor could outpace anyone unfamiliar with the terrain.

❖

The kidnappers' trail led east. Cordelia couldn't help a groan. She hoped they weren't heading for Celeste to seek sanctuary from the Sun-Moon. Cordelia had seen enough of them to last a lifetime, not to mention the fact that Fajir lived there, and Cordelia would die happy if they never laid eyes on each other again.

From the branches of Pool's moving tree, the rolling plains seemed to be racing by. Cordelia wished they had time to stop and visit Wuran, but that was just her wanting to put off the inevitable. A lot of bad shit had happened to her in the east: she'd nearly been burned alive, had been kicked around by Naos's gnarly mind powers, had her mind severed from her body for a few days, and she'd missed several big fucking fights that would have cut the tension nicely. Yeah, it was a nonstop parade of fun in Sun-Moon territory.

Nettle's slender arm snaked across her shoulders. "Your face is troubled, Sa."

Cordelia leaned into Nettle's lithe body. "Is it selfish that I don't want to go back to Celeste even to save a baby?"

"Ahya, yes."

Cordelia stepped away, surprised. "I thought you'd say no."

Nettle wrinkled her narrow nose. "The thought may be of the self, yet you take the action. That defies selfishness." She brought Cordelia back into her embrace. "And the thought is entirely within understanding. I share it."

Cordelia chuckled. "Well, if I didn't want honesty, I shouldn't have asked a drushka. Anyway, a larger part of me hopes the Sun-Moon's city is in flames."

"I do not believe that, Sa. You might wish for harm to come to the Sun-Moon, but you would never wish it for an entire city. When we were there, you defended the common people and hesitated even to kill those Sun-Moon worshipers who threatened you."

"Damn it, stop knowing me so well," Cordelia muttered, but she didn't push away.

Nettle laughed and planted a kiss on Cordelia's temple. "It takes much skill to know the difference between human jokes and human lies. You should feel fortunate that I am so very skilled."

Cordelia turned her head to kiss Nettle's thin, soft lips. "Believe me, I know just how fortunate I am to have you. And how skilled you are."

She was fortunate to know all the drushka. And not just for the speed of the tree. The last time she'd gone to Celeste, she'd had to take one of the geavers, large animals that the plains dwellers used for transporting goods and people. Aboard Pool's tree, she spotted several lumbering across the plains, their long necks sweeping over the ground as they searched for food. Slow and ponderous most of the time, they could run when necessary in a miles-eating gait that managed to upset the entire digestive system. And it had still taken days to get to Celeste.

Pool's tree nearly flew in comparison. The roots propelled it as if they were tentacles, and it stepped over ravines and uneven ground with ease. But it stuck out like…a giant tree in the rolling plains, so when a group of plains dwellers rode toward them, Cordelia wasn't surprised.

She hoped they didn't want a fight. Not so long ago, she would have been excited at the thought, but she was in a hurry, and they had a huge fight looming in their future. She would have suggested that Pool ignore these newcomers, but she hated the thought of them following the tree across the plains.

Cordelia felt Pool's summons rather than heard it. Unless she was astral projecting, she had a hard time hearing Pool's words, but she could always feel when the drushkan queen was near.

The tree slowed to a halt. "If we're going to talk to them, let's take Reach," Cordelia said. Reach was a shawness, a drushkan healer, but she'd also been the ambassador of the drushka to Gale. She had all sorts of useful skills. And she'd loved Cordelia's late uncle. In drushkan terms, that made them family. Reach also had the habit of adopting stray humans. Her own son was an orphan she'd found during the boggin attack on Gale. She put many people at ease even if they weren't used to drushka.

"Ahya," Nettle said. "And Horace or Simon? In case we have need of human healing?"

Those two could do a lot more than heal, but to a drushka, a shawness was a healer first. Cordelia held her wooden sword to her waist until it sprouted tiny tendrils that kept it in place, a living weapon given to her by Pool.

"The queen has sent scouts," Nettle said.

A trill of alarm passed through Pool's connection, and Nettle hissed.

"What's happening?" Cordelia asked.

"The plains people are not stopping. They ride hard for the tree, weapons out."

Cordelia ground her teeth. "Idiots! What are they thinking?" One of Pool's limbs curled around her, and she stiffened, trying to relax as the limb lifted her to Pool's riding place. It was convenient, but she didn't know if she'd ever get used to being moved like a doll.

"Sa?" Pool asked. "What shall we do with these fools?"

Cordelia shook her head. "I don't want to kill them." That wouldn't be good for inter-species relations, no matter that most Galeans wouldn't care. "Their bows can't really hurt the tree."

"A minor sting," Pool said, lifting one elegant shoulder.

"Put me down there," Cordelia said. "I'll talk to them."

Nettle stood beside her, ready as always, though an arrow would do a lot more than sting either of them.

"Could we not ignore them?" Reach asked as she swung down to join them. "If we continue, they will fall behind."

"We can't leave an enemy at our backs," Cordelia said.

"My scouts send me a vision," Pool said. "These plains dwellers bear the sign of a single red eye."

"Fucking Naos," Cordelia grumbled. Not only did she come down from space to fuck with them, she made sure she had a welcoming committee on hand.

Pool's branch grabbed the three of them, but instead of setting them on the ground, she brought them to a lower branch where Horace and Simon waited. Horace frowned in concern, but Simon looked grim. Cordelia remembered his promise to fuck up the Sun-Moon if they ever messed with his friends again. At the moment, he looked as if he'd carry out that threat without hesitation.

"Get me close," he said.

Cordelia nodded, thinking of a plan to put him in the plains dwellers' midst, then realized he wasn't talking to her. He had a similar connection to Pool, and before Cordelia could ask what he had in mind, Pool lifted him free of the branches and held him out, shielding him as several arrows winged his way.

Simon flashed all the way back to college, to a course in ancient literature where he'd read a translation of *The Iliad*. The epic poem had started with the word rage. He'd always thought it an odd way to open a tale.

Now he understood. Anger washed over him, at the world, at every single person who'd ever pushed him around, at himself for taking it all those years from colleagues, from family, from acquaintances and friends alike. From Dillon.

And here came some assholes who'd decided to shoot instead of talk. Humanity should have moved past such attitudes, but here on Calamity, ignorance was alive and well. It was probably the same on Earth, too. Well, it was high time such violent people learned that actions damn well had consequences.

Even though they sported Naos's symbol, these people weren't possessed. Simon had cut that power from Naos's repertoire. She could have ordered them to attack random strangers, but that still gave them a choice. When Pool held Simon forward, the sound of their arrows punching into her bark and the pain spiking from her tipped him from anger into rage.

His power shot from him in a burst, and he interrupted them as he'd done to people several times before. His power impacted every part of their bodies, freezing each cell in place as if they were in stasis. Not even their brains could function without his permission, and they couldn't die unless he let them.

He left the animals alone, their riders slumped in the saddles. The drushka leaped down and herded the animals until Pool's human allies could round them up. Still, their riders didn't move, held by Simon's power.

He strode toward them once Pool set him on the ground. Cordelia would want to know what they had to say. A tiny part of Simon wanted to snuff them like candles, but he wouldn't let his power drive him mad. Still, as he looked at them, held so completely, he knew why some feared him and everyone like him.

"Simon?"

Horace stood behind him. Simon didn't trust himself to respond, not liking what he might say. He reached out blindly and felt Horace's warm hand close over his. He needed that connection to ground him, though Horace had to be as tired of people fucking with them as Simon was.

When Cordelia had the plains dwellers' weapons, she said, "Okay, Doc."

Another reminder that he was still human. With a sigh, Simon bottled his power, though he kept it ready, right next to his anger so they could feed off each other if necessary.

The drushka had lined up the plains dwellers on the ground. When Simon let them go, they jerked, their muscles responding to signals he hadn't let their brains send before. They hadn't been able to see or hear anything, and now they sat up and whipped around with wide eyes and shocked faces. They'd never be able to remember the missing moments, and now that they were surrounded by a host of armed drushka, they seemed less willing to fight.

"Who's in charge?" Horace asked in the plains language. Simon stood close to Cordelia so he could translate. Even with as much time as she'd spent on the plains, she'd never learned the whole language; she'd claimed she was good at enough other things to make up for her lack of linguistics.

One of the plains dwellers lifted their chin. "The goddess is in charge here and everywhere."

Simon sighed after he passed on this tidbit.

"She didn't stop us capturing you," Horace answered.

Simon glanced at him in surprise. Horace had always been a peacekeeper, the first to call for everyone to calm down, but lately, he seemed to be spoiling for a fight. Or maybe he was just restless. Too much action crammed into too small a timeframe could feel like a drug.

The plains dwellers bristled, but some looked worried.

"We don't have time for bluster," Cordelia said. "Ask them about the Galeans, the baby."

The plains dwellers didn't want to answer questions. They blathered about Naos and her all-seeing eye and how she was going to take over the world now that she'd come to the planet. So, she'd told them about the crash, told her followers to wreak as much havoc as possible so that Simon and all the other *Atlas* crewmates were nice and distracted.

Now that Simon thought about it, hostile plains dwellers might be keeping the Sun-Moon contained in Celeste; these had been headed toward Gale. If they weren't going to attack the city, they might have been commanded to keep anyone from coming out.

"What do we do with them?" Horace asked as Pool joined them.

The easiest answer was to kill them, but Simon could tell by the tense faces that no one wanted to do it. The fact that they weren't cold-blooded killers was comforting even if it carried a host of problems.

"We can't take them back to Gale," Cordelia said. "Even if the keep had a big enough jail, we're not the wardens of Calamity."

"Turn them over to other plains dwellers?" Horace asked. "Someone like Wuran?"

"They hold leaders responsible for the crimes of a clan," Reach said. "And Naos is not here."

"Are they brainwashed?" Cordelia asked.

Horace shrugged. "I'd have to do a deep dive in one of their minds to see. And Naos is more powerful than I am. Even if she did something, I might not be able to spot it or undo it. The Sun-Moon might be able to help."

Simon snorted. "But they won't."

Cordelia raised her arms and dropped them. "Well, we can't just give them their weapons and tell them to behave!" She looked at Simon, and he knew the anguish she was feeling. She didn't want to hold someone's life in her hands, not when so many questions remained unanswered.

And he didn't know what advice to give her besides the option to delay. "Let's take them with us, find the Galeans and the baby, then make a decision."

She smiled, and he could feel the relief rolling off her. "And if we have to take them all the way back to Gale, we can try to unscrew their minds if they're…screwed. Maybe Liam will be back by then. He's had more experience being diplomatic with the plains dwellers. He can talk to them."

Pool spread her hands as if to say anything was possible. "Perhaps they are like a drushkan tribe, and once their queen is dealt with, they will change their ways."

It was a possibility. But as the drushka bound the captives and lifted them aboard the tree, Simon knew it wasn't going to be that easy, not with the fervor shining in their eyes.

They hadn't gone far when they spotted a smaller group approaching from the east. Simon sighed, wondering if they were going to have to fight every step of the way, but this group waved as if happy to see them. Simon sent his senses out and couldn't help a wide grin when he detected Samira. Even though it'd only been weeks since he'd seen her, she was a welcome relief.

He went down to greet her and stopped cold when he saw her captive. Lydia and Mamet also rode with her, but it was Fajir marching with her hands bound who drew the eye.

"Motherfucker!" Cordelia shouted as she came down from Pool's tree. She pointed an accusing finger in Fajir's direction. "What the fuck is she doing here?"

After giving Simon a huge hug, Samira stepped aside with a calculating smile. "You remember Fajir, I see."

Cordelia stalked forward, her hands clenched menacingly. Lydia's mouth opened, but she seemed hesitant to get in Cordelia's way. Fajir took a deep breath, a beatific smile coming over her face as if this was exactly what she'd been waiting for.

After a look at Lydia, Mamet stepped in front of Fajir and flung her arms around Cordelia's neck. "My friend! It's so good to see you!"

Cordelia pulled up short, blinking, and Simon sensed her confusion as her emotions tipped. She hugged Mamet in return. "Good to see you, too, kid."

"Is Nettle here?"

"Ahya, young one," Nettle said, reaching them. She didn't resist when Mamet pulled her into the embrace, too, though she spared a glare for Fajir.

Lydia moved to Fajir's side, and it was only then that Simon noticed the bundle Lydia carried, something completely swathed in linen. As Simon watched, it squirmed.

"Is that…a baby?" he asked.

Lydia smiled. "Yes. Did you lose one?"

He rushed forward, his senses flying over the tiny form, easing its suffering, its hunger, and verifying that it was Miriam's child. And Dillon's. He hadn't realized until then just how worried he'd been. He didn't bother with words, reaching through his connection to the drushka and telling Pool to send Miriam at once.

She came to them as if on wings, the tree setting her at Simon's side so she could reclaim her child. Her face transformed from steely to wondrous in an instant.

Mila and Victoria came after her, cuddling their own children, and Horace brought Evan so all of Dillon's children could be together. Horace's power flowed out, signaling a communion, something the yafanai of Gale often did: mingling their powers in a meditative state. With a smile, Samira joined them, and Horace extended a hand to Simon. He flowed with the rest of them, intertwining their powers in a way he hadn't done since he'd fought Naos. This time, it was only for the sake of community.

Still, he never would have done it if he wasn't the most powerful person among them.

Samira held out a hand to Lydia, but she pulled back. Samira had said that Lydia hardly ever took part in any yafanai rituals. Her unique power set her too far apart. Among a temple of those with preternatural abilities, she was the only one who everyone viewed as mystical.

Simon let himself sink into the bubble but only for a few moments. They still had so much to do.

Chapter Four

So, someone finally caught your ass." Cordelia had been ready to rip Fajir's head off, but Mamet had leapt on her like an amorous prog. It had given Cordelia's temper time to cool. Having Nettle beside her helped, too. As frightening as the drushka could be in battle, most of them projected an air of calm, probably a side effect of their connection to plants. Something as slow as a tree had to keep its cool.

As the power users joined in some kind of happy bubble, Cordelia had moved to stand in front of Fajir, looking her up and down. "You look like shit."

Fajir only smiled.

"What did she do?" Cordelia asked Mamet. "Where did you catch her?" Maybe if they talked about Fajir as if she wasn't there, she'd have some words for them.

Mamet shifted nervously and glanced at Lydia.

"Don't worry," Cordelia said. "I won't kill her if you need her alive, but I might slap her around a little."

"Try it," Fajir said.

Cordelia grinned. That was more like it.

"She attacked Samira and Lydia near our camp." Mamet cast a nervous and disgusted look Fajir's way. Cordelia flashed back to Mamet's bruised and battered body when Cordelia had found her in Fajir's dungeon. She had a lot to be angry about.

Cordelia leaned close to Nettle and nodded toward Fajir. "Watch her."

"Ahya."

And if Nettle was watching, the rest of the drushka would be, too. Cordelia led Mamet a few steps away. Mamet's shoulders lowered, and she took a deep breath as if she'd found cleaner air.

"Spill it. What happened with her?"

Mamet's words came out in a rush. She seemed relieved as she told how Fajir had been caught by Samira, how the Engali chafa and elders had declared that since Fajir's only provable crime against their clan had been the torture of Mamet, that Mamet should decide her fate. That sounded like a raw deal. Pin a possible execution on a twenty-year-old? Cordelia had never killed someone outside the heat of battle. She didn't know if she could do it if her blood wasn't up and pumping.

She looked back at Fajir. Well, maybe.

"Lydia had a dream of Fajir's future," Mamet said. "An unbreakable prophecy, so she must live." She breathed deep again, no doubt relieved that she wouldn't have to execute anyone.

Cordelia nudged her shoulder. "I understand."

After a grateful smile, Mamet said, "When Fajir escaped, Lydia chased her to keep her from killing innocents."

"Commendable," Cordelia said. There might be more to Lydia than she thought.

"Until Fajir tried to kill her," Mamet said. "When we found them, Fajir was strangling her, so Samira knocked her unconscious."

"Some people never learn."

Mamet hung her head. "Now we're traveling with her to keep her in check, and I...don't want to!" When she picked her head up, she had tears in her eyes, and her fists were clenched. "I just want her to go away!"

Cordelia put a hand on her shoulder, her heart going out. "It's all right; relax. I'll take her off your hands." She wasn't even sure why she said that except that Mamet was in pain, and Cordelia could help. But what the hell was she going to do with Fajir? Put her with the plains dwellers they'd caught? Maybe they'd all kill one another. Problem solved.

A few tears fell down Mamet's cheeks, and she wiped them away before smiling shyly. "Now you've saved me twice."

Cordelia felt heat in her cheeks. She waved away the worship shining in Mamet's eyes. "No big deal." She patted Mamet on the shoulder, and they turned to watch the power users' huddle.

A moment later, the happy power bubble broke up, and Mamet practically ran to Samira, giving her the good news. Maybe she was planning on some serious make-out time now that they didn't have to guard Fajir. Thinking of young love, Cordelia wished them well and winked at Nettle. Nettle grinned from where she stood behind Fajir.

The yafanai were headed back toward the tree. Cordelia and the drushka followed, leading Fajir. Samira and Mamet stayed where they were, and Lydia looked between them all as if unsure who to join.

"No!" Lydia finally said. "Fajir needs to stay on the plains if she's going to help!"

Samira narrowed her eyes. "If she leaves the plains now, she'll find her way back. You said that's how it works."

Lydia bit her lip; she'd gone a bit pale and started to sweat. She slicked her dark red hair back from her forehead. "I can't go back to Gale."

"Why?" Cordelia asked.

Samira gave her a dirty look. "It's too painful after her losses."

Cordelia fought the urge to sigh. She was so tired of emotional garbage, but she kept her mouth shut. After all, she'd had trouble going back into the swamp, the place where her parents died.

But the only way to get over pain was to face it.

"Come with us," Mamet said, holding out a hand to Lydia. "Back to the Engali camp."

"Yeah." Cordelia nodded toward Fajir. "She won't kill anyone she's not supposed to under my watch."

Fajir bared her teeth but said nothing. Cordelia bet there'd be a long line waiting to kill her after she fulfilled her so-called destiny. Nettle might be first, though she was keeping herself in check.

Lydia bowed her head, and Cordelia couldn't guess what she was feeling. Whatever it was, Cordelia was going to get a cramp from resisting the urge to yell at her to make a fucking decision.

Nettle crossed over and touched Lydia's shoulder, making her jump. "Come with us, young one, but remain aboard the queen's tree. We can hold this…monster there in complete safety, and you will not be directly in the place that caused you such pain."

Lydia smiled widely and threw her arms around Nettle's slender waist. Nettle chuckled and hugged her back. Mamet sighed as if grateful the whole thing was sorted out, but now *Samira* seemed torn, looking from Lydia to Simon to Mamet. More fucking feelings. Great.

Cordelia led Fajir into the tree, letting them work it out.

❖

Lydia felt as if the world had been lifted from her shoulders. She was still going to Gale, but with the drushka, she wouldn't have to go inside, wouldn't even have to see the city if she stayed far inside the branches. She should have thought of the tree before. She'd loved living with the drushka on the plains; she found them warm and welcoming and open. They never lied, and they didn't see the point of her power, so they never asked her to use it. And Fajir wouldn't be able to move without their permission, let alone kill anyone.

Even if she got away, there was Cordelia and the paladins as well as Simon Lazlo and all the yafanai to catch her. She'd sit nice and tight until she was needed, and Lydia could see that no one else got hurt.

But now Samira seemed to want to come to Gale, too, though Mamet clearly wanted to go home. She hadn't had a peaceful night since Fajir had come back into their lives.

Lydia crossed over to them, desperate to help them make up their minds if she could. "What's going on?"

"She wants to go with you," Mamet said, her eyes hard.

Samira sighed. "I only think that I should...see this through." It sounded weak, as if she wasn't certain of her own words. Lydia flashed back to a conversation she'd had with Samira right before this whole adventure started: Samira thought Mamet was getting too serious about their relationship too quickly. She'd been scared that Mamet was thinking marriage while Samira was having a fling.

And now, maybe Samira saw a way out. She never tried to hide her feelings, and they shone through now. But breaking Mamet's heart would be like denying a child a hug.

Maybe that was the problem. No matter if Mamet's anguish was justified, maybe Samira needed someone stronger.

Mamet gestured toward the ossor, her hand out. "Samira, please."

Samira took Mamet's hand but stayed where she was. "I...I need to see this through, Mamet, and I want to go back to Gale, to see how it's changed, to help Simon. He's been through so much—"

"So have I!" Mamet yelled. She lowered her voice. "So has everyone. And there will be more trying times in the future. With these goddess worshipers running rampant, my people need us now more than ever."

Samira seemed sheepish, but in the end, Mamet was asking her to choose between people and a town she'd known her whole life and people she'd just met. Lydia didn't know what she'd do if forced into such a choice. When staying with the Engali had been a sort of vacation, Samira had seemed happy, but now that her dear friend and her old people needed her help...

No matter what she decided, there was no choice in Mamet's dark eyes. If Lydia could see it, Samira surely could. Mamet wanted Samira to choose her over everything, everyone else.

But Samira seemed to always need more than one person to care about. Lydia wanted to hug them both or run away from the tension, but she was rooted to the spot.

"I'm sorry, Mamet." Samira had a hitch in her voice, but not enough to overwhelm her. She was too strong for that, the type of person who could easily become jaded and hard if she let herself. "I think you should go back to the Engali, and I should go with Simon and the drushka."

Lydia couldn't tear her eyes off Mamet's anguished face. Samira hadn't pleaded with Mamet to come with them. That would be too hard for Mamet, so Samira was letting her go, but Lydia doubted Mamet would see it that way.

"After all this is over—" Samira began, driving the final nail into the coffin.

"Don't bother," Mamet said as she turned and stalked away.

"Mamet!" Samira said, taking a few steps. "Wait! Don't walk away angry, at least say good-bye."

"Good-bye!" Mamet said over one shoulder, the vitriol in her words cut with a sob.

Samira sighed and seemed as if she might take a few more steps, maybe use her power to stop Mamet, but she faltered. Tears stood in her eyes, but they didn't fall.

"Find her again when the trouble's over," Lydia said. "Maybe she'll be ready to forgive."

"I hope she doesn't ride right *toward* trouble."

Lydia nodded. If Mamet avoided the rampaging plains dwellers, she should be all right. Lydia didn't have time to yell good-bye before Mamet was lost in a cloud of dust.

Aboard the tree, Samira and Lydia told Cordelia and Simon about the Galeans they'd met, those who'd stolen the baby. Simon wanted to go after them, but Cordelia argued that they had other things to worry about.

Simon spoke about trouble in Gale. The temple had burned down. Lydia didn't mourn it. Freddie had died at the gates, and it had never felt like home. It chilled her that someone had tried to kill

Simon Lazlo and had kidnapped the baby from the mother's womb. Disgusting. She was relieved that the drushka now protected the mothers. If they were all living aboard the tree, Lydia could get to know some of them better.

If they didn't badger her with questions about the future of their children.

Fajir stayed quiet as she listened, even when Simon told them Naos had landed her ship. When the drushka finally tucked Fajir away in a cubby, she remained silent. Lydia followed, surprised when the drushka removed Fajir's bonds.

"Are you sure that's a good idea?" Lydia asked Reach, the former drushkan ambassador.

"Ahya, yes," Reach said. "The tree itself will be her shackle. Only a fool would seek to run." She looked to Fajir. "You hear this, yes?"

Fajir didn't respond. Reach spread her hands as if to ask what more could they do before she walked away, leaving a few guards nearby.

Lydia sat cross-legged on the branch in front of the cubby, wondering why she was still bothering with this monster, the woman who'd tried to kill her once and vowed to one day finish the job.

"Are you pleased, Nemesis?" Fajir asked. "Now I am as good as caged, waiting for your day when I will be a hero."

Lydia didn't know what to say. She *was* pleased, but more than that, she was thoughtful. Fajir had saved her from the Galeans. She'd done it by threatening to strangle someone and drop her on a baby, but she'd done it nonetheless.

"Why did you save my life?" she asked. "When the Galeans attacked us, you could have fled into the night."

"With my hands bound?"

"You could have gotten out of that sooner or later. We weren't far from Celeste. Or you could have joined the Galeans against us. You saved me instead."

Fajir shrugged, face turned away so that her long black hair hid her expression. "I told you. You are mine to kill."

"I don't believe that."

Fajir sneered in profile. "Do you think me in love with you, Nemesis?"

"I think you've forgotten how to love."

Fajir faced her at last, eyes blazing. "I loved more deeply than you will ever know."

"Once, sure. Now?" Lydia shrugged. "So, why?"

For a moment, Fajir said nothing, then she leaned forward, her gray eyes boring into Lydia's face like metal shards. "You claimed my life with your power. I claim yours."

Lydia knew she should be frightened, but just as when Fajir had threatened her before, it amused rather than scared her. Fajir had tried to back up her words once, and Samira had stopped her. Lydia might not be so lucky a second time, but still…nothing.

Lydia smiled. "I think you're full of shit."

To Lydia's surprise, Fajir threw her head back and laughed, a crazy sound more like a roar than a note of joy. Maybe it was the insanity that put Lydia at ease: Fajir said "kill," but she might as easily save Lydia or boil an egg or declare that she wanted to weave a rug for everyone in the world. The further she got from sanity, the more unpredictable she became.

To someone who could see the future, that was…comforting.

"I'm tired, Nemesis."

Lydia didn't know if Fajir wanted a nap or if she meant she was tired of life, but it didn't matter. "Lie down. I'll make sure no one bothers you."

Fajir gave her an odd look, something between touched and amused before she snorted and lay down in the cubby, stretching her limbs and sighing. It had to have been hard to sleep as trussed up as they'd kept her, but Lydia wouldn't have dreamed of untying her out there in the wilderness. Fajir wasn't unpredictable all the time.

Dillon tried never to get lost in sentimental bullshit, but being back in a body felt as good as when he'd first come to this backward, fucked-up planet. After years of living on the *Atlas*, the wind had felt so good. He'd relished the air in his lungs and the sun on his face, and now, after being trapped in Dué's mind, it felt really good to stretch.

Standing on the plains, he allowed himself one more look at the waving grass and the rocks that dotted the landscape like herds of sheep. It reminded him a little of his great-uncle's farm in Ireland, one of the few places on Earth that hadn't gone fully industrial.

Dillon sighed and turned back to the mine, fighting a stab of grief that he'd never go home again, and everyone who'd ever known him on Earth was long in the ground.

Then he reminded himself that he'd hated most of Earth and most of his relations after his old man passed. And on most planet-side missions, he'd been overcome with nausea or some other ailment. There weren't enough push-ups to cure him of a sensitive stomach or a shit immune system, and to maintain the respect of his troops, he'd had to pack his own meds or see the company medic on the sly.

Now he had a new fucking body, one acclimated to this planet. There was no need for Simon Lazlo, that backstabbing little shit. This body was young and fit. He'd have some time before it started to fall apart. And once it did, well, there was always Patricia Dué.

The thought of her powers should have made Dillon smile, but she was a problem waiting to happen. Panicked because of Naos, she was safely under his thumb. But if she got comfortable, she might turn her powers on him. He'd probably given her enough shit while sharing her head that she'd leave him be. Her own pride would keep her out of his head.

He rubbed his chin as he passed through the gate into the small town sitting before the mine. Patricia was enamored with his old body; maybe she'd start to feel that way about this new body with his old mind.

So…would he screw her in order to keep her close? He'd manipulated women that way before. If he pretended to fall for her, she'd lap it up. But…her new body was so *young*. In his old body, people in their twenties and early thirties had seemed young to him. Patricia's new body was about fifteen, if that. Really young women hadn't done it for him in years. He wanted a woman with experience, and Patricia looked like a girl, at least on the outside. If he'd had a kid as a teenager, a fifteen-year-old could have been his fucking grandchild.

On the other side of the camp, she stood talking to his old body with its new, sycophantic mind. *That* burned him; she'd made Jonah such a tool. With a sigh, Dillon told himself to let it go. Patricia was attached to Jonah. If Dillon went around badmouthing him, it would only push her away.

But Jesus fucking Christ…

Patricia waved him over. He could practically smell her desperation, see it in her mismatched eyes, one brown, one blue. She looked moments away from panicked as she tucked her long brown hair behind her ears. The worry on her teenage face made him want to use a nickname with her, something soothing that would calm her down. When he'd been stuck in her head, it had been sarcastic, but now the nicknames naturally came to mind because of her youthful looks, something like pumpkin or honey or sweets, his old standby.

His old body glared like a cartoon, and it almost made Dillon burst out laughing. He'd unnerved many a recruit with a well-timed look, but outside of his body, the glares were a fucking joke. He supposed it was a good thing that he couldn't intimidate himself.

"We're talking defenses, but no defense is going to be good enough," Patricia said, the words running into each other as she spoke too quickly. She gathered the hair off her neck and tied it into a hasty knot, but a few sweaty strands stuck to her jaw. "Nothing's going to be good enough. She's going to roll right over us."

"Easy," Dillon said, barely keeping back the term of endearment that wanted to follow. He picked one of the damp strands off her face. "You know what we have to do."

She nodded. "Go to Gale." She blinked, and there were goddamn tears in her eyes. "But I don't want to."

He had to laugh. "None of us want to, sweet…Patricia. But we both know Naos didn't come here to sit on her ass in the mountains. And it's going to take more than you and me to beat her. If we go to Gale, you can shield my mind from any nosy interlopers, and I can watch your back." He nodded at Jonah. "I'm afraid the old bod will have to stay here."

She looked even more stricken, and Jonah's brows practically met, he glared so hard. Dillon had to cough or he would've brayed a laugh. "My old bod walking into Gale would cause too much trouble. Some would want to worship it, some to kill it, just like always."

"Jonah," Patricia said softly. "He's right. You're going to have to wait for me outside Gale."

"Mistress," Jonah said, nearly a whine. Dillon wanted to kick him. "I'll always do as you ask, but I'd rather be by your side."

"Does he know what he is?" Dillon asked. "Who he used to be?"

Jonah ignored him. Patricia gave Dillon a warning look. He guessed that was a no.

"You'll wait on the plains with some of my followers," Patricia said. "And watch for Naos's approach."

That was a good idea, proving yet again that her body and mind didn't match.

"He can watch the road to the mine, too," Dillon said. "That way the Galeans won't be able to sneak around and retake it."

She smiled, clearly pleased by the praise. And now that she was calmer, Dillon led her to the house where they were keeping the two paladin captives. He hadn't wanted her working on them before, not while she was so keyed up, remembering when Lazlo had tried to augment Natalya while angry. He'd ended up turning her into a little Naos: lots of power with a dash of nutjob thrown in. He'd ended up augmenting a healer, too, which would have been nice if that healer hadn't abandoned Gale with the rest of the renegades. Dillon's takeaway had been that power users needed to be calm before they did anything, no matter how powerful they were. Runaway emotions bred recklessness.

Now that they had a plan, Patricia walked with her head up, her eyes clear if still a little pinched. She kept her frown, and he bet that if he could peek inside her head, he'd see someone desperately trying to convince herself that everything was going to be okay.

The inside of the little house was dim. It had been a shabby place to begin with; the whole mine had a temporary look that Dillon remembered from many a bailiwick out in the field. Though with the old tech he'd had under Pross Co., their soldier encampments looked a lot better than some colonist outposts, especially those who were slow to receive tech and went back to the land, so to speak.

Patricia had tried to spruce it up. She'd stopped the miners from keeping equipment in their sleeping shacks. Instead, she'd had them double up the bunks and turn the most tumbledown wooden structures into storage sheds. Now the bunkhouses contained only beds, small chests, and a few chairs.

Everyone had been shooed out of this bunkhouse except two still forms on the beds. Patricia had kept the paladins asleep, and Dillon had stripped their metal and leather armor. He knew both were uncomfortable to sleep in. Patricia could heal any aches and pains they developed, but Dillon wanted to save them pain if he could. They were going to be his people again, after all.

Patricia knelt by the first cot, the one with the lieutenant. She stared at him, her eyes losing focus as she used her power. Dillon's scalp tingled, and he was so glad she'd been distracted when she'd put him in this body; she'd let his power come with him, though he wouldn't be able to use it in front of the Galeans.

Or maybe someday he could, when certain people had been gotten out of the way. Maybe he could claim that the yafanai had come up with a new process to give powers to those fully grown, a process that usually started in early adolescence. Any older than that, and there was a risk of madness, the brain not being able to stand such radical changes.

"You have to let me into your mind," Patricia said, and it took Dillon a moment to realize she was talking to him. He tried not to smirk. She could force her way in anytime she liked, but after his lessons, she was asking permission.

"Go ahead." He didn't add that she should take care where she wandered. There was no need to threaten her now.

The tingle over his scalp increased, and he got flashes of memory, the lieutenant's memories, playing in fits and starts like a corrupted vid. His name was Porter. He was popular, everyone smiling when they spoke to him. Even Cordelia, the mayor's niece, seemed to like him, and she seemed a bit of a battle-ax, from what Dillon remembered. Porter had gone with the renegades, and Patricia sorted through his memories looking for Liam Carmichael, Dillon's new body.

Porter hadn't had many conversations with the new mayor. He'd seen Liam with a drushkan girlfriend; that could be a problem, though girlfriends could easily be gotten rid of with a little indifference.

Patricia sped through the memories, and Dillon watched the battle against the plains dwellers and the Sun-Moon from Porter's perspective. It was quite a show, even with the drushkan power winging about that Porter hadn't understood. Dillon watched the return journey to Gale, and his hand curled into a fist as Porter helped the humans that the drushka had poisoned. Fucking drushka! He'd known they'd be trouble. He wondered if Enka, the envoy who'd tried to seduce him, would ever come to Gale again. If she did, he'd fry her ass, secret powers be damned. No one poisoned his city and just walked away.

But Porter and the paladins hadn't let the drushka get away. Cordelia had organized a rescue and revenge party, and Dillon found himself admiring her. She was a pain in the ass, and she was tight with Liam, so he had to get rid of her, but fuck, what a waste. While Liam waited in Gale, she led a rescue party for the ages, going off on her own at last with only a handful of drushka to face the head honcho face-to-face. He wished he could have seen it.

Instead, Porter was part of a team of decoys that drew parties of drushka away and killed them or kept them busy so Cordelia could get inside the final drushkan perimeter. Porter was a brave guy, loyal, and Dillon saw plenty of ways to make use of him.

At last, Porter had a memory of returning to Gale with the rescued hostages, and Dillon finally saw more of Liam. He'd been elected mayor while Porter had been gone. He'd made great strides in putting the city back together. Point to him. He'd let the Yafanai Temple get burned down. That was a mark against. He'd come up with some scheme to feed the town—probably with Lazlo's help—another point, but he'd neglected to check on the mine, allowing Patricia to dig in. Mark against. Starting off even stephen with the people of Gale, Dillon could work with that. Feeding and sheltering the common folk would always go further than the yafanai being homeless, and most people had never seen the mine; out of sight, out of mind. Plus, Liam's connection to Cordelia would help Dillon ride high on her rescue effort.

"That's it," Patricia said, sitting back with a sigh.

Dillon nodded. "Good job. Can you make up some excuse to cover the time Porter's been out? Like, we were all caught in a collapse at the mine, and you've just now managed to put us back together?"

Patricia nodded slowly. "I could work in that you've had a little brain damage, and I've done what I could. That will explain why the mental blocks that Cordelia's healer put in your mind are no longer in place and will cover up the ones I'll put in to shield you from the yafanai."

He frowned at having brain damage, but it might account for some of his inevitable "odd" behavior. And he could say her blocks were holding his mind together. As gross as that seemed and as incompetent as that might make him appear, it was for the best. He kept his grimace down. "Sounds good."

She gave him a shy smile, letting him know he was still on the right track with her.

They dug into the private's mind too, identifying her as Sunny Swanson. As a new recruit, she wasn't known strictly by her last name yet. People kept comparing her to Cordelia Ross, which both delighted and annoyed her. Cordelia was her idol, but she wanted to make her own name, too. Dillon grinned, always happy to have a gung-ho soldier on his side. With the right mentoring, she could become *his* Cordelia Ross one day, his loyal guardian of Gale.

But as for info about the mayor, she had almost nothing except what she'd observed on the trip here. Fuck.

Dillon decided to stay while Patricia built new memories for Porter and Swanson. He knew his presence would comfort her.

When Patricia was done, she sat back. "I'm surprised you're okay with building new memories. I thought you disapproved of all telepathic manipulation."

"Mind fucking," he said with a grin. "Call it what it is."

"But this is okay?" Her tone turned defensive. "As long as it's in your interest?"

His instinct was to get angry right back at her, lob more accusations, but he kept his temper, summoning the tactics he'd used on irritated senior officers. He sighed and leaned forward on one of the bunks, clasping his hands. "I don't claim to be perfect, sweet…Patricia. And I believe one should use every tool in one's arsenal to survive, and that includes mind powers. All I meant before was that you don't have to use powers all the time. Sometimes, a good speech will do." He nodded at the sleeping paladins. "But not in this case, obviously."

She stared, probably wondering if he was only trying to control her. He had to make a stronger case. "You lived without mind powers on Earth," he said. "Just like the rest of us, you had to convince people to give you what you wanted the old-fashioned way."

"I was never any good at it." She stood and paced. "With telepathy, I can guarantee loyalty instead of just trusting that I have it!"

He shrugged and leaned back, feigning nonchalance. "Then do it. Travel the world and mind fuck everyone to your side. Then when you come against Naos, you'll have a whole world full of people to throw at her. That'll work, right? I sure as fuck hope so because that's what an army of zombies would do, just keep leaping at the target even though it doesn't do any good."

The bluntness and the profanity seemed to snap her out of her own head. She stared again, stock straight, fury in her drawn brows, her quivering shoulders. He sat still, not daring to interrupt her thoughts, knowing she'd realize he was right. Her true nature, that one that never thought of her as the kind of person who hurt other people, would reassert itself. Finally, she sagged, and he nearly smiled.

"I just want to be safe," she mumbled.

He crossed the room to put one affectionate hand on her shoulder and rubbed slightly with his thumb, working the tension out. "And you will be. We'll work together, and we'll get Gale to help. None of them can match you in power, not even Lazlo, so they'll be reluctant to fight as long as you keep a confident face and don't let your power leak out."

She smiled, a lopsided grin that had an air of familiarity. After having him in her head, she was no doubt thinking she knew him well. "'It's enough that he knows you have the biggest dick,'" she quoted. "'You don't have to swing it around'?"

"Exactly." He nodded toward the door. "Now, if you want to wake up our paladins and give me some room, I'll explain what happened when the mine fell on them, and we all got a little brain damage."

She nodded, but her smile edged into a frown. "Are you sure you don't want me to implant a directive in their minds to always do what you say?"

Tempting, but it seemed akin to telling an outrageous lie, one that could quickly snowball until the liar had to tell one more lie after another, building a wall around themselves that would one day collapse. "I can manage them. Have faith in me."

"I do, God help me," she said, sounding a lot older than not just her youthful face, but whatever age she'd been when the *Atlas* first left Earth. Of course, they were all far removed from then.

CHAPTER FIVE

Cordelia began to wonder if running from one crisis to the next would be normal from now on. When she'd lived on the plains for nine months, she'd occasionally been desperate for something exciting. She'd participated in wrestling matches among the Uri to get out of digging wells or settling petty disputes. She supposed that was always the way: the calm times were too boring and the busy times too hectic.

As she caught sight of Gale, she lined up everything she had to do. Step one: make sure the city was operating as it should. That included double-checking that the new Shi was keeping her promise to stay clear. Two: get Liam back. Three: make a plan for Naos. Four: make a plan for Patricia Dué? Could that be the same plan?

So, number four but possibly five was: do *something* with the plains dweller captives to see if they'd been brainwashed, and if so, find out if the yafanai could fix them. If not…well, first things first.

And last, figure out what to do with fucking Fajir. Any future crap had to have something to do with Naos. Maybe Lydia's prophecy meant they were going to take the fight to her rather than waiting for her to attack Gale. That was a fucking relief, at least.

As before, when they'd returned from the swamp, people poured from Gale to welcome them home. Cordelia let herself relax slightly. The city wasn't flooded or covered in giant bugs or anything; no one appeared to be in the process of dying. Private Jacobs, who'd been invaluable to Simon while Cordelia was off fighting drushka, pushed through the crowd, scattering the well-wishers.

"Captain Ross," Jacobs said, snapping off a salute. "You and the doc should come to the keep. You have a visitor. It's a…" Her eyes shifted to the drushka.

Cordelia suppressed a groan. Fucking wonderful; one of the old drushka had come calling. And there was never just one lurking around. "I'll send a message to Pool, and—"

"No, Cap!" Jacobs coughed and lowered her voice. "She asked me not to let that happen."

Cordelia frowned, wondering which drushka wouldn't want to speak to a queen, but that was an answer in itself. Another queen wouldn't want Pool to know she was here, and only one queen came without a tree taller than the keep.

Cordelia found Simon and bent to whisper in his ear. "I think Shiv is here. She doesn't want her mom to know."

Simon's mouth compressed into a thin line. After he had a quiet word with Horace, Simon and Cordelia hurried through the crowd to the Paladin Keep. Cordelia spread the word as she went for all paladins to fall in and get their gear together for a trek back to the mine.

Problem seven—eight, if she counted guarding the Storm Lord's brood—if Shiv didn't want Pool to know she'd come back, it wasn't a social visit. For over a week, Shiv had been with the old drushka as a kind of ambassador, so someone besides Pool would know the old drushka and their ways. Cordelia hoped the old drushka weren't pissed and massing for an attack. Of course, if they were, maybe Cordelia could figure out a way to throw them in Naos's path.

She snorted a laugh.

"What's funny?" Simon asked.

"Life and its myriad fucking problems."

He sighed. "After living so long, I shouldn't get surprised, but it happens all the time." He stared ahead. "I hope she's all right."

The thought that Shiv might be injured made her shoulders clench. But why wouldn't Shiv want Pool to know? Maybe she intended to seek revenge on her own? Then why ask for Cordelia? Both she and Pool would want to kick ass for Shiv's sake. As Pool had often said, if someone became a friend or enemy of one drushka, they could count all drushka the same.

The Paladin Keep jutted from Gale's western side like a spear, a shard made of wood, metal, plastic, and stone, materials from Calamity and from the original colonists' landing pods. Cordelia had thought it a thing of beauty, a testament to the strength of her ancestors. They used everything they had; they adapted and fought and tamed the land for their own. She still felt a tremor of that pride, but it was for everything her people had overcome since the Storm Lord had come in person, bringing all the shit politics of her ancestors from far-flung Earth.

And it reminded her that there was a great heap of metal and plastic now sitting in the mountains to the north, and all that stood in their way of claiming it was a mad goddess. Easy.

Jacobs directed Cordelia to the captain's office. "She only got here this morning, but she's pretty upset," Jacobs said. "She found me, said I smelled the most like you, Doc." She frowned, but it had a bit of humor in it. "I didn't know what to say, but she didn't give me much chance, babbling about how she had to see you, Cap, and how her mother couldn't know. I hid her. She's probably ready to bust out of that room."

"Thanks, Private, we'll take it from here," Cordelia said.

After another crisp salute and a nod of gratitude from Simon, Jacobs hurried down the stairs. When Cordelia opened her office door, Shiv launched herself forward, and Cordelia barely caught her. She wanted to whirl the kid around, always pleased by her exuberant greetings, but Shiv clung to her, breathing hard. Her skin seemed waxy, the whorls standing out like cracks. She'd been letting her green hair grow since Cordelia had first met her, and now it hung limply around her head, and her bright green eyes sported a dull film.

"Sa," Shiv croaked, her voice brittle.

Cordelia's scalp tingled: Simon's power covering them both. Cordelia's aches and pains eased, and she felt as if she'd just donned her armor rather than having worn it for days. Shiv took a deep, shuddering breath, and her color improved. She licked her lips and buried her face in Cordelia's chest, smacking dully against the armor.

"What's wrong, Shiv?" Cordelia asked.

"You did not bring him." She took a step back. "I thought you would."

"Who?"

"Lyshus!" The word was practically a scream. "I did not ask Jacobs because I did not want Shi'a'na to know, but I thought you would realize my need, Sa!" She took a step back, her eyes going hard. "Have you become a fool in my absence?"

Cordelia wanted to fire back, but she was savvy enough to know something fucked up was going on. This wasn't just a teenage temper tantrum. Drushka grew up quicker than humans, but Shiv was a queen and only fifteen. She'd live a long time, so maybe she stayed a child longer than others, but this sudden shift to anger was far beyond normal.

"Shiv," Cordelia said, holding out a hand. "It's all right."

"It will never be all right again! If you had brought him, I could have taken him and been away." She muttered a few words in drushkan. "Go, and do not return without him."

Simon's eyebrows shot up. "What the hell happened to you in the swamp?"

Shiv held her chin up, but soon after, her mouth turned down in sorrow, and she dropped onto the rug as if all the strength had left her. Drushka didn't weep, but she was still the picture of sadness as she curled into a fetal position, crying Lyshus's name over and over.

Cordelia looked to Simon and mouthed, "Pool." He nodded. No matter what Shiv wanted, Cordelia was out of her depth here. Simon's eyes went half-lidded.

"No!" Shiv leaped up, teeth bared, leading with her claws.

Cordelia jerked Simon out of the way, nearly flinging him across the office. He tripped over a chair and crashed to the floor. Shiv banged against the wall and pushed off as if she was made of rubber. Cordelia caught her wrists, not bothering to tell her to calm down. Her eyes were wide, crazed, her mouth open in a snarl, sharp teeth snapping at Cordelia, at everything. Cordelia tried to swing her around, to grab her from behind, but Shiv bucked and grunted, screaming. Footsteps and shouts came from the hall outside.

"Stand down!" Cordelia cried, fighting to be heard. The last thing she wanted was some frightened paladin, fresh with memories of the swamp, to bust in here and shoot Shiv before they could figure out what the fuck was going on.

Simon's power rolled across the room, and Shiv went limp so fast, Cordelia dropped her. She breathed a sigh of relief as silence descended.

"I'm all right; everything's all right," Cordelia called, breathing hard. "When Pool, the drushkan queen arrives, send her up."

Murmurs of acknowledgment came through the door. Cordelia looked to Simon. He shook his head and righted the chair he'd tripped over. "If she's sick, I don't know with what." He tapped his head. "I told Pool we need a shawness."

Cordelia nodded and hoped Nettle came, too. When Nettle followed Pool through the door, Cordelia put an arm around her, happier just to be breathing the same air. With Nettle, Reach, and Pool in the room, Cordelia laid Shiv on the desk and moved the other furniture into the antechamber to give everyone room.

"She attacked us," Cordelia said.

Pool held up a hand. "Better I see for myself, Sa."

Cordelia didn't know what she meant until Pool reached out her hands. Drushkan telepathy, right. And Pool clearly wanted to see the memories from Simon's and Cordelia's perspectives. Cordelia sat on the floor, and Nettle cradled her body even though she was still wearing the damn armor.

"I'm heavy," Cordelia said.

Nettle's narrow lips brushed her forehead. "Never, Sa."

Cordelia breathed a laugh, but it had more nerves behind it than humor. She wasn't afraid of the touch of Pool's mind—well, not much—but she was worried for Shiv, so she eased out of her body as quickly as she could and heard Pool's voice in her mind.

"Show me."

Cordelia relived the scene for Pool, sensing it as Simon did the same. As a drushkan queen, Pool could divide her attention among many people at a time, always connected to each member of her tribe, all but one: Lyshus.

She sensed Pool's irritation. "This is because of that child."

The memory transfer done, Cordelia floated back into her body and sat up. There was no need to tell the story to any of the drushka now. Unless Pool barred them from those memories, they'd all know. Nettle helped Cordelia stand and looked at Shiv with worry on her narrow face. Reach rubbed Simon's shoulders.

"I am glad you were not hurt, shawness."

"Me, too," he said. "Is she sick, Pool?"

"Something to do with Lyshus, her tribe of one," Pool said. "I had hoped the old drushka would help her, that they would have some wisdom, but it appears that being apart from him has weakened her, altered her. He has not been well, either. His parents call him depressed. But this…" She smoothed the hair from her daughter's forehead. "Perhaps she will feel better when she is with him and her sapling. I will bring her to the tree."

She carried Shiv herself, and as soon as they were among the soil outside the keep, Pool's roots broke through the ground and carried the two of them away through the ground. Cordelia opened her mouth to say she wanted to go with them, but she kept the words back. Maybe this was something the drushka had to do alone.

"Do not worry, Sa," Nettle said. "I will tell you what occurs."

"Even if it's a secret?"

Nettle frowned. Keeping secrets was almost like lying, and no drushka liked that. But Pool had told a few lies in her life, had kept more than a few secrets even from her tribe. If she didn't want something to get out, it didn't. "I would not lie."

"I know," Cordelia said, kissing her temple.

Reach followed Pool, so Shiv was in good hands. Shiv had once been afraid that her mother would kill Lyshus for developing the green hair of a drushkan queen. And from what Cordelia had heard, his powers extended beyond those of even a normal queen. Queens bonded to one tree at a time, that tree serving as the focal point for their tribe. From what Nettle had told her, Lyshus might have the power to communicate with other queens' trees, which sounded not only rude but forbidden.

Cordelia exchanged another worried look with Simon. Pool abhorred the thought of harming a child, but if Lyshus was hurting Shiv, killing her…

Maybe Shiv was right, and she and the boy should run off and be a tribe alone together if that was the only way they could survive and not give other drushka the creeps. But then what would happen when there was only one of them left?

Shiv drifted among an endless green sea. She was home, back in the swamp where she belonged, but this time, she was not surrounded by the scent and feel of strange drushka with their old-fashioned ideas and twists of braids that hid their faces. She was not pummeled with eager questions or touched by curious, unwanted hands. She did not have to fend off the thoughts of queens who wished to commune with her and were confused when she denied them.

Better than that, better than the comforting presence of Shi'a'na, her mother, she could feel her sapling and Lyshus, her tribe of one. When she had first felt the sickness, she thought she simply missed him, that the feeling would fade, but the longer she went, the farther she got from him, the more it felt as if she had not taken a sip of water in days. But no water could soothe her, and no meat could tempt her. She knew a truth she had only guessed at before: she would die without him.

It had not been long since they had seen each other. Not yet one of the human weeks, but it was too much time. He would be suffering, too, and that had finally convinced her to run. The old drushka had chased her, wanting to know what had gone wrong, wanting her to return, promising that whatever had happened could be cured; all ills could be corrected. She did not listen, and they did not catch her, and in the end, they ceased trying to keep up.

When Sa had not brought Lyshus, something in Shiv had gone dark. She remembered her actions as though she had seen them at the bottom of a pond. Dimly, she felt shame, but that could not override the need. Now, he was here in her lap, his young mind intertwining with hers like a vine, and she knew peace.

"Daughter?" Shi'a'na's voice. She did not pry, had long ago ceased trying to force her way in. As a queen, Shiv could stop her, but Shi'a'na only hovered. "Tell me, daughter, how can I fix you?"

Shiv felt the healing songs of the shawnessi comforting her, but she had no need of them, not with Lyshus so near. She sent that thought to Shi'a'na and felt a jolt of frustration. The shawnessi wanted to aid her, maybe break the link with Lyshus. That did not upset her. She had once wished for the same thing. Even if it hurt, she would suffer if it would free him, make him more like other drushka, but if it would not work, that was fine. So, they were not like other drushka. When had she been, after all? They were their own truth.

Her mother felt around the problem while Shiv relaxed in the song. Lyshus relaxed, too, asleep and dreaming, his mind quiet now that it was with hers, but he had suffered. She could feel his slight body; he had lost weight when he should be gaining. When they had been together, he had grown faster than a normal drushkan child, but that was simply a new truth, too.

"Can you make him a tree, Shi'a'na?" Shiv thought. Then they could run off to the swamp where they would bother no one. And they would be content with their trees and with each other. And when they died, the drushka could come claim the trees, or maybe the trees would die with them, the four of them in the same grave.

Her mother recoiled. The trees were eternal, no matter what. The life of each drushka was important, but the trees were paramount.

Shiv did not care; she was with Lyshus, and they would never part again.

"I...do not know, daughter."

But Shiv could tell this meant more than one thing. Her mother had always been better at hiding her true self than any other drushka. She might not know how to make another tree, might have made Shiv's by accident, or she might not wish to make another.

Even that did not anger Shiv as it should have. Since Lyshus could touch the trees of other queens, she would share hers with him.

She knew that idea should have repelled her, but she felt nothing but happiness.

"That is the song of the shawnessi," Shi'a'na said. "When you awaken, you will feel differently."

The song stopped, and Shiv's eyes opened. She enfolded Lyshus in her arms as he murmured against her chest. The anger and desperation of the past few days faded, and Shiv felt herself again.

Mostly. Her mother had been right. Without the song, the worry came back.

Shiv did not know how she would share her tree. It had never been done. But someone like her, the child of a queen's body, was not supposed to exist. And when she had fed Lyshus her blood after his birth, everyone thought it would not be a bonding, that she was simply sustaining him as the blood of her mother's blood. They had done no other ritual, but he was as bonded to her as any tribesman was to Pool. And taking her blood had made him a queen. That had to be why queens were not allowed to have children of their own bodies: the thing that made them a queen carried on. Among the old drushka, queens were born only when another queen died, a great call going through the whole. They were born with the green hair, with powers, from parents who had never been queens themselves. And then their line died with them, but Shiv, Lyshus, this...

Shi'a'na helped her sit up, not touching Lyshus, afraid of a link between him and her tree.

But there already was one. Shiv felt despair wrap her again, and even the idea of living alone with Lyshus in the swamp could not chase it away.

"We will solve it, daughter," Shi'a'na said. The shawnessi retreated, all but Reach who knelt by Shiv's side among the soft green of her mother's inner branches.

Shi'a'na folded her long legs beneath her. Her green hair cascaded around her much like the hair of the old queens, and though her mother was shorter than all but the second and third queens, she loomed over Shiv, over most drushka and humans. When she was younger, Shiv had thought her mother the most beautiful thing that existed, and then she had resented her mother as the power that kept Shiv from doing all that she wanted. Now she saw the fear in her mother, knew one day that her splendid mother would die, and the love she felt for Shiv, that carried through all her mother's drushka, would also die. The humans Shiv knew would be dead then, too, and no one but Lyshus would be left to love her.

Shiv could feel her mother's thoughts winging through the branches, but she could not hear them, not unless Shi'a'na let her in. Some were no doubt everyday thoughts, making sure her people and her tree had all they needed, but some were closer, flowing to Reach, and outward, to Simon Lazlo.

"What are you saying?" Shiv asked, fear and loneliness pulling tight around her.

"Seeking a solution," her mother said.

"It seems simple enough," Reach said, spreading her hands. "Shiv and the child must remain together. So, if the child cannot go among the old drushka, Shiv must remain here."

Shiv caught her mother's frown. She did not want Lyshus near her, but she had kept him while Shiv went to see the old people. She could warm to the idea.

"I thought being apart from you might weaken his power," Shi'a'na said, responding to Shiv's agitation. "And it seemed to be so, but now I see that was because you were both weakened. Perhaps we should try to separate you again, only with both of you tended by a shawness."

"No," Shiv said, hugging Lyshus fiercely. She let her mother into her mind enough to see how much she had suffered. Shi'a'na shivered and reached out with mind and body, soothing, reassuring. Lyshus made her nervous, but her love was still there.

Shiv wanted to fold herself into that love and let her mother take care of everything, but she was a queen, with a tribe of her own, and she could not afford such luxury.

"Perhaps that is the answer!" Reach said, catching the emotions flying between them. "With more members in her tribe, the bond between Shiv and Lyshus might not be so strong."

Shiv pondered this, liking the idea. It was the purpose of a queen. "But…" She stroked Lyshus's green hair. "What if they become as him?"

"Perhaps that happened because he was newly born. With an adult, it might be different."

"And if it is not?" Shi'a'na asked. "If we only compound our problem?"

Reach spread her hands, and she was right. Anything was possible, and they would never know if they did not try.

"Then I will take my tribe and go into the swamp," Shiv said. "We will be a small tribe, but we will be together, and no one will be nervous by our presence."

She felt shame from Shi'a'na, a rare emotion indeed, but it did not lessen the fear. Shiv felt conflicted herself, angry with her mother for not giving her unconditional approval and understanding her from a queen's perspective. Her bond with Lyshus made it hard to be angry with him for being able to touch her tree, but the thought of another queen doing so... She would be incensed.

Reach rested a hand on Shiv's shoulder, giving her a reassuring squeeze. "I think you would go mad alone," she said. "We will try all we can before you leave us to suffer." Her tone was a little teasing, and Shiv felt that rush of conflict again, happy that Reach felt close enough to tease her and angry that no one shared her anguish. She wondered if she would ever have the luxury of a single emotion again.

"Now all we have to do is ask for volunteers," Reach said. She and Shi'a'na exchanged a look. Shiv knew the meaning of that, too, and it added more anger. Shi'a'na's tribe had been with her for generations, another thing that rarely happened. Drushka were supposed to mix and mingle among the queens, not bond with a single queen for birth after birth after birth.

But when Shi'a'na put out the call, two voices answered, those who had had a taste of their child but had found it unfulfilling because of his bond with Shiv.

Lyshus's parents ran through the branches to stand anxiously before Shiv, hands intertwined, hungry eyes on their son. Even though he had changed, they still sought a bond with him. Their reverence for queens would not let them be angry with Shiv, and for some reason, that infuriated her more. She wanted their anger; she wanted all their emotions, and she realized then just how much she craved a larger tribe even as she reveled in her attachment to Lyshus alone. She wanted these two to be hers.

And she knew what to do because she was born to it. She stood and reached for her sapling that stood nearby, cradling Lyshus's sleeping form with her other arm. She found a line in the bark and sharpened it with her mind so she could slide the edge of her hand along it, cutting into her skin. Reach began to hum, a song that venerated this moment. Lyshus's parents' eyes fixed on Shiv, their own greed apparent but also glazed over, all of them knowing this ritual without having to be told.

The parents took Shiv's hand and lowered their mouths to the wound, drinking her blood. At the same time, their minds opened to Shiv, and she flowed into them, linking to them in a deeper way than when she had to go through Shi'a'na. Now, Shi'a'na was no longer part of them unless Shiv wished it.

Shi'a'na winced. No one had ever left her tribe before. Shiv felt her mind flowing around the gap, seeking a remedy. Luckily, Reach was there with her song, soothing the transition for everyone. Lyshus's eyes flew open and met those of his parents. Shiv felt their thoughts flowing back and forth, welcoming each other, bonding through her, and it felt so right.

A tremor went through the parents' limbs, and their faces turned from wondrous to confused. Shiv felt something within them, a change, and she despaired, for if they were going to become as Lyshus, they would be four queens, and how would there ever be enough trees?

The parents fell to their knees, and Shiv felt their agony. She dropped beside them, Lyshus tumbling from her arms. He began a high pitched keen. Shi'a'na cried out. Reach's song changed in pitch, but the melody was confused, switching from one to another as she sought the source of the problem.

Shiv's mind was on fire, screaming with agony as her tribemates writhed in pain. The call went out for more shawnessi, for Simon Lazlo, who was already on his way and who now sent his power ahead, looking for damage but finding none. Shiv heard his words through her mother: "Something's changing them! It's inside!"

What did that mean? Shiv grabbed them, trying to fight through their pain to ease it, to find the cause, but there was nothing, nothing. No wounds, no sickness. Their hair fell out in clumps, and she realized they were trying to change as Lyshus had, but since they were grown, it was not working.

"Their systems are rebelling," Simon's voice said. He was in the tree now, the branches winging him skyward until he was among them. "I can't stop it."

"Shawness, you must!" Shi'a'na's voice, and she was in agony, too, connecting to Shiv, trying to ease her pain, to spread it amongst the other drushka so the suffering would be less.

Shiv tried to cut off the connection, to save others this misery, but she feared being alone with it. "Shi'a'na, please!"

Her mother's helplessness surrounded her. They were doing all they could, but it would not be enough. The two bodies at her feet shuddered and bucked. Tiny tendrils of roots broke from their skin as if they were drushka and tree combined. Their eyes rolled back, sinking into their heads as their hair continued to fall, and tiny limbs took its place.

"It's too fast, too fast," Simon mumbled. He turned his power from them to Shiv, seeking to cut her off from their agony, and she breathed in relief even as she cried out for him to forget her and save them.

At last, Lyshus's parents lay still, their lives faded as if they were hunks of wood. Shiv stared in horror. When Lyshus crawled into her lap, mewling, she hugged him close, rocking back and forth. Reach's long limbs folded over both of them as she sang in a low voice, her sorrow like a balm.

"Shiv," Simon whispered. "Pool, I'm so sorry."

Shi'a'na was staring at the bodies, eyes wide, her mind seeking theirs and finding no answer. "Why, shawness, why did this happen?"

"I don't know. I've been following what I could from your telepathic sending, but…" He swallowed. "I can try to find out."

"Do so."

Shi'a'na turned to Shiv, anguish and fear in her eyes, fear for the rest of her tribemates, but also for her daughter, for the life she would lead if no one else could ever join her tribe. Shiv cowered in Reach's arms. She wanted to fling herself at her mother, but she would not be able to take Lyshus with her, and she needed him even more. She buried her face in Reach's shoulder and wrapped herself in her pain.

CHAPTER SIX

Horace fought the urge to put his head in his hands and groan out loud. At Cordelia's insistence, he'd done a deep telepathic scan on the plains dwellers who'd attacked Pool's tree, but so far, he'd only found a fanatical devotion to Naos. No telepathic tampering, not even a slight suggestion. Either Naos's touch was far lighter than he'd ever expected, or these plains dwellers hadn't been tampered with at all.

Lying along Pool's branch in a sleeping line, the captives should have been radiating peacefulness, but more than one scowled in their sleep as if even their dreams were tainted with fervor. After the huge confrontation near Celeste where so many had died, Horace would have thought they'd grown tired of killing and fighting.

Like he had? Even with all the trouble lately, something in him still craved action. He'd thought more than once about how he'd nearly died in the swamp before a quick thinking paladin had pulled him out of the water, jerked the spear from his gut, and demanded he heal himself. He'd been too out of his mind with pain to do it at first, and he would have drowned without the paladin's interference.

Afterward, when he'd healed the captives from Gale, he'd been thankful to be alive, exhausted, and looking forward to getting home again. When he'd finally returned home to something approaching normal, there'd been this…emptiness inside.

With a sigh, he stood and looked to the drushka who waited, watching the captives carefully. "Shawness?" one asked.

"Nothing," he said. "They're just…homicidal."

The drushka spread his hands. Unlike female drushka, he had no poisonous claw, but the gesture was the same: anything was possible. "Some simply enjoy the kill."

"But what are we going to do with them?"

The drushka grinned, showing sharp teeth. "We should release them inside the swamp, ahya. Many dangerous creatures for them to fight, and they will have their fill."

And it'd be nice to give the old drushka a pain in the neck since they'd given Gale so much trouble. But these plains dwellers wouldn't make it anywhere near the old drushka. They'd get eaten by something long before that. He chuckled. Cordelia would probably look on that as a good idea.

"I'll talk to Cordelia. Maybe we'll take them into the plains and let them go while they're asleep. If they come for us again…we'll deal with them."

"Ahya." The drushka gestured to his fellows, and they continued to watch the sleeping captives.

"Will you ask Pool to put me down?" Horace asked, wishing he could tell her like Simon could. Maybe a connection to the drushka would help him find some peace as it seemed to have done with Simon. Maybe learning how to fight would give him something instead.

When one of Pool's limbs lowered him to the ground, Horace spotted Jon Lea waiting near the trunk of the tree. Jon offered a hesitant smile, but when Horace gave him a cursory brush of power, Jon wasn't nervous at all. It seemed his taciturn face just wasn't used to smiling.

"Jon," Horace said with a nod. "Are you following me again?"

Jon's smile widened just a touch as he held his hands up. He'd relaxed slightly since the last time he'd been caught following Horace around. "Just wanted to make sure you were all right."

"I can take care of myself." Horace wanted to walk away, irritated, but something made him linger. After Horace had saved Jon's life in the swamp, Jon had taken to following him out of a sense of obligation. Horace first thought there had to be more to it, that Jon was in love with him or something, but he detected no sexual feelings, just a keen sense of admiration.

"I know," Jon said, but he still stood there as if knowing something and acting contrary to it was the most normal thing in the world.

Horace supposed it was, especially to someone who seemed new to feelings in general. Or maybe he was just new to acting on them.

"Walk with me," Horace said, heading for the gates of Gale.

Jon fell in step beside him.

"Have you ever…" Horace paused, not knowing how to phrase his question, afraid of giving offense or maybe opening himself up, but if anyone was likely to react calmly, it was Jon. "After a fight, after you've gotten past the relief and the adrenaline, do you miss it? I mean, do you ever find the rest of life…boring?"

Jon took a breath and narrowed his eyes, apparently thinking. With difficulty, Horace kept himself from taking a peek inside Jon's mind; that was illegal as well as immoral. He couldn't expect honesty if he wasn't willing to take a chance on it.

"After a few fights," Jon said at last, "you remember how tired they make you. But if you feel like fighting is your purpose, you start to look for them, and it can be hard when you don't have one."

"The tired feeling passes too quickly for me," Horace said. "Don't get me wrong. I don't like seeing my friends get hurt, and I'd never wish a physical struggle on anyone, even if I was there to heal them, but…"

"Maybe you're looking for purpose," Jon said. "Another job might help."

"Scrubbing the barracks like a new recruit?" Horace asked with a smile.

Jon shrugged. "I like to build models."

Horace had a sudden vision of taciturn Jon Lea's room being filled with complex wooden models, a side of himself that many people probably didn't know.

"I don't think building things would give me the rush I'm craving," Horace said.

"Then it probably won't help if I keep listing hobbies." Jon stopped in the street. "Take a swing at me."

Horace took a step back. "What?"

"Take your best shot. I won't hurt you."

Horace glanced around. The street wasn't very busy, but everyone would gawk at two people fighting. Someone swore as she dodged around them, and one of the merchants who'd stepped outside was eyeing them curiously. "I…don't think…"

Jon glanced around, nodded, and walked away. "Follow me."

Horace did, his heart rate picking up, and his excitement building. He didn't know what would happen when they got where they were going, but he was looking forward to it in a way he hadn't looked forward to anything in days.

Jon led him to the Paladin Keep and around the back, to a large field of grass with some wooden equipment and a dirt track. A training field.

"Now," Jon said. "Don't worry. I'm not going to strike back."

Horace's irritation spiked. When would people finally learn, *really*, that he could take care of himself? It didn't matter if Jon struck back or not, with his powers—

"No telepathy," Jon said as if reading his mind. Horace's face must have shown his feelings more than he intended. "No micro stuff. Just you and me. Take a shot."

Horace put his fists up. Jon didn't follow suit, so Horace took a halfhearted swipe at his chin.

Jon moved his head out of the way, and Horace hit empty air. "Keep your shoulders square, and turn a bit to the side, like this." He shifted his stance. Horace followed suit, and when Jon invited a hit again, Horace put a bit more force behind it. Again, Jon evaded easily. As Horace's excitement built again, he tried harder, but Jon barely had to move to stay ahead of him, giving advice in his even tone.

When Horace's energy began to flag, he pushed harder, resisting the urge to reach for his power. As he began to slow, Jon's tone shifted, becoming louder, more insistent, the tone he no doubt used when training recruits.

"Push!" Jon shouted. "Come on! Punch! One, two, one, two."

Horace grunted and tried to hit with one fist then the other until he stumbled. Jon caught him and lowered him to the ground. "That's enough."

Horace breathed hard. "Am I...allowed to use...powers now?"

Jon nodded with that same tiny smile. Horace used his powers to refresh himself and give Jon a little bump, though Jon barely needed it.

"How do you feel?" Jon asked.

"Better."

"Keep some of the tired. It might calm you down to live through a few sore muscles."

Horace barked a laugh. Maybe that was his problem: his powers made fighting too easy. "Thank you, Jon."

"Anytime. We can practice on the regular if you want. You should spar with someone knowledgeable until your form improves."

Horace sneaked a micro tendril his way to see if he was teasing, but no. Horace's form was terrible, but Jon's words made it seem as if he could be better. That made him indescribably happy. "I should go report to Cordelia now," Horace said. "She's offered to show me some stuff, too."

"She's a good teacher." Jon stood and reached as if he was going to offer Horace a hand, then dropped it. Horace chuckled and stood. So, Jon was finally learning he wasn't helpless. It was a start.

Cordelia supposed she should be grateful Horace had solved one mystery. The Naos captives weren't part of any telepathic plot, just murderers on a rampage, and she had no idea what to do with them. Pool couldn't keep them captive forever. Rather, Cordelia didn't want her to. Gale wasn't the police force of the world. And Cordelia couldn't execute an entire group of people for nearly attacking her. She'd tried talking to them, convincing them that Gale wanted to be left alone, but she didn't have Liam's charisma.

The drushka watched for his return, but so far, no luck.

The captives shouted at her and threatened her, even when shown Simon's power. In the end, Cordelia had no choice but to take Horace's suggestion to knock them out, take them far into the plains, and drop them off. It was another stumbling block in her plan to go get Liam back. She had the drushka warn Wuran, letting him know these people might be coming through. She wasn't surprised when Wuran brought his entire clan closer to Gale so they could all keep an eye on one another.

Cordelia wanted to press on and go after Liam, but Simon and Pool convinced her to wait, to give Liam a chance to make an alliance. It wouldn't do Patricia any good to torture or kill him. And Gale was still shaken by recent events. They needed their paladins to stay put for a little while.

As a few days passed, the pall of anticipation hanging over Gale lessened. Naos hadn't come, and people still had to live their lives. Crops needed to be tended; people needed to be fed, and life had to continue. Cordelia met with Simon, Pool, and the others to plan for Naos's eventual arrival, but they kept coming back to not knowing what to do. The best option they'd come up with was to have the yafanai and Simon unite their powers as fast as they could through Cordelia, then launch a spiritual attack. They'd try to keep Naos as far from Gale as possible. While that was happening, the paladins and the drushka would attack her physically.

And if Naos attacked from a distance, too far out for them to get to her quickly, well, they were screwed. Cordelia had to laugh. Accepting that everyone might be screwed let her see each day as less of a slog at least. It was strangely comforting to know some situations were hopeless.

After she'd spent too much time pacing and arguing about marching on the mine, she threw herself into training new recruits with Lea. The mothers of the Storm Lord's children stayed aboard Pool's tree along with Horace and Simon. The ruins of the Yafanai Temple were pulled down, and reconstruction began. Simon went out to bolster the crops every day, and the paladin trail masters had organized several hunts with the drushka, so the people had enough to eat. Cordelia hadn't seen Shiv since her reappearance, but Pool said she was alive, though a drushkan couple had died trying to find a solution to the Lyshus problem. Besides offering a shoulder to cry on, Cordelia didn't see how she could help. She did her best to comfort Nettle, but like the humans, the drushka had to keep putting one foot in front of the other.

Even with all the normality, Cordelia felt...poised. The air had been turning cooler before surprising everyone with a heat wave, and Simon reminded them that after years of the Storm Lord's tinkering, the weather would be unpredictable for a while.

The air over Gale turned stifling, making tempers flare. Cordelia increased patrols, but even she got a mad on every time she went outside and felt as if she was trying to breathe inside a cooking pot. Not a gust of wind disturbed Gale, and she felt certain the crops would have died without Simon. After the third stifling day, Cordelia was more than tired of feeling hot and sweaty and angry. She began to hope Naos would come over the horizon just so all the tempers in Gale would have a target.

After a week of sniping and fighting, a cool wind blew over the city as if someone had flipped a switch. Cordelia had been outside, breaking up some stupid argument between two shopkeepers, when the wind rolled over her. She breathed deep, and everyone on the street sighed as if they'd scripted the scene. Grumbles still abounded, but now they sounded more like apologies, so Cordelia walked away without giving a warning. She turned into the wind, closing her eyes and lifting her chin. In the old days, she would have thanked the Storm Lord, but now she knew any good luck was only despite him.

She headed for the keep at a stroll, not wanting to miss a second of this breeze. She felt this same elation when she slipped free of her body, but she wouldn't have left it now for all the sweet rolls in Gale.

"Captain Ross!"

With a sigh, Cordelia opened her eyes to see Private Jacobs careening toward her, face delighted. Well, at least the excitement in her tone wasn't bad news. Maybe more luck than a shift in temperature had arrived.

"What is it?"

"The mayor's home! The scouts just spotted him!"

Cordelia grinned, her spirits lifting further. She followed Jacobs to the northern gate and spotted the approaching party: Liam, Private Swanson, and Lieutenant Porter.

And Patricia Dué.

Cordelia slowed. "Shit. The fuck does she want?" She hadn't expected a visit from the mine's usurper. But Liam was smiling. Hopefully, the blocks Horace had put in his mind had kept anyone from fucking with him.

She was definitely getting Horace to check him out as soon as possible. "Tell Simon the mayor's back," she said to one of the drushkan scouts. "And ask him and Horace to come to the keep."

"Ahya."

When Liam came close, Cordelia threw her arms around him. She resisted the urge to squeeze, not wanting to crush him with her armor even if it was unpowered.

"Happy to see me?" he asked.

"Of course, asshole," she said softly. "You brought company?"

"To talk about Naos. I convinced her that we should be allies."

She eyed him skeptically, but he seemed confident, more than she would have expected, given the circumstances. "And the mine?"

"All in good time."

What the fuck was that supposed to mean? Cordelia supposed that when Naos had flown overhead, discussions at the mine had gotten sidetracked. According to Simon, Patricia had originally shared a body with Naos, after all. She had to be freaked out.

When Liam gestured Patricia forward, she shifted her feet and seemed to have trouble making eye contact, miles from the confident two-hundred-year-old Cordelia had met before. The way she leaned toward Liam said that she'd come to depend on him, too. Maybe his convincing had been more than verbal.

Cordelia snorted. "Sly fucking dog," she whispered as he fell in step with her.

He blinked and smiled, shaking his head. "What?"

"I'll give you shit about it later, don't worry." She nodded toward Patricia. "I don't know how welcome you'll be in Gale." She raised a hand before Liam could argue. "I'm all for being allies, but you did steal our mine. I'm not ready to trust you."

"If I wanted your town, I'd take it," Patricia said, narrowing her eyes.

"It's all right," Liam said, holding his hands out to both of them. "Trust is earned; I think we all understand that. Patricia can stay in one of the apartments above the warehouses. I can stay nearby just in case any hypothetical fires need to be put out." He winced as if only just remembering Gale had been horribly scarred by fire less than a year before.

Cordelia frowned but nodded. Patricia would have a guard day and night, including drushka and Simon, who was currently walking toward them. Seemed he'd decided that seeing them in the keep wasn't soon enough.

Liam grunted. Cordelia glanced over to see his jaw clenched and his eyes narrowed. She swore under her breath. Liam had been jealous of Simon before, had acted as if Simon was stealing his friends, but Cordelia thought he'd gotten over that shit. Maybe something about Simon sitting here in Gale while Liam had been at the mine brought it all back. But it wasn't as if any of them had been on a fucking vacation.

"Mr. Mayor, welcome back," Simon said, smiling warmly despite Liam's frosty posture.

Liam swallowed visibly as if forcing down the words he wanted to say. "Happy to be home." His smile was a little smug, a little brittle. Cordelia needed to get him drunk as fast as possible.

But to her surprise, Liam was reluctant to leave Patricia at all. Horace met them soon after Simon showed up and waited while they got some apartments ready.

"You sure you want to stay here?" she asked, trying to think past the unease wiggling inside her. She tried a grin. "Or do you want somewhere new and fairly spruced up?"

After a blink, he grinned back. "I am the mayor, after all."

She snorted and rolled her eyes. "And just how many of your constituents are going to get an invitation to your new place for a *private* meeting?"

His eyebrows rose almost to his hairline, then he smiled as if he really liked that idea. Just a little time away had seemed to have gotten him over Shiv, at least a little.

"I noticed Porter's been giving you the eye," she said.

He swung his head toward where she nodded, then made a grunt of surprise before he was seized by a coughing fit. She thumped him on the back, wondering if thoughts of Porter had overwhelmed him, or maybe he wasn't as over Shiv as she'd thought.

"Never mind," she said. "There's no rush."

"Hooray for that," he said, his voice scratchy. He cleared his throat again. "So, tell me what's been going on."

She started with the ship, but he knew about that. She tried to make it clear that she had wanted to rush off and save him but couldn't. Instead of giving her shit or reassuring her that he'd been okay, he nodded and said, "Understood."

Well, maybe he *was* hurt by her non-rescue, or maybe it was still Simon bothering him, or… She sighed. She didn't have time for his childish shit before, and she didn't now. If he wanted to be cold and formal, so be it.

She told him the rest of the news bluntly: that the plains dwellers were riled up again and that they'd recovered Miriam's child. His head snapped toward her at the last news, and he stared intently as she explained that all the children and mothers were staying in the drushkan tree for now.

He took a deep breath, and his face went eerily still. "Sure that's wise? Are these…kidnappers trying to kill the children or protect them?"

She frowned. "Protect them from who? I think they're trying to start a Storm Lord cult and make sure the kids don't grow up under our evil influence."

He looked away as if he didn't know how to process that. "You're right," he said softly. "The kids will be safer among the drushka. That way, no one can push or pull at them. When they're old enough, they can decide what to be."

Something he'd never gotten a chance to do with his hard-ass of a mom. She clapped him on the shoulder. "Right."

"Just don't…" He swallowed and cleared his throat. "I don't think we should vilify their father."

She snorted a laugh, wondering where the fuck this was coming from. "The man who killed your mother, my uncle, Jen Brown, and who knows how many others? Don't vilify him?"

He ducked his head, and the wind gusted, bringing Cordelia's skin out in goose bumps and lifting the hair on the back of her neck.

"Thought you agreed that they could make up their own minds. That should include what they think about their father."

"What the fuck—" she started, then Patricia sauntered over, glancing back and forth between them.

"Mayor Carmichael," she said, "one of the workmen had a question for you."

Liam stalked off, fists clenched at his sides.

"I couldn't help but overhear," Patricia said softly. "The mayor and I have had many conversations the past few days. His father lives at the mine; did you know?"

Cordelia's jaw dropped. "No! Did they meet? What happened?" She forgot who this woman was for an instant before shutting her mouth. She should not be standing around gossiping about her best friend with this...Naos half.

Patricia shrugged. "He said his father had his reasons for leaving when he was a baby; maybe they were able to work some stuff out. I know it's got him thinking about fathers."

Liam confided in Patricia? Or had she dug those memories out of his skull and called it conversation?

"Excuse me." Cordelia stalked away, mentally calling out for Horace and hoping he had his telepathic "ears" open. She saw him standing with Simon, speaking to a group of people, but his head whipped toward her, and he grasped Simon's arm.

"What is it?" he asked in her mind. Simon looked at her, too, and her scalp tingled as their powers played over her.

She strode to them and spoke softly. "I'm fine, but I need to know if that mind-bending, mine-stealing fuck is in Liam's head."

"I scanned him," Simon said. "I didn't detect anything physically wrong, but I didn't do a full scan."

"And I gave him a cursory look," Horace added. "The blocks are still there."

"And you're sure they're *your* blocks?"

He blinked a few times, then shrugged. "I mean, there's no telepathic signature, but..."

"So, you can undo them and see if he's been tampered with? Something's off."

"I guess I could," Horace said, looking to Simon, who shrugged.

"I could do a deeper scan," Simon said. "If she broke through Horace's blocks, she might have left scars." He frowned. "But if she did change him, she's not going to sit back and let us heal him."

Cordelia's face burned with rage. "We'll have to sneak up on them."

"Before Naos arrives?" Simon asked. "I mean, if you don't think we can trust them to help us fight Naos, I'm all for picking a fight, but didn't we want Patricia's help?"

"Fuck." Cordelia kicked at the ground. If they were able to disable Patricia but Liam had nothing wrong with him except for some emotional turmoil, they were fucking up a major alliance for nothing.

But it was *Liam*. She had to make sure he was okay. "Do what you can without getting her attention. I'll find a way to distract him. If I can get proof that he's been fucked with, we'll spring a trap."

CHAPTER SEVEN

Dillon walked down the dusty street and tried to slow his heart rate, tried to tuck his power back where it belonged. At a distance, he'd been able to disperse the humid miasma surrounding Gale, but he couldn't go summoning storms or throwing lightning bolts in the middle of the goddamned town. Nothing would give the game away faster than that.

He was getting on so well with Captain Ross, then she had to bring up his old life, his kids. All he'd asked was that the Galeans not tell his children he was a piece of shit. They could talk about him in neutral tones, let his kids have some affection for their old man. They didn't have to list everyone he'd wiped out on his way to the top.

Especially Brown. That one still hurt. She'd just shot Lazlo, and he was seeing red, so he struck out, just as he'd had with Paul Ross. Shit happened. Hell, kids were well acquainted with accidents.

And did anyone ever mention his many admirable qualities? No, it was always a litany of fuckups. He bet no one brought up how Lazlo had engineered the boggins that almost destroyed Gale or how he'd fucked up augmentation and created Natalya, Naos's old host. Or how he'd held Dillon still while some fucker stabbed him in the back. Dillon would give a lot to know who had actually knifed him, but Patricia claimed not to know him, and the killer had buggered off. Maybe whoever it had been was currently prowling around Gale, and if Patricia smoked him out, Dillon could repay him in kind.

He took another deep breath and tried to calm his temper. As soon as he turned away from Ross's view, he walked a tight circle, hands on his hips as he looked at the calm blue sky. He wished he knew how Liam acted when he was angry, then at least he'd have some way to vent. He'd seemed pretty pissed when he'd shot Dillon six times, but he had to have some speed between diplomatic and murderous. Maybe it took him a while to work up to anger. That meant more smiling practice, digging deep and bringing out his natural charm.

But holy shit, the people in this town were going to try his fucking patience with Ross and her cronies shit-talking his former life on one side, and the people who still worshipped the Storm Lord on his other. And his old followers would be against him in this body. He supposed he should be thankful that someone was trying to avenge his memory.

But he'd have to kill them if they got in his way.

This was going to be Liam's last term as mayor, that was for damn sure. Dillon would ease into this new life, separate himself from Ross and the rest of them, claim they'd just grown apart, then he'd become...

What? Not a paladin; they were crawling with renegades. A mercenary? A fucking shopkeeper? He snorted. Maybe he'd drift around the world, take Patricia to keep him in one piece, and they'd chart this fucking planet, spread humanity around a bit. He'd watched Calamity from his window on the station many times, and he remembered every inch he'd seen, a side effect of Lazlo's treatments. They'd taken plenty of scans from the *Atlas*, and now those were waiting in the mountains. If he could get his hands on them...

Or the metal. It wouldn't matter who he'd been if he could take possession of the metal. Storm Lord or not, the whole world would be begging for a fraction of his time and attention.

Now that was interesting. As he was, he could be overwhelmed by Lazlo and friends, but if he was the king of metal on this godforsaken rock, no one could touch him, especially not with Patricia by his side.

And Naos? He laughed and glanced around to make sure no one was watching, but the dusty alley stood empty, the bustle of the warehouse district masking every sound. If he could somehow get Queen Nutter on his side, he'd be fucking invincible. She'd enjoyed toying with him from space, but he didn't know how much of that had been Patricia's influence. But Naos *was* Patricia, at least on some level, and it wasn't as if Naos was the bad twin and Patricia the good twin. They both had aspects of each other. From what he'd been able to figure out, Patricia had been overwhelmed by the power she'd acquired after the accident, and to cope with that, her personality had split, trapping the part of Patricia she'd always thought of as herself and letting her darker side free, mad as it was.

When Patricia had escaped her own mind, she'd taken some power with her, but not as much as Naos, who still bore the madness for both of them. But maybe Naos could be fixed, as Lazlo had fixed Horace, as he'd been trying to fix Natalya. If her power could be brought to heel, her mind could heal itself. Hell, that was probably why she'd come down: she wanted her sane half back.

If Dillon could find out just what Patricia had done for Naos, he might be able to figure out Naos's endgame.

He strode into the converted warehouse where a group of people were rapidly setting up living quarters. One of the women in a workmen's smock caught his eye and winked. He winked back, wondering if she was an old flame of the mayor's that could be rekindled. A nice thought, a reason to enjoy this body.

Shiv felt more comfortable aboard her mother's tree than she did on the ground, even after the deaths she had caused. Dimly, she thought of what it was like before she had her own tree, before Lyshus, before she had met a single human. She had longed for new faces, for adventure and the unknown. When she had met Cordelia and Liam, she had wanted to spend every moment with them. Liam's embrace had been powerful, ahya, but it was more than that. She wanted to wrap herself in human sights and sounds, to breathe in all the life she thought she had been missing.

Now, those memories were cloudy, nothing compared with the feeling of having a tribe. The contentment radiating from Lyshus was almost enough to drown out the memories of his parents' horrible deaths and the terrible realization that she could not have a tribe larger than one.

Reach said the parents had died because their bodies were trying to change like a queen's, but they were too old, not malleable enough. Shiv could have infant tribemates, but they would all go the way of Lyshus, becoming queens with the ability to connect with any tree. Shiv sat on a branch and swung him around in front of her. He perched happily on her knee, grinning his nose away and putting his face close to hers so they could breathe in each other's scents.

She ruffled his green hair, loving him, but some other feeling wormed just below the surface.

Hatred.

She gasped, denying the thought as soon as she had it, but the feeling did not flee so easily. Indeed, it bloomed. What kind of future lay ahead for her?

She wanted to sink into the calm of her mother's branches, to feel at one with her people, but she was apart from them now, a visiting queen. And they knew of the deaths. She sat among the branches alone except for her tribemate. Lyshus made her mother nervous, and so all drushka were nervous. Shiv could go among the humans. Simon and Cordelia would always make her welcome, but they were not drushka. They did not understand her feelings, and they were busy with their own troubles.

She wished she could let time flow backward to when Shi'a'na had gone to fight the Shi and left Shiv in Gale. She had three children to care for and plenty to distract her. Her time apart from Lyshus had solidified how dim her future was without him, and now it seemed dim *with* him, too. She would have to wander the swamp alone with the feel of him clogging her mind. They would be lucky if they were not killed within an afternoon.

Shiv stood and swung Lyshus around her back again. She could not sink into despair. The anger within her flared, trying to direct itself at Lyshus. She trampled it; he was still a child. He could not help what had happened to him. He could do nothing to change it. She would find a solution, and they would not be outcasts, and they would not be eaten.

Lucky for her, there was much to look at among her mother's branches these days besides drushka. She ventured higher, to where a dangerous human was guarded by several drushka as well as the human Lydia, who did not mingle with other humans. Shi'a'na said that Lydia remained aboard the tree because the humans would want her to use her mind power, and she refused. Shiv wished her the strength to remain apart and yet be happy. Maybe watching the dangerous human gave her purpose.

And then there were the mothers. Most were comfortable among the tree; others were not. Shi'a'na had moved some of her branches close together to form something more like a human floor, and the mothers spent their time there in little cubbies that Shi'a'na crafted from her bark. Some had infants. Evan lived among them, though Reach often cared for him when Simon and Horace were busy. Others had the swollen bellies of impending human motherhood, and those complained very loudly.

Shiv slipped easily into their midst. Maybe this was where she should stay. She was not a mother, but maybe they would understand how she could delight in her tribemate one moment and wish to fling him from her the next.

Miriam, the mind-bender who had once saved Shiv, nodded to her. Shiv followed the human custom and nodded back, but Miriam had too few words. Shiv had had enough of quiet. She went instead to Mila, who often fed Evan. She held her own infant now as she spoke with one of the other mothers, a woman with red hair that was brighter than a drushka's. She held an infant, too, and Shiv recognized her as one of Simon's friends, the fire controller Victoria. As Shiv settled near them, Miriam came over, too, and Shiv grinned. Miriam was only fun when she and Victoria were together and could fight with their words.

"Shiv," Mila said, "how's your little one?"

"We both enjoy health. As do you, I see, or you would be much distressed."

Victoria snorted, but Mila threw back her head and laughed. "It's just a way to start conversation."

Shiv sighed, happy conversation was started, at least. "I seek distraction. My future thoughts are too dire."

"We heard about what happened," Victoria said. "It must feel a bit like you'll never have another child."

Mila gave her an angry look, but Victoria had only spoken Shiv's mind, at least how a human would understand it. "Ahya, but that is what I would be distracted from. Tell me tales between you and the rest." She gestured toward the other mothers.

"Gossip, you mean." Miriam inclined her head at Victoria. "If you're looking for petty, look to her."

"At least I have the good manners to talk behind people's backs," Victoria said. "I don't insult anyone to their faces." She sniffed. "Unless they deserve it."

"You two are a mess," Mila said.

They both grumbled something about why she chose to spend time with them.

"That's easy," Mila said. "You're also the only ones who have popped."

Shiv sucked her teeth, not understanding. "Popped?"

"Given birth," Mila said. "I guess it's mean of me, but I like talking to people who are at the same stage as I am, not terrified of the birth coming up."

"Terrified?" Shiv asked. She had never seen a human birth, but if it involved popping in some way, no wonder the mothers were frightened. "But shawness Simon will see that they are well."

"Being told a thing and knowing it are different," Mila said.

Shiv repeated these words, tried to absorb their wisdom. Yes, someone could tell her that her future would be all right, that Lyshus would be all right, but they could not know. No one could know the future.

Except Lydia. Shiv went still, happiness blooming inside her. She had never seen the point of knowing the future until now.

The others began speaking again, but Shiv's mind raced away. If Lydia could show her the future, Lyshus's future, her fear could finally depart. Even if that future was that they would die soon, she could bear it. If the future showed them living long lives, she could bear it. If they lived, they would be content. No one could live for years with sadness hanging over them.

But Lydia did not want to use her power. Shiv could threaten, she supposed, but Lydia was used to dangerous humans. She might not be swayed by dangerous drushka. Pleading? Bargaining? Shiv could state her fears, but if Lydia refused, she would then be on her guard to another plea. As for bargaining, Shiv had nothing to give. She could have words with one of Lydia's enemies. Or she could fight them if necessary. Perhaps Lydia wished to fight the dangerous human but feared to. If Reach would watch Lyshus, Shiv could do it for her. She did not relish killing a human, but when one death would put her future at ease?

She would find a way.

An argument broke out among the mothers who had not yet popped. Shiv turned toward it, as did the others. The argument rose in volume, then a crack echoed through the branches as one mother slapped another.

Shiv rose to her feet, craning her neck. One of the mothers with short blond hair held her hand to her cheek. Her brown eyes blazed as she glared at her attacker, a tall woman who wore a colorful scarf tied around her head. Both had the bellies, but the scarf woman's belly was much larger.

"You..." The short-haired woman threw herself at the scarf-wearer while the others sought to keep them apart.

Miriam sneered. Victoria seemed amused. Mila passed her child to Victoria, who squawked at suddenly having two infants in her lap.

"Shiv, come help me," Mila said.

"Ahya." Shiv followed as Mila stalked toward the fighting mothers. She bade Lyshus drop from her back, and he did, padding silently behind her. Were they going to join the fray? She must be careful of the bellies. And she must not scratch. She tucked her claws into her palms, her excitement growing. First, she had a plan to see her future, and now she would have a wrestling match? It was a good day.

The mothers were still trying to hold the struggling combatants, but they seemed more protective of their bellies than the two fighters. Mila waded into their midst, and Shiv followed, sending a mental signal to Lyshus to stay outside the crowd.

"Hold her back!" Mila shouted, pointing at the woman with short hair. She took herself toward the scarf-wearer, putting her hands on the taller woman's shoulders.

Shiv eased in between those holding the short-haired woman. Before any of them could react, she wrapped her long arms around the woman's shoulders while whipping a leg around the woman's knees and arching back on her other foot. The short-haired woman squawked at being so pinned.

Shiv rested her chin on the woman's shoulder and spoke in her ear. "Submit, little mother, or I shall carry you to the ground."

Shiv was both proud and disappointed when the short-haired woman went still. She trembled, and Shiv could practically smell her rage. "She slapped me!"

"Ahya, and you wish revenge, but Mila wishes you not to fight, and I agreed to help her." Shiv sighed, the idea that she *must* help Mila shuddering through her. It felt similar as to when another human asked her assistance, and she had pledged it, a strange attachment to those she barely knew. She sent the errant thought to Shi'a'na, seeking a name for this feeling.

"It is being a queen, daughter," Shi'a'na said in her mind. "The feeling that you must protect all who seek the safety of your branches. The humans do not know what they ask when they seek help from a queen, but we feel the need to protect them all the same. You will have to learn when to fight it where humans are concerned."

Shiv sighed again as Mila reprimanded the scarf-wearing mother. Shiv held on to the short-haired one, not trusting her to keep still.

"Do you need assistance, daughter?" Shi'a'na asked, and Shiv felt drushka waiting in the branches, ready.

"No, Shi'a'na. This one is easier to hold than an infant hoshpi." She felt her mother's amusement, and the channel between them closed slightly, though Shiv felt her mother watching.

"Rest easy, little mother," Shiv said aloud. "Revenge can take another form."

This made the short-haired mother relax, and Shiv released her. When the mother nodded to her, smiling eagerly, Shiv nearly laughed, wondering how she would get her revenge. She could not kill the scarf-wearer, not with the drushka watching.

"Now," Mila said as the crowd quieted. "What's this nonsense about?"

"She slapped me!" the short-haired mother roared.

Mila held up a hand. "I know, Shana. I'm not blind." She turned to the other. "Why did you slap her, Kara?"

"Mind your own business, Mila," Kara said, ice in her voice.

Mila put her hands on her hips. "You're obviously not equipped to handle this like civilized people, so it *is* my business, even if I have to be the only civilized one here. You're upsetting the others, upsetting yourself, and you're interfering with my calm!"

As if to echo her, one of the babies began to cry. Mila stabbed a finger in that direction. "And I know that sound is putting all of us on edge right this moment, so you better tell me what the fuck is happening, so I can deal with that, too!"

The volume and the human swear word seemed to shock all of them, though Kara's lips pinched together until they turned white, and she did not speak.

"Shana was going on about the Storm Lord," one of the others said. "And out of nowhere, Kara slapped her."

"She should keep her filthy mouth shut," Kara said, leaning toward Shana.

Shana leaned forward, too. "He is our god, Kara!"

"He seduced us, then left us, Shana! He was just some man."

As they bickered, Shiv frowned, no longer wanting to stop the fight. This Shana still worshiped the man who had nearly destroyed her town? Who enslaved shawness Simon and attacked Shi'a'na? Shiv *wanted* Kara to destroy her.

"Whatever anyone thinks," Mila yelled. "It's over now!" When they quieted, she took a deep breath. "Whether you believe he's dead or not, he's gone. There's no point talking about it and definitely no point arguing. Just keep to your corners."

"We shouldn't need to," Miriam said softly as she joined the crowd. The rage in her voice carried more than any yell ever could. "We wouldn't need to be in this tree if people like you could let go of that…coward." She nearly spat the last word, her dark eyes locked on Shana. "Were you part of the scheme to kill Simon Lazlo? Did you help burn the temple with all of us inside? Did you help them rip me open and steal my child!"

Her voice rose and rose until the last word echoed through the branches. Everyone winced, and Shiv guessed Miriam was using her mind powers. Shana had gone pale, backing away and shaking her head. "No! I promise, Miriam. I wouldn't do that. I wouldn't. I just want…my baby's father to be good." Tears dribbled down her face.

Shiv stepped toward Miriam. No wrestling hold could keep her from using her power, but her telepathy could not affect a drushka. "Does she speak the truth?" Shiv asked.

With a blink, Miriam transferred her glare. "What?"

"Before you destroy her mind, see if she speaks the truth. Truly, Miriam, if she was one of the ones who stole your child, I will help you kill her."

"Daughter," Shi'a'na said in Shiv's mind. "Take care with such a pledge."

Shiv did not respond. This went beyond the feeling of a queen for one who sought her protection. If Shana had stolen a child, she had caused deep anguish. That had to be repaid.

As Shana babbled about how Miriam could look inside her mind and see if she was lying, Miriam let out a breath. Shiv could not read her expression, but she turned and stalked away, taking her child into the branches. Victoria hurried forward, returned Mila's child, then followed Miriam.

The mothers broke into groups, some comforting Shana, and Shiv noted these to her mother. If they still worshiped the Storm Lord, they would need to be watched. Mila continued to speak with Kara, so Shiv gathered Lyshus and wandered away, her mind whirling. She would have to watch these mothers more; they provided a fine distraction, and perhaps she would uncover a new plot to venerate the Storm Lord.

First, though, she would speak to Lydia about her future.

Fajir didn't think she could hate her nemesis any more, but every day when she woke, there was that smiling face, waiting, wanting something from her that neither of them seemed to understand.

Fajir had tried yelling, sneering, even pretending Nemesis wasn't there, but after a week or more passed, her hatred cooled into frustration and then ambivalence. She asked what Nemesis wanted again and again, but the woman only said, "My name is Lydia," then spoke of other things.

She must be desperately lonely. Samira had spent most of her time on the ground, and few humans seemed to want to live aboard this massive hunk of wood. Maybe Nemesis didn't like speaking with the drushka, and she wouldn't go to Gale, afraid of being forced to use her power. But with all that, it seemed as if Nemesis couldn't stop talking, either.

Fantastic.

This morning, Fajir had stayed in her cubby, waiting for the chirpy sound of Nemesis's voice to become so grating that Fajir had to emerge to tell her to shut up, but no sound came. Fajir had waited, but the morning wore on, and she didn't like staying inside all day. At night, she could pretend her life was different, but with no deep shadows, she was reminded of all she had lost, including her freedom.

She climbed out. "Well, Nemesis—"

No one waited except the drushka who always hovered in the shadows, watching her. Fajir looked along the branch for the familiar dark red hair, the slight form, the smiling face, but she saw nothing.

She nodded to the nearest drushka. "Where is Nem...Lydia?"

The drushka spread their hands. Fajir didn't know what that meant, but when no other answer was forthcoming, she walked a few steps away. She heard the drushka close in, a slithering sound as their skin rustled against the bark. Still, they made no other noise, didn't speak, and she knew they would be on her if she took another step. She didn't relish being trussed up like solstice dinner again.

Fajir plunked down, an unforeseen cloud of despair engulfing her like a plunge into icy water. Now she truly had lost everything and everyone, abandoned by every person who had ever bothered to love or hate her. Even her nemesis had grown tired.

Through a gap in the branches, she saw hints of Gale below, a fall that could kill her. Would the drushka catch her? Leap after her as she plunged to her death? Perhaps the tree would catch her, but how agile could such thick, clumsy branches be?

And then...nothingness. There might be an afterlife with Halaan. Or maybe she would become as the stars, her thoughts just a winking light in the void of the night sky. Perhaps she would meet this Naos again, finally see what all the fuss was about.

Her legs twitched. From the corner of her eye, she tried to see the drushka. Since she'd sat, no doubt they'd relaxed. If she could get enough of a start, she could be over the branch and dead.

What would Halaan think of such an end; what would Nico think? Would he mourn?

She sneered at herself. She hadn't risen among the ranks of the guard to ponder suicide like some teenager, imagining the pain on friends' faces when they learned of her demise, wondering if they'd feel guilt for not treating her better. If she was going to fling herself to her death, she should do it for no other reason than that life had become tedious and unbearable without her sword in her hands and her enemies' throats opened before her.

Stupid Nemesis. Why wasn't she here to keep these thoughts from Fajir's mind?

In their last conversation, Nemesis said the drushka had been upset for days because of some tragedy. Nemesis wanted to visit her drushkan friends, find out if there was anything she could do, prying into business that wasn't hers. Perhaps she was speaking with this friend instead of distracting Fajir. Or maybe she'd seen the friend the night before. If Nemesis was lonely, maybe she'd stayed the *whole* night. Fajir hadn't missed the wistful looks Lydia had directed at Samira and Mamet. Maybe she wanted more than just conversation.

Fajir scowled. Lydia's former lover had died, and she would lie with another? When thoughts of her dead love still caused tears? How could she? But Nico had done the same, fallen in love with Fajir. Didn't they know that everyone had one great love in their life, and every other feeling was…

Infatuation? Lust? If they didn't call it love, maybe it was a forgivable sin.

When Nemesis appeared farther down the branch, Fajir didn't return her cheery wave, glaring instead.

"What a morning," Nemesis said.

"How could you?" Fajir said, unable to keep the scorn from her voice.

Nemesis reared back and blinked. "What?"

"To sully your lover's memory with one of them!" She pointed toward the drushka. "Are you so lonely, Nemesis?"

"My name is Lydia, and I have no idea what you're talking about, but I can see you're mad at the drushka for something."

"For…seducing you!" But by the confusion on Nemesis's face, Fajir knew her own thoughts had run away with her. If Nemesis had lain with a drushka, she would have blurted it out by now, probably would have drawn Fajir a picture since she couldn't keep anything to herself.

"You think I was having sex with a drushka?" She grinned widely. "Which one? Or was it all of them?" She called something in the alien language and received several hooting calls in return as well as laughter.

Fajir stood. "Stop laughing at me!"

The drushka fell silent as quickly as if they'd vanished, but the sound of their movement still carried through the tree. The idea that someone could go from laughing to deadly in half a heartbeat unnerved her.

"Something's got you upset," Nemesis said slowly. "Don't tell me you were...jealous." She frowned, then half of her mouth quirked up.

Fajir turned away and tucked her knees up. If she was jealous, it was only because she had no one to talk to. But she couldn't admit that. She didn't want to be so...changed.

"Hey, I'm sorry, Fajir. I didn't mean to...make you angry." She sounded closer, but not too close, not within reach. Once taught, Nemesis remembered a lesson.

Fajir exhaled slowly, letting her rage die. Nemesis had also learned that anger was Fajir's most comfortable emotion. She could always admit to that. "Did you go to Gale?"

"No, I was visiting a drushkan friend, and some of the former renegades came up the tree and told me about some new people in town." When Fajir turned back around, Nemesis sat and told a tale about the mayor of Gale returning with a powerful woman named Patricia. The Galeans hoped she'd make a good ally against Naos. Fajir listened attentively, always anxious for news of battle. If the Galeans defeated Naos, the plains dwellers could be subjugated, and her people would be safer.

"Patricia," Fajir said. "The name is familiar." She thought back to a lonely night under the stars when she'd been Nemesis's captive. "Naos appeared before me and asked me to kill her. She must be a good ally to have. Will she help me save the world, Nemesis?"

"Maybe," Lydia said with a shrug.

Fajir had to admire her certainty even as she loathed the source.

"You never told me about seeing Naos," Lydia said.

"You never asked."

Nemesis gave her a dark look. "What else am I not asking that I should?"

"Are you never tempted to look far into the future on purpose?" Fajir asked.

Nemesis sat back, blinking again. "When I first left Gale, yes. But the temptation fled pretty quickly. My power didn't keep Freddie from dying. It won't help anything."

Fajir nodded. The death of love colored all that came after. "If you'd been born worshiping the Sun-Moon, and your partner had been killed by a creature, you would have spent your life wiping those creatures from the planet."

Nemesis's mouth turned down. "I don't blame the prog for Freddie. It was an animal doing what animals do. The Storm Lord was responsible for what happened." She sighed. "I couldn't have killed him either. Not sorry he's dead, though."

"You're weak."

"That's shit," Nemesis said. "I was strong enough not to surrender to grief." Her face flushed, and Fajir had to smile. She so rarely became angry.

"Prove your strength. Fight me now."

Nemesis's face relaxed into another smile. "It's proof of my strength that I'm *not* going to take you up on that. And proof that I'm not stupid, too."

"You're afraid."

"To fight you? Absolutely."

Fajir smirked. "I suppose it's smart to know when you can't win."

"Oh, I could win," Nemesis said, a note of affront in her voice. "Watch." She stood and began to walk away.

Panic fluttered through Fajir's chest. "Where are you going?"

"I'm winning," Nemesis said over her shoulder. "Because I'm walking away, and you want to ask me to stay." She grinned. "Even if you never admit it. I know it's true."

Fajir's mouth worked, but she said nothing. If she demanded Lydia come back, she would be laughed at. The drushka would cut off any pursuit, and if she begged…

Never. She ground her teeth. Stupid Nemesis.

CHAPTER EIGHT

Lydia couldn't help but feel pleased with herself, as if knowing Fajir missed her was some sort of coup. She knew the feelings were nothing more than loneliness on Fajir's part or some other reaction to captivity. As soon as Fajir was released, she would return to being nothing more than a murderer.

But in the moment, it felt like progress.

Now all Lydia had to do was decide when and if she would speak to Fajir again and what they should talk about if she did. She didn't know what, if anything, would do the most good, but pondering it gave her something else to think about besides the fact that Pool's tree stood just outside the place where Freddie had died.

Lydia shook the thought away as she saw Shiv standing on the branch ahead. A drushkan child hung from her shoulders like a backpack. Lydia was reminded of the recent drushkan deaths, how they were connected to Shiv and the boy, though she didn't know how.

And she saw no reason not to give Shiv a big smile. After all, it wasn't likely that she'd murdered anyone if she was still walking around free. "Young Queen," Lydia said in drushkan. "How may I be of use?"

Shiv cocked her head, wrinkling her nose. "Your drushkan is good," she said in Galean. "But we will speak the human way."

Lydia swallowed her amusement at being given a command instead of an option. Well, Shiv was a queen, after all.

Shiv leaned against a branch, and the boy slipped from her shoulders to sit and play with a handful of small leaves. "I would ask that you...trade."

When drushka paused in the middle of a sentence, they were usually leaving something out, and judging by Shiv's wince, she didn't like the omission. She had a long way to go if she hoped to one day speak as smoothly as Pool.

Lydia held out her hands. "I'm afraid I don't have much. What are you looking for?"

"Something you will not give at first," Shiv said with a sigh. "I do not like this…dragging of the feet, as Sa would say, but I know that if I ask, you will say no."

Lydia's belly went cold. It could only be one thing. "You want me to use my power."

"Ahya."

"But every drushka I've spoken to doesn't see the point of knowing the future."

"Every drushka is not a queen."

Lydia glanced at Lyshus. Something about Shiv's face or tone had obviously alarmed him. He looked back and forth between them with a frown. "Does this have something to do with the deaths I heard about?"

"Ahya," Shiv said softly, hanging her head.

Lydia hazarded a step forward. "If you tell me more about what happened, maybe I could give you some advice, but—"

Shiv threw back her head and laughed, but it had a hollow sound. Lydia wondered if she'd picked that up from her human companions. "If my mother has no answers, how could you?" She gripped Lydia's shoulders, her claw tucked away, but the slender fingers were strong, maybe a bit more forceful than they needed to be. "Ahya, I knew you would say no, which is where the bargaining begins." She smiled, but the sight of the sharp teeth didn't make Lydia feel any safer. "There must be some object you want or some task you cannot fulfill yourself, some trade you will agree to."

Lydia swallowed hard. She hadn't known that the drushka had the concept of everyone having a price. Maybe Shiv was learning more than the rest of the drushka. She tried to smile. "Um, well, I have everything I want, food and shelter."

Shiv let go and tapped her chin, going from threatening to childlike in an instant. "No human baubles?"

"Like…jewelry, that sort of thing?"

Shiv's green eyes brightened. "Jewelry, ahya! You have but to speak its name, and it shall be yours." She thought again. "Ahwa, no. I will bring several from some human places, and you shall choose." She whistled to Lyshus and began to move away.

"Wait!" Lydia cried with a laugh. "I don't want jewelry." And how did she plan to get it, anyway? Steal it? Did the drushka have some cache of coins no one knew about? "I don't want anything, Shiv, really."

"If not any*thing*, perhaps any*one!*" She spread her hands. "Since you stay aboard the tree, you must prefer drushkan company to human. I can introduce you to several very fine lovers. It will be between the two of you to decide what to do with one another." She wrinkled her nose. "Sing your stories of past lovers who pleased you well, and I will tell you who matches best."

Lydia sputtered a laugh. This was one of the most intriguing, ridiculous conversations she'd ever had. "I'm…flattered? I don't know. No, thanks. If I want a lover, I can find one on my own." She felt herself blushing. "Probably."

"No bauble, no lover, and you have your food and shelter," Shiv mumbled with a frown. "A conflict, then. Surely you have one. Everyone does. Tell me of your conflicts, and I will solve them."

"My…"

Shiv spread her hands again. "Enemies that need words or enemies that need a strong fist." She punched one hand into her other. "Enemies that have threatened your life?" Her gaze flicked past Lydia's shoulder toward Fajir's prison. "Enemies who should see the sun no more."

Lydia's mouth worked again. Could all drushka treat death so casually when they wanted?

"Or," Shiv said as she stepped closer, "you could become my human tribemate." Her gaze took on a different cast, not only strong and determined but caring as well. "Pledge yourself to me, to the safety of my hands and branches, and I will care for you always." As soon as she said the words, her mouth turned down, and she jerked her head to the side as if shooing away an irritating insect.

Lydia swallowed, feeling the weight of those words, though she knew they had to mean something different to a drushka. Pool had never spoken that way to Lydia; maybe she'd said something similar to Cordelia Ross, but Lydia had experienced a…feeling in Pool's presence, an assuredness of protection that she hadn't felt since her parents' death. In the tree, Pool's presence surrounded her, made her feel safe.

Shiv didn't have such presence, not yet. She had her own tree, but it was only slightly taller than she was. In time, she'd probably develop the same aura as Pool, but in Lydia's lifetime? Not if drushkan trees grew as slowly as others. And what would Shiv's protection mean while they still lived under Pool's branches?

But none of that mattered anyway.

"I'm sorry, Shiv," Lydia said. "That was a beautiful offer, truly, and I'm happy to call you friend or tribemate or whatever you'd like, but it doesn't change anything as far as my power's concerned. Whatever your problem is, knowing the future won't solve it."

"I only want to know if we live or die!" Shiv said, turning a circle. "Either outcome would bring me comfort!"

"Then take comfort," Lydia said, brightening. "Because whatever crisis you're thinking of, you're either going to survive it or you're not." She smiled, hoping Shiv would see the sense other drushka saw, but Shiv glared, and Lyshus moved to stand beside her, growling in Lydia's direction.

Lydia backed up even as Shiv held a hand in front of Lyshus to keep him still. Another chill traveled up Lydia's spine. When she heard a whisper of sound behind her, she turned to see another drushka, one of Fajir's guards.

"Ahya, be easy," he said, holding up his hands. He stepped close around Lydia, his hands still raised as he put himself between her and Shiv. He smelled like new grass, and Lydia was surrounded by that sense of Pool's comfort again.

Shiv turned her glare on the newcomer, but before she could speak, the branches lifted Pool herself into sight, placing her lightly on the branch. Even as tall as she was and as fearsome as she could be, Lydia had never been afraid of her, not like she'd just felt around her daughter. Pool turned bright green eyes on Lydia, and her narrow lips quirked briefly upward, a reassuring smile. Lydia couldn't speak, too confused. When Pool nodded down the branch, a path of retreat, Lydia turned and nearly ran.

She didn't even know she was heading toward Fajir until she saw the familiar lean shape and long black hair. Fajir quirked an eyebrow before she squinted at Lydia's face and frowned.

"What happened, Nemesis?"

Lydia stammered for a few seconds, still trying to process Shiv's offers, the growl of the boy, the appearance of Pool. Never had the drushka seemed so...alien. "My...name is Lydia, and...I'm scared."

"Of what?" Fajir stepped closer, and Lydia didn't retreat, didn't even notice if the drushkan guards crowded closer.

Lydia shook her head and tried to tell herself she couldn't afford to be stupid where Fajir was concerned, but under the circumstances, any human presence was a comfort. "One of the drushka," she whispered. But what was she supposed to say? A child growled at me, and I ran?

Fajir lowered her voice. "Have they turned on the humans?" Her eyes darted from side to side, probably weighing her options. "If they attack, stay behind me. If you can pick up a weapon, pass it to me."

Lydia nearly barked a laugh, her astonishment growing. "You'd protect me from the drushka?"

Fajir disturbed her even further with a lopsided grin. "I've told you, Nemesis. I'm the only one allowed to kill you."

Then why didn't she do it now? She was close enough to try, but her posture, her gaze, was directed at the drushka, and Lydia guessed she was calculating odds and running fight scenarios in her head.

After a deep breath, Lydia cleared her throat. "They haven't turned on anyone. It was just a…brief conflict." She took a step away. Fajir frowned, but there was something besides suspicion and anger in her gray eyes. Worry?

Lydia sighed as she tried to process two confusing events at once. Now she had another emotion swirling within her, but she couldn't even name it. One thing was clear, there was too much shit going on for her to start having any sort of feelings for a monster.

Shiv faced down her mother as the rest of the drushka faded away. She felt an itch stirring in her belly, a feeling she had often experienced when trapped by her mother, her people: the feeling of rebellion.

But this was more. This was challenge. She had never known this desire to fight another queen, but it felt like a fire inside her that nothing but combat would quench.

"Be easy, daughter," Shi'a'na said, inching closer. Her hands were up, unarmed, and Shiv sensed nothing from her except care and concern. "The instincts of a queen are burning hot inside you. Let me help you as other queens once helped me."

Memories flowed from Shi'a'na of the night she became a queen, ascending to the Anushi tree for the first time. As her tribe had come to take her blood and let their thoughts entwine with hers, she had experienced a rush of emotions unlike any she had ever felt, but she had the other queens to guide her, to explain and soothe.

And instruct. Shi'a'na had chafed a bit under their strict rules, and Shiv laughed to see her mother struggling with the same rebellious feelings she had felt her whole life.

But Shi'a'na had learned how to pass emotions through her tribemates, how to relieve the suffering by sharing it, how to be with all her people at once.

"But I have only one," Shiv said quietly. "And will forever unless I take more children."

"I know, daughter." Shi'a'na sighed, her face sorrowful. She let her emotions continue to flow, and Shiv saw that while she was fearful of Lyshus, she was also sad for him and for her daughter, for all the tribemates who would never be. "It is why your feelings are so... scattered. You do not have the calming influence of wise elders or a host of minds to help bear your worries. And I have not helped you as I should."

The hot feeling of challenge was fading, leaving more room for worry after worry and fear and anger at stubborn Lydia for not wanting to look into the future. Lydia had denied the safety of Shiv's hands as she never would have denied Shi'a'na.

Shi'a'na drew back. "She is human, daughter. She does not understand. You must not give your pledge to them so freely."

"If not them, who?" Shiv walked up and down the branch. "They are the only tribe left to me!"

"They cannot know your mind, not truly."

"Sa can! Shawness Simon can. Give them to me, Shi'a'na."

Her mother drew back, eyes wide, and Shiv felt the flickering of challenge rising within her, too. She quickly quenched it, but the hot emotions made Shiv grin. She could not best her mother, not with strength or with her mind, but to try would at least purge some of the rage within her.

But Shi'a'na went as still as a pond on a breezeless night, and the anger flowed away from her, dissipating among her tribe. "They are not *mine*, daughter. They pledge themselves to whoever they care for, and they care for you as well as me."

"But you took my words as challenge, Shi'a'na; do not deny it! You think of them as your own despite your words, despite the tribe that bears your anger." From her side, Lyshus growled again.

Now, Shi'a'na's mouth opened. "He would dare?"

No tribemate was supposed to interfere in a fight between queens. It was why Shi'a'na had been able to free the queens of the old drushka and fight the great Shi. Lyshus's growls did not affront Shiv. Instead, she grinned, happy someone at least could share her feelings. "But he is a queen, too."

Shi'a'na frowned, and Shiv felt her disgust. She could accept the child of her body being born a queen. At the time, she had not imagined rejoining the old drushka and thought someone would need to take her place one day, but Shiv's tribe of queens was too much to accept.

She would *never* accept it, no matter what she said.

Shiv's anger and sadness and fear melted inside her to become like a human forge. A haze fell over her vision, and she leaped at the creature in front of her, the queen who would take all that was hers, who would deny her a tribe, a life of her own. The lash of her mind was turned aside easily, and her leap became a fall as the other queen threw her to the side. Calming words and feelings were flowing from this queen, but Shiv did not want to hear them, feel them. She wanted to stoke that ember that lived deep inside this rival queen, the one that wanted to respond to challenge.

Shiv leaped again, and again she was turned with ease. Her fury mounted. As she prepared to attack again, the other queen cried out in anguish, and Shiv sensed a different attack. She felt for the source, wondering which queen had involved herself in their fight, but the attack wasn't coming at Shi'a'na. It stabbed at the Anushi tree.

Lyshus knelt on the limb, his mind battering the heart of the Anushi, using the power unique to him to attack the tree, and through it, its queen. Shiv snapped out of her rage as if she had been caught in a sudden storm. The trees were sacrosanct. No matter what happened to individual drushka, even queens, the trees would remain.

"Lyshus, no!"

Shi'a'na was on her knees, and Shiv could almost see the inky tendrils of Lyshus's peculiar power winging through branch and limb, poisoning the sap, the blood of the tree. All of Shi'a'na's drushka cried out, but Lyshus looked on the kneeling queen without pity. Before Shiv's eyes, he blurred, growing, and Shiv felt herself growing too as he passed some of the power into her and her sapling. From where she had left it in the branches, she bade it climb down before it fell. When it reached the ground, it would be large enough to carry her.

"Enough!" Shiv put her mind behind the word, making it a command. Queen he might be, but he was still tied to her, her tribemate, and too young to not obey.

His power ceased, and he looked to her. He was as tall as her waist, taller than a child three times his age, maybe more, as she was taller than she had been. Not as large as Shi'a'na, but nearly as much as the youngest of the old drushkan queens.

Shi'a'na wrapped her arms around herself and looked at Shiv, at Lyshus, with horror in her eyes. Shiv wanted to comfort her, but she felt the shawnessi coming, felt her people beginning to recover. She had to get away, to get Lyshus away. The drushka did not have many crimes, but attacking the tree was one of them. She grabbed Lyshus and sprinted, winging through the tree so fast she was nearly in flight. Her own tree caught her as she leapt free from Shi'a'na's branches. It now stood as tall as the palisade of Gale, and she bade it carry her and Lyshus to the swamp as fast as it could.

Lydia gawked when the drushkan guards fell to their knees, howling in pain, but Fajir moved like the wind. She was on one downed guard in a moment, smacking an open palm into his face so that he plummeted from the branch.

"Stop!" Lydia ran to where he'd fallen, relieved to see him alive on a branch below. She reached for Fajir, knowing she was reaching toward her death, but she had to at least slow the woman down.

Fajir kicked another drushka over the side. The third struggled to draw her weapon, but she was staggering and keening. Fajir tried to wrench the wooden spear from her grasp, but it clung to her hands, and Fajir punched her in the face, making her nose erupt in a golden river.

"Come, Nemesis." Fajir didn't wait for an answer but ran along the branch.

Lydia didn't hesitate. If Fajir wasn't going to kill her, that made her the only one who could stop Fajir from killing anyone else. She followed, calling out for Fajir to wait, wanting to check on the drushka howling around them, but Fajir gave her no chance. She began clambering down the tree.

"You won't get away!" Lydia called. "There're too many drushka."

"We must find a way down. They'll kill you when they recover, kill us both."

"You don't know that!" Lydia shouted. "We don't know anything. I have to help them."

"They've gone mad, Nemesis!"

Maybe Fajir was right; maybe whatever had prompted the rage Lydia had seen in Shiv's eyes had spread to the other drushka.

"We've got to get to Simon Lazlo and Cordelia Ross," Lydia said. "They'll know what to do." She headed toward the nearest branch and used it to climb to the one below, Fajir following her. If they could get as low as they could, maybe they could shimmy down the massive trunk. It probably had plenty of handholds, but Lydia was not a climber. She'd scaled a few trees in her youth, but none had been as large as this monster. Still, she and Fajir eased their way down, and soon, the keening from the drushka faded and stopped. The limbs of the tree drooped as if exhausted, and Lydia was able to scramble down, almost sliding, but the ground was still very far away.

"There," Fajir said, pointing.

One of the branches sagged nearly all the way to the ground. It would still leave them with quite a drop, but it seemed safer than trying to climb down the trunk itself.

When they began the descent, Lydia's foot slipped. Her heart nearly leapt out of her chest, but she managed to catch herself. The branch was more slippery than the trunk, the cracks in the bark not as large, and Lydia skidded more than once, grating the flesh from her palms.

Fear made her giddy, and the world seemed to tilt around her. "We need to go back!"

Fajir caught her wrist. "Careful."

Lydia's breath came in short gasps. She caught a glimpse of the ground below, and it seemed hundreds of feet away, falling farther right before her eyes. She clamped them shut and tried to breathe deep.

"Go, Nemesis," Fajir said, her own voice breathless.

"I'm going as fast—"

"Now!"

The branch began to move, shuddering. It didn't have the slow, careful movements Lydia had seen before; it shuddered and creaked, the tip flicking like a whip. One of Lydia's hands came free, and she scrambled for another hold, digging her fingers in until they either had to go through the bark or break trying. Fajir was yelling at her to move, but she couldn't, her fear pushing her until she embraced her power out of the need for somewhere to flee.

The future was always silent, leaving her room to breathe. She saw herself from a short distance away, watched as the branch whipped to the side, and she went flying. Oh, this was going to hurt.

The air rushing from her lungs broke her concentration, and pain cascaded through her body. She tumbled through something rough, dirt and grass and bushes that grabbed at her hair, her clothing. The world became a blur of light and shadow and agony. When she skidded to a halt, she tried to breathe, but it wouldn't come easily.

Stars danced in Lydia's eyes, and her throat felt as if it had been stuffed with hot lead. She coughed weakly. Something wet slid across her face, the slight movement igniting other blips of pain. Her nose ached like fire. When she moved her head, stars swam in and out of focus. Was she using her power again? Why else would the world become a long tunnel? A black haze creeped over her vision but not before she glimpsed a hand reaching for her.

❖

As Fajir saw it, she had two choices: leave Nemesis where she lay or kill her. She had studied many injured soldiers in the field, deciding whether they would survive being moved. Nemesis's face was bloody, her eyelids flickering before closing. She was no doubt concussed, but her limbs seemed unbroken. The labored breathing was a concern but might be a simple product of the fall and not a broken rib poking into a lung. There was a good chance she would awaken on her own and stumble back to Gale and an even better chance that the drushka would come for her first.

But if they had gone mad, they might kill her. Why not save them the trouble?

Fajir knelt beside the still form, ready to pinch Nemesis's nose and mouth shut or put a knee to her throat. Perhaps she'd flip Nemesis over and grind her face into the dirt until death shuddered through her.

Fajir lifted the small body in her arms and stood. She wondered at herself as she carried Nemesis north, away from Gale and the drushka. Nemesis hated Gale, and the drushka had turned on her, so...

She hurried northwest of the city, out of sight of the palisade before she laid Nemesis in the grass beside her. Neither one of them was dead, and that was...not how this encounter was supposed to go, at least not in any of Fajir's dreams. She'd pledged to kill Nemesis, and she'd had a chance, and now...

Ever since Nico had left, Fajir's purpose had been clear: kill every plains dweller she met until one of them killed her. Then she'd been captured, but her purpose was still with her. She'd fulfilled it for a while under the bondage of Nemesis and her friends. Then when she'd been a guest of the drushka, escape turned all but impossible. She was doomed to captivity until she fulfilled Nemesis's silly destiny. After that, if she lived, she doubted Nemesis and the drushka would let her go back to killing plains dwellers. Nemesis would see her captured again since she could not stomach killing Fajir herself. She did not even want to see it done. Nemesis venerated life in a way that turned Fajir's stomach.

And so, she had to die.

Fajir stayed where she was, her limbs stubbornly refusing to kill.

Well, in captivity, perhaps she'd found another purpose. She'd comforted herself with dreams of killing the drushka, of killing Nemesis, but as she tried to recall those dreams, small details of another dream returned to her.

It had started with Nemesis standing in the long grass of the plains. Fajir had briefly thought of leaping on her, killing her, then they'd been dancing and laughing atop a white boulder under an endless sky.

Fajir sneered. Had a few weeks of captivity made her so weak? She should kill this piece of trash now, and her confusion would stop.

Still, her limbs would not obey.

Fajir shuddered. Perhaps… She stroked her chin as she stared at Nemesis's bloody face. Perhaps she was only keeping Nemesis alive until this destiny had come to pass. Then Fajir would kill her. Fajir, and no one else.

With a nod, Fajir lifted Nemesis again and carried her farther from Gale. She didn't know how much further in the future this destiny was, so it was best to be prepared for a long wait. They'd need food, water, and some way to start a fire. That meant…plains dwellers.

Bile filled Fajir's mouth. She would rather kill both herself and Nemesis than beg from them. But she could *steal* from them. From when she'd first tracked Horace and Simon for her Lords, she knew a clan lived close to Gale. She'd see what they had to offer. Nemesis had begun to shift as if dreaming, a sign that she would wake soon. If Fajir was going to kill any plains dwellers, best to do it before Nemesis woke so she wouldn't have to listen to any subsequent whining.

She headed farther west, bearing Nemesis easily. The woman was far shorter than her and small, though her curves put Fajir's to shame. No wonder she eschewed fighting. Her balance would be all over the place if she didn't build up the right muscles. Her hair had come undone from its tidy knot and blew around her face, the effect spoiled by the blood leaking from her nose. The nose wasn't crooked, probably not broken, just slightly squashed. She'd have a mighty bruise. After Fajir stole some water, she'd wash Nemesis's face, but before then, maybe her injured state would come in handy.

Fajir headed toward a large rock in the distance, the spear-like tor that the plains dwellers used as a meeting place. Fajir skirted around it and soon found what she was looking for, evidence of a camp nearby. She ranged away from it, scanning for tracks. At last, she found a smaller group of tracks, fresh. A hunting party.

She grinned as she sneaked closer to them. They laughed and joked as they walked, scaring away game. Perhaps they were youths at play. She left Nemesis where they couldn't help but spot her, then knelt in the grass and waited.

Four of the plains vermin walked together; they had the blush of youth and were probably out to practice their skills but were chattering instead. She craned her neck. Their weapons were real enough and wouldn't refuse to leave their hands as drushkan weapons did. They carried bags across their shoulders; they'd brought her weapons and supplies. How thoughtful.

When they saw Nemesis, the youth in the lead cried out and rushed forward, the others following. Their elders should have taught them more carefully, chided them for leaping into the unknown. Now they'd never live to hear those lectures.

A shame.

The thought almost made her pause, but she let her instincts take over as the group bent over Nemesis. A doubled fist to the back of the neck laid low the one in the back. The second began to turn, and Fajir's open palm connected with his chin, sending him after the first.

The third was kneeling at Nemesis's side, so Fajir rocked back on one leg and kicked, hitting her forehead and knocking her down, too. The fourth was wilier, drawing a bone sword and stumbling back, but his feet connected with Nemesis's body, and he tripped, falling flat on his back, sword tumbling from his fingers. Fajir snatched it up and bashed his face with the pommel.

All four lay still, and they were all…breathing.

Fajir took off their packs, stuffed as many supplies as would fit into two of them, then swung those around her shoulders. She took the sash from one so she could tie the sword to her waist, then she hefted Nemesis and hurried to the north, huffing under all of her burdens.

She'd left the plains dwellers *breathing*, a fact that made her growl as she jangled along. It was the haste, she told herself, but that wasn't all. Nemesis was infecting her even while asleep! When they'd gone far enough to suit Fajir, she dumped Nemesis on the ground and used the water from one canteen to splash her roughly in the face.

Nemesis's eyes flew open. She tried to sit up, then groaned, holding her head. Fajir's anger was still up; she could feel the heat in her neck, but she leaned forward, easing a hand under Nemesis's head. "Here." She held the canteen out.

Nemesis sipped from it slowly. "Where...what?"

"Be silent." Quickly, Fajir told her what had happened from the moment the tree flung them. She'd been fortunate enough to roll upon going airborne and had landed safely.

When Fajir spoke of the plains dwellers, Nemesis's head snapped up. She winced but kept her steady gaze. "Did you kill them?"

"No," Fajir said. "Are you happy?" She tried to be as snide as she could but was unsure what answer she was looking for.

Nemesis sat back, gaze unreadable. "Yes. Thank you."

Fajir breathed out. Good; that reaction was good. If Nemesis thought Fajir had spared those plains dwellers just to please her, it might make her more controllable. "Fine." She rooted around in the packs until she found a rag. "To clean your face," she said as she handed it over.

Nemesis raised a hand to her nose and winced. "How bad is it?"

"Not broken. And though you were unconscious, you have only a small wound to your head. You may have a broken rib. You were lucky, Nemesis."

"My name is Lydia," she said as she put a hand to her side and winced. "What do I do for a broken rib?"

Fajir smiled, happy to be speaking of something besides feelings and not killing. She helped Nemesis bind her ribs with one of the straps from the packs. "Even if it's not broken, being bound will remind you to favor that side."

"I don't need the reminder, thanks," Nemesis said as she tried to stand. "Did the drushka chase you out here?"

"No. I didn't wait to see what they did after they went mad."

Nemesis nodded slowly and glanced around. She seemed afraid. Good, that would make her easier to control, too. "So, what's the plan? I'm guessing you won't go back to Gale, and since you brought me out here, you don't want me going back either."

"They might have killed you, too, but are you thankful for my rescue? Clearly not."

Nemesis snorted a laugh. "Sure, thanks for saving me from the drushka, who are probably fine now, and who you *definitely* didn't run away from just because they were holding you prisoner."

Fajir shrugged. "You could have looked into the future to see, but you didn't. If you're going to deny your power, Nemesis, you're going to have to trust your instincts, as you did when we fled the tree."

"I thought we could get to Gale," Nemesis whispered.

"I was never going to Gale. Surely you knew that when we began to climb."

Nemesis nodded.

"And still, you didn't object when I followed you. You don't want anyone to kill me." The words caused an uncomfortable warmth in Fajir's chest, and she searched Nemesis's face for confirmation, but Nemesis looked away.

"Why am I here?" Nemesis asked. "Were you waiting for me to wake up just so you could be a sarcastic ass? So you could cut my head off with your new sword?"

Fajir's stomach turned. "I'm not some barbaric, plains-dwelling vermin."

Nemesis quirked an eyebrow. "You tried to strangle me once with your bare hands."

The memory made Fajir shift uncomfortably. The deed now seemed to belong to someone else. "Is it wise to remind me of that now?"

"So, what am I doing here?"

Fajir sighed. "I…need you…to be alive when this fire comes, so…I can see if your power is real." She waved vaguely. "Before I kill you." She looked away, not knowing which expression on Nemesis's face would anger her more: fear or gratitude or hope or something else entirely. She stood. "Come, Nemesis. We will walk my road for a time."

"My name is Lydia, and if you try to kill anyone who doesn't deserve it, I'm going to find a way to stop you." She stood, her legs shaky but her expression determined.

That would do. "Rest assured, everyone I kill will deserve it."

CHAPTER NINE

Patricia had forgotten what it was like to be around a crowd. The warehouse district of Gale bustled with people shouting and lifting, building, and tending animals. Their heartbeats surrounded her; the susurrus of their minds flooded her own. The press of Gale came so much closer to swamping her mind than the small numbers at the mine. Moment to moment, she could almost enjoy it, losing herself in sound and sensation, imagining herself among a great swarm of butterflies. But when she tried to think, it felt like struggling to move through that very same swarm. She couldn't see, and the feelings became frightening in their enormity.

When the feel of struggling reminded her of being trapped in Naos's head, she fought down panic. They weren't one anymore. She didn't have to split herself in half in order to deal with this power. She breathed slowly and blocked out the denizens of Gale inch by precious inch.

She was not Naos, even though they'd once been the same. She could hardly believe it, but Dillon had been right, and that annoyance helped center her. Before him, it had been so easy to cast Naos as the villain and herself as the escaped prisoner, but Dillon argued otherwise, and she'd been forced to believe him. She wasn't better or worse than she used to be, and Naos was just a megalomaniac because that was who she'd had to be in order to deal with her enormous power. But what if Naos's motivations had dwelled deep inside Patricia herself: her mild obsession with Dillon, her desire to have everyone do what she said without argument, her dislike of subterfuge, and her desire for everyone and everything to make sense?

So, Patricia's reasons were why Naos had tried to subjugate the world before, but what about now? Patricia shivered. Naos wanted

Patricia back so she could keep a rational thought from one moment to the next. She'd dipped into Patricia's corner of their mind all the time to bathe in rational thinking. Without that, Naos would probably drift through space wherever the music of the universe took her.

Patricia took another breath. It didn't matter. Simon had defeated Naos before; he could do it again, and she would help, then she would be free. She'd be the most powerful person on or above Calamity.

She only hoped she didn't have to kill Simon before he turned his power on her.

At the converted warehouse, workers were putting the finishing touches on her new rooms, something opulent enough for visiting guests. Someone had tried to hide the construction with colorful throws tacked to the walls or furniture placed in front of stacks of boards or bricks. She drifted to the window overlooking the street and stared at the bustle below. Maybe she'd ask for a skylight and a ladder so she could climb to the roof and see the city spreading below her like a buffet.

Smiling at the thought, she wondered where Dillon was. In the days they'd been in Gale, he'd avoided Liam's old friends like the plague. He seemed happy to oversee the construction, and she was happy to let him. She'd kept contact with Jonah out in the plains, but he hadn't reported anyone coming from the north, just some minor agitation with the plains dwellers, but no concerted attack such as Cordelia Ross had warned them about. Patricia didn't bother to tell anyone about a minor scuffle, not wanting to let slip that she had scouts. Who knew what the Galeans would do if they discovered Dillon's old body up walking around?

They were already poking around too much. Patricia was growing tired of shooing away Horace's telepathic probes. For someone who was supposed to be in love with Simon, he certainly spent a lot of time trying to pry into Liam's mind. She'd tried to make her new blocks resemble Horace's old ones, but so far, every time she thought he was satisfied, she'd catch him sniffing again. When Cordelia or the others tried to visit, Dillon put them off, claiming he was too busy for chitchat, but that couldn't hold forever. Cordelia stunk of suspicion, and Patricia knew she wanted to grab the mayor so Horace could do a deep dive into his psyche. She thought Patricia was manipulating him.

She didn't know the half of it.

Patricia wandered down the hall to the mayor's new office. Dillon sat at a desk, looking at some paper. The sunlight slanting through the window picked out strands of his dark hair and turned them gold. When he looked at her with eyes as bright as emeralds, she smiled. She couldn't have picked him a more handsome face if she'd tried. Liam's body was leaner, without the command inherent in Dillon's old muscles, but Liam's body seemed to have charm genetically implanted behind its high cheekbones.

"I never enjoyed paperwork before," Dillon said, "and that hasn't changed." He tossed the paper aside.

"Don't you have people to do that? Mayoral aides?"

He grinned. "I have to learn some of it if I'm going to fake being the mayor, at least for a little longer."

That was a surprise. "Not planning to keep the job?"

He mumbled something, and she had to clench her hand to keep from reading him. She'd have to break her own blocks to do so, but more than that...she couldn't let him be completely right about her! She'd changed, damn it.

And she didn't want to ask what he was planning to do if it wasn't being the mayor. "Cordelia and her friends are going to come for the mayor. Soon. They haven't stopped fishing."

Dillon leaned back in his chair and scrutinized her. The color might be different, but there was something about the intensity of his stare that she remembered from before: charisma he'd managed to take with him. "You got all that from surface thoughts?"

She rolled her eyes. "I haven't gone prying and tinkering. Cordelia Ross happens to think very loudly. I'm still playing by your rules. No 'mind fucking.'"

He sighed. "You're still using your power when you don't need to. One look at that woman's face will tell you she doesn't trust you."

Patricia's anger flared. "So, I'm only supposed to use my power when you give me a direct order, *Colonel?*"

He stared at her like a parent waiting for the end of a temper tantrum. Patricia took a deep breath. She was getting tired of playing his games. As soon as she didn't need him...

She forced herself to take a breath. Contemplating three murders in one day had to be her limit. She was not going to kill Naos just to become her. "What are we going to do about the mayor's friends?"

Dillon stood. "Head them off. Come on, you and me are going out."

He led her to a bar in one of the nicer areas in town. She wasn't sure alcohol was a good idea, but as they settled amidst the tables, and people said hello to the mayor, Patricia began to relax. A distraction was just what she needed. She even sipped the local mead and enjoyed the smell of fresh flowers arrayed in a clay vase on the table. The place was only a quarter full, and the conversations around them were background murmurs. The walls were a light sky blue that put her in mind of a spring morning.

Patricia hadn't tried the alcohol at the mine. As she sipped, she found that she'd missed the burn, the way the tongue went slightly numb in its wake. It was like a signal for better times to come.

On her second glass of mead, Patricia felt someone prying around the edges of Dillon's telepathic blocks. She nearly dropped her cup before slamming it down, splashing the table and Dillon's sleeve.

"Hey!" he cried, frowning at her.

"They're doing it again," she said, wanting to shout but keeping her voice down. "Someone's trying to get in your head."

He sighed and put his own cup down. "It's my fault. I'm not doing a good enough job fitting in. I should have come here before you and eased the way."

She blinked, beyond surprised that he would admit such a thing. "That's...they would have just broken your blocks without me."

"But they might not have suspected anything if you weren't with me."

So, he was blaming her after all. Before she could yell for real, he held up a hand.

"Don't worry. I thought this might happen. I've got an idea."

"Run for it?"

He snorted a laugh. "As if Ross the bulldog would just let the mayor go."

The psychic probe came again, irritating her like a splinter embedded too far under her fingernail to reach. "Is now when you order me to use my powers? Or are you still trying to prove you're *not* a hypocrite who'll say whatever he needs in order to get what he wants?"

To her surprise, he laughed again. "Doesn't make me wrong."

"What are we *doing*, Dillon?"

He frowned hard and leaned forward. "Louder, please. The whole fucking town didn't hear you."

Patricia clenched a fist and took another breath. She did not have to lash out. She was not Naos. "If they gang up on me, they could overwhelm me like they're planning to overwhelm *her*." That niggling tendril came again, and Patricia felt along it to Horace's power on the other end. "I've got him in my sights."

Dillon drained his glass. "Lead me there."

Patricia's hackles raised at being ordered about, but she did as he said. Maybe he was going to pummel Horace into submission. Whatever happened, she was certain he'd be begging her to use her power by the end.

Patricia led the way out of the bar and down the street, following Horace's signal until it snapped off; Horace sensed her coming, but she had the pattern of his brain down now. She could follow him anywhere.

When she and Dillon turned the next corner, Horace was standing by a rug stall on the edge of the market, Cordelia Ross with him. They were pretending to *shop*. Simon Lazlo must have had more important things to do, but Patricia bet he was waiting somewhere, power at the ready for the slightest telepathic call.

"Horace, Cordelia!" Dillon shouted, raising an arm.

They turned, but their smiles were hesitant, caught in the act.

Cordelia took a step forward. "Liam, what—"

"What's with the mind probes?" he asked as they reached each other.

Her eyes widened while Horace glanced at the ground. Neither bothered to answer.

"I was just sitting and having a drink with our new friend and ally." Dillon nodded at Patricia. "Then she tells me someone's trying to wiggle into my mind. I asked her to trace it, and here you are." He smiled, but even Patricia could tell that the look seemed wrong. It didn't reach his entire face.

As if realizing that himself, he settled on a frown. "What gives?"

Cordelia frowned right back. "I should ask you that. You've been avoiding me."

"Maybe I have more important things to do."

She tsked. "And you've been making more pissy comments. If something's wrong, blow up at me, for fuck's sake." When Dillon took a deep breath, Cordelia pointed at his face. "See, that's what I mean. Something's holding back your anger, and I think it's her." She switched her glare to Patricia, who shrugged, so ready to shut her down.

Dillon reached up slowly, put his hand on top of Cordelia's, and lowered it. "Yeah, you got me. I think it's bad form to fight in front of our allies."

"That's a load of shit. She's in your head. She got around Horace's blocks and replaced them or something."

Or something was right. Patricia smiled, starting to enjoy herself. She kept her power coiled, unseen, around Horace's brain, ready for when Cordelia tried something physical. It would feel so good to let loose, even here under Simon's nose. Without Horace as his right hand, maybe Patricia would be able to best him.

Dillon was saying something about diplomacy. Cordelia shoved his shoulder. Horace's power rose but didn't flow, not yet. Dillon staggered one step and put his arm out across Patricia's body as if holding her back.

"I'm fine," she said, telling him she wasn't using her power, not yet, not until Horace did.

"If you're not under her influence, prove it," Cordelia said. "Let Horace scan you."

"And lose the blocks?" Dillon asked, frowning. "The only thing keeping our new ally from…" He cleared his throat. "Manipulating me?"

"He put them up; he can put them back. So?" Cordelia lifted an eyebrow.

Dillon stared her down. His mind was probably racing. He so clearly thought Cordelia would back down when confronted. He'd been too used to that in his old life. Patricia risked a probe toward Cordelia's mind. If she could pick some childhood memory, she could feed it to Dillon. Maybe that would placate her, and then…

Her gentle probe hit a wall, the same sort of block Liam had in his mind when she'd first met him, the reason she'd had to scatter his consciousness instead of just putting it aside.

Horace's wide eyes turned toward her. His mouth opened.

Patricia slammed into his telepathic power with her own, blocking his signal, but he pushed back, ready, and he wasn't a fool. He grasped Cordelia's arm. Swearing under her breath, Patricia took control of his body, the first thing she should have done, but Cordelia had already seen his face, the direction of his gaze.

"Motherfu—"

Cordelia grabbed for Dillon, but Patricia took her legs out from under her; she tumbled to the ground. Patricia's control over Horace slipped. A signal went out.

Patricia mentally grabbed them again, but she already felt Simon Lazlo's power sweeping over her. She grunted as waves of pain stabbed through her, her nerves on fire. "We have to run."

Dillon hauled her tight to his side, and they left Cordelia and Horace in the street. "Fuck, fuck," Dillon said. "I had that! I had—"

A crack like thunder boomed in the cloudless sky. Patricia looked to Dillon, thinking he'd struck with his lightning, but he seemed as confused as her. A flash of light came from the west, and Patricia winced. The flash resolved itself into a burst of flame, and Patricia was barely able to make out the meteorite streaking through the sky to slam into the fields outside Gale. She stumbled as the ground shook, and people screamed around them. Dirt flew into the air as if sprayed from a giant fountain, and several market stalls shuddered as if threatening collapse.

Patricia realized she was hugging Dillon for dear life; he had an arm around her, too, but his eyes were locked on the dirt falling from the sky like rain. Patricia's heart thudded in her chest so hard, she wouldn't have been surprised to feel it punch through her shirt. Simon's attack had ceased, but now she felt something new, a tingle across her scalp, and buzzing filled her mind as if her skull was full of bees.

All around them, the people of Gale grabbed their ears and shook their heads. As the sound grew louder, they shouted at one another, but Patricia couldn't hear them. Her heart sank. The sound wasn't outside of them; it was inside, and she knew of only one telepath with the strength to send such a message to so many at once.

"I'm tired of waiting, chickadees," a voice said, Naos's low purr. "I thought you'd have come in droves by now. Well, since you're all so terribly shy, how about a gift? The first group to come find me in my mountain hideaway gets all the metal that their hot little hands can carry. And if you don't come…" Patricia received a flash of images: Naos's power hunting through the stars until she found an asteroid that would suit her purposes. "Not too big, not too small. My own little baby bear." She had yanked on that flying rock, altering its course, steering it like a goddamned ship until it crashed just where she wanted it. Maybe Celeste had gotten the same.

"And that's just the beginning. See you soon, lovelies."

"No," Patricia said with a sob. "It's a trick. She won't give you anything." She muted her power to almost nothing, but Naos wasn't speaking to her specifically, not yet. First, she wanted to see how many enemies she could get out of the way.

The sounds and images faded as swiftly as they'd come. Naos might not be able to possess anyone, but her power was still too awesome to comprehend.

"Fuck," Dillon whispered.

"Indeed," a voice behind them said.

Patricia spun around. Simon stood behind her, a revived Cordelia and Horace at his sides and a host of yafanai and paladins at his back. Patricia snapped her telepathic shields tight around her and Dillon.

Simon held up a hand. "We can't afford a fight right now," he said, "if we're going to go after Naos. Who knows what she'll do with all the people she's now luring to her hideout?" He looked between them, a frown on his face. "But we need to know the truth."

"And you have to let Liam go," Cordelia said, glaring at Patricia.

Patricia swallowed and looked to Dillon. She opened her mouth, desperate for something Simon would believe, the brain damage excuse he'd come up with. Since he wasn't a telepath, the damage was all he'd see if he looked.

From the confident look that stole over Dillon's face, he was thinking something similar. Time to find out if they'd ever have made it as actors.

"I've got good news and bad news," Patricia said. "The good news is, I'm not controlling Liam."

"And the bad?" Simon asked.

"He's not exactly…himself anymore."

Cordelia didn't want to believe it. According to Patricia, when the *Atlas* crashed, the mine collapsed, sending tons of rock down on Liam's head as he took a tour. By the time Patricia and company had gotten to him, his brain had been damaged on the deepest level.

"I fixed what I could," Patricia said, "but there was some memory loss, and I don't know him, and your paladins only knew him a little. I had to…improvise."

Cordelia glanced at Horace and Simon. Horace gave her a little nod as if to say it was possible. Simon's face was carefully blank.

"Is that why you won't let Horace in?" Simon asked.

"I was hoping to find out enough about him to fill in the gaps I missed, but…" She shrugged. "You're all tightly shielded yourselves."

"You should have fucking told us from the start!" Cordelia shouted, unable to contain her anger any longer. "You should have sent a telepathic message to us when it first happened! Simon could have fucking fixed him."

Horace put a hand on her arm, but he didn't send any calming waves her way. Good, she wanted to feel her anger. She stared at Liam, caught up in a mix of pity and horror. How much about her did he actually remember? Being kids together? Being partners? There was a time when they were practically the same person. Did he remember that at all?

That probably depended on how much shit Patricia was full of. She could easily be using this brain damage story to cover for how she'd fucked over his mind in the first place.

"Let me." Simon stepped forward, hand out. Liam pulled his head back as if alarmed, and Cordelia tried to remember if Simon had ever healed him before. They'd never been the best of friends. Liam probably still had some resentment about when Simon had healed the Storm Lord after Liam had gone through all the trouble of shooting him six times.

If he even remembered that.

"I see the damage," Simon said quietly, his eyes searching Liam's face. Liam's expression relaxed as seconds ticked by. Simon's healing had a soothing effect that even Liam couldn't ignore, no matter how pissed off he was.

Simon turned a pitying look Cordelia's way. "There was substantial damage, and the brain's a tricky organ. Even if Patricia had been intimately acquainted with his neurons and all the pathways of his brain, she would have had a difficult time rebuilding it exactly as it was."

"I did the best I could," Patricia said, sounding sulky but also guilty. "I'm sorry."

"It's all right," Liam said, turning to her. "I told you it was." With a sigh, he looked to Cordelia. "She asked me if we should tell you, and I said no. I remember…bits and pieces of my life. I thought that, as time went on…"

Cordelia swallowed hard, not knowing if she should mourn the lost memories while he was standing right in front of her. He was dead, and he wasn't: a walking corpse. "No, it's okay. I'm sorry. I didn't…" She breathed deep. "You should have fucking told me, Liam!"

"You would have looked for a solution that isn't there," he said.

She pointed in his face, anger taking over every other emotion again. "I will decide just how much shit I can handle. Nobody can do that for me. If there's a problem, I want to know."

His gaze was steady, but she caught a hint of a smile. "Understood."

"I can help," Horace said. "I've worked with amnesia patients. There might be more there than you realized." When Patricia turned a resentful glance his way, he raised his hands, drushkan fashion. "Not saying you did a bad job, but unless you were the healer or the psychiatrist among the *Atlas* crew, I have more experience."

She put on a smile. "The blocks are there to protect what memories I could retrieve from the paladins and whatever else he's currently building. It's too late to start over. Who knows what else he might lose?" She looked to Cordelia. "I'm not lying. I don't have a personal interest in him, not like you, but with Naos here, I knew...I had to make amends after how I treated you. Fixing the mayor is how I'm doing that. Please, we might have handled this badly in the beginning...and just now...but I know what I'm doing, really."

She said, "we might have handled," including the brain-damaged guy in her fuckup. But he'd said he hadn't wanted to tell anyone. That sounded like the old Liam. He would have been afraid they'd make him give up being mayor.

And Cordelia supposed they were lucky that Liam wasn't actually her puppet. He was walking and talking on his own. A few people had told Cordelia that Liam and Patricia had had several long, loud arguments, so he wasn't just doing whatever she told him to do.

"Where do we go from here?" Cordelia asked Liam. "If you want to start over with Horace, we can find someone to take over the mayoral duties. You'll have time to heal, and then, you can be mayor again."

"With everything I have to do in the city and Naos in town?" He grimaced. "No thanks." He affected a pose she'd never seen from him, relaxed but on guard. She knew a lot of paladins who never seemed to go off duty, but he'd never been one. When he relaxed, he did it all the way, at least on the outside. Inside, he was the same bundle of knots as everyone else.

She didn't know whether to hug him, hit him, or introduce herself.

"We need a plan," Simon said. "For Naos. All cards on the table."

Cordelia had no idea what that meant, but if it was about showing secrets, she was in. She told herself there'd be time to repair Liam's fractured memory after they'd dealt with Naos. She'd sit on him if she had to, but she'd get the old Liam back.

CHAPTER TEN

Shiv wrapped her arms around herself and keened, keeping to the shadows of the tree that had been part of her former home in the swamp. Never had she felt such sorrow, such horror. Her tribemate had attacked a queen and a queen's tree. He had done it in defense of her, but even so, it was wrong! Her mother had shared stories of her fight with the Shi, and even when that great queen was threatened, the drushka had only sought to bar her mother's path or restrain her, never to harm, and it had not even been in their thoughts to harm the tree.

Now, Lyshus had done both, and he did not seem to understand the crime he had committed, one that would not even blossom in the thoughts of any other drushka. It had to be her fault; she had turned him into a monster.

Sitting on the floor at her side, he stared at her with worried eyes, his body much longer than it had been scant days ago when they fled from her mother. He had only seen two full moons. He should have been as high as her knee, but his head reached her waist. And with the power he had pulled from Shi'a'na and put into Shiv, she was nearly a foot taller than she had been. Her trousers halted halfway up her lower leg, and her sleeves stopped at her elbows.

She would not have cared save that it was a reminder of how everything had changed. When she had fled from her mother and into the swamp, she thought of nothing except escape. The journey and the few days following had been a nightmare of running and stopping only to listen for signs of pursuit. The swamp seemed to be listening, watching, judging. They had eaten sparingly as they journeyed farther into the thick ropy branches of the swamp trees until they reached Shiv's former home.

The small camp her people had once lived in stood in ruins, abandoned nearly nine months in the past. The drushka had made a small village that humans could visit before they knew about the queen and her tree. The houses they had built among these trees had been reclaimed by the swamp, even in so short a time. Vines covered them, and tiny sprouts sprang from the walls.

Shiv crouched in the middle of the house she had called her own, but the roof had caved in under a deluge, and her scent had been replaced by the smell of mold. Outside the window, her sapling waited, tall enough to carry her now. It did not feel as drushka felt, but she called to it anyway, unwilling to seek comfort from Lyshus, not yet.

When the tree reached a branch through the window and touched her shoulder, Lyshus breathed out, a sigh and a keen. He sensed her sorrow and her reluctance to take comfort from him. It confused and frightened him and made him even sadder.

"Do you not see?" she yelled. She shared with him the memories of what he had done, trying to impart her horror and the idea that he must never attack a queen's tree again.

He ceased keening and cocked his head. His own memories countered hers: she had been in pain, and he wanted to stop it. His was a child's understanding with too much power behind it.

Shiv groaned and took his shoulders. "Lyshus, you must never harm a queen's tree. I should have taught you this lesson before, I suppose, but..." She should not have had to. It should have been part of his blood, her blood that she had passed to him. "Perhaps my blood is tainted, but whatever the reason, you must see how the trees connect us." She fed him images that her mother had offered her when she had asked for tales of the old drushka, how a great tree had split the world in the very beginning of things. Its seeds broke open and became the creatures of the world, and one of those creatures was the drushka, the first Shi.

She shared memories of her own childhood. She had felt how Shi'a'na's tree was connected to her drushka, that without it, they would have no connection to the living world or to one another. Without it, they would die. No drushka could live without that connection, without a tree to sustain them.

He sat still, his green hair hanging limply around his face. It had grown with the rest of him. She smoothed it away from his silver eyes. His gaze flicked to her tree, then back to her. "Tree," he said softly, learning speech now that he was large enough to use it.

She sucked in a breath, but as oddities went, speaking at just over two months seemed the least dangerous. "Ahya," she said. "The trees are important."

He frowned, and she received the impression that her tree was most important, connected to them as it was. Shi'a'na's tree was less important, could be sacrificed.

"No! If that tree dies, all its drushka will die! Shi'a'na, Nettle, Reach, your…" She had been about to say his parents, but they were already dead.

Lyshus did not grieve. They were nothing to him. And he only recalled Shi'a'na as a thorn to Shiv and to him, someone who had tried to keep them apart and then—as he saw it—had tried to hurt Shiv. Of Reach he had several fond memories but only as the mother of Little Paul, with whom he liked to play.

"Yes, yes!" She latched on to that memory. "You must…help protect Little Paul's mother!" She could not think of the right words. He should venerate the trees on his own. It should simply be part of him. Even though she loved to hear the stories sung aloud, Shiv had known from birth that the queen's trees were sacred. As a queen, she would fight another queen if she had to, but she would never harm a queen's tree. The very idea made something deep inside her shudder.

Lyshus had no echoing shudder. He sucked his teeth, still not able to see beyond the two of them. He was broken, and it was her fault. Her blood had done this to him. She wanted to wrap her arms around herself and keen again, but she had to do something with the two of them. They could not keep running blindly, but if he could not understand why the trees were untouchable, he could not be around other drushka.

She caught a thought from Lyshus. Little Paul was human, not drushka. Even if Shi'a'na's tree died, taking Reach with it, Little Paul would live. He grinned, happy his friend would be safe.

Shiv nearly threw him from the house. He simply could not see beyond his circle. He loved her. He loved her tree. He even cared for Little Paul, but beyond that, he did not understand why he should care for anyone else. It did not seem part of him.

Her thoughts turned dark. He was an abomination and could not be allowed to live.

Shiv's insides ached at the thought. She clasped him to her and keened anew, punishing herself for wanting his death but believing it all the same.

They should both be thrown into the swamp to drown.

Lyshus patted her back in lazy circles. She could still feel his confusion, but he had no guilt over what had happened. His sorrow was all for her and her pain. She felt his power reach out, but instead of connecting to her tree, his reach extended further.

She pulled back. "What are you doing? Are you reaching for another tree?" She shook him lightly. "Do not!"

His power kept going, his eyes losing focus. She raised a hand to slap him and bring him back to himself, but his reach passed the other drushkan queens, not even slowing as it raced along, seeking someone, something.

"Oh my, my." The human voice sounded funny in her head, echoing, distorted, as if it was shouted down a hollow log filled with whining insects.

Lyshus's grasp tightened on Shiv's arm, and he smiled, though his eyes remained glassy. "Help," he whispered.

"Certainly, certainly," the echoing voice said. "I'll help if I can. I never expected to hear from one of the tree folks. I thought your minds were…off limits."

Shiv could not close her mouth. The only humans she knew who could speak with the drushka as they could speak with one another were Sa and Simon, and that was because they had bonded with the drushka through Shi'a'na: Sa with her spirit self and Simon by taking in queen's blood. Horace had tried to use telepathy with them, but he could not succeed.

And this was not Simon or Sa or even Horace. "Who are you?"

"You knocked on *my* door, honey. I think it's only right you start the introductions."

"Help," Lyshus said again.

Shiv stared, searching his small face for any emotion beyond earnestness. Could he reach out to telepathic humans as well as other queens' trees? But why reach out to this voice? Why not find Sa or Simon or Horace, all of whom he had met? Who was this…

Lyshus shared his reasons. Shiv had needed help, and she did not want him to reach for other drushka, so he sought the most powerful human mind he could find, and some power of his let him connect. Shiv had heard the humans speak of this powerful mind, one they feared, the one who had come from the sky. "Naos."

"Righty-o! So, now you know me. And you are…" Shiv felt the telepathic fingers reaching for her, but just as with Horace, they could not penetrate her mind. The contact went through Lyshus, and he was sending only her loudest thoughts as queens did with their drushka. She felt the frustration of this Naos, and it pleased her. Through Lyshus, Shiv had control, and that meant she had what Sa would call a bargaining chip. Naos could not invade her mind, could not even really sense her, so no hurt could be done that way. And it seemed as if Naos wanted something from her, and if that was so, they had a place to bargain from.

"I am Shiv, daughter of Pool. I seek your assistance."

Mind fingers danced along their connection, seeking a way in like burrowing worms. "You've come to the right place, honey. I'm sure we can figure something out." Naos sent images of a place in the mountains to the north where a great bulk of metal waited. "But I can't leave just yet. I invited a lot of company. You're welcome to join. I can tell that you're special, so I'll make extra room for you. I'm sure we can come up with a solution to any little problem you might be having. And in return, well, I'm sure you can find a way to be useful."

Shiv looked for human deception but found none, not knowing the mind markers for such. She would have to look this Naos in the eyes and see for herself. If she could help, so much the better. And if she could not, Shiv supposed she would have to get used to traveling the land with only Lyshus and her sapling for company. They were not safe living this close to so many drushka.

And the drushka were not safe from them.

Cordelia tried to stay close to Liam as they put together a team to journey north. Everything was in the shit. Pool was upset about Shiv's rebellion and Lyshus's attack on her tree. All the drushka were freaked out by it. Nettle had been so shaky and jumpy that Cordelia had just wanted to hold her and tell the world to fuck off.

To make matters worse, fucking Fajir had taken the opportunity to escape, and the drushka were unable to say whether Lydia had left on her own or if Fajir had taken her. Samira wanted to go after them, but Fajir was no fool. She'd stay on the move, and she'd be watching for pursuit. She'd either kill Lydia or hide them both so they'd never be spotted.

A group of drushkan trackers reported that Fajir had gone north. All Cordelia could promise was that they'd keep their eyes open for

Lydia on their way to visit a mad goddess who would pummel them with asteroids if they didn't play her stupid fucking games.

And Liam had brain damage and might never be the same again.

Cordelia wanted to punch someone for that alone. Too bad she'd given up her drunken street brawls.

Liam had been watching her from the corner of his eye all morning as they collaborated on getting supplies together and outfitting the paladins. He'd had some good ideas on how to put teams together. It would be really weird if all he could remember from his former life was the lessons his mom had tried to beat into his head.

Now they sat in the Paladin Keep, reading over supply lists. "You all right?" she asked as he sighed.

"Yeah." But he sounded tired.

She went to clap him on the shoulder but hesitated, not wanting to…hurt him or anything, even though Simon said he was as healthy as he could be under the circumstances. "It's okay to rest." When he glanced at her, she shrugged. "Or whatever. Have a mead, relax."

He smiled slightly, and it seemed a little sad. Well, why the fuck not? Everyone was a little sad at the moment. "Too much to do."

She cleared her throat, not wanting to push. Maybe she should get Reach to speak to him. Drushkan healers didn't take any shit when it came to who needed a rest. "Well, um…" She gestured to the list of supplies. "At least the shortages here are under control. Now that the weather's leveled out, the plants are doing better."

He smiled a little wider. "True. Lucky that."

"Well, luck and Simon. He's been working with the plants and says we'll have an early harvest."

Liam only grunted, but his shoulders seemed tight, his body poised as if to run or strike.

Cordelia rolled her eyes but said nothing. At least he remembered his nonsensical jealousy of Simon. Every little bit helped, right?

"And the drushka have brought in some hoshpis, so we have meat."

"And mead."

She grinned. "And mead, thank…" She'd been about to say the Storm Lord, old habit. "Goodness."

"Yep." He drew out the word, and she thought she noticed a flush starting around his collar.

"Hey." This time, she did put a hand on his shoulder. "Why don't you let me take care of these supply lists? I know you like the schmoozing part of being a mayor way more than this shit. I can find someone who loves to make fucking lists."

He laughed, and it seemed genuine, the flush disappearing. "Fucking lists, huh?"

She snorted a laugh. "I hadn't been thinking that, but sure. Marches can be boring, right? Gotta spread the love around, make sure everybody gets some."

He laughed harder, and she joined in, both of them snickering over sex jokes as if they were twelve again. It was the first real connection she'd felt to him in days, and it lightened her heart.

"I'll finish this," he said, lifting the list. "Aren't you supposed to be meeting with the drushka anyway?"

"Yeah." Pool wanted to speak with her, but Cordelia didn't really want to go among her branches and surround herself with drushkan sorrow. It broke her heart.

He nodded to where Pool's tree stood beyond the palisade, and with a sigh, she stomped off, glad she could at least leave Liam on a happy note.

The drushka were quiet in their tree. Pool sat on one of the branches just outside the bark cupola where she rode when the tree was in motion. She had her knees drawn up in front of her, and her crossed arms rested atop those as she stared at Gale. Her long hair fluttered in the wind, and her face was still, but this close, Cordelia could feel her turmoil.

Cordelia sat beside Pool and mimicked her pose.

"My thoughts are chaotic, Sa," Pool said.

Cordelia nodded. Even without their bond, she would have noticed that. "We're all having chaotic thoughts right now. But Shiv will be all right, Pool. She's a survivor."

"Ahya. I wonder if merely surviving an event is the same as moving past it. Her tribemate has attacked a queen's tree and not by accident. Such a thing should have been forbidden in his deepest heart. How will my daughter live with that?"

Cordelia couldn't answer. Even Simon admitted he was stumped where Shiv was concerned. He'd consulted with Reach and other shawnessi after Lyshus's parents were killed. He said something about drushkan DNA mixing with Lyshus's unique telepathic abilities to fuck up everything the kid touched. And he was warped, too, if he was able to rebel against something that should have been in his genetic code.

But being stranded in the swamp with a little psycho who loved her still made Shiv safer than anyone currently dealing with Naos.

"We have to go into the mountains," Cordelia said. "Even if Naos is lying about giving out metal, others will be going to see her, and who knows what she'll do to them? Plus, there's the fucking meteors to consider." She sighed and scrubbed a hand through her hair. "I wanted to wait for her to come to us, but now I think it's better to go in with our eyes open and our fingers on the trigger."

Pool didn't look Cordelia's way. "I have heard that my daughter's former mate is also suffering. A sickness of the mind?"

Cordelia shrugged. "Yep, everything's shitty."

"Ahya," Pool said with a slight wrinkle of her nose. "Liam once helped save my life. I will aid him if I can, for more than my daughter's sake."

"I appreciate that. He will, too, I'm sure." Maybe. Cordelia swallowed, feeling like an ass, but she had to ask. "About traveling north…"

"You wish to ask me to come with you, Sa, to pit the might of my mind against Naos as I did before, and that will be easier if I am close to her."

Cordelia sighed. "I don't want to put the drushka in danger, and I'm not quite sure what the fuck we're going to do when we get there. At least she's here on the ground, so if we need my astral form to deliver the payload, I won't have far to go."

"Nettle wishes to go with you. I know her heart already. And Reach. She sees in you the face of her past love. Others wish to go for their human friends, and some will go simply for the spectacle. Before my daughter fled, I would not have hesitated, but Lyshus left me feeling…vulnerable."

Cordelia snorted a laugh and spoke without thinking. "You took your tree to war with the Shi, but one tiny child scares you?"

Pool went still, and Cordelia thought she'd really put her foot in it, then Pool sighed. "The old queens would not have hurt the Anushi."

Yeah, Cordelia had forgotten that part. And Naos wouldn't think twice about destroying a tree.

"I know this Naos can strike from anywhere at any time," Pool said. "I know I am no safer here than there. The mind knows, Sa, but the heart?" She waved a clawed hand. "It fears."

"We'll do everything we can to protect you and the tree, Pool."

"If I die, there is no queen within my branches to succeed me."

Cordelia sat back. She hadn't thought of that. "But hasn't that been true since you gave Shiv her tree?"

"Among the old drushka, when a queen dies, a new one is born to random parents. And the one who was born when the last queen died, the one who has been growing up a queen-to-be, assumes the new role of queen." She spread her hands. "But since I live, no queens have been born, so I made Shiv, as you say, but I gave her a tree because… she longed for purpose. I thought, perhaps upon my death, she would assume both trees, but now…"

"Your people will have to get a queen from the old drushka."

"With old ways and old values."

"But," Cordelia said, "they'll get new tribemates, too, and you'll all…flow together again or something." She tried to tamp her awkwardness down, but this was all beyond her, and Naos was hanging around her thoughts like a ghost. "Come on, Pool, you're just…in a funk." That seemed a callous way to describe Pool's only child running off with a psychopath, but any words were better than shaking Pool, which was her next best idea. "This happens to humans sometimes; you start to think about everything that's wrong with your life or that could go wrong, and pretty soon, all you can think about is potential disasters. You have to do what you can to shake off that feeling, or you'll just sit here paralyzed." She grinned and touched Pool's shoulder. "And you've got it better than most humans. Your drushka can help you move past this."

Pool chuckled. "You are partly right, Sa. We drushkan queens cope with our long lives by sharing our experiences through our drushka, but if I do not know how to think about my daughter, my drushka certainly will not."

"So…maybe don't share that with them, but you can share it with me and Simon. He's got a longer life ahead of him than me *or* you. What you can add to his knowledge might help drushka for generations."

Pool cocked her head. Finally, she stood, effortlessly pulling Cordelia with her. "You are right about that, Sa. It was a thought I had not had. And perhaps after I have distracted myself fighting Naos for you, I will think of a way to help Shiv."

Cordelia barked a laugh. "Oh, you're going to fight her *for me*, huh? Very generous of you."

Pool wrinkled her nose. "Ahya, I am a slave to helping humans win their battles."

"Like that one I helped you with not long ago. You know, defeating the entirety of the drushka and their queens."

"You are owed for that, I suppose." Pool knocked her arm lightly into Cordelia's, and Cordelia felt her amusement, her teasing. Drushka didn't keep score. Cordelia wondered if that was supposed to be Pool's impression of a human. The drushkan sense of humor could be a hard one to grasp, though she'd heard many drushka say the same thing about humans.

So now they had an army to march on Naos. At least something was starting to go right.

CHAPTER ELEVEN

Horace walked through the plains, his friends arrayed around him. It was a pleasant day, except for the fact that they were marching toward the mountains and what could be their doom. It should have made him nervous, but even after all his sparring practice, he was still looking forward to another fight.

It had been a nervous two days. Cordelia had told him they were finally heading out, and Horace had been seized by fierce excitement. He'd grabbed Simon and hauled him to Pool's tree for a round of lovemaking so passionate, they'd both been left breathing hard and grinning from ear to ear.

When they'd first set out, Horace had been happy still, holding hands with Simon as they walked. Even through the first night of camping on the plains, Horace hadn't lost his smile. He'd sparred a little with Cordelia and Jon, and they'd all been laughing.

Then Naos had appeared in his dreams, the same nebulous presence who'd once neatly severed his telepathic connection to Cordelia and swatted him away as if he was of no more consequence than a gnat.

Now, on the second day of marching, he couldn't stop thinking of her, wondering if he was ready and wishing it were all over. It would be so much better if they could only walk faster. He glanced back. Pool's massive tree followed at a slight distance, enough so that the walking humans wouldn't be crushed by its roots. Horace would have loved to be aboard it so they could hurry to the party, but Patricia didn't want to ride, afraid of being trapped, maybe. And Liam didn't want to leave her on her own, and Simon and Cordelia wanted to be close to Liam, and Horace wanted to be close to Simon, so they walked, and it was starting to feel as if they'd never get to the mountains.

When Patricia had attacked in Gale, Horace thought that spelled an end to this alliance. But Simon and Cordelia had accepted the brain damage story. He still didn't buy it, a side effect of his new desire to look for trouble, he supposed. He couldn't wait to do a deep scan on Liam, certain he could fix whatever had happened inside that brain no matter what Patricia said.

He watched the others walking through the grass. They had to go around ravines and ditches that Pool could have stepped over. Everyone seemed more subdued than they'd been on the first day, but no one complained. Maybe he was the only one in a hurry to fight a mad god. And the rolling hills were pleasant with the soothing waves of the green grass and the stark white of the rocks standing out like stars. They'd passed Wuran's clan on the way, and Samira had left them there, wanting to go after Lydia. She and some of Wuran's trackers sped away on ossors, and Horace wished he could have gone with them. At least they were doing something besides walking.

"You can ride, you know," Simon said from Horace's side.

"Hmm?"

Simon chuckled, and Horace looked around to find him smiling. "You keep looking at the tree."

"I'd feel better if we were all aboard." Before Simon could argue, Horace held up a hand. "I know, I know. She wants to walk, and you have to be down here to keep an eye on her, and I want to be with you." Simon squeezed his hand, but Horace frowned ahead to where Patricia walked with Liam. "If she acts up, the tree will catch her faster than we will."

Simon stepped closer and lowered his voice. "I hope to prevent any 'acting up.'"

"She's a telepath, Simon; she doesn't need to eavesdrop. You don't have to whisper."

Simon's eyes widened. "Is she listening?"

"Not that I can detect." He stretched his neck, thinking about the fight at the market and letting that piss him off. His defenses had been up, then, and she'd breezed right through them. The only reason he'd been able to get a signal out was because she'd had to leave off shielding him in order to incapacitate Cordelia. If he'd charged, one of them might have knocked her flat, but he'd relied on his power instead of his body, just as he always did. What good was training if he forgot to use it?

Simon's touch on his arm made him jump. "What's up with you today?" Simon asked, his own voice taking on an annoyed edge. Simon could be terrible when comforting angry people. With tears, he was all hugs and soothing words, but he could only reply to anger with anger, as if assuming it had to be aimed at him when he'd done nothing wrong.

"I'm just frustrated," Horace said, and Simon's tone made him even more so. Horace fought the urge to frown harder.

"About what?" Simon asked, defensive again, as if Horace had no right to anger.

"Everything," he said, not knowing how to explain.

"Me?"

"Not everything is about you," slipped out before he could stop it.

Simon reared back, his chin nearly meeting his chest as his eyes went wide. "I—"

Horace shook his head roughly, guilt mixing with the emotional storm inside him. "I'm sorry, Simon, I didn't mean that. I just…I feel…"

Simon didn't look mollified by the apology. With a sniff, he faced forward again. "You've been out of sorts for a long time now. You weren't when I met you."

"That was a long time ago."

"Less than a year. And I can only think of one thing that's changed since we met and now."

Horace rolled his eyes. "A lot has changed." He counted off on his fingers. "The boggin attack, leaving Gale, living on the plains…"

"I know."

"My getting abducted, you getting shot, the fight with the Sun-Moon, with the plains dwellers, with Naos…"

"Yes, but—"

"Gale getting poisoned, going to fight the drushka, almost dying in the swamp—"

Simon's head whipped toward him. "You never told me you almost died."

Horace sputtered for a moment. "I told you I got hurt."

"But not that you almost died. What…" He shook his head. "Do you…want to talk about it?" He sounded unsure but less defensive, his anger chased away by the fear rolling off him.

At least he cared. "I'm fine," Horace said.

"Well, now you are, but…" Simon's face brightened. "Oh! So, that's what it is. Almost dying does change a person."

As if all the other events didn't? Maybe it took death to really shake someone who'd been alive for over two hundred years. Horace shook his head. "No, I was feeling this weird restlessness before that." True, almost dying had made it worse. Jon thought his restlessness was an addiction to adrenaline that wouldn't be cured until Horace let himself feel some of the ache and fatigue of battle.

Simon was still nodding as if he hadn't heard. "The longer you're all right," Simon said, "the better you'll feel. That's how it was for me."

Him again. Horace knew he wasn't being fair, but it felt good to have a target for his anger. He tried not to get lost in that feeling, tried to shake it off, be angry at the fact that he wanted trouble, angry that this latest trouble could easily overwhelm him, and angry that even though he knew it was dangerous, he was still looking forward to it.

Angry that he was walking.

Maybe he was really angry at Patricia. Deep down, Horace didn't believe she'd be of any help. She would turn on them at the first opportunity; they should have just gotten her out of the way.

The breeze careening over the plains chilled him. The weather had taken a cool turn since her arrival. Simon said that Naos didn't have Dillon's power, but maybe she'd been hiding it. If so, Patricia had it now. That made her even more dangerous.

He regarded her once more. He'd only ever killed a boggin, and it had sickened him. He'd refused to kill Naos's vessel even when he knew that doing so might end the war. This was beyond craving action; he felt…bloodthirsty.

His bile rose. Well, he couldn't be that bloodthirsty if the thought still turned his stomach. Watching her young body with its old, devious mind, he knew the world would be safer without her. Even when she laughed at something Liam said, the feeling didn't dissipate. She was a problem. He didn't want to kill her himself, but he wanted her…gone.

"…not to mention meditation," Simon said.

Horace shook his head, realizing that Simon had been talking for the last few minutes, but Horace had barely heard a word. He stopped himself from asking. He didn't want to get in more trouble. "Sure."

Simon took his hand, enclosing his fingers in warmth. "I'll help you."

"What are we going to do about her?" He nodded toward Patricia.

"What do you mean?"

"Even if she helps defeat Naos, she still took over Gale's mine."

Simon blinked ahead. "I guess…we'll figure it out. There's nothing we can do about it now."

"I can think of something." He almost blurted it out, but as Simon stared, Horace didn't want to say it, ashamed he'd thought about murder so casually.

"Are you…you aren't…" Disbelief filled Simon's voice as he whispered, "You mean kill her?"

Shame flooded Horace anew. "We're going to have to in the end."

Simon pulled on him, but Horace kept walking. "Kill them before they kill you? Do you know who you sound like?"

Horace rounded on him. "Don't you dare say the Storm Lord."

People were walking around them, giving them curious looks. Simon kept staring, his eyes hard and unyielding. "Even if it's true?"

"I am nothing like your ex-boyfriend." Horace started walking again.

"He was never—"

"Oh please," Horace said, and there came that feeling of satisfaction again, the bliss of having a target. "You couldn't have been more in love with him."

Simon marched up to his side, all anger now. "If you think that, then you have to accept that I knew him better than anyone, and you're singing his tune."

Horace flushed, knowing it was true, but he couldn't stop, as if he'd walked too far, and now he had to keep going or the whole trip would have been a waste. A voice inside cried out to let it be a waste, to apologize for being touchy, apologize for taking his anger out on the man he loved, apologize for whatever he had to apologize for in order to get that look off Simon's face.

But another voice argued that he hadn't done anything but speak the truth, and that he had a right to his anger, and that, well…well…

If he had to walk, it felt good to fight.

And he was using his power to assuage his guilt. The only emotion allowed free rein was anger, but he could stop that. He could calm himself down.

He just didn't.

When the guilt came again, he tried letting it be, clenching his fists to keep from flicking the feeling away as easily as Patricia had dismissed his power away before, but when it came time to speak, what he said was, "I need to be alone for a little while."

That was not the apology he'd been planning. He couldn't make himself look at Simon's face; there was probably nothing but devastation there. Having been rejected for so long, slights like that broke Simon's heart, and that made Horace even angrier.

He marched away into the plains, far enough that he couldn't see anyone else. He could still see the tree, but a small rise separated him from those walking, and he dipped into a shallow ravine to put more distance between them.

When he spotted movement to his left, he thought it was one of the scouts, but it was Jon, following him again.

"I want to be alone, Jon," Horace threw over his shoulder.

"We don't have to talk."

"If I can see you, I'll pick a fight with you."

"Fine by me."

Horace stuttered to a stop and laughed, the tension leaking out of him, leaving him feeling deflated. Jon stopped just outside of reach as if expecting a physical fight. But unless Horace used his power, he couldn't hurt Jon, and not just because of the armor. The man was too good.

"I meant that I'm likely to start an argument. I'm in a very prickly mood."

Jon shrugged. "I don't know how to argue, so you'll just be yelling at me."

Probably true, and the prospect didn't excite Horace at all. He started walking again, and Jon fell in beside him as they picked their way down the ravine. The white, chalky walls bore swirls of brown and sandy gold. "My restlessness has gone beyond craving a fight. I'm becoming an asshole."

"Like you're caught up in your own head."

That was certainly true. Horace was angrier with himself than anyone else; he just wasn't letting himself feel it. And he didn't want to start now. "I was a jerk to Simon."

"Say you're sorry."

Horace barked a laugh. "That's not going to cut it. He's going to want an explanation."

"I can explain."

Horace glanced at him in surprise. "How?"

Jon looked at nothing for a long moment. "I'll tell him about wanting to fight even when you don't want to feel that way. I'll say that, because of your power, you don't know how to be exhausted. I'll say that a lot of soldiers use alcohol or sex to cope. He should feel good you're not doing that."

Horace snorted. "I don't know. He might approve of the sex approach."

"Not that kind of sex," Jon said, unsmiling. "From what I heard, it's when you use someone just so you can get out of your own head for a little while. The other person is just a…tool."

Horace blinked; he'd never heard Jon open up so much before. Of course, Jon might not see his speech as particularly revelatory. It probably meant more to him that he'd shared his love of models, his own method of coping with a dangerous job.

"How you doing at not using your power after sparring?" Jon asked. "Did you do it last night?"

"That's not what's bugging me." In fits and starts, Horace told him of the confrontation with Patricia and Liam, how he'd been thinking with his power, the strongest part of himself, and he'd still been bested.

Jon shrugged. "Even if you'd rushed her, she probably would have taken you out. If she's controlling Liam, he could have stopped you. He used to be a paladin."

"I know." Horace spoke a little louder than he meant to, but Jon didn't seem to mind. "But I should have tried."

"It's been a long time since anyone's beaten you power to power, hasn't it?"

Horace went still. "Not since the Sun-Moon." He swallowed. "And Naos."

Jon pointed back over the lip of the ravine. "Patricia used to be a god like them, right?"

"So, you're going to tell me I shouldn't feel bad because they're powerful?"

"You can feel bad about whatever you want. I'm just trying to help you determine why that one fight is upsetting you more than those others." Jon stared at nothing, face as placid as usual, and Horace was tempted to peek into that head, but he kept himself in check.

Being kicked around by powerful assholes *was* a good reason to be upset. It was one of the reasons he'd been eager to learn how to fight, so he was less likely to be surprised. But Jon was right. That wouldn't have helped with Patricia. He hadn't been scared; he'd used what he was most familiar with. And part of him knew it wouldn't work.

Maybe that was it. He was angry because all the fights he kept getting into were with mega-powerful gods.

Jon put a hand on his arm, gaze locked on the rocks in the distance where the ravine was covered in shadow.

"What?" Horace whispered.

"I saw someone."

"Probably a drushkan scout."

"No."

The definitiveness in his voice made Horace look again, this time with power. Jon was right. A group of humans was waiting in the ravine. He went through them one by one, people he didn't know, until he came to one man.

Disbelief and fear rushed through him. The Storm Lord. "No, it can't be. He's dead."

"Who?"

Horace tried to fight down his fear, but if the Storm Lord knew he'd been detected, he'd hit them with lightning. "We need to run." Horace pushed through his own emotions and sent out a desperate, telepathic call. "Simon!"

Patricia swore, stumbling as she walked. She'd been regretting her decision not to ride aboard the tree. She was curious about the drushka, but Dillon had been right: if something went wrong, and they were high off the ground, it would be harder to get away.

Not that it would be easy now.

She'd kept a lazy telepathic and micro-psychokinetic net over the whole company, alternating between the two so that no one became suspicious. And she thought her touch light enough that no one would notice, especially since she didn't bring it near Simon or Horace.

But when Horace stormed off over a hill out of sight, Patricia followed him with a light telepathic tendril, not invading his mind, just ready in case he used his power.

When his power reached toward Jonah and his people, she tensed, but she didn't act quickly enough to shut it off. He detected Jonah, and Patricia knew he'd realize whose body that used to be. She threw a telepathic shield over him as he put out a call for help.

"We need to get over there," Patricia said. "Horace found Jonah."

"Fuck." Dillon followed her gaze, but so far, no one else seemed to notice. She'd instructed Jonah to stay far to the east, and he'd been hiding in ravines and ditches when he could. The drushkan scouts mainly ranged north.

"Take him out," Dillon said.

Patricia gawked, her fear rising like the tide. "They'll kill us!"

"Not if they don't find out. Take him the fuck out before he comes running over that hill, and you have to explain your little science project with my old bod. And don't think they won't want to know what happened to my mind."

He was right. It was too many questions, but he wasn't thinking far enough ahead. Horace was Simon's lover. He was worth more alive than dead.

But Simon would feel it if she used her power with enough force to incapacitate Horace and the man with him. She sent her own telepathic signal, something Simon couldn't spy upon. "Jonah, take that man and his friend prisoner. Stealthily."

He obeyed. Patricia continued to block Horace's signals, but she feared that stopping him from using his power would be too detectable.

"Is it done?" Dillon asked.

"Jonah is handling it. Distract Simon."

She continued to block Horace's telepathy as it became frantic. Horace used his micro powers against one of Jonah's men, knocking him unconscious. Patricia caught the thoughts of another man who leapt upon Horace, but the man's thoughts turned panicked as he was attacked in turn. Everything was going wrong.

Dillon glanced back to where Simon walked. "Wait a few seconds, then do something that makes it look like Naos is attacking."

"I can't pull a goddamned meteor from the sky!" She didn't think so, at least. Maybe she wouldn't have to go that big. "Just go talk to him."

Dillon faded back, hailing Simon and engaging him in conversation, a distraction for her distraction. She threw another telepathic shield around the yafanai in the tree, then struck everyone with a telepathic blast, hoping Simon wasn't alert enough to know it was her.

Everyone staggered, Simon and Dillon included. She reeled, too, as if she'd felt the same assault. It disrupted all the yafanai, and Simon was tottering, so Patricia risked a micro-psychokinetic blast for Horace and his friend. One of them had been injured; now Patricia put them both down, telling Jonah to carry them into the nearest limestone cavern. This close to the mountains, many such caverns connected to the mine, and Patricia could collapse the entrance behind them.

Until she needed them.

Chapter Twelve

A flashback played through Simon's head like a vid at slow speed: when Dillon had kidnapped him by socking him in the jaw before a telepath had knocked him out, all because he'd let down his guard.

Now he grabbed Liam's arm, struggling to regain his thoughts. He'd been so discombobulated by the fight with Horace, then Liam had called his name, and he was trying to listen to Liam instead of brooding when a telepathic attack had stabbed him in the brain.

"Something's…it's…" He couldn't get the words in order. Panic rampaged through him like a wild animal, but he had to get hold of himself, had to tell them that someone had attacked.

But Liam bent double beside him, and as Simon looked around the field, the world tilted crazily. Everyone seemed in various stages of distress, including Patricia.

"Shawness!" Reach took his arm. More drushka were racing through the grass, supporting the humans. Reach began a healing song, the melody mixing with the other shawnessi, but Simon's body was fine. His mind was on fire. Still, the song let him breathe through the lingering effects of the telepathic attack. His vision returned to normal, and his thoughts finally got in order.

"All of us," he muttered, clinging to Reach. "She hit all of us."

"Was it Naos?" Reach asked.

"Had to have been," Liam said. He'd gone a bit pale as he pressed the back of his hand to his mouth.

Patricia staggered over. "Maybe we're not going fast enough."

"And so she slows us down with an attack?" His head snapped to the right. Horace had marched off alone. Simon ran, relying on his legs to know what they were doing without guidance from him. They'd had a stupid fight, and Simon had let Horace out of his sight, and now he was probably suffering alone or incapacitated or…

Simon topped the rise. The plains stood empty, but there was a ravine below. He ran and looked along its length. Nothing. "Horace?" He took a slow turn. He just had to look more carefully, that was all. "Horace!"

"Shawness?" Reach asked.

"He must have fallen. Maybe she hit him harder than the rest of us." He sent his distress to Pool, reaching for the person who could see the farthest and act the quickest through her drushka.

"We will find him, shawness," Pool said in his mind.

Reach caught Simon's arm and helped him walk. Cordelia had followed and was calling orders to the paladins to fan out along with the drushka.

Nettle leaped into the ravine and loped along it. Simon sent his power out and tried to ignore the people around him. Horace couldn't have gotten far. He wouldn't have walked away into the wilderness, no matter how upset he'd been. He knew how dangerous that was.

Hadn't someone followed him? Simon remembered one of the paladins breaking off. Jon Lea.

Simon whipped around, searching for the glint of metal armor while his power still sought Horace. He tried to stretch his senses further, but a headache throbbed through his temples, and he pulled back. Why had Naos hit them with such a powerful blast? Had she been waiting for one of them to separate from the others so she could pick them off one by one like some maniac from a slasher film?

"Here, shawness, a way down," Reach said.

Simon let her guide him down the side of the ravine. She sniffed the air. "I smell blood."

"What?" Simon focused harder, making pain rage through his skull. "I can't…I should be able to detect him even if he's injured, even if he's…"

Dead.

Simon fought the urge to sob and clung to Reach. "Where?"

Reach waved ahead. Simon ran, hearing Cordelia and several others skitter into the ravine behind them. What the hell had Horace been thinking? They never should have had that stupid fight. Simon should have just said how much he loved him and that he was there for him, and…

A few red smears decorated the ground where Nettle waited. Horace had been injured, then he'd…walked away? Crawled? Simon cast his senses about again but found no one except those surrounding him.

Nettle went farther and stopped next to a divot in the ravine wall. "Here."

The word seemed as loud as a shot, though she spoke in a normal tone. Cordelia stepped to Nettle's side, and her expression tightened into worry.

Simon tottered forward. A large rock hid their feet from view. "Did you…find him?"

The back of the rock bore a crimson stain and a puddle of blood at its base. If the person who'd shed that much blood wasn't dead already, they soon would be.

"Horace!" Simon yelled, turning a circle, pushing through the pain.

Dizziness overcame him. He tried to brace himself, to call a warning, but the same telepathic attack as before stabbed at him, bringing him to his knees. His thoughts tumbled beyond all control.

Nearly lost in the haze, he heard a voice say, "Don't keep me waiting." Naos's voice, but it sounded different. Angry or annoyed. Simon fought to get hold of his power, his thoughts, trying to use his anger.

His mind suddenly cleared as if scrubbed clean, and he looked up into Patricia's face, feeling her power.

"I hope you don't mind," she said softly. "I was ready for her this time."

He blinked, realizing she'd used her telepathy to clear his thoughts. He used his power on himself, but it felt worn, pummeled in a way he couldn't counter.

"Why is she doing this?" Cordelia asked as she leaned on the bloodstained rock.

"Didn't you hear?" Patricia asked. "She's trying to hurry us along."

"Not without Horace," Simon said.

"Can you sense him?" Reach asked.

"I would have told you if I could!" He knew he should rein in his temper. It had cost him too much already. "I'm sorry. I can't sense very far, not with these fucking telepathic attacks!"

"How fast does she want us to go?" Cordelia yelled.

"You can track Horace, right?" Simon asked Nettle.

"Ahya, shawness, but his attackers are moving swiftly."

"Lead on."

"Hold it!" Cordelia said. "A handful of us can't go racing into the plains. Besides, the drushka are already on it, right?"

Simon looked to Nettle, who wrinkled her nose with a sympathetic smile, and Simon realized how stupid he was. Of course the drushka were on it. They'd fanned out, and once Nettle had found them a starting place, a simple thought had alerted the rest of them. They ran up and down the ravine and even up the sides and over the plains, searching for clues.

Before Simon could take a step, a trill of alarm came from Pool.

"The trail has gone into a cave, shawness," Pool said, "and then farther underground, to a tunnel that has collapsed."

Simon looked to Cordelia, his heart sinking.

"It will be all right, shawness," Reach said. "We will find him."

In a tunnel that had collapsed. "Can you tell who took him?"

"Perhaps he fell and injured himself?" Reach said, but it didn't sound as if she believed it.

Cordelia stared at the ground. "And then he and Lea crawled into some random cavern instead of shouting for help?"

"There are other scents here," Nettle said. "Some seem almost… familiar, yet I cannot place them. Some were plains dwellers, by the leather they wore."

Cordelia grabbed Simon's arm, and he didn't need to be a telepath to read the guilt on her face.

"Oh hell," he muttered. "It might be the ones we let go."

"What's this?" Liam asked as he finally reached them. "Who did you let go?"

Cordelia rolled her head from side to side as if readying herself for a fight. "We caught some plains dwellers not long ago, and we didn't know what to do with them, so—"

"So, you handed Naos's army right back to her?" Patricia asked.

Cordelia frowned hard. "We weren't just going to fucking kill them."

Liam wiped a hand down his face, and Simon sensed his aggravation, but he was trying to keep it under wraps. He hadn't seemed this quick to anger before his brain damage. If Patricia had to rebuild him at that fundamental a level, maybe they'd never get the real Liam back.

Horace could still try.

If they ever found him.

"You should have kept them locked up," Liam said, shaking his head.

Cordelia spread her arms. "Where, exactly?"

"Somewhere they couldn't attack and kidnap people!"

Simon stepped between the two. "What's done is done!" He hated that he had to take on the role of peacekeeper when he wanted to rage, but Horace needed him to keep everyone on track. "We have to find Horace now."

"If we don't leave and hurry, Naos will keep attacking us," Patricia said quietly.

Simon rounded on her to say he didn't care; nothing was more important than Horace's safety, but Cordelia stopped him this time.

"Let's go back to the tree and think it through," she said.

He took a deep, shuddering breath, but his anger could quickly grow beyond his control. He'd had a lot taken from him in his long life. Horace would not be another loss. *The Iliad* came floating to him again, the poem that started with rage. "If he dies while we're thinking, I will burn this whole goddamned planet to cinders."

Lydia ran through her dream. She saw the flames again as they careened across the plains, gobbling up people and animals, all of it playing in slow motion like some obscene torture.

She couldn't hear them, the future forever silent, but this felt different from what she'd last seen. Now, she was in the middle, and her heart pounded in terror.

"Nemesis!"

Fajir was here somewhere, but Lydia's mind rejected that idea. She shouldn't have been able to hear her. Maybe the future was finally fading into a normal dream? But the flames still roared soundlessly around her.

"Nemesis, stop!"

Lydia turned, hearing Freddie's voice along with Fajir's. Was Freddie in the flames, too? Her future and her dreams pulled at each other, blurring around the edges, and Lydia saw Freddie crushed by the prog's foot, heard the horrible sound of crushing bone. She tried to scream, tried to get to Freddie, but just as in real life, she could only watch.

"Nemesis, you will fall!"

Just as Freddie had fallen. Someday, she'd witness the fire in all its glory, hear the cries of terror as she'd heard Freddie scream.

No, no, no, she had to get away!

"Nemesis!"

Lydia gasped as something smashed into her, and her feet lost contact with the ground. She had a moment to wonder if the flames would consume her before the ground smacked into her, driving her breath from her lungs. She rolled, and a sharp slap to her cheek made her eyes fly open.

"Lydia!" Fajir yelled, their faces inches apart, bathed in moonlight. Her eyes were wide with fear and concern. "Wake up!"

Lydia gasped. She could hear her heart in her ears, felt not only the sting in her cheek but the ache of Fajir's tackle and the hard ground beneath her. Her bruised rib ached, as did her nose. Tears left wet streams down her cheeks, and she couldn't breathe. She tried to force herself to calm, but a low sob escaped her. "What…is this?"

"You dreamed." Fajir hauled her upright. "And then ran as if haunted. Maybe your injury…" As Lydia sobbed harder, Fajir patted her awkwardly. "You're safe now."

Lydia wanted to laugh at the sheer discomfort on Fajir's face, but she didn't feel as if she had control of her own body; she couldn't stop crying.

The night after they'd left the tree, Lydia had slept deeply, only awakening when Fajir shook her roughly in the morning. Fajir had stared at her with concern all the next day. This night, their second on the plains, it seemed her dreams and the future had melded somehow, but instead of simply thrashing and calling out, she ran. It had felt too real.

"Why?" she asked with a sob. "I'm doing what I should be. I'm trying to find this future. Why won't it leave me alone?"

Fajir sat beside her in the moonlit grass. Their campfire was an orange glow not far away. "I…I don't…"

"I'm trapped, Fajir. My power told the Storm Lord where to put his troops on the palisade at Gale, and the boggins snuck in the other side. If I didn't have power, maybe things would be different." She sobbed again, knowing most of her words weren't coming through clearly, but she couldn't seem to stop them either.

"And I saw Freddie get stepped on, and I knew it was hopeless without even looking. Why couldn't I have some other power or none at all? I keep running from it, but it keeps finding me, and people will never stop asking me to use it, and I'm so tired, Fajir!" Lydia tilted sideways until her forehead rested against Fajir's breast. She'd never felt so hopeless. Maybe she'd damaged more than just her skull when she fell, breaking something else inside herself. "Please just hurry up and kill me."

Fajir's arms went around her slowly. "I understand. No matter what you do, you're forced into this…circle, and you can never reach the end."

Like Fajir and her vengeance. Lydia's breath was ragged as she tried to rein in her sobs.

Fajir's embrace tightened. "You're a widow like me, but no one ever taught you how to be one. No animal killed your love; your power did that, and so you seek to fight your power."

Lydia pulled back but didn't scoot away, shocked by the understanding in Fajir's voice. "I don't kill people."

Fajir snorted a laugh. "I didn't say that we're exactly alike, Nemesis."

"My name is Lydia. I heard you say it."

Her smile grew warmer. "To conquer your power, you must rid yourself of it."

Lydia rolled her eyes. "Sure. I'll just go back to the day I was born, and—"

"Don't be tiresome, Nemesis." She stood, and her unarguable grip pulled Lydia with her. She led the way back to the campfire. "Healers can burn out power. The Lords told me Simon Lazlo once did so to himself."

"But it came back." Simon's *and* Horace's powers had returned. Because they were micro-psychokinetics. Healers. They had enough power left to slowly heal themselves, but for Lydia… She started to laugh, a stutter that grew to a guffaw, chasing away the last bits of her dream, the last dregs of horror.

"Fajir, you're a genius!" She grabbed Fajir's shoulders, pulled her head down, and kissed her quickly on the lips.

Fajir gaped like a fish, her eyes practically bulging out of their sockets. Her face went scarlet behind her tattoos, and she took a step back as if she feared Lydia might attack. "You…you must not…"

"I should have thought of that!" Lydia cried. "Long before now. I'm a widow, and I have to fight my power by getting rid of it. Then I'll be free." She took a step forward, and to her further amusement, Fajir backed up again. "And you'll help me."

"I will?"

"You just tackled me to keep me from hurting myself. You haven't killed me yet, and you're not going to."

"I'm not?"

"Nope. We need each other. That's why we keep coming back to each other."

"Ah." Fajir nodded, but her eyes were still wide as if she was struggling to understand. "You need me to save the plains and to help you rid yourself of your power, and I need you for…"

Lydia took a deep breath and thought about that one. She was good at reading people after spending so much time looking at various futures. She knew Fajir was developing feelings for her, but whether they were truly romantic or just the attachment one drifter felt for another, Lydia didn't know.

"I'm your project," Lydia said softly. "You needed something else to do with your life, so why not help another widow? Maybe you'll even prove to me that some people deserve to die." Though she didn't believe that was possible.

But Fajir smiled and nodded, and that was enough. They returned to camp but didn't sleep, sharing a short silence until dawn when they began walking again. Fajir said she would deliver Lydia to Gale, but after walking in that direction, Fajir spotted the trail of the drushkan tree.

"They must be going to the mountains, to Naos," Lydia said.

"Do we follow?"

Lydia nodded and saw the relief on Fajir's face. It seemed Fajir had developed a superstition about Gale that was similar to Lydia's. Nothing good happened there.

Everyone was still reeling from Naos's attack, but Cordelia didn't believe Naos had orchestrated her assault for the very same instant that Horace and Lea disappeared. Patricia knew something, no fucking doubt.

After they'd climbed out of the ravine, Simon ranted that they needed to do something to get Horace back before they could even think about moving, but Cordelia found it hard to plan with a traitor in their midst.

"There are tunnels through this whole area," Patricia said at last. "I found some connected to my…the mine." She glanced at Cordelia and cleared her throat. Cordelia was tempted to correct her about whose mine it really was. "And many of them branch together. It may take days to track them."

"How convenient," Cordelia said. "As convenient as the fact that the only telepath we had who even approached your strength is now missing."

Patricia snorted, but she was wise enough to say nothing. Cordelia didn't know if her snort was in response to the very thinly veiled accusation or the thought that Horace could ever come close to matching her.

"Who gives a fuck how long it takes?" Simon yelled. "Pool can start digging out the tunnel, and we'll go from there."

"The drushka are already scouting for another way in," Liam said.

Simon waved his words away and resumed his march toward Pool.

Nettle spread her hands. "Some of the abductors were plains dwellers. Perhaps others in the area will know where they are going."

"Unless 'others in the area' are more captives you've already let go," Liam muttered.

"Don't fucking judge me," Cordelia said. "We didn't have anywhere to keep them, and we couldn't kill them."

He didn't back down. Patricia stepped up beside him. "What do you think we'll have to do now if not kill them?"

Cordelia glared, ready to tell her to mind her own business, but Nettle spoke first. "Battle is different than killing unarmed captives," Nettle said. "When their leader has been dealt with, they may submit as drushka do."

"And in the meantime," Patricia shot back, "they'll pick us off one by one like in a damned horror vid."

Cordelia frowned. She hadn't understood that when Simon mumbled something about it, and she didn't understand it now. Liam barked a laugh as if he was firmly on Patricia's side. Brain damage or not, she'd gotten to him.

"Who cares who did what in the past?" Simon said, some of the words spoken through his teeth. When they hadn't followed him, he'd come stalking back. "Horace has been taken, and now we go get him."

"Shawness," Nettle said softly. "We cannot linger here and wait for Naos to attack again."

And they still didn't know why Naos was doing that. Cordelia looked around, hoping a clue would appear out of midair; a thought tickled in her brain. Horror vids. She turned a hard look on Liam. He shifted his gaze away as if embarrassed.

Or guilty.

Liam glared when she didn't stop staring. "What? You got something to say?" He sneered, clearly trying to put her off with anger, but coming at her mad was never the way to get her to back down.

And he knew that.

Had known it, anyway.

Horror vids. What was it about...

Cordelia felt eerily calm. "Yeah, I've got some questions."

As they continued their staring contest, Simon started railing again. He asked Nettle and Reach to go to Pool in person and plead his case. After Cordelia nodded, the two drushka headed back. Patricia argued, but Cordelia kept her eyes on Liam. She watched for an expected reaction, anything familiar, but she didn't picture any, her mind carefully blank.

"If you're waiting for me to give you a hint about how he should act," she thought as "loudly" as she could. "You're shit out of luck."

Patricia's gaze jerked to her. So, she was listening. Horror vids. She didn't know what that meant, and neither should Liam. It sounded like one of those references a person had to really understand before they'd laugh.

Unless they'd been brainwashed by someone who understood completely.

Cordelia reached for him, going in hard. Her legs went out from under her, but she'd expected that as Patricia flexed her power. But Simon was there, and Patricia yelped in pain. Cordelia let herself fall and rolled, slower in her armor but still fast enough. She grabbed Liam's legs and knocked him to the ground.

"I don't know what Patricia did to you," Cordelia shouted. "But if you can hear me, Liam, fight back!"

She grabbed him before he could roll away and pulled herself on top. She couldn't sit on him forever; she needed to help Simon. One quick punch to the chin should do the trick.

He put a hand to her chest, teeth gritted, no doubt in pain from her weight.

She pulled back a fist. "I'm sorry."

He got a look in his eye she'd never seen, a casual cruelty. "I'm not."

A white flash filled her vision, and her head snapped back, teeth clacking together. The smell of ozone filled her nostrils, and she couldn't move.

Why was she tumbling, then? Rolling over and over before hurtling into the sky. Before she reached the stars, something jerked her to a halt, her strengthened lifeline.

Cordelia gasped. "What the fuck?" Had Patricia done something? Naos? It felt like…

When she'd been standing outside the palisade and the Storm Lord had come for Liam. He'd hit her with his lightning instead.

But Patricia didn't have that power. No one did. Just the Storm Lord, and he was dead.

When was the last time any problem of hers had stayed buried?

"No!" she shouted. "No fucking way!" They'd never found his body, but Simon had been so certain of his death. She should have known better. She grabbed her lifeline, trying to pull herself back. Where was he? Hiding? Then why hit her when he did? Why give himself away to protect Liam?

Unless…

Mind fuckery, just as she'd suspected. Patricia or Naos or who the fuck ever had salvaged the Storm Lord's mind or something. And now he was a passenger in Liam's body just like Patricia had been in Naos's?

The thought made her want to vomit. Liam must have been going crazy in his own head, forced to share his fucking body with the asshole that killed his mom. Cordelia had to get back and dig that fucker out before Liam went as crazy as Naos.

She felt a tickle in her brain before a shadow loomed over her mind. Just as before, she felt the titanic presence that heralded Naos's arrival. It was getting closer, coming from the planet rather than from space as Cordelia followed her lifeline down, out of the atmosphere.

This time, Naos wouldn't want to have a jolly conversation, not after Cordelia had tried to kill her.

Simon had just enough time to be grateful he could still act on instinct.

He'd known Patricia was using her power, but since he wasn't a telepath, he couldn't read her mind, and he didn't sense her power reaching out to anyone, so he assumed she was either shielding herself, or she always kept her power ready.

Then Cordelia leapt at Liam, and Patricia's power flexed. Without even realizing it, Simon attacked her power center and gave her enough of a shock that Cordelia got loose.

"What the hell is—" Simon grunted as Patricia pushed back, a wild look in her eyes. He didn't know what had happened with Cordelia and Liam—not to mention Horace—but he was putting an end to it right now.

He faced her down, their powers clashing. Her telepathy was her most dangerous ability, so he kept his focus on that part of her brain. She was fast, and it was obvious she'd had some practice switching "gears" when it came to power, an ability she'd no doubt perfected after sharing a brain. He'd just have to be faster.

A scream and a burst of pain distracted him. His power stuttered as anger and fear rolled through him along with recognition. He knew that pain, that power.

Dillon.

He felt an answering scream inside his own chest, a cry of disbelief and rage. He reached deeper than he thought he could and summoned every ounce of power, knocking Patricia down, almost knocking her out. He looked for Dillon, wondering just how in the actual fuck this was happening.

Ultimately, it didn't matter. Simon would kill him personally this time and make sure it took.

Cordelia lay on her side, unmoving. Liam sat next to her, breathing hard. Simon sent his senses out, looking for that body he knew so well.

When he reached Pool, she was distracted. Something was happening aboard the tree; the drushka had all withdrawn to Pool's branches. Faintly, he felt the panic of Cordelia's astral form. He reached for her through Pool.

"Naos is coming!"

"The human mothers are in turmoil," Pool sent, nearly on top of Cordelia's thought.

A rumble came from the tree, and a group of branches blew apart on the side. A shriek of pain came from Pool's mind, nearly bringing Simon to his knees. He staggered that direction before he remembered Patricia.

And Dillon.

When he turned, Patricia was gone, along with Liam, and Dillon was still nowhere in sight. Cordelia had been right about Liam, at least. Patricia hadn't just talked him into going with her. He sensed the two of them scrambling over the next hill. She threw a bolt of telepathy his way, and he strengthened his own brain, only blinking at her weak attack. He knew he should hit back, but Pool and Cordelia were still screaming for his help.

And Dillon was still out there somewhere.

Fuck.

❖

"Fuck!" Dillon cried. Patricia wanted to yell at him to shut up, but she saved her breath. "How in the fuck—"

"It doesn't matter," she snapped. "Just keep running. She didn't know what had fucked up her plan, but Cordelia had obviously figured out that something was wrong.

"You didn't kill Horace," Dillon said. "Why the fuck not?"

"He's worth more alive."

"Unless he managed to send a telepathic signal and fuck this whole op!"

Anger burned through her. "He didn't send a signal. I made sure. If anyone fucked this *op*, it's you!"

He didn't respond, but she could feel his anger, one more bit of bullshit she did not need.

"Go back if you want," she said, done with him.

"Too late for that."

"Right. Because you had to go throwing lightning around."

He snarled at her like an animal. "I wouldn't have had to if you'd had my fucking back!"

She rounded on him, and it didn't matter that the paladins and the drushka were practically breathing down their necks; she'd slowed them down by sending a signal to the yafanai that their god was alive. And a huge telepathic signal was moving toward the tree, but none of that mattered because all the built-up tension inside her needed somewhere to go.

"You want a fight?" she said to Dillon's surprised face. "I will knock you on your ass!"

"Only because of your power," he said, giving her a disdainful once-over.

"That's you," she said. "Talking shit about something until you need it. Manipulation 101, right? Well, I'm not taking your—"

A white flash knocked her sideways. Stars burst in her vision, and she barely felt her body hit the ground. She tried to find air, to grab hold of her power, but everything inside her, from muscles to neurons, was in full spasm.

Dillon leaned into sight. "Wait, were we *not* using powers?" He had the nerve to smile, the bastard.

Patricia pushed, finding her rage.

"That was just a taste," Dillon said. "If you want—"

Patricia found a strand of power. It was enough. She hit him with a micro-psychokinetic burst, a jolt to his entire system that mimicked his power. With a cry, he stumbled away. As soon as Patricia could access that power, more came, and she healed herself.

Dillon was up on one elbow, gasping for breath. The sky had darkened, and lightning flashed in the distance as the wind picked up. Thunder boomed, and the grass slid together in soft, rattling whispers.

Patricia stared at him as he watched her. Most of her anger had fled now that she'd gotten to hurt someone.

"We finished?" Dillon asked, as if he had the same thoughts *and* the upper hand. Pure bravado, fake as a daydream.

"I am if you are," she said. But if he put one more foot wrong…

He glanced toward where the paladins and the drushka waited. "Why aren't they chasing us?"

She let her smugness show. "I told the yafanai aboard the tree that you're alive."

He glanced back at her quickly. "And they believed you?"

"Obviously some did if they're making enough trouble that no one's come after us."

He threw back his head and laughed, making her jump. "Oh perfect." He stood and offered her a hand.

She let herself be pulled up, still wary.

He grinned. "Nice to know they care." As quick as the grin came, it faded. "I hope they don't get hurt."

She rolled her eyes. Leave it to him to think of that *last*. "Come on. We need to catch up with Jonah and our bargaining chip." She wondered why she was inviting him at all, but he was in the body of the mayor, a second body to bargain with.

He glanced back the way they'd come before giving her a calculating look. She thought he might refuse, but he finally gestured for her to lead the way. She smiled as she did. Between the two of them, he was the one with nowhere else to go.

CHAPTER THIRTEEN

Fajir had been thinking a lot of Halaan. That didn't bother her; his death was always close to her thoughts. Lately, though, instead of mourning or fighting to remember the exact color of his eyes by dim lantern light, she kept recalling things he'd loved: a favorite dessert, a skilled dance troupe, or the way he'd grow giddy with anticipation at the prospect of a night off from guard duty. Fajir couldn't help a smile as she remembered.

If Nemesis noticed, she gave no sign. After her dream, Fajir watched her closely all the next day. Nemesis had been right: taking care of someone felt good. Halaan had always said so. Was that why happier memories wouldn't leave her now? Because she was living as Halaan would have wished?

Or perhaps he was complaining from the afterlife, saying Fajir should remember that she'd loved him beyond any other, and that she could never find happiness with anyone else.

Nico, Fajir's second in the palace guard, would disagree. Before he'd abandoned Fajir, he'd said that their lost loves wanted them to be happy, but only after their vengeance was done, of course. Once Halaan's killer was dead, Fajir could move on, or so Nico had said.

But he'd only said so because he wanted Fajir for himself.

The man responsible for the death of Nemesis's love was dead, and she seemed…happier. Once her power had been taken away, she might become even more lighthearted.

And intolerable.

"Why do you not still mourn?" Fajir asked. They still walked in the wake of the drushkan tree.

"For Freddie? What makes you think I don't?" The words sounded harsh, but only curiosity shone from Nemesis's dark eyes. Even with the bruises marring her face, there was something in her that was... compelling.

"I don't doubt that you wept for her," Fajir said. "But I've never seen it."

"You're not weeping either."

Fajir ground her teeth. "You often know my thoughts before I speak them, Nemesis! Why don't you know them now so I don't have to speak them? I do not have...all the words!" She scrubbed a hand through her hair.

"My name is Lydia," Nemesis said with a sigh. "And I'm too tired to draw you out anymore."

"Draw me?"

"Make you come to your own conclusions about your problems. But because you're new to introspection when it doesn't involve murder, and I'm tired..." She sat on the grass and patted the space beside her.

Fajir was still trying to untangle her words when she ignored the invitation and hopped up on a boulder. "I think about much besides *vengeance*."

Nemesis's eyes widened. "Do tell."

Fajir shifted, uneasy. Nemesis's words could easily turn cutting, and she had a way of laughing... "I'll tell you, but don't mock me," Fajir said, hoping her tone carried enough threat.

Nemesis nodded solemnly, not a trace of humor on her face.

Fajir still couldn't look at her. "I've been thinking of...happier times with Halaan, and I wondered if that meant my mourning was done, but it should never be done!" She smacked a fist into her palm. "Does he lament or rejoice from whatever lies beyond this life?"

Nemesis was silent. Fajir risked a look. She seemed to be staring at nothing as the wind blew her hair across her face like a curtain. "If the people we loved, those who died, feel anything, I've never known it. Or felt it. I can't follow someone's future after they've died. Maybe that's because they don't have one, or if they do, maybe they become..." She shrugged. "Something far different than what they were, like random molecules or blades of grass or starlight." She smiled, but nothing mocking lurked in it. "Or something far beyond anything we could comprehend, leaving all cares behind."

Halaan not caring for her anymore?

"No!" Fajir hopped down to pace. "What is the point of our partnerships if they don't transcend death? We may as well have a hundred partners! A thousand!"

Nemesis stilled, and Fajir could tell she was wary. That might have pleased Fajir not long before, but now she found it frustrating. "Speak, Nemesis! I will not strike you."

"Are you asking me to take apart your religion?" Nemesis asked, anger creeping into her tone. "All right. Why shouldn't you have a thousand partners if you meet that many people you want to share your life with? You haven't spoken about your gods in a long time. If you've let them go, why are you holding on to this notion that the person they assigned you to at birth is special beyond what grew between you?"

Fajir's mouth worked, but no sound came out. Halaan and all her ancestors cried out for her to slap Nemesis across the face, promise or not. She turned away to keep the feeling inside.

Nemesis sighed, and Fajir heard a rustle as she stood, but she was smart enough to stay out of reach. "I know your people have been doing the partner thing for generations, but mine have been listening to prophets for generations, and it hasn't helped them. I don't doubt that you loved Halaan, or that the Sun-Moon can make a great personality match with powerful telepathy, but aren't there people who fall in love outside partnerships?"

Many. There were those who married outside it, but they were not separated from their partners. Sometimes, large groups of people lived in the same house, partners and couples became one huge family. It made those who fell in love only with their partners look almost…lonely.

"And there must be some widows who fall in love," Nemesis said.

Like Nico, but that had felt like betrayal. She'd never had happy recollections of Halaan in Nico's company.

"We must keep walking if we're to catch your healer," Fajir said, turning for the trail once more.

Nemesis sighed again, but she didn't push. Wise Nemesis. Fajir strode ahead before she recalled Nemesis's dream and consequent outburst and slowed, the better to keep a watchful eye and make sure she didn't fall.

"So many toys to play with!" Naos's voice was a shout in Cordelia's mind. "Is it my birthday?"

Cordelia flew as fast as she could for her body, but when she'd been expelled from it before, Naos had always thrown her back into it again. Except when Naos had *severed* her from her body. Then Cordelia had to struggle back all on her own. The plains never seemed so far away. Cordelia felt as slow as when she'd been underwater in armor, fighting against the mud. And a monster had been trying to eat her then, too.

She wished she was back there. She'd take a prog over Naos any day.

"Simon!" Cordelia shouted as loudly as she could. She couldn't see Naos, but feeling her was so much worse, as if something was sucking up all the air. "Stay back, asshole, or we'll hit you like we did before!"

"My body's not here, genius. And Dr. Lazlo will have to wrangle some telepathy before he can attack my mind." She cackled. "And his lover boy telepath is currently MIA."

"Fuck," Cordelia said. She reached for Simon again, for Pool, but she sensed their distraction. As she finally came within sight of the tree, she saw why.

A scattering of broken branches lay beside Pool's tree. The fractured ends where they'd broken jutted from Pool's leaves like spears.

"What the fuck?" Cordelia muttered. Naos's mind would be on her before she could find out.

Unless she was distracted.

"Don't count on it," Naos said.

Except for the inconvenient fact that she could read minds.

But with no other options...

"Why did you attack us?' Cordelia asked.

"Join minds with me, and I'll tell you all my secrets." She laughed again. "But I didn't break your queen's branches."

"Before this! The telepathic attack." The air felt thinner even though she had no lungs. Naos would squeeze her spirit until she imploded. Something had to distract her, something she couldn't resist.

"Was it Patricia?" Cordelia asked. "Did you attack her and get the rest of us, too? Or did she attack us herself?" That made more sense, especially if Patricia had allied with the Storm Lord. They'd probably gotten rid of Horace, too, since Patricia knew the tunnels and mines.

"Patricia?" The force of Naos ceased bearing down as if waiting. "She's with you?"

"Yeah, go get her!" Cordelia yelled, hurrying for Pool. If she could shield Cordelia, there might be a chance.

Simon caught flashes from Pool. Some of the yafanai, including a few of the mothers, were using their powers against one another and the drushka.

"They say the Storm Lord lives!" Pool thought. "I am trying to restrain them, but—"

But she couldn't let them hurt the tree. A branch reached for Simon. "I'll take care of them," he said. "You help Cordelia."

Before the branch even set him down above, Simon sent his senses out, looking for the yafanai. They weren't hard to find. He let all his anger out, using that to interrupt them, freezing them in place like a stasis chamber.

He couldn't keep them that way for long. It took too much concentration when there was so much to do: help Cordelia, find Horace, and root Dillon out from whatever rock he was hiding under.

Simon hurried through the branches and found a scene of barely contained chaos. Drushka and humans lay scattered through splintered hunks of wood. Many were wounded, but the humans couldn't bleed if he didn't let them.

Shawnessi were tending the drushka with healing songs. Simon wanted to help, but interruption took all his concentration. He looked for Mila, Miriam, or Victoria. He needed to find out which yafanai were on the Storm Lord's side and which weren't.

He found the three women lying on the branches with their babies beside them. He let them go from his power, and they jerked, no doubt startled. With a cry, Mila snatched up her baby. The other two followed suit. Victoria glared at Simon, and Miriam surged to her feet, saving her glare for the other yafanai.

They spoke over one another as their babies started to cry.

"Who started this?" Simon shouted. "I can't heal anyone until—"

"Restrain them all!" Miriam said. "You don't need to keep them like this; just mute their power."

He opened his mouth to retort, then shut it. He should have thought of that.

Keeping their powers suppressed, he let their bodies go. With so much power freed, he could heal as the drushka restrained all the other yafanai. They resumed shouting at one another.

Simon trusted the drushka to hold them. The stress had several women perilously close to labor. He used his power to put it off and searched for Cordelia.

"Where is she?" he thought to Pool.

He needn't have asked. Naos's consciousness chased Cordelia through Pool's branches, confused by drushkan telepathy. Simon couldn't hear Naos's thoughts unless she wanted him to, but he could sense the signal, the massive output of power.

And she didn't need all of it to chase Cordelia. It was searching for something else, too.

Simon pushed his power through Cordelia, the easier to track Naos's signal. With Cordelia acting as an antenna, he saw that the signal led into the mountains, but he couldn't reach all the way to her body; it was just too far.

And he didn't have Horace's telepathy to attack her mind.

"Miriam, I need to borrow your power."

He sensed her wariness and ground his teeth, but he kept himself from just taking it. He couldn't do that to an ally, not if he ever wanted her to trust him again.

But time was slipping away.

She'd barely said, "All right," when he took her power, entwining it with his own. She gasped, and he knew she probably wanted to include some conditions.

"No time!" he shouted. She fell into the trance that came over people when he communed with them this way. He sent his senses out again and as Naos's mind sought Cordelia's, he struck.

Naos swore in his head. "So, there you are! You don't have as much juice as before."

"Leave us alone!" Simon said with a snarl. "You want us to play your stupid games? We can't do it if you keep fucking with us. Between you and Patricia, you're only slowing us down!" He hit her again with a telepathic strike, but she barely paused.

"Patricia, Patricia, Patricia, that's all you people talk about. It's almost enough to make me push through these ant bites you're giving me and snuff you out."

For all her words, Simon glimpsed something through Miriam's telepathy. There was something preventing Naos from taking them out, maybe a drain on her power as she used it for something else, but before he could dig, she shoved him further from her mind.

He felt her anger, but she had no witty retort or torture-filled threat before she withdrew, maybe to go looking for Patricia. Whatever. Cordelia's path was now free to her body, and Simon could get back to finding Horace.

When he opened his eyes, he let Miriam's power go, and she staggered. Victoria was holding her own child as well as Miriam's, and she hadn't ceased glaring at Simon.

"She almost dropped little Luke," Victoria said. "What did you do to her?"

He hadn't even realized Miriam had named her son, but of course she had. He shook off his shame and turned to go. His senses swept over the bound mothers and drushka, making sure all the injuries were healed. He was going after Horace. Cordelia could sort out what had happened here.

But once he left, those near labor might begin. He was pulled in every direction.

"Fuck!" he yelled, making everyone take a step back. This was all Dillon's goddamned fault.

Again.

"I don't suppose you're going to take Evan while you're up here," Miriam said as she gasped. She took her baby back and added her glare to Victoria's. "You've been leaving him with the drushka more and more."

Oh, he did not need that guilt on top of everything else. "I'll pick him up after I put out all fifteen thousand fucking fires raging at the moment!" He stomped away, remembering his pledge to burn the world if he didn't find Horace. If everyone insisted on being a total asshole, why couldn't he do it, too?

He marched toward where the shouting was still happening. "Think of your children!"

The yelling faded to muted mumbling.

"No matter what you believe, you want your children to be safe, right?" Simon said, only slightly quieter than his yell. "Then you have to take some deep breaths because several of you are on the cusp of labor."

The mumbling ceased. Only a couple of them had given birth before in their lives. No matter what they'd heard, the prospect of the actual experience was a frightening one.

"Are you going to help us?" one of the women asked quietly.

Simon met their gazes. In all the emotions flying around, he couldn't tell who was on Dillon's side. He supposed it didn't matter. He wasn't going to let the Storm Lord worshipers suffer even if their god didn't give a shit whether they lived or died.

❖

Horace couldn't remember much, just that he was tired of being punched in the face. It had happened several times now. He'd opened his eyes, had enough time to remember the last punch, then another came from out of the darkness, and he started the whole process over again.

Finally, he opened his eyes, remembered the last hit, and managed to croak, "Wait!"

No punch. That was different.

His face burned, throbbing along with his side. He reached for his power and found it denied, that part of his mind shielded behind a telepathic wall.

"Shit," he said.

"My sentiments exactly," Patricia's voice said behind him.

He turned slowly, not wanting to aggravate his injuries. She sat against the wall of a tunnel, and he lay on the floor. The area around them was lit by lanterns, enough light to see the Storm Lord sitting just behind her, scowling. His hair was grayer, and he'd acquired a scar down the side of his face, but there was no mistaking him.

Horace bit back most of his questions, knowing they probably wouldn't be answered. "Is Jon all right? The paladin who was with me?"

"I kept him from dying. If you cooperate and behave, he'll be fine, blah, blah, blah." She picked a piece of dirt from her trousers.

Horace couldn't help a burst of anger. "Good to know you can be so flippant about life and death."

She yawned. "I've been shamed by people far older and wiser than you. Do your worst."

The Storm Lord just watched Horace intently. Horace stared back, surprised. From what he'd seen, the Storm Lord didn't often let others do the talking. Seven other people stood farther down the tunnel, talking amongst themselves. Liam was one of them, and he didn't seem like a prisoner.

Horace sighed, completely unsurprised. "I guess it's too late to say that I knew your story about the mayor having brain damage was a sack of lies. We shouldn't have even talked to you."

"What did you want to do? Kill me and be done with it?" She still sounded more tired than anything.

He put all the vitriol he had in his voice. "That would have been better for everyone."

Her bored look turned into a glare at last.

"Are you controlling him, too?" Horace asked, nodding at the Storm Lord.

She snorted. "Just be content with the fact that you don't know anything and shut up."

Horace tried to stretch, but his aches and pains didn't let him move far. "How come you healed Jon and not me?"

"Oh, there we go! Another jerk who's happy for me to use my power as long as it benefits him." She threw a pebble at the opposite wall. "Forget it."

Interesting. Maybe if he kept goading her, she'd elaborate. "I have been a therapist, but is now the time to talk about your problems?"

Her glare increased, and the Storm Lord shifted as if he might attack, but Patricia put a hand on his arm, and he stilled, thoroughly controlled.

One more nugget of information to be tucked away.

"Where is Jon?"

"If it'll shut you up, he's there." She nodded down the tunnel, and Horace spotted a shadow that could have been a person on the floor. "I'm keeping him unconscious."

Horace's anger bubbled again. Of course they were keeping Jon unconscious. He was the paladin, the dangerous one. What could Horace do besides shut someone down with his power or send out a telepathic signal that would bring Simon and Cordelia and the drushka? He opened his mouth, then shut it, remembering Jon's lessons about not telegraphing one's attacks. Patricia was doing worse than that by underestimating him. He couldn't let her know about her mistake.

Horace breathed deep, trying to determine the extent of his injuries. Something had rammed into his side; he remembered the dull ache. But it hadn't broken the skin. His leg had a bandage around it that was stained with blood, but it was dry. He wiggled a bit, trying not to think of every action before he did it, even though Patricia didn't seem to be reading his mind.

If forced, he could execute some of the maneuvers Jon and Cordelia had taught him. But the Storm Lord was watching, and he'd been a soldier before he'd been a god.

"Can I go see Jon?" Horace asked softly, trying to think of Patricia as someone who'd been wounded. The injured could be irrational and dangerous even as they wanted to be soothed.

"He's fine."

He took a deep breath. "I believe you, but he's still my friend. Please?"

With a wary look, she stood, the Storm Lord with her. "Follow me."

The Storm Lord kept himself between them as she led the way down the tunnel. This was going to be tricky. Taking on this many opponents required powers. To get his own back, he needed Patricia to loosen her grip. To do *that*, he needed to get her away from her meat shield. Horace supposed he should be grateful the Storm Lord wasn't throwing lightning around. Maybe he was the one with brain damage.

At a bend in the rocky tunnel, Jon lay on the floor. They'd stripped his armor, but his chest rose and fell. Horace knelt at his side and took his hand. He seemed uninjured, but it had been a long time since Horace had to look for injuries with only his eyes.

Patricia leaned against the wall and crossed her arms. "I thought you were with Simon Lazlo. Is this guy your secret lover, or are the three of you..." She waved a hand as if inviting him to fill in the gap.

He wanted to retort about the differences between friendly and sexual touching, but he needed to be smart, calculating. He'd already pissed her off, and he had to undo that damage if he was going to get out of here. Even Cordelia could playact when she needed to.

He'd just have to find out what appealed to her. She hadn't seemed talkative in Gale; her puppet Liam spoke for her most of the time. When Naos attacked with the meteor, she'd gone bloodlessly pale, terrified, but they were all scared of Naos. He thought of the first thing she'd done when free in her new body: taken over a mine and invited trouble. And she'd somehow resurrected the Storm Lord, another source of trouble if she lost control of him.

So, she wanted a home, wanted power, wanted a helpmate, possibly a lover.

She coveted.

"Haven't you ever wanted something you couldn't have?" he asked, stroking Jon's face and hoping to be forgiven for all this touching. He heard a rustle of fabric as Patricia sat, closer than before, but the Storm Lord was still in the way.

"Hasn't everyone?" she asked.

"Probably."

She snorted. "Some people won't admit it, but there's always that better job or boyfriend or piece of jewelry." She sighed. "Or an entire life."

Horace licked his lips; his head started to ache from the strain of thinking fast without thinking "loudly." "Why did you come here? Originally." When she frowned and tilted her head, he added, "Simon came to this planet to get away from Earth, but I never knew what the rest of you were looking for." He glanced away as if embarrassed. "If that's not too personal."

"No, it's just been a while since I thought about it." Her gaze went far away. "There's no great mystery. I was the copilot. It was just a flight for me. I was never going to be a colonist." She shut her eyes. "And then I was her."

Horace didn't want her to go there, not if they were going to be *friends*. "Was being a copilot all you wanted? Or did you want to work your way up the chain of command?"

She barked a laugh. "I had visions of being a fleet admiral one day, running missions behind the scenes. I liked the numbers a hell of a lot more than I liked the people."

Probably why she controlled people rather than led them. She'd relaxed, drawing up one leg and resting her arm along her knee. Now, if he could only get the Storm Lord to loosen up.

Before he could try, a voice called for Patricia down the tunnel. Horace tensed, looking to see if the Storm Lord turned at the sound, too, but all he did was stare at Horace as if he'd been given one job to do and was going to do it better than anyone had thought to do it before. Horace could have screamed at him.

"Here," Patricia called.

Liam walked out of the dark, looking glum. When he caught Horace's eye, he frowned harder. "I thought our guests were sleeping."

"I wanted to make sure he was all right," she said, a bit of rebellious anger in her voice.

Liam's smile was brittle. "A few injuries will make him less likely to run away."

At once, Horace's face tingled before it hurt less, and the throb in his side and leg faded to nothing. Healing as argument: he could get behind that.

"I wanted to make sure his brain wasn't damaged," she said with a smile as fake as his.

He sighed, and Horace wondered what was going on here. Was she controlling him yet still fighting with him? Was Liam trying to reassert himself? Or maybe she wasn't as good at mind control as Naos.

Horace cleared his throat. "Jon and I are alive, so nothing's been done that can't be undone. Clearly, I wasn't supposed to find out about him." He nodded at the Storm Lord. "But you wouldn't have been able to keep him a secret forever. Cordelia and Simon are never going to let him join the alliance, but Jon and I, and you, Liam, should go back. Or did Naos stop being a problem while I was unconscious?"

Liam barked a laugh, a hollow sound. "We're not going back."

Was that him speaking or Patricia? If she wasn't controlling him completely, maybe she'd promised him something too wonderful to refuse even if it meant abandoning his friends and allying with the man who killed his mother.

"Simon will keep looking for me."

Liam sneered. "Because he loves you?"

"Yes."

"Don't count on that," Liam said, crossing his arms. "One day, he'll stop without warning and leave you in the shit."

Horace sat back on his heels. "What?"

"Enough," Patricia said. "Horace, you and your friend are going to be our guests for a little longer, and that's that." She stood and brushed off her trousers. "And judging by your face," she said to Liam, "I've got more tunnel to dig." She stood on her tiptoes and had a word in the Storm Lord's ear before kissing his cheek. She strode down the tunnel, leaving the Storm Lord glaring down at Horace and Liam glaring in her wake.

CHAPTER FOURTEEN

Cordelia wondered how many times she'd look at her life and think everything was fucked. She didn't know what she'd do if she woke up to a morning with no problems. Probably get nervous and punch someone.

When she'd returned to her body on the plains, she'd felt as stretched as a mound of dough. Nettle had returned to lean over her, a worried look on her face. "If Naos is going to chase me every time I leave my body, astral scouting is out," Cordelia said.

"I will not mourn." Nettle helped her to her feet and provided a shoulder to lean on as Cordelia learned to walk again. They started through the long grass toward Pool's tree. "Simon has calmed some yafanai who started a fight in the tree while you were gone. The queen reports that some of the mothers are near birth."

"Great." It was only half sarcastic. "Maybe labor will distract them. Was Pool hurt? The tree? How are you?" She cupped Nettle's face, lamenting that she was still wearing her armor. They both could have used a hug.

"I am well, Sa, but the queen still suffers. The yafanai tore a large hole in her branches. Perhaps they were aided by Naos or Patricia. The wounds to the tree are being sealed."

"Fucking gods! Is there anything I can do?"

Nettle wrinkled her narrow nose and kissed Cordelia soundly. "Simply be as you are. If you wish to offer the queen comfort, I am certain she would not object."

"Okay," Cordelia said as they continued toward the tree. "But I'm not kissing her."

Nettle chuckled. "No? But through our connection, she is aware of all your kisses."

Cordelia snorted a laugh. Kiss one drushka, you kissed them all, she supposed. Liam would have made a joke about orgies.

Liam. She'd nearly forgotten him. She told Nettle her suspicions, confirmed by the lightning that had struck her: the Storm Lord was sharing Liam's body. Pool absorbed this knowledge through Nettle, and by the time Cordelia saw her speaking with Simon, everyone had shared it.

"I felt his attack," Simon said. Just beyond him, some expectant mothers milled around, denied their power. Miriam stood guard over them, and the look on her face said no Storm Lord worshiper was getting past her watch.

"I thought Dillon was hiding nearby in his own body, but in Liam?" Simon asked. "Holy shit."

"How is it possible, shawness?" Pool asked. "The old Shi once forced the younger queens to do her bidding, but to live inside them?" She frowned as if she'd eaten something sour.

"Must be a trick Patricia learned from Naos," Simon said. "We can't figure it out until we get him back, and even then, we'll need a skilled telepath, so…" He spread his hands drushkan fashion. "We need to get Horace."

Pool spread her hands, too. "I cannot move the tree, shawness, not with so great a hole in the branches. Many still suffer from the shock."

Simon's stare seemed desperate, even crazed. "Can't some of the drushka—"

"No one will leave the queen while she is wounded." Nettle put a hand on Simon's shoulder. "Wait but a little while."

He shrugged out from under her grasp. "I've already waited! Cordelia?"

She didn't want to leave the drushka either, but the tunnel wasn't far. "We could start digging, but it'd be safer to wait." She kept her voice as calm as possible. Simon had freaked when he'd seen blood in the ravine, but the attackers wouldn't have bothered to cart dead bodies away. "Horace and Jon are alive, so Naos or Patricia or the Storm Lord or whoever probably plans to use them for—"

"I'm not going to let Horace be *used* by the crew of the *Atlas*!" Simon yelled. "I know exactly how that feels."

He stomped up and down the branch, and Cordelia remembered his fiery threats. She kept her hands down, her posture relaxed. She did not want to give him the impression that he needed to power his way out of there.

But she also didn't want him to abandon them. He was the linchpin of their whole anti-Naos plan. "Okay," she said calmly, "you stay here with the moms, and we'll start digging."

When he stopped to stare, he seemed slightly less manic, and she wished they had the power to soothe him as he did for everyone else. Her heart went out to him even as he was making her very nervous. They'd had too many unstable power users around lately.

"We'll find him," she said quietly. "As fast as we can, then you and I will kill the Storm Lord, get Liam back, punch Patricia in the face, and put Naos on her ass."

He smiled, but for a moment, he looked all of his nearly three hundred years. She wondered when he'd last slept for real and not because of his power.

"Thanks," he said. "I'll enjoy all that and the drinks afterward."

"Fuck yeah."

As he turned toward the moms, Cordelia went back the way she'd come, Pool and Nettle with her.

"Maybe you better have Reach keep him company," Cordelia said.

"Ahya," Pool said. "She is among the mothers already. She will comfort him."

And watch him, but Cordelia didn't say that. Pool would pick up on her anxiety through their connection.

"I will help in the digging," Nettle said. "And some others as well since it is not far, but most will remain with the tree."

"Understood," Cordelia said. "I'm going to leave some paladins here, too, since I know you'll be distracted, Pool."

Pool ran the outside of her hand down Cordelia's cheek. "Sa, you are dear to me."

Cordelia knew she meant dear in more of a family way than as a lover, but Nettle's words about kissing echoed in her mind. To her horror, she had to fight a blush.

By the teasing glance Nettle and Pool exchanged, Cordelia knew *that* embarrassing conversation had already been shared. She fought both a harder blush and the urge to wipe her cheek. Flirting with people—drushka included—wouldn't normally bother her, but this was *Pool*.

"Better get digging!" she said loudly. She strode away, Nettle with her. "I know you helped her tease me, and you better believe I'm going to have my revenge."

Nettle brushed her short, deep red locks off her forehead. "Ahya, Sa, I have no doubt you shall try."

❖

Lydia wondered what Mamet was up to at that moment. Her people lived north of Celeste, almost where the plains met the sea, and the rockier terrain this close to the mountains made Lydia nostalgic.

Not that there had been many days before Fajir came and turned her world upside down.

And now, marching toward the unknown, there was little to think about besides the past...or Fajir.

Something had happened between them; some corner had been turned. Lydia tried to pinpoint exactly when she *knew* Fajir wouldn't kill her; she couldn't remember. She was still a little scared of Fajir's unpredictability, though.

Who built a relationship on such unsteady ground? If a friend had asked Lydia's advice about starting a relationship with someone like Fajir, Lydia would have told them to run away fast.

Still, Fajir had said she wouldn't strike, and that meant... something. Lydia rolled her eyes as she walked, skirting a boulder and watching her feet for loose stones. Yes, *that* was healthy.

Fajir had tried to *kill* her.

Twice.

"Watch your step," Fajir said. "The slope is deceptively steep."

Maybe Lydia should ask why she was being so helpful. Fajir would probably babble about widows and duty and destiny. Those were all good answers, true ones, but they weren't the main reason Fajir had turned a corner.

She was in love.

Lydia had realized it before, ignored it, called it vague names like "feelings" or a "crush." But someone didn't help a crush through hostile territory filled with people she hated on a mission that made no sense for her to care about.

"I've never been into the mountains," Lydia said, distracting herself as much as anything.

"Nor me." Fajir's hand hovered as if ready to take Lydia's elbow, a fact Lydia tried hard not to find charming. She made herself remember the feeling of Fajir's hands around her throat.

"Stop," Fajir said, eyes locked on something in the distance.

For a moment, Lydia had the panicked thought that Fajir was reading her mind, but she had to have seen something. "What is it?"

Fajir drew the bone sword from the sash at her waist. "They hide, Nemesis, so no doubt they have already seen us."

"Lydia. And who?"

Fajir's smile reminded Lydia of the one time she'd seen a grelcat, a large predator that hunted the plains. "Shall we find out? Stay behind me." She ran, and after a moment of gawking, Lydia stumbled after. Clearly, Fajir wouldn't wait for an ambush.

Or to see if those she'd spotted were friend or foe.

When Fajir raced around a boulder and a leather-clad form leaped to accost her, Lydia was relieved to spot a red eye emblazoned on their clothing. She'd worried that all her thoughts of Mamet's people had caused one to appear.

Her relief fled as several more Naos fanatics sprang from their hiding places, but Fajir moved for them like the wind. Her eyes went half-lidded; her hair was like a black flame dancing around her shoulders. Lydia faltered, losing pace as Fajir whirled amongst the grass and boulders, a dust storm given human form.

Some she killed, and Lydia's stomach wanted to rebel, but others she wounded, and Lydia began to see a pattern. Fajir only killed if her attacker left her no choice or when a wounding blow would have left her open.

Lydia had done that, changed her. It was…special.

She had just enough time to call herself an idiot when one of the fanatics found a way around Fajir and into Lydia's path. She'd fallen too far behind. The fanatic stared at her, the lower half of their face hidden behind a scarf. They must have been riding hard through the dust before they'd reached this place.

Idiot, she thought again, thinking about dust instead of moving and falling into her power before—

The fanatic pitched forward, the back of their neck split like a ripe fruit. Fajir spun away, but the attack had left her exposed, and another fanatic slashed her arm. Fajir didn't let the wound stop her as she scored a hit across the attacker's belly and moved closer to Lydia.

Lydia spotted a dust cloud in the southeast. More were coming, and Fajir already had one wounded arm. The blood trickled from her sleeve.

"Fajir!"

"I see them." She kept the last two fanatics at bay.

"We have to…" Run? They couldn't hope to outpace what was probably a pack of ossors. But if these scouts had ridden hard, they had to have mounts, too.

Lydia pulled Fajir to the base of a boulder, then scrambled atop it. She scanned the nearby rocks and ravines, her heart racing. Her power sat at the back of her mind, desperate to be used, promising she could at least see if they got away.

"Shut up," she said with a snarl. "I already know Fajir does, so just shut up!"

"Nemesis?"

A hint of movement caught her eye, and she nearly crowed. "There, that ravine! Their mounts!"

Fajir didn't wait. She feinted left, and when the fanatic on the right came at her, she slashed his knee, toppling him. She dispatched the last one quickly, and Lydia slid down, running for the ossors.

"Careless Nemesis!" Fajir said as she ran to catch up. "They may have a guard!"

Lydia slid to a stop just as she saw the fanatic hidden by the rocks. He lifted a knife as if to throw it, and Lydia didn't need her power to know that her life was about to end.

She hoped there'd be starlight.

An arrow sprouted in the fanatic's side as if summoned, throwing him to the ground. Lydia dashed for the ossors. No matter who'd saved her, they couldn't wait around and confront the horde that was coming.

She pulled herself into the saddle, Fajir beside her, when a voice called, "Seren?"

Fajir froze as if someone had dunked her in ice. A group of mounted warriors milled not far away, all of them armed with shortbows.

And all of them in Sun-Moon robes.

The one in the lead pulled down a dust-covered scarf, revealing tattooed cheeks. "Seren Fajir, it is you!"

"Nico," Fajir said softly, her eyes wide, voice nearly trembling.

Lydia looked between them and wondered what Fajir could be so afraid of.

❖

Shiv began to wonder if she even needed the help of this much-feared Naos. It was hard to hold on to despair as her tree nearly flew through the swamp. The roots curled around the taller swamp trees and moved her tree in leaps that tickled the insides and made Shiv laugh in delight. As Lyshus laughed with her, she forgot his failure to understand the importance of the drushkan trees. He became a normal child, thrilled by sensation and the joy of another.

Soon, they would break free from the swamp. Shiv had never been so far north, had no idea what sort of terrain awaited her. She recalled Sa's stories of mountains, but what lay between the swamp and those rocky peaks? Perhaps she would be so happy at discovering it that she would avoid Naos, avoid everyone, and continue on her own with Lyshus.

Forever?

She shook the thought away. She had no time for despair. For all her delight, she had to be wary. She had kept close to the eastern border of the swamp, wanting to remain far from the Shi, but this territory might belong to another queen.

As if summoned, Shiv felt a questing mind. She ignored it. The queens could feel her presence, probably sought her, but her smaller tree could move far faster than theirs.

A flurry of movement caught her attention. Far to the side, a group of figures flashed through the air like a disturbed flock, but birds did not fly so low, and insects were not so large. It could only be a band of drushka. She should have known the queens would not be content with her lack of interest. They sent scouts to see what could be seen.

The old drushka had been very interested in her when she had stayed among them. She denied them full access to her mind, not wanting them to know about Lyshus. A child born of a queen was interesting enough; frowned upon but not expressly forbidden. One had not been seen in even the longest memories.

Still, there had been stories, tales Shi'a'na had never learned because she never asked. They did not end happily.

Shiv commanded her tree to turn away from the oncoming drushka. They would not hurt her, probably would not even bar her path, but she was not in the mood to be fodder for their eyes, did not want tales sung about her. She would not be another unhappy tale.

The drushka turned, keeping pace. Since they were not hers, Shiv could not speak directly to their minds, and shouting seemed undignified. But as she continued and still they followed, her anger grew. She did not want to fight them; that would only give them another story. Surely they had enough tales to sustain them. They did not need hers!

But she might find *theirs* helpful.

The thought made her pause. They had tales of queens' daughters. Perhaps they had others even more forbidden. All the tales she had heard ended in tragedy before the daughters ascended to a tree, but that did not mean such stories did not exist.

Shiv slowed and stopped, and the band of leaping drushka came to a halt. She waited, and after a moment, their hunt leader approached, walking along the branches of a swamp tree with her palms up to show herself unarmed save for her claws.

The wind gusted across her, and Shiv caught a hint of scent, something familiar. She had met this silver-haired female among the old drushka but had smelled her scent even before they met. This was Enka, once envoy of the old Shi, now a hunt leader with the Seventh. The old queens had introduced them, saying Shiv might be more comfortable speaking with a drushka who had also been to Gale.

If only to poison it.

Shiv told Lyshus to stay aboard the tree while she went out. If Enka felt any guilt for harming the humans, she had never shown it. The old Shi had commanded it; now the new one commanded her to leave the humans alone. It mattered not to Enka.

"Young queen," Enka said, eyeing the tree curiously. "Your tree is larger than I imagined."

"You will come aboard and travel with me," Shiv said, trying to fill her voice with Shi'a'na's tone of command.

Enka spread her hands, but the gesture seemed hesitant. "If you will it, but…"

"I do not ask you to give yourself into my branches," Shiv said, though the desire to do so beat inside her.

Enka smiled softly. "We will escort you—"

"No, only you. The others may leave. We will have a journey, you and I, and then you will return to the swamp." There would be time enough for a few stories, then Enka's task would be done. She could return and tell the old queens whatever she wished. After Shiv had visited Naos, all problems with Lyshus would be solved.

Nemesis's predictions had prepared Fajir for tragedy, but not for the lurch in her heart at the sight of Nico's face. He was dressed and mounted as if stepping from her memory, and yet he seemed like something from another world.

Nemesis's eyes were wide with questions. Since she and Fajir had their own ossors, they could flee from Nico. But Nico and his troop didn't seem fazed by the approaching dust cloud. It had to be an army from Celeste, a force great enough to catch her and Nemesis if they fled.

"Nico," Fajir croaked again.

"Seren," Nico said, a myriad of expressions flashing over his face even though his voice was steady and formal. No calling her his *Faja* in front of others, not that she would have allowed it. She still felt the sting of betrayal over his confession of love, still felt the pain of his abandonment.

She sat straighter in her saddle. "Well—"

"The Lords will want to speak to you." He gestured over his shoulder, and her heart sank further.

"The Lords are with you?" She stared again at the dust. Gusts of wind came from the west, sweeping the cloud over the waving grass like a discarded veil. A few drops of rain pattered down.

Nico nodded and gestured for them to follow.

Nemesis's eyes grew even wider. Fajir nudged her ossor close. "We cannot outrun *them*," Fajir said. Nemesis nodded, and Fajir could practically smell her fear. The Lords were much maligned by her former people.

For good reason.

"I will not leave you," Fajir pledged, gratified to see some relief on Nemesis's face.

Fajir kept their ossors close as they turned with Nico's group. She had a flash of memory: Nemesis riding and leading Fajir, whose arms were bound. She'd pledged to kill Nemesis, Samira, and Mamet a hundred times over during her imprisonment.

That, too, felt like a different age.

They rode through the first ranks of Sun-Moon soldiers. Fajir heard whispers in their wake, but she had never minded whispers. As a widow, she was used to them, and most were respectful enough.

It wasn't until she heard a stray comment calling her the former seren who'd abandoned her duty that Fajir whirled around, hand going to her sword. One of the soldiers shied back.

"Come say that to my blade," Fajir said. She wanted to add that the Lords had abandoned *her* in her darkest moment, but she wanted to give them the chance to answer for that first.

Nico shooed the offending soldier away, but he did not deny the accusation. Fajir wanted to strike him. So he believed it, too, even though he'd been the one to leave. He'd clearly spread his own tale when he should have told everyone that she'd died. Only the Lords needed to know the truth.

Even if only to deny her aid.

The Lords rode in the center of the pack atop a geaver, no doubt the spoils of some plains dweller skirmish. The large creatures didn't often come close to Celeste, preferring the stumpy trees that grew centrally in the plains. When the creature stopped, its long neck moved over the ground, and it pulled up a large hummock of grass, massive teeth grinding loudly. It blinked a long mane out of its huge eyes and didn't seem to mind anything going on around it.

A handler tapped the beast with a pole, and it folded its four legs, lying down. The Lords leaned out from a canopied box that sat atop the geaver's pebbled hide. The dribble of rain continued, but only the Lords were shielded.

"What's this?" they said in unison. They bent their heads together, one dark, one golden. They looked well enough, but Fajir remembered their haggard faces after Naos had attacked Celeste. "Our widow returned." They looked to Nemesis, and she bowed, always the wise one. Fajir followed suit before she realized it.

"Will you not introduce us?" the Lords asked.

Fajir started. They normally read the minds of those nearby, but she obeyed, speaking Nemesis's language since the Lords seemed disinclined to insert the language of Celeste into Nemesis's mind.

"This is Nem—" Fajir cleared her throat. "Lydia, lately of Gale."

"But not anymore," Nemesis said with a smile. "I'm Lydia Bauer of No Affiliation now." After a moment she added, "A pleasure to meet you, Lords."

"So, you are not scouts for the Galean army marching on the mountains?"

"I only wanted to check on some friends I have there," Nemesis said hurriedly. "And Fajir was kind enough to accompany me."

It wasn't wholly a lie, but Fajir still sighed. Hiding things from the Lords was useless.

They smiled. "We have determined your abilities before, Lydia, ex-prophet of Gale. Your power will be useful to us in the future."

Nemesis's smile disappeared as she bared her teeth in a snarl. "I won't—"

"Your cooperation will not be necessary." They gestured to Nico. "Guard her until we have need of her."

He bowed from the saddle. "Lords."

Fajir's temper rose, but she put a restraining hand on Nemesis's arm. Something was amiss here.

"Lords," Fajir said, "Simon Lazlo is among the Galeans. You once told me you would never risk his wrath. Now you follow him?"

They glowered at her. "We will not discuss Simon Lazlo or anyone else with you, now or at any time. Either take your proper place again or leave." They gestured, and their geaver stood.

Fajir followed numbly as Nico led Nemesis away. The Lords had abandoned her, and they didn't even remember? But they remembered everything, knew everything. If it wasn't a lapse of memory…

They didn't care. All the nights she'd lain awake lamenting her fate, knowing she'd let the Lords down, and they hadn't thought of her at all. Her hands tightened on the reins. They hadn't bothered to disarm her, either. She was immaterial. She couldn't do anything to them, not while they could read her mind.

Or could they? Crazed thoughts were flying through her head unchecked.

The army began to move, and Fajir and Nemesis went with it, watched over by Nico in a pocket of mounted widows, none of whom had been part of her former force.

Nemesis scrubbed her hands over her head and leaned close. "My scalp is tingling like crazy. Your Lords must be using their power in a big way."

"Reading your mind?"

"If they are, they're not saying anything. And I didn't feel a spike when they said they knew my power—which I will *not* use for them— so maybe they already knew because they'd read my mind when we were closer to Celeste?"

If they had, they'd neglected to help Fajir then, too. "Normally, I would say that the Lords can make you use your power, but if they're already using that power to such an extent that they did not read us…"

Nemesis whistled softly. "I bet they're creating a telepathic shield around this whole army, hiding from the other gods. It's got to be taking everything they have."

Not just reading minds but making those minds invisible *and* seeking to keep their output of power undetectable? Yes, they had to be very distracted.

Enough for an escape? That depended on their plans.

Fajir fought down anger and disappointment and turned to Nico. She dearly wished Cordelia was there to lie for her. "Where are we going?"

He barely glanced at her, shifting in his saddle. Good, maybe he was ashamed of any rumors he'd started. "To the mountains. The Lords say we will receive metal there."

Fajir glanced at Nemesis. They'd both heard Naos's voice in their heads, inviting whoever could reach her to claim the downed spaceship. It seemed everyone in the world had heard it, too. And the Lords had believed it.

It sounded dangerous, foolhardy even. The Lords' main enemy, the Storm Lord, was dead. Perhaps they feared his followers would claim the metal, make fearsome weapons of old, and seek revenge.

And since they'd brought an army, they knew there would be competition for the metal.

If it wasn't simply a trap.

CHAPTER FIFTEEN

Dillon was tempted to pump a few bolts of lightning into the tunnel walls. It would vent some of his frustration and maybe give Patricia a reminder about why she shouldn't fuck with him.

It could also give away who he really was to Horace, but that cat was out of the bag already with almost everyone else. And maybe the healer could use a reason to be afraid of him, too. Dillon had seen him cozying up to Patricia, even if she was too blind to notice. A person could do a lot of things with a captive, but trust was not one of them, especially one as powerful as Horace. It didn't help that Patricia seemed determined to keep him awake and healthy against Dillon's wishes.

A move made out of spite, pure and simple.

How could he have ever felt sorry for her? Youth. A pretty face turned to him in crisis; it had always been a weak spot. Lessan—navigator of the *Atlas* and over two hundred years dead—had looked at him that way, and he'd pitied her, too. Until she'd defied him. He hadn't meant to kill her, but Patricia...

As he watched her dig chunks out of the partially collapsed tunnel, he didn't doubt the usefulness of her *power*, even if it did paint a giant target on their backs. But her obstinacy was getting out of control, and it was harder and harder to make nice.

He shifted his gaze to the healer again. At least Dillon's old bod was watching Horace like a hawk. And the way Horace's eyes darted around the tunnel meant he needed watching. Dillon caught his gaze and held it. A calculating look flitted over Horace's face before he smiled hopefully.

Oh, this was going to be interesting.

Dillon wandered over, grateful to be getting away from the noise of shifting rock.

"What happened, Liam, really?" Horace asked, and Dillon wondered if he and the mayor had been friends, maybe even exes. The mayor had quite a few of those.

Dillon sighed and leaned against the wall, letting the old bod watch them both. "At the mine, you mean? You won't believe me if I said people change."

"But what could possibly make you switch sides? Mind control?" He frowned and broke eye contact as if he hadn't wanted to say that last part out loud.

Dillon smiled. "You're trying to reconcile your theory with my little spat with Patricia?" He shrugged. "Like I said, people change."

"Did she threaten you? Threaten Gale?"

Best to say nothing, but if Dillon had to get Patricia out of the way, he'd need more power in his corner. He took a slow look down the corridor to where Patricia was, then flicked his gaze to Jonah. When he looked again at Horace, he raised his eyebrows, hoping he looked like someone who was afraid to speak openly.

Horace's eyes widened, and he nodded slightly.

Dillon nearly smiled. All it took to fool someone was finding out what they wanted to believe. "There's…a lot at stake," Dillon said, words that meant nothing, but Horace would no doubt read volumes in them.

"Like people's lives." Horace smoothed the hair off the unconscious paladin's face. What would Lazlo think of that? The idea of Laz with a broken heart was both pitiable and gratifying. And by the way Horace glanced at Jonah after the touch, he was probably asking for "Liam's" help escaping.

"If Naos keeps running around free, we're all in danger," Dillon said.

"You really think that's a war anyone can win?"

"I think it'll take everyone to beat her." Dillon made himself nod at Jonah. "Even him."

"And you know Cordelia and Simon would never work with… him." Horace frowned as if uncomfortable talking about someone else in the room, even if that someone didn't react.

Dillon swallowed hard. He'd already pulled a storm down on them outside, and he didn't want to kick up a tornado, but thinking about the past shredded his calm more than anything else. "I knew it wouldn't happen right away."

Horace snorted. "Try ever." Now he looked Jonah in the eye. "You've got a lot to answer for, even with whatever's wrong with you."

Jonah just glared.

"You could have at least asked about your children," Horace said. "If you cared at all."

Dillon's stomach churned as he wondered what Horace was playing at. Was his indignation real, or was he trying to provoke "the Storm Lord?"

No matter which, it was giving Dillon a headache, and now he felt guilty on top of everything. Maybe "the mayor" should have paid a visit to those kids, but he was scared he'd give the game away, and there'd been so many other things to do, and…

Fuck it. He could find out how they were doing now. "Tell him about them," Dillon said. "The kids." Jonah wouldn't react anyway.

Horace glanced at Dillon, probably thinking their intentions were aligned. "Simon and I have been taking care of Evan, your child by Caroline. Well, much of the time, anyway. The drushka have been looking after him when we can't." He returned Jonah's glare. "Your faithful worshipers have been trying to kidnap the children, use them as pawns. Miriam was almost killed."

As if Dillon could have done something to prevent that. He'd never wanted any of the mothers to be hurt, even if he couldn't remember who Miriam was. They might have only had one night together, and there'd been so many.

Horace sniffed at Jonah's lack of expression, clearly ready to give up, but Dillon found himself hungry for more.

"What are their names, the other children?"

"Evelyn," Horace said. "She's Victoria's daughter. Then there's Kena, Mila's daughter. And Miriam's son is named Luke." He thought for a moment. "I know one other died in childbirth with the mother."

Dillon struggled to keep his face impassive but had to turn toward the wall. How much would it give away if he asked her name? Had the mayor known? Shit, he probably wouldn't remember her anyway. God, he felt like an asshole. At least most of them got to keep their babies. All the dead one got was the cold ground.

Dillon cleared his throat. "I'm sure he'd be sorry if he wasn't…" What were the words Horace had used? "Wrong in some way. I'm sorry, for what it's worth."

"Me, too," Horace said.

Patricia called from down the corridor, coming to the rescue. "I'm getting something strange," she said softly when she reached Dillon's side. "I've been keeping my power down, trying not to attract Naos's attention." She wrung her hands, catapulted from petulance back to worry at the mention of that name. "But I can feel something coming this way."

"A signal or a person?"

"I'm not sure." She glanced upward as if expecting the ceiling to collapse.

"If Naos has come out of the mountains, this is the perfect opportunity to strike." He smiled just thinking about it.

"She's not stupid. It's someone else, and if they come any closer..." She scrubbed her hands through her hair. "It keeps fading in and out. If we don't want them to sense us, we need a distraction." Her eyes slipped shut before he could ask what she had in mind, and he almost snapped at her to wait for his input.

"I just need to bounce the signal like so, and..." She opened her eyes and smiled. "There. Signal meets signal. That'll give them enough to worry about."

"Who? What did you do?"

Patricia smiled widely. "I introduced a potential rock to a confirmed hard place, or a confirmed group of soldiers and drushka, in this case."

Dillon fought the urge to shake a better explanation out of her. She'd done something to the Galeans, but that party wasn't just battle-ready soldiers and drushka. And now he couldn't stop thinking about those kids. He might be an asshole, but he was still a father, still had a responsibility even if he forgot it now and then. He had to start thinking further ahead.

Simon tried to lose himself in the sound of wind sighing through the branches, in the smell of greenery that surrounded the drushka, and in the comforting notion that he was surrounded by friends who had quickly become family.

All except Horace.

No, he told himself. He had to stay away from that thought. It was the most upsetting development, a worry greater than Naos or Patricia.

Or Dillon.

Simon took a deep breath through the anger. He had to get ready to deliver some babies. Wielding his power while angry was dangerous, as he'd proven while augmenting Horace and Natalya. He also didn't want to bring a life into the world while ensnared by a fit of rage. It didn't seem right.

Using his power, he cleansed his hands. He took a few more breaths to center himself, but the worry wouldn't leave his thoughts. It wasn't just that Horace was missing; it was their stupid fight. Simon couldn't figure out why it had happened. Horace was clearly dissatisfied, maybe even with his entire life, and Simon couldn't help thinking it had something to do with their relationship. But Horace had implied that was selfish, then—

"Shawness?" Reach asked. "Are you ready to begin?"

"No," he said with a sigh, but more time wouldn't help. He stood from the branch where he'd been sitting and turned toward where his patients were waiting. Three of them couldn't wait much longer.

"I am interested to see a human birth," Reach said. "Caring for human children is very different than tending drushka."

With how quickly drushka grew, he knew that for a fact. Because they developed in pods, drushkan newborns were larger and could walk and eat solid food from birth. They were easier to deal with because they could feed themselves, but they also tended to wander off.

And bite everything.

Simon took another deep breath. His thoughts were all over the place. He nearly gave Reach a hug when she began a soothing melody. She followed him to the first expectant mother, who lay in a small basket of branches. She eyed him warily as she breathed hard. He didn't ask if she was a Storm Lord worshiper. He couldn't afford to think badly of her while trying to help.

"Don't worry. There won't be any pain." He sent over some soothing vibes, happy Reach's song was there to back him up. "Do you have any friends to be with you?"

"We didn't know if it was allowed." She sounded a heartbeat away from crying.

Simon laughed shakily, guilt adding to his misery. "Of course it is! Call them over."

She called, and one of the other mothers, not so far along, came over and sat behind the patient, propping her up.

"What are your names?" Simon asked.

"Kalith," the patient said. "She's Shana."

"Relax, Kalith, breathe." Simon fell into his power and sent it over her, searching for possible problems. He felt her contractions ready to begin and encouraged them as he lifted her shift and let the amniotic fluid come forth.

"Like queen's blood from the pods," Reach whispered before continuing her song.

Simon muttered an affirmative, but all his focus was on mother and child, easing both, making sure the baby faced the right way, then coaxing it into the birth canal.

"Push," he said softly, feeling a tentative movement from Kalith. "Harder, please."

She obeyed, and the baby began its journey. Simon shifted more focus to her, trying to calm her fear. A tickle nibbled at the corner of his mind. No one else was supposed to be using their power, so who was this?

It didn't matter. He brushed the thought away. If he lost focus, Kalith would begin to feel the pain, and he wanted her stress-free. Now that the birth had begun, he kept thinking of the mother and child who'd died while he'd been away from Gale.

The tickle came again, and someone grunted. Simon looked for the source of Kalith's pain, but it wasn't her. Shana muttered something, and one hazy thought floated to the surface in Simon's mind: these weren't just mothers; they were yafanai.

And some of them were dangerous.

And his control had slipped.

Not all of them were as concerned for their current state as he was.

The force wave hit him like a hammer, sending him spinning end over end until he slammed into Pool's trunk. The world continued to tilt crazily even after he stilled, and the voices around him seemed to come from a long tunnel.

Someone was screaming. Kalith, still in mid-labor. Simon felt around him, willing his brain to still, to tell up from down. Reach was on the branch near him, moaning in pain. Shana was on her feet, and anyone who approached her flew into midair.

"Shana, help me!" Kalith cried.

"The Storm Lord needs our help first," she said, her face set in a determined frown. If she felt bad about abandoning her friend for an egomaniacal asshole, she didn't show it.

After tossing away another drushka, Shana grabbed her head as if suffering a telepathic attack, but she dashed a hand out, and another scream sounded from the branches. Shana straightened again, eyes locked on Simon.

He reached for his power, seeking to attack hers, but another wave of force hit him from the side, and he tumbled over the branch, plummeting for the ground.

❖

Nettle cried out, and this time, Cordelia was in her body to feel Pool's pain. Her knees nearly buckled at the telepathic shriek, but it had to feel ten times worse to a drushka.

She tried to breathe through it as she held Nettle up. Staggering toward Pool's tree, Cordelia tried to tell herself this wasn't her pain. She could block it out; she could move. One step, two...

It helped. The vibrations pinging up and down her skeleton calmed, and she walked a little easier, dragging Nettle with her. "Grab the drushka and haul ass to the tree!" she cried. At least she'd taken off her armor to dig. Several others had done the same while those remaining in armor guarded them with sidearms and the last of the ammunition. Everyone laid hands on a drushka and followed in Cordelia's wake, the questions flying fast and thick.

"Muzzle it and keep walking!" Cordelia shouted. She didn't have the time or the words to explain, knowing only that Pool was hurt. Maybe it was Naos; maybe the yafanai were rebelling again.

That meant Simon was hurt, too.

"Fuck!" Cordelia said with a roar. Was anything ever going to go right again?

The tree was staggering as if drunk. Cordelia spotted flames coming from one of the branches. As she watched, a body plummeted from on high and screamed all the way to the ground. Cordelia picked up the pace, hauling Nettle partially onto her shoulders.

"Get that body," Cordelia yelled to one of the leathers, and the man darted away through the grass. Cordelia kept going for the tree, calling in her mind for Pool to give them a hand up. For a moment, she didn't think Pool would respond. Screams were coming from high up, both drushkan and human, and Cordelia caught a glimpse of other people falling. The tree couldn't catch all of them.

Finally, a branch reached down, sweeping Cordelia off her feet, and hauling her and Nettle into the sky so fast, her heart flew into her mouth, and her stomach nearly emptied. She was dumped on another branch without ceremony and looked up to see Pool lifting one of the yafanai by the neck.

Pool's eyes were glazed, and she snarled, looking more inhuman than Cordelia had ever seen. Cordelia cried, "Wait!" but Pool dashed the woman's head against a branch, opening her skull. "Pool!"

Pool said nothing, her rage-filled face searching for other targets. Cordelia knew she had to get there first, not knowing if Pool would choose her targets carefully in her current state. Cordelia laid Nettle down, then ran past Pool, looking for hostile yafanai, but the whole place was a chaotic struggle, and Pool's agony beat against Cordelia's brain. She finally spotted Miriam through the tangle.

Miriam glared at another yafanai as if locked in an epic staring contest: telepathic power. Cordelia ran for them and punched the other yafanai in the side of the head, dropping him. She hoped like fuck that most of the attacking yafanai weren't pregnant women.

"Who's attacking?" Cordelia shouted.

Miriam gasped and clutched her child to her chest. "Follow me," she said, and Cordelia had never been so grateful for someone who didn't waste time talking. She pointed out various yafanai who'd attacked, and Cordelia knocked them out while Miriam distracted them. Cordelia started toward a redhead who was standing near the fire, but Miriam stopped her.

"She's snuffing the flames!"

Cordelia let the redhead be and sent a thought to Pool to leave that one alone, but she received no reply. Hopefully, Pool had turned her attention toward her drushka.

Cordelia turned to where three women were screaming, their faces red with pain, but no one was hurting them, and they had their hands pressed to their abdomens. Giving birth?

"Oh shit," she said, having no idea what to do about that. Reach knelt beside one, and other shawnessi were staggering around, but with Pool in such pain, how much help could they be? "Shit, shit, shit." Cordelia looked to Miriam. "Do you know how to deliver a baby?"

Miriam looked scared for the first time in Cordelia's experience. "No! Why should I? Just because I've given birth—"

Cordelia turned away, not having time for a discussion. "Is that all the attackers?"

Miriam turned in a circle, her eyes slightly glazed. "I don't see any others, and I can't sense very well with all these turbulent thoughts. Shana isn't here, and she started this whole thing."

Cordelia would much rather hunt this Shana through the trees than deal with births. Rounding up the last of the attackers would help Pool stay calm and thereby give the shawnessi the wits to act. "You up to finding her?"

Miriam smiled grimly. "Absolutely."

The smell of greenery still filled Simon's nostrils. The tree. He'd fallen. The air rushing past was a feeling he'd always remember. His head had still been swimming, a feeling that chased away the terror and left him with a euphoric sense of freedom.

Then Pool had caught him, and he'd been happy to be alive.

As he lay on a branch, the tree moved beneath him as if dancing; a lovely, false idea. Recent events fell into place like pistons: the births, Shana, the screams. Above him somewhere, people needed help.

And Horace was still missing, Dillon was still alive, and as Cordelia would say, everything was still fucked.

He marshalled his power, coalescing his foggy thoughts and healing himself. When he stood, he felt far beyond anger to a weird sense of calm. It'd been nice to picture himself napping in the branches of a dancing tree.

Pool's limbs waved about. He hopped onto one that took him higher, his power reaching out to heal what he could. He let his senses flow through the limbs and sap, repairing burnt or blasted branches. He eased the suffering of the drushka until he came to Pool at their heart and pictured his power as a rush of cool water flowing over her.

"Ah, shawness," she thought, "you are the dearest of balms." She shared a memory: losing herself to pain and anger, she'd killed one of the yafanai, one of the mothers-to-be. As one who'd often lost himself, he forgave her, but others might not. One of the branches placed the body at his feet.

Simon didn't know her name, but there was no saving her. But the child within? She lived. Simon restarted the circulation in the mother's body, hoping the child hadn't been deprived of oxygen for too long. He needed a knife and sent a thought to Pool. She dropped down beside him, handing him a sharp sliver of bark.

Pool put her hands where he instructed and crooned almost like a shawness as he cut the baby free. She stripped off her shirt and wrapped the squalling infant as Simon sealed the umbilical cord. When she held the baby, he didn't offer to take it, letting her send him where he was needed.

In the branches above, he found that Reach had delivered one child. He helped with the other two and heard about how some of the attacking yafanai had escaped and were now being pursued by Cordelia, Miriam, and some of the drushka. The yafanai—including all the mothers—had separated themselves into two camps: those who'd given up the Storm Lord and those who held out hope. The latter group were further split into the escapees, those knocked unconscious by Cordelia, and several deaths.

Simon checked the unconscious people but left them sleeping, deepening their unconscious state. He kept his power pumping into the tree, too, sparking the broken limbs to regrow, but that would take time. When he strode over to the yafanai who'd given up on the Storm Lord, he felt calm, almost wondrous, lost in his power and certain of his course. Maybe he should get knocked in the head more often.

The yafanai jumped when he laughed, and he curbed his mirth. "I need a telepath, please."

They glanced at one another, but when he sent a soothing wave over them, one stepped forward, shyly holding up her hand. "I'm Kara," she said. "I'll help if I can."

"When I was delivering the first baby," Simon said, "there was a signal."

Kara nodded eagerly, as did a few of the others. "A message saying the Storm Lord needed help again. It got stronger and stronger."

And then his control had slipped. "Could you tell where the message came from?"

Kara closed her eyes as if that would help her remember. "I still feel something, but I'm not powerful enough to—"

"That's fine. Just stay with it." His senses flowed over Kara, finding her power center, then following her power outward, beyond her reach. Something flickered at the edges of his senses, a monumental output of power that danced teasingly in and out of focus, possibly telepathic in origin.

Horace? He didn't know, couldn't "hear" telepaths unless they wanted him to. Perhaps Miriam could help, but she was with Cordelia.

The answer floated up through the calm haze that enveloped him: he could go see for himself.

He walked away without a word, silently asking Pool to lower him to the ground. Reach caught up to him as he waited. "Shawness, where are you going?"

"To look for Horace and see what that signal is. Pool?" he asked aloud. "Down, please." She was probably very busy.

"Is that wise, shawness?" Reach crooned softly around the words. "The queen can take you to Sa, and once the last of the miscreants is caught, and the tree has had time to heal—"

Simon laughed at her attempt to calm him. Couldn't she see he was already as calm as could be? The coolest cucumber. "Now, please, Pool." She couldn't be that busy. He'd hate to have to climb all the way down. Maybe if he jumped, he could prepare himself for the impact and heal himself on the ground.

Then he'd experience that lovely rush of freedom again.

A supple branch plucked him up, Reach with him, and lowered him to the ground.

"You don't have to come if you're too busy," Simon said to Reach as she stayed with him in the fading sunlight.

"Ahya, of course I must! You will need your power for other things besides relaying all you see to the queen. She will follow soon." Her cheer sounded false, though he didn't know why. Nothing bad could happen when he felt so good.

CHAPTER SIXTEEN

Night fell on the longest three days in Fajir's life. She'd started a captive of the drushka, then had escaped, been snared by her nemesis, walked from dawn to dusk, fought a few vermin, and now had come back to where life had begun: in the hands of her Lords.

Nico offered Nemesis and Fajir separate tents, saying their owners could bunk together. Nemesis seemed torn, and Fajir was strangely proud. Fajir wouldn't hurt Nemesis now—she felt that in her bones—but she had before, so Nemesis was wary. But when surrounded by potential enemies, it was always safer to face the danger one knew.

"We'll share," Fajir said, deciding for them both. And despite her earlier pride, she felt a thrill when Nemesis looked relieved.

Nico turned away, but Fajir caught a look of shock, perhaps jealousy. Fajir ignored him and shepherded Nemesis into the tent. She lit a small candle and surveyed the blankets and rugs. Nico hadn't given them a lamp. Maybe he feared they'd start a fire.

Nemesis leaned close, smelling of grass and sweat. "Are we going to sneak away in the night?"

Fajir chuckled. "Like secret lovers?"

Nemesis's cheeks went slightly red, and Fajir's stomach fluttered.

"Nico is an accomplished guard," Fajir said. "We would be caught and would no doubt spend the rest of the journey bound."

"Why are they keeping us at all?"

"So we do not tell others of their presence. That would be my reason."

Nemesis snorted. "You would have killed us." She waved vaguely. "Or two hypothetical people who got in your way."

"Not if I had a use for them." And that begged the question, but she feared discussing too much, not knowing who might be listening. "But I have never had much use for hypothetical people."

Nemesis swallowed rather than laughed, her gaze roaming over the small tent. Fajir tried to think of some way to soothe her, but it had been so long since she'd had to put someone at ease. Ever since Halaan died, she'd thought of others' emotions as none of her concern. Or if those emotions belonged to an enemy, they were something to be used.

As if she was any better at that than soothing.

Then she noted the blood still spotting Nemesis's face and remembered one instance when she'd spoken longingly of baths.

"Wait here a moment."

Fajir ducked out, seeking their guard. She knew him of old, and when she barked for a washbasin and soap, he obeyed, and it arrived mere moments later.

Fajir placed both inside the tent. "It's not a bath, but…"

Nemesis regarded her coldly. "Are you saying I smell?"

"No! I only…" Fajir groped for words, stomach plummeting.

A wide grin appeared across Nemesis's cheeks. "Kidding! I *know* I smell. This is fantastic. Thank you, Fajir."

Fajir's cheeks burned, and her insides heated. Why couldn't her organs just stay normal and still? "I'll give you privacy." She stepped out and let the flap fall behind her. "And you're welcome, Nemesis."

"Lydia!" came the cry from within.

Fajir smiled and stood to guard the tent, trying not to listen to the gentle splashing. Perhaps Nemesis would require someone to scrub her back.

"Seren?" Nico's voice asked.

Fajir nearly jumped, shaken from her strange reverie. She tried to keep any wistful emotions off her face. "Yes?"

He cleared his throat and stepped forward, a lamp in one hand and a bundle of cloth in the other. "I'm…I'm sorry, Seren. For leaving you in that house and every mournful thought I've had about you since." He couldn't meet her eyes. "I wanted you to know that I didn't speak of you to anyone. I started no rumors, but I must apologize for not quelling those I heard."

Fajir took a deep breath and didn't know what to feel. "I understand." She stepped closer, desperate for at least one person from her old life to know the truth. "When I was alone, captured by the enemy, I asked the Lords for aid, and they denied me, Nico. They feared angering Simon Lazlo."

He blinked, his mouth falling open. "That...that cannot..."

"Do I ever lie?"

"No, Seren, but..."

She kept her gaze steady even though she wanted to shake him. "They would not help me escape. They didn't offer to kill me. They abandoned *me*, Nico, not the other way around."

He swallowed so hard, she could see it in the dim light. "Then... now is your chance to make peace."

She leaned back on her heels, not expecting that. He held out the bundle of cloth, and she took it, unfolding it to reveal a warrior's robe that tied tightly around the waist and had close-fitting sleeves. An embroidered moon graced the back, and someone had quickly lined the symbol in charcoal, the mark of a widow.

As if her tattoos were not enough. But the garment was also for her to see when she took it off at night. As if she needed reminding. But that was the point of widows; they were never to forget.

She expected to feel anger at such dark thoughts. It would be so easy to don this robe, forget the past few weeks, and return to the comfortable rage that had guided her in the months since Halaan's death. Soon, he would be dead a year, but that didn't matter. Grief and anger could go on and on and on.

She swung the robe around her shoulders, wearing it over the clothing the drushka had given her. The fit was slightly off but could be adjusted.

Nico smiled proudly, and she read an offer in that look: to behave however she wished. She could return to being a palace guard. She could hunt the Engali responsible for Halaan's death again. Nico would follow her regardless. And perhaps one day, he would repeat his pledge of love. Perhaps not. And perhaps she would accept him. Perhaps not.

She breathed, waiting for rage to come, but it denied her, leaving sadness instead. Rage had been her closest companion since Halaan's death, but now it felt as far away as the moon.

Fajir opened her mouth to crush the hope in Nico's eyes, but she felt as if Halaan whispered in her ear, urging her to wait. He'd always been so much better at deception.

She didn't want to lie, so she simply nodded, letting Nico think whatever he wished. He beamed and nodded awkwardly before walking away without a word. If he thought she'd returned to the fold, she had a better chance of slipping away. Someday, if she survived this coming catastrophe, she would journey to Celeste and tell him why she'd chosen this path, why widows should be allowed to choose.

If she could ever think of the words. Perhaps Nemesis would help her.

❖

Cordelia followed Miriam's directions through Pool's branches. Everything might be fucked, but at least hunting criminals was fun. It had always been one of her favorite parts about being a paladin.

Nettle soon joined them, proving Pool was feeling better. Cordelia paused long enough for a quick kiss.

"Shana's moving quickly," Miriam said. "And I sense she's not alone."

"Can you slow her down?" At Miriam's cold look, Cordelia added, "Never mind." She'd been around ultra-powerful people for too long. Even Horace, who'd been specially augmented, had trouble connecting to a mind that wasn't in front of him.

Miriam kept leading them down. Pool wouldn't have lowered Shana to the ground, but she appeared to have made it on her own. Maybe she'd been planning an escape the whole time. Her trail through the grass led away almost due east, and the sun was disappearing in the west.

"I can track them in the dark, Sa," Nettle said.

Cordelia shook her head. "Not without me and my armor—which I'll have to go get—and more backup. If Shana and her allies had an escape plan, they could have people following from Gale. Let's hope the Storm Lord calling for help put their plans into effect earlier than they'd hoped."

"Did you see him?" Miriam asked. Her baby hadn't made a peep on the journey through the branches, and Cordelia wondered if she could soothe him telepathically. Handy.

"If you mean the Storm Lord, he's not in his body," Cordelia said. "He's sharing Liam's." She cracked her knuckles, trying to stave off the desire to chase *someone* through the dark. "But we'll put it right."

Miriam seemed thoughtful, but Cordelia saw the way she clutched her child tighter.

Nettle must have seen it, too. She rested a hand on Miriam's shoulder. "Worry not. He shall only have the children if the drushka lay dead."

Cordelia shuddered. This day had proven that the drushka weren't invulnerable. She turned back into the branches. The drushka lit candles that bobbed like stars in the darkness. When Nettle grunted, Cordelia barely had time to brace herself as she got another worried thought from Pool.

Simon was venturing into the plains on his own.

Cordelia shouted a curse as she got the rest of the story: Simon had done some healing before marching off, Reach in tow. Pool had feared he'd harm himself if made to stay, and she'd hoped oncoming night would turn him back, but no such luck. Reach had been forced to light a candle when Simon kept walking in the dark.

"He's risking a broken neck," Cordelia said. "Exactly the reason I didn't want to go!"

"He thinks the telepathic signal was from Horace," Nettle said. "He risks all for love."

Miriam shook her head. "It wasn't Horace. It was way too powerful. If he would have stuck around, I could have told him."

"Fuck!" Cordelia said.

Pool lifted them all higher, into her presence. Another drushka stood beside her with a candle, bathing them both in soft light.

"What the fuck does Simon think he's doing?" Cordelia said.

"I would send drushka after both him and the captives, Sa," Pool said, "but they fear to leave me."

Cordelia nodded. She didn't want to leave Pool either. "If we leave Simon alone out there, he might get into trouble he can't handle, and if we leave Shana and her cronies, we're handing the Storm Lord a bunch of yafanai. Fucking perfect." She walked in a circle, weighing her options. "Okay, I'm going to armor up and go after Simon. I'll take a few paladins with me."

"I am with you as well, Sa," Nettle said.

Cordelia's gaze flicked to Pool, and she lowered her voice. "You sure?"

"Ahya." Nettle wrinkled her nose. "The queen will be better protected with Simon returned. And Reach is out there already. I cannot be afraid to tread where she has gone before."

Cordelia laughed at the rare show of drushkan pride. "Okay." She regarded Miriam and Pool. "Can you wake up one of the captives and squeeze their plan out of them?"

"Are you approving a deep scan?" Miriam asked. "Because I'm not one of these gods who can change people's thoughts like they change shoes. There are risks for a deep scan when it's done by mere mortals like me. That's why it takes the mayor and the paladin captain to agree for a deep scan." She cocked an eyebrow. "Unless you're the Storm Lord."

"Well," Cordelia said, trying to control her temper. "The mayor's come down with a case of jerk-in-the-brain, so he's not available, and I'd say this situation meets the life or death rule about deep scans." She stepped close. "And if you ever compare me to the Storm Lord again, I will knock you on your ass."

Miriam's lips quirked up. "Just checking."

Cordelia was tempted to hit her anyway, but she'd come far from her brawling days. She restrained herself to an eyeroll so extreme, it stung. "Get to it, then."

Miriam turned away, still smirking. Cordelia hoped one of the paladins had remembered to bring her armor back to the tree. Oh, how things had changed. There was a time when she'd have rather left her limbs behind than a suit of armor.

"Wait, Sa." Pool's long fingers completely encircled Cordelia's bicep. "Wounds and all," she said, looking down with a serious expression, "call for me, and I will come."

"No offense, Pool," Cordelia said covering Pool's hand with her own. "But stay here and heal your ass." She chuckled as she blushed, doomed to always be a little embarrassed around her queen. "And every other part of you."

Pool grinned and bent down. Her hug lifted Cordelia clear off the branch. Cordelia squawked, laughing, until Pool set her on her feet. For all her words about healing, Cordelia knew she would carry Pool's promise with her into the night, and it made the going easier.

The constant stumbling and tripping cut into Simon's good mood. He began to see his emotions of the past hour the way Horace would: an overreaction to stress masquerading as no emotion at all. Beyond rage was an eerie calm, a flat ocean in the eye of a hurricane. But sooner or later, he would have to deal with the rest of the storm.

At least walking through the dark was better than waiting for Pool to heal or a yafanai to knock him around again. He stopped, looking at the hints of terrain he could see by the light of Reach's candle: an inhospitable lot of grass and rocks and holes in the ground.

"I know I'm being a fool," he said.

Reach stepped up beside him and lifted her unencumbered hand. "We have all lost our reason now and again. When Paul was killed, only Sa could keep me from killing the one I held responsible for his murder, even after I knew her to be blameless. I simply wanted blood."

Simon put a hand to his chest, feeling as if his heart had seized. "Oh God, what if Horace is dead?"

"No, shawness! I only meant…" She put the palm of her hand to her forehead. "And now I have proven that not even shawnessi have the right words all of the time."

"Don't I know it." He tried to swallow his fear as he cast his senses out again, but the signal seemed to be fading. It couldn't be Horace. Whoever held him had to be powerful enough to suppress his power, and if they were that strong, their control wouldn't keep slipping.

Unless they wanted it to, and this was a trap.

"Will you turn back now, shawness?" Reach asked.

Simon thought for a moment, but trap or no trap, he'd come so far already. And doing something still felt better than waiting. "No, I won't, shawness. But I won't blame you if you do. There's still something out here, and it's better to know what it is than to keep guessing."

She grinned, wrinkling her nose. "Let me lead the way." She bent low in the grass and rocks, one hand shielding the candle. Simon tried to mimic her, but she was so much more surefooted. He focused on keeping his feet, easing the ache in his back, and giving her the occasional boost of stamina.

Soon, she stopped, and he barely kept from crying out when she blew out the candle.

Simon bit back his questions and used his power to make his eyes adjust quickly. The moon had not yet risen, but the myriad rocks of the plains were bright in the starlight.

He jumped as Reach touched his arm and spoke close to his ear. "I smell many humans, and I see the flicker of lights."

"Where?"

Her hand trailed up his arm, and she touched his head, her middle finger tucked away. He let her turn him slightly and scanned the darkness. The telepathic signal skittered like a centipede over his skull, but he saw nothing.

"Where?" he asked again.

She moved him, putting his hands on a boulder. "Just over the top there."

He felt to the top of the rough stone and squinted into the darkness but saw nothing still. "Your eyes must be better than mine."

"The lights, shawness! Surely you must see them."

He didn't know how he could miss lights even from far away, but he saw nothing but emptiness.

Unless...

He opened up his power and sought the signal again. It flickered only slightly now, barely there. If he hadn't been looking for it, he might never have found it. Only significant distance gave it away.

"Does it smell like a lot of people?" he asked.

"Ahya."

"Like plains dwellers?"

She and the other drushka weren't familiar with many clans, but there were probably similarities in clothing or animal smells. "Some perhaps," she said, "but there are unfamiliar smells as well. Do you know who they are, shawness?"

"A group of people that I can't see? That sounds like a giant, telepathic shield. And even Naos might not be a telepathic match for the Sun-Moon." He bit his lip. If he was this close, they had to know he was here. Unless the massive power output from hiding what was surely an army was taking all their attention.

But they couldn't hide from the drushka.

He had half a mind to march into their camp and see if he could scare the hell out of them again. They'd kidnapped Horace once already. Maybe they'd decided to ignore his warning and try again.

Or maybe they'd be ready for him this time and kill him before he went two steps. Then who would help save Horace and stop Naos? It wasn't just ego saying that Cordelia and the others were counting on him.

"I'm not sure what to do," he said at last.

Reach squeezed his arm. "Good. Then I will not have to wrestle you back to where Sa awaits us."

He breathed a chuckle, not even surprised. "I should have known she'd follow."

"Ahya. Now, for plans of battle, let us go consult a soldier."

CHAPTER SEVENTEEN

Cordelia listened to Simon's story and didn't know what to feel. She leaned against a boulder, the handful of her people bathed in warm lantern light, and the night seemingly full of people who wished her harm.

And now the Sun-Moon were added to the mix. They'd no doubt heard the call to metal as clearly as everyone else. Whether they were after it or just sought to stir things up with Naos, she didn't know. The fact that they were hiding said they didn't want a fight, but they couldn't think Naos would just give them the *Atlas*. Maybe they wanted to hide and wait and see who else would fight Naos, then they'd mop up the tired winners.

That matched Cordelia's experience with them. And it meant that after she and Pool and Simon had beaten Naos, they'd have a second fight on their hands.

"It is good that they are close, ahya?" Nettle asked Simon. "You can borrow their power as before when it comes time to face Naos."

"Unless they've figured out a way to stop me," he said. "Also, they were pretty tired when I did that and weren't prepared to put up a fight."

"They will be tired now, too," Reach added. "If this display of power is as taxing as you suspect."

"We can't just pretend they're not here, whatever we do," Cordelia said. "We can't leave a threat like this at our backs." She really didn't want to go talk with the high-and-mighty Sun-Moon, who'd once lit her on fire and held her friends hostage, but she had to know what they had in mind. "I say we go in confident and see what we can find out."

"Drushka and all?" Simon asked. He'd been strangely calm through his story. She wanted the pacing anger bomb back. At least then, she knew what he was thinking.

Nettle and Reach both sucked their teeth and looked at each other.

"Not the tree," Cordelia said quickly, knowing she wasn't just putting these two at ease. "We take a small party with the threat that the tree will come after us if shit goes sideways."

"Better to do so in the daylight, Sa," Nettle said. She turned to Simon. "I know you do not wish to wait, shawness, but…"

"No," he said with a sigh. "I can't stop thinking, what if they have Horace? I know it's not likely, but the thought won't let me be. If I leave now, I might be abandoning him."

Cordelia knew it was more than unlikely. The timing wasn't right, and if the Sun-Moon wanted to keep their heads down, the last thing they'd do would be to kidnap someone who would definitely be missed.

But if Horace *had* stumbled across them somehow…

Well, she had her small party now, she had a significant drushkan connection, and she had Simon, whom the Sun-Moon feared. But the idea of going in blind—literally—put her guard up. The Sun-Moon couldn't hide from the drushka, but Cordelia wasn't about to send Nettle and Reach scouting on their own.

But no one had to put their body in danger while she was around.

"I'll take a peek in my astral form," she said, lying on the ground.

"No, Sa!" Nettle said. "Recall what happened before when you were pursued by Naos."

"She can't be everywhere at once," Cordelia said, trying not to think about that very thing. "And I'm not going far. Pool will be able to see the camp through me, then you'll know it, and she can share what she sees with me and Simon."

"And if the Sun-Moon detect you and attack your mind?" Reach asked, her tone as measured and patient as if she were speaking to a small child.

"Then Simon and Pool can get me loose, right?" Cordelia said, returning her condescension.

Simon smiled. "I'm honored and terrified by your faith in me."

Nettle still frowned as she knelt by Cordelia's side. She'd never liked the fact that Cordelia could leave her body, but this was a journey that called for every weapon in their arsenal.

Cordelia kissed Nettle's hand. "I'll be back before you know it."

"Impossible, Sa, but know that if you do not return, I will kill the Sun-Moon to retrieve your spirit."

Cordelia chuckled. "If I speak to them, I'll tell them to watch their asses."

"Ahya, and every other part." Her lips brushed Cordelia's forehead.

Cordelia was grateful for Nettle's patience as she slipped loose from her body. She didn't know if she could have given Nettle the same gift.

A combination of fear and exhilaration swept through her as she floated above their little party, the colors and shapes sharper to her astral eyes. Cordelia reached for her connection to Pool and through Pool to Simon. As soon as she made both, Nettle's eyes lifted as if seeking her spirit, and Cordelia had to turn away from her beloved face.

"I am with you, Sa," Pool said.

"Me, too," Simon said, "though I'm not sure how well this will work. If Pool can only see through your eyes…"

"But that is not so, shawness," Pool's voice said in Cordelia's mind. "I can touch Sa as if she was a drushka, a long root indeed."

Cordelia didn't know why that struck her as funny; it must have been the giddiness that came with being outside her body. She floated in the direction Reach had indicated, her lifeline floating behind her as a silvery-white cord.

The plains seemed as empty as before, though they were brighter, and from above, part of them seemed to have a slight blur, like something seen at the very edge of her periphery. Before she could ask what to do, the scent of greenery suffused her. A shiver ran through her, a feeling she'd never thought to experience without a body. She would have said someone was lightly caressing the back of her eyes, one of the strangest sensations she'd ever felt.

The blur beneath her cleared, but her vision was even more different than before, the colors sharper still, and any movement in the camp that stretched out beneath her drew her attention even if she wasn't looking at it directly. Everything in motion seemed to have a halo of light surrounding it.

"Fantastic!" Simon said, awe in his voice. "Is this how drushka see, or is it some amalgamation of human and drushkan senses?"

"Save it for later!" Cordelia said. There had to be at least two hundred tents, maybe more, and who knew how many people each tent contained? There were ossors penned here and there, as well as geavers. One large tent sat in the middle.

"If Horace is here, that's where he is," Cordelia said. "They kept him with them the last time."

Simon's power pushed through her as if she was an antenna. "I'm not feeling…oh shit."

Cordelia's mind filled with sound, and a deep ache spread through her as if her spirit was being wrung like a wet cloth. She cried out, and that smell of greenery filled her again, shoving away the pain.

"I think we got their attention!" Cordelia cried as she turned back for her body. The Sun-Moon's attacks stabbed at her when they could find their way around Pool. They didn't even try to talk. Simon's power rushed through her, healing, then striking, a punch of power that made the telepathic surges finally stop.

Cordelia leapt back into her body and gasped as her eyes flew open. It had always felt like slipping into warm water or her favorite set of clothing, but now it felt like jumping into a lake to escape a raging fire.

Nettle lifted her, cuddling her close, armor and all. Nettle mumbled something about being right yet no one ever believed her.

Cordelia coughed as she sat up, clutching at Nettle. "I'll never argue with you again."

Nettle kissed her temple. "I will forgive you that falsehood, Sa, out of worry for you."

Simon knelt beside her, and her heart rate returned to normal. "I thought they'd talk first." His eyes practically blazed in the dim light. "Makes me want to march in there and—"

A faint scream from the darkness cut him off. Cordelia staggered to her feet, and they all looked in the direction of the Sun-Moon camp.

"Just a moment," Simon said. His eyes glazed over as he used his power. "I'm still not detecting the camp, but…" He snorted a laugh. "Oh dear."

Cordelia repressed the urge to shake him. "What?"

"It seems as if our rebellious miscreants from the tree have stumbled upon the Sun-Moon army. Perhaps we even masked their approach with our scouting."

Cordelia froze, trying to think of ways this news could be bad. Finally, she barked a laugh. "I can't say they don't deserve one another."

The news spread to the rest of the paladins, and soon everyone was laughing as they listened to the distant yells.

Finally, Cordelia called a halt to the mirth, feeling a little sorry for the rebel yafanai. "They're going to be annihilated."

"Ahya," Nettle said, satisfaction in her voice.

"The Sun-Moon will probably get involved," Simon said. "If they can manage an attack with their shield up." He looked at Cordelia. "They'll be distracted."

She grinned. "Perfect time to sneak in."

"For a drushka," Nettle said. "Without the queen's help, you will not be able to see through this shield."

Cordelia frowned, but Nettle had let her take a risk. Fucking give and take. "All right, but I'll get close with the paladins, and I'll be waiting just outside my body so I can speak with Pool. One bad thought, and we come running."

"I'm going with you," Simon said to Nettle. "I can speak with Pool while still in my body, and I'll have you to guide me besides." He shrugged. "And I can handle the Sun-Moon up close."

"Follow our lead well," Reach said, hooking her arm through his.

Cordelia kissed Nettle soundly, and Nettle nipped at her bottom lip, a promise for later. Cordelia made herself focus on what she had to do rather than on thoughts of anyone getting hurt, though it was as hard as she remembered.

Nettle led the paladins forward, then bade them wait in a shallow ditch before hurrying away with Reach and Simon. Cordelia leaned against a rock, slipped just outside her body, and waited, anticipation and worry running through her like a rising river.

Lydia didn't know how she could sleep in the middle of an armed camp with a couple of self-proclaimed gods who were planning to use her like a puppet.

And again, her stupid power was to blame.

When Fajir had come back inside the tent wearing a Sun-Moon robe, Lydia hadn't known what to think. Thankfully, her shock had worn off quickly enough for one word to filter through the dread squeezing her chest: run.

Then Fajir had looked at her and smiled, and her eyes bore the same soft quality they'd had since her escape, and Lydia knew that even though the wrapping had changed, the internal transformation Fajir had been going through continued unabated.

Fajir had shrugged. "I thought to return to how I was but couldn't." She sighed as she sat. "It must be you, Nemesis."

"Lydia," she mumbled.

Now they sat in the tent together, listening to the noises of the camp settling around them. Would someone bring them dinner? Fajir could get some, Lydia was certain, by shouting another order to a passing widow.

"Would you like to use the bathwater?" Lydia asked. "It's still relatively clean."

Fajir smirked. "Compared to what?"

Lydia snorted a laugh. "As if you're any cleaner than I was!"

"I will get some more." Fajir stepped outside again, taking the basin with her. Lydia expected her immediate return, and then she would stand outside to give Fajir privacy.

Or maybe she wouldn't. Maybe Fajir wouldn't even ask but would begin to bathe in front of her. There probably hadn't been much privacy when she'd patrolled with her widows before. Lydia would have to decide where to look. Probably at the wall. Fajir would laugh at her sense of propriety, even though she'd given Lydia privacy in the first place. Maybe Lydia would sneak a peek at the lean muscle hiding under that robe.

Lydia clenched a fist. Fajir had tried to kill her! She did not need to be fantasizing about strong arms and thighs and whether or not Fajir made love the way she fought, as an unstoppable force of nature.

After a deep breath, Lydia forced herself to calm down. She needed to focus on getting out of this camp before the Sun-Moon used her for whatever they were planning. And she had to go with or without Fajir.

Except she wouldn't go without her. And she couldn't keep telling herself it was because of the prophecy. She didn't have to keep random people safe from Fajir anymore. Fajir had changed because of her. The woman who'd once tried to kill her was now living *for* her, at least a little, and Lydia couldn't just ignore that.

She didn't want to.

And where was Fajir anyway?

Lydia scooted over to the tent flap just as Fajir pulled it aside and knelt on the rugs covering the ground. She pulled up short, blinking as the flap fell shut behind her. Lydia gasped at their sudden proximity.

Fajir held her hands to the side. "Better?"

Her face was free of dirt, and her hair was slightly damp. Lydia caught the scent of musky soap. A slight blush darkened Fajir's cheeks around the tattoos.

Lydia told herself to sit back but didn't.

Fajir's gaze flicked to Lydia's lips, and she seemed almost... hungry.

That was all it took.

Lydia wrapped her arms around Fajir's shoulders and pulled her close until their lips fit neatly together. Fajir stiffened, so Lydia turned her head farther sideways and deepened the kiss, her tongue gliding along Fajir's lips until they parted. Fajir moaned, and her arms snaked around Lydia's waist and flexed into a bruising grip.

Lydia tangled her fingers in Fajir's damp hair. Fajir crushed her harder still, her touch roving over Lydia's back and arms as if she was a climber seeking purchase.

They fell sideways, and Lydia had a spare thought about the candle in its holder, but Fajir's hands had found their way under Lydia's shirt, and she didn't care if the whole world burned down.

Fajir flipped both of them effortlessly, a force of nature indeed, so that Lydia was underneath. Lydia wrapped one leg around Fajir while they fumbled with each other's clothing, mouths only parting for moments before crashing together again. The touch of Fajir's calloused hands sent tingles racing to Lydia's core. Her skin was softer than Lydia had imagined, but underneath, she was as hard and powerful as paladin armor. Lydia reached low on Fajir's body, desperate to hear her cry out with passion.

Outside the tent, someone screamed.

Lydia fought the urge to curse.

She and Fajir paused at the same time, faces less than an inch apart. If the sound wasn't repeated—

Another scream, joined by shouts.

Fajir pushed up and away. Lydia rolled to her knees, both of them straightening and refastening their clothes.

"Stay here, Nemesis," Fajir said as she made to duck outside.

Lydia scoffed. "Sure, that's going to work." She jerked Fajir to a halt and spoke in her ear. "Lydia."

Fajir gave her a lust-filled look before biting her own lip and stepping outside. Lydia followed but stayed close, letting Fajir lead. She wasn't going to stay behind, but she also wasn't stupid.

The Sun-Moon camp was scrambling, people running toward the sounds of commotion and calling to one another in a language close to that of the plains dwellers. Lydia couldn't pick out enough to understand.

"What are they saying?"

"They want to know what's going on." Fajir had her sword in hand. She glanced at where the noise was coming from, then in the opposite direction. This was the perfect opportunity to escape, but these were also Fajir's people. More than that, the noise was close to the widows' camp, and Fajir had worked closely with them since her partner died.

Lydia touched her arm. "Let's help them. Then we sneak away."

Fajir smiled. "Always compassionate, Nem—Lydia."

Lydia beamed, her stomach fluttering, and she knew her growing feelings were going to get her into trouble very soon. She couldn't even fool herself and say she was staying because the plains and mountains were dangerous for someone alone. She could acutely recall the feel of Fajir's hands on her body, and she wanted more.

They threaded through tents and campfires. Lamps and torches bobbed through the dark, and Lydia had flashes of her vision. Maybe it had finally begun. Before she could voice that horrid thought, a person screamed ahead, and Lydia's mouth dropped open as a body went flying through the air as if thrown by a giant hand.

Samira? Lydia picked up speed, pushing around Fajir, who called for her to slow. Lydia ran harder, desperate to help her friend if she could, hoping Fajir would do the same. When a dark shape flew toward her from the gloom, Lydia cried out, and Fajir crashed into her, carrying her to the ground.

"Caution, I said!" Fajir hauled her up as the shape landed behind them, revealing a wad of tents twisted together.

Lydia looked up and spied someone dressed in Galean clothing: loose trousers and a voluminous shirt hiding a large belly. Her short blond hair seemed to stand on end as she looked around with wide eyes.

Not Samira, but Lydia recognized her from the temple. They'd never spoken, and Lydia couldn't recall her name, but she was a yafanai.

Fajir pulled Lydia behind another tent as several other Galeans joined the blonde. The night was filled with the cries of wounded people as well as the keening of ossors. One of the pens must have broken open, and the animals were bolting, crying out, and tripping over tents and people. Off to the side, one of the campfires had caught a nearby tent, and the flames were climbing higher.

"Where did all of this come from?" one of the Galeans called.

Another had a hand to her temple. "I don't know! It must have been hidden by telepathy, but—"

"Look out!" The blond yafanai slashed a hand through the air, and an arrow fell to the ground.

A cadre of widows followed it, weapons drawn. The blond yafanai glared, and the widows tumbled away, victims of a macro-psychokinetic push.

"We have to get out of here!" a Galean yelled.

"They're from Gale," Lydia said to Fajir. "But why are they out here alone?"

"Scouts?" Fajir looked toward where the widows had fallen and frowned.

Lydia shook her head. A group of yafanai wouldn't be scouting alone, and the blond leader was clearly pregnant. Lydia wouldn't have wanted to go running and bending and scouting while suffering the exhaustion that came from carrying a child.

They must have stumbled through the telepathic shield. Lydia remembered the Galean kidnappers she'd fought with Samira, Mamet, and Fajir. Were these Storm Lord worshipers, too? Maybe they were also trying to get to Naos for the metal or whatever she'd promised them.

The blond leader's eyes went wide, and she pointed. "Cam, piss off that geaver!"

Lydia stood on tiptoe in time to see the geaver pen rattle and the gate fall over. The animal bellowed, a sound like hundreds of pots grinding together. It shook its flat head and reared, long neck reaching for the sky. It landed with a rumble, and Lydia felt the vibration all through her body.

The geaver turned for the camp, lumbering into a run. It threw several people aside with its neck, and its lashing tail tore more tents from the ground. Two handlers ran to calm it while several soldiers attacked the yafanai, but all were thrown.

"We have to warn people!" Lydia said.

Fajir shook her head and stood calmly. "No need."

The geaver lifted into midair, and Lydia thought it was leaping, but it hovered and kicked its thick legs. The Sun-Moon walked beneath it calmly, their steps in perfect sync, and their hard gazes fixed on the yafanai.

The fire that had grown out of hand vanished like a snuffed candle as the duo passed. The blond yafanai glared, but the force wave that lifted the edges of several tents faded into a slight breeze before the Sun-Moon's power. The Moon raised an arm, palm up as if opening a window, and the handful of yafanai rose into the air like the geaver, limbs flailing. They ceased moving immediately, their eyes glazing over. The Sun-Moon let them fall, and they lay still in the dirt. Lydia had to turn away from the sight.

Fajir breathed a sigh of relief. And even though she was horrified by the Galeans' slack faces, Lydia joined her. She didn't care for the Sun-Moon or their worshipers, but she didn't want to see anyone get trampled.

Like Freddie.

"Friends of yours?" the Sun-Moon asked as they turned in Lydia's direction.

She shook her head. "I didn't really fraternize with the other yafanai."

"They probably feared knowing their fates."

Lydia nodded, unnerved and not knowing how they'd gotten that information or if they were reading her mind right now. "What are you going to do with them?"

Their heads tilted as one. "Do you care about everyone you haven't…fraternized with?"

She looked to Fajir, whose blank expression held no answers, but her hands were clenched into fists. Fear or worry? Whichever, Lydia saw no reason to lie. "I care about people in general, yes. I don't like to see anyone get hurt."

"What a strange companion for our Fajir." They turned and gestured to a group of widows. "Bind them in one of the wagons. They will stay insensible."

As the Sun-Moon put the geaver pen back up and deposited the stunned animal inside, Lydia repressed the urge to shout that Fajir wasn't *theirs* anymore. But Fajir stared at them almost wistfully, making Lydia's temper rise.

There'd be no more kissing that night.

CHAPTER EIGHTEEN

Simon kept one hand on Reach's back. He'd never known a telepathic shield could be so large. It stopped smells, sights, sounds, everything, like a blanket thrown over the whole that told outsiders there was nothing there.

Human outsiders, anyway.

Simon felt Pool in his mind, but he still couldn't see any camp. Maybe that ability was something about Cordelia's connection to the drushka or the way she could free her mind from her body. But when he still saw nothing, he regretted coming along. He didn't relish having to be led as though blind, and it was only a matter of time until he tripped.

He opened his mouth to say he should go back, when the world seemed to shudder, and a camp sprang into existence: tents and fires, the smell of latrines and cooking meat. Somewhere, a voice called out, and he caught the keen of ossors.

"Incredible," he whispered. "How did they base it on distance and not—"

"A question to debate later," Nettle said, a warning in her voice.

A scream cut through the camp, and the nearby people rushed toward the sound. No one would notice the three of them with screaming going on.

But in the commotion, he noticed a small group of people surreptitiously making their way to the center of the camp just as he was. Nettle had her weapons out and eyed the other party suspiciously. Simon sent his power their way, trying to determine how many there were: five, and the one in the lead was—"Samira!"

Her head jerked up, followed by the four plains dwellers of the Uri clan who'd offered to help her track Lydia.

"Simon?" she said as her group hurried over. "And Nettle and Reach?"

"What are you doing here?" they asked at the same time.

"There is a time to ask questions, and it is not now," Nettle said as Reach touched Samira's shoulder. "Do your eyes deceive you about where we stand? Your mouths may only move if they are instructing your legs."

With unspoken questions, Simon and the two groups continued toward the center of camp. Simon squeezed Samira's hand, happy to see her and to have backup. If he'd known they were going to end up in the same spot, he might have made the journey with her from the beginning. It would have saved quite a bit of aggravation.

But then, what would have become of the drushka when the Storm Lord worshipers rebelled?

"Best not to consider such things, shawness," Pool said in his mind.

"I tracked Lydia here," Samira whispered, glaring at Nettle's back as if happy to have someone to defy. "Are you scouting?"

"I wish. Horace has been taken. I hope he's here."

She returned his squeeze, always ready to respond to someone else's problematic love life, never mind the state of her own.

The large tent Cordelia had seen loomed ahead. Nettle put up a hand, halting them as she looked about, then she gestured ahead quickly. Simon spotted the dark and golden heads of the Sun-Moon moving toward the sounds of screams and the glow of a large fire before the tent hid them from view. Nettle peeked inside before ushering everyone in.

Two of the plains dwellers stayed by the door. Simon scanned the first room but saw only divans, cushions, and blankets. He peeked into a second room: a desk, no people. The third contained a large bed. He didn't know whether to be disappointed or relieved.

Angry was nice. He could go there again.

Behind him, Samira sighed. "I was hoping they were keeping Lydia in here."

"Same for Horace."

"Are you sure he's here? Lydia's and Fajir's tracks joined up with some Sun-Moon scouts, then came here."

Simon's head began to ache. "I don't know." And now they were back at square one, except in the center of an enemy camp. Square zero.

"We must go, shawness," Reach said. "Nettle has searched the furniture for important papers to bring to Sa but found none."

Simon turned away from the sparse bedroom. "Telepaths don't need to send missives. Hell, I don't even know why they brought a desk."

Nettle met them in the first room. Its plush superiority made Simon want to gag. Leave it to them to believe that war was no reason to leave comfort behind.

"Shawness Horace is not here," Nettle said. "Let us go back to Sa and speak more of what to do."

Samira shook her head. "I'm going to find Lydia."

Simon's worry and anger mixed, feeling too much like a panic attack from his past. He flexed his power, numbing the feelings. "No, Samira, it's too dangerous. Come with us, please. I..." He scrubbed a hand through his hair. "I can at least save one person. I know you don't need saving, not really, but..."

She kissed his cheek. "I know what you meant, but I have to find her."

"Whatever we do, we should go now," Nettle said, her voice low.

He supposed they could all look for Lydia, but a larger group would be easier to spot, and if they were gone too long, Cordelia would stumble in after them.

Of course, then she'd be able to see the camp, too.

"Come with us for a little while, Samira," Simon said. "Cordelia can come back with us, and we can split up and look."

She frowned but didn't argue, and they followed Nettle outside. The screams had ceased. The glow of the large fire had disappeared. They'd taken too long. The Sun-Moon had probably dealt with the rebel yafanai with laughable ease.

Simon wasn't even surprised when they'd only gone a few steps, and a dual voice called, "Dr. Lazlo, what a pleasant surprise."

They didn't speak in his mind, probably saving the bulk of their power for maintaining their shield, but their voices made him grind his teeth. He'd never forget being their prisoner or how good it had felt to see them thrown around the room by Samira. And it still brought him joy to think of how he'd taken their power without permission in order to subdue Naos.

But they were ready for him now.

"Pool," Simon thought, "tell Cordelia we've been spotted."

"Already relayed, shawness."

Nettle had her weapons out, as did the plains dwellers. Reach hadn't carried her weapon in recent memory, but she rocked slowly on her feet as if ready to burst into motion. Simon sensed Samira's power rising, but she didn't lash out, not yet.

Simon snapped his own power around all of them. He couldn't stop the Sun-Moon's telepathy unless he attacked their brains, but he could fortify everyone else against attacks. He hoped. He'd never faced the Sun-Moon's power head-on, not while they were prepared.

So far, they simply watched. They'd been a calming force aboard the *Atlas*, but since coming to Calamity, they'd proven themselves to be arrogant assholes, just like Dillon.

"Shawness," Nettle said softly. "The camp is poised."

He risked a look. The entire camp had gone silent, the inhabitants watching with eyes that flickered in the dark like dying stars.

"We didn't come to attack," Simon called, trying for peace. "The Galeans who stumbled into your camp are enemies of ours; they attacked us before they came here, and we wanted to see if anyone else from Gale had...become your guests."

They smiled but kept back by fifty feet or more. Well, he had threatened to destroy them if they ever attacked him or his friends again. By their rigid posture, they remembered, too.

"No," they said. "No other...guests."

Samira bared her teeth. "Liars! I know Lydia is here."

Their gazes shifted to her, then back to him. If they were thinking of a witty retort, they kept it to themselves. Maybe they had changed. "Since you didn't come to attack," they said, "you're welcome to leave."

"Where is Lydia?" Samira asked.

"Samira," Simon said, his neck itching from all the eyes in the gloom. "We need to regroup and discuss." Or they could attack. He could neutralize the Sun-Moon if they hadn't figured out a way to counter him, and he could interrupt a great deal of their followers.

He clenched a hand, fighting down the urge. They weren't trying to push him around now; they were offering a way out. And who knew how many enemies there were? All it would take was one blow to his head to incapacitate him, and he'd had enough of those lately.

Samira continued to glare. Maybe she'd developed a death wish in their time apart.

"Samira, please."

The Sun-Moon took a step forward when Samira didn't back down. "Well?"

"That's close enough," Cordelia's voice called from the edge of the light. She and her armored paladins marched into view, sidearms drawn. The Sun-Moon worshipers gave way before the weapons, and Simon didn't know whether to laugh or cry.

"You might have the numbers," Cordelia called to the Sun-Moon as she and her people surrounded the others in a protective circle. "But we've got guns, and your weapons won't do shit to this armor."

Simon itched to remind her that her face was still vulnerable, that she and the paladins *could* be overwhelmed, and that they hadn't much ammunition, but she knew all that, and with their telepathic spying, so did the Sun-Moon.

Still, Simon was certain that none of them wanted to lose people.

For a moment, all was still. If Lydia was here, the Sun-Moon clearly weren't going to give her up. Samira had her fists clenched, her power poised. Simon didn't know if she *could* retreat at this point, she radiated so much anger. Maybe he should cut *her* power off and have Cordelia carry her out of here. They could always sneak Lydia out some other time.

The Sun-Moon smirked, actually freaking smirked, and Simon didn't know if they were reading his thoughts or if they just felt invincible, but it brought his rage back in a boiling rush.

He stepped forward to look at Cordelia, and the glance she gave him spoke volumes. He could almost hear her asking, "Are we gonna do this?"

As an answer, he whipped his power toward the Sun-Moon, staggering them, and their people answered in a howling rush.

Cordelia had known it would come to a fight since she'd first spied this camp, and though she didn't relish combat like she used to, it was going to feel good to finally kick the Sun-Moon around. She'd never paid them back for nearly killing her and pulling her into their fight with Naos.

The two gods staggered, but Cordelia didn't count them out yet. "Fall left!" she cried as the worshipers rushed them. She fired into the crowd, wounding one in the leg and hitting another when that bullet passed through. The rest of the enemy scattered before the sound and the violence, her ultimate aim. The other paladins fired, too, and their guns got them into a cluster of tents just as the worshipers who'd been trying to follow them flew away as if in a hurricane, the force wave coming from the Sun-Moon's direction.

So, they were still up, though Simon seemed to have spoiled their aim.

"Can you take them out?" she called as she put her sidearm with its three remaining bullets away and took out her blade. She parried a strike from the worshipers who stumbled through the tents to get at them.

"I'm suppressing their outer telepathic power," he said, the words sounding as if they were coming through his teeth. "That's hard enough!"

"You did it before!"

"They were exhausted and wounded before!"

"No time for arguing," Samira said as she flung some worshipers into the night. "We have to find Lydia. Come on."

She led them deeper into the camp. Cordelia supposed she had to commit, but if they stayed too long, they were going to be overwhelmed.

As if in answer to her thoughts, one of the plains dwellers was cut down fast, his neck laid open. Nettle's fast blades barely saved another from the same fate. An arrow rang off Cordelia's armor, and she saw the archer drawing back for another shot, aiming for Reach. Cordelia grabbed her and spun, taking the shot in the back on her armor. She winced at the bruising force. She wouldn't be fast enough to take every arrow. One of the paladins shot the archer, but there would be more.

"Do you know where Lydia is?" Cordelia asked between breaths as she continued the fight.

"I...think..."

"You do not know!" Nettle said.

"She can't be far," Samira yelled. "I didn't see her on my way in, and if you didn't either—"

"We did not search the tents." Reach ducked under a swing and gouged her attacker with a claw. He stumbled away, clutching the wound and gurgling under the fast-acting poison.

"I know she's here!" Samira shouted.

"They're coming, the Sun-Moon." Simon's eyes were unfocused as if holding the Sun-Moon was taking all he had. When another plains dweller was wounded, it took Simon a few moments to heal him where it would have been instantaneous before.

To the side, a swath of tents and people blew away as if the Sun-Moon were firing randomly.

"We have to get out of here." Cordelia spun to count how many attackers they still had, but the worshipers were fading into the night. Getting ready for a big push, or had the Sun-Moon found them?

"Dr. Lazlo," the Sun-Moon called, "Naos has been searching for us, and without the telepathic shield, she will find us. We don't want to fight on two fronts; do you?"

He looked to Cordelia. She shrugged. She certainly did *not* want two fights, but the Sun-Moon might be lying. "Let's end this if we can," she whispered. "It's too big of a fight."

"You're near the edge of the camp," the Sun-Moon said, still out of sight. "Go now, and there will be no more death."

Samira turned, mouth open as if she was about to tell the Sun-Moon to fuck off.

Cordelia hit her once, a sharp jab to the chin. As Samira fell, unconscious, Nettle grabbed her and hauled her over one shoulder.

"Captain's prerogative," she said to the others' shocked faces. "Anyone else?"

They shook their heads hurriedly, and Cordelia grabbed hold of Simon with one hand. "We're leaving," she called. "The doc will let your power go once we're clear. Don't come after us. We've got an army of our own."

"Understood."

Reach's nose guided them toward fresher air, and Cordelia kept her guard up, knowing their escape couldn't be this easy, not after blood had been shed, but that had happened on both sides, and maybe the Sun-Moon really had enough.

They made it out without challenge and were hurrying back toward the tree when Simon sighed. "I let their power go."

Cordelia looked back, wondering if the shit would fall now, but she couldn't see the camp anymore now that the shield had gone back up. And the only tingles she felt were from Simon's power, healing and bolstering.

"Think they meant it?" she asked Simon. "They'll leave us alone?"

He shrugged. "Only time will tell. We can take comfort in the fact that their telepathy can never affect the drushka." He glanced at Samira's limp form. "She is not going to be happy."

"I'll leave her to you."

He gave her a wry smile. "Thanks ever so much."

Cordelia kept glancing back as they walked, her worry not over despite what she said aloud. From her memories of the Sun-Moon, they weren't keen to accept an insult, never mind an attack on their camp.

❖

Shiv halted at the edge of the large trees. They had grown ever sparser the farther north she had come, and the ground became firmer, though a thin film of water covered everything. Ahead, the trees disappeared, leaving ribbons of water running like roots over a plain of green. The mountains began not far distant, and while daylight had remained, she had spotted trees here and there along the slopes. They were not the behemoths she was used to; the green blobs of their leaves covered them from base to crown.

Night had fallen now, and Lyshus slept in her arms. Shiv kept her eyes on the mountains, darker shapes in a dark world. Tomorrow, she would seek the unknown.

Enka stirred below in the branches. Shiv had kept her there, not wanting her to see Lyshus. Shiv could feel her every breath, it seemed. And since she was not of Shiv's tribe, it was easy to think of her as an intruder, one of the fleas found on the rocky plains.

"Have you eaten, Queen?" Enka called from below. "Shall I hunt?"

Now that Lyshus slept, Shiv left him in a cubby of bark and climbed down. "There is no need." She lowered a catch she'd made earlier that day, one of the joora birds that waded through the shallow water. She let herself be smug; she could take care of her tribe and her visitor with no help.

Enka offered neither surprise nor praise as she took the bird. "Do you prefer raw or cooked meat?" Without waiting for an answer, she began to strip the feathers, a necessary task either way.

Shiv considered. The drushka did not venture this far north, and Shiv had seen more birds than large predators. "Cooked, I think." She commanded her tree to lower them to the ground, then she started a fire on a small patch of dry ground while Enka prepared the bird and set it to cook.

All day long, Enka had been silent, and Shiv had not ventured down to speak with her. Shiv thought to ask for stories many times, but Lyshus's presence and her own fear had stopped her before the words escaped. As much as she yearned to hear tales of people like herself, the likelihood of bad endings doused that fire. She supposed it was better to hear them now on the edge of this treeless, friendless wasteland. The words could simply float into the nothingness and disappear.

"I have heard tales of queens who bore their own children," Shiv said. "And how all those children were daughters, and those daughters came to bad ends. Are there any tales of those daughters becoming queens?"

Enka sat back and studied the flames, her head tilted as if thinking. After many moments passed, Shiv almost barked at her to answer, but Enka was old, just under one hundred summers, and she had no doubt heard many stories.

The firelight glinted off her long, silver braids and sparkled in her yellow eyes. She tapped one claw against her drawn-up knees. The clothing she wore was nearly the same dusky gray as her skin. Among the trees, she disappeared. No wonder she had lived so long.

"I recall one tale." Closing her eyes, Enka began to sing, her voice low and soothing, rising and falling with the words. "The world was young, the great tree not long broken, the plants and animals new, the drushka running among them."

Shiv settled in to listen, but impatience gnawed at her. Too many tales took place when the world was young. It must have been a busy time.

"The world was young," Enka sang, "with the drushka even younger. The first Shi took her tree and tribe into the swamp to partake of its bounty. The swamp was young and plentiful, and the drushka were happy."

And then came more drushka and more until one reached the point of the story. Shiv wondered if Enka could be hurried, maybe as one herded a fat hoshpi.

"The swamp was young and the drushka happy, but loneliness took root in the young queen, and she could not know joy in life or limb with no other queen to share it."

Shiv dropped the blade of grass she had been fidgeting with. This was new.

"The first queen was young and tried to make a queen of the others' children, but none had the knack, not born to be a queen. She took a mate and bore a child, and the swamp rejoiced in the way of all things young.

"The world aged, as did swamp and drushka and queen and child until the queen made a tree for her daughter."

Shiv licked her lips. The other tales never got this far. Usually, queens' daughters developed a mind sickness and killed other drushka or ran into the swamp, never to return.

"The daughter was young but eager. She became a queen and felt the lack of a tribe all her own, for a queen must have a tribe above all things."

"Above all things," Shiv whispered.

"The daughter was young and too impatient, and she became as impulsive as her mother. She took from her mother's tree too quickly, and the minds of her tribe melded into one, their own minds lost to chaos."

No.

"And the young queen and her young tribe *were* chaos, and they roved the swamp, madness their weapon, and killed what they saw, drushka or not, and the swamp mourned."

Shiv clenched her fists. No, no, no.

"And the queen mourned with the swamp, and she knew—"

Shiv stood. "She knew her daughter had to die, and she was very sad, and it was for the good of the drushka!" She kicked a stray stick. "Useless! That is not what happens!"

Enka opened her eyes and stared.

"This is what happens!" Shiv commanded her tree to lower Lyshus. He blinked sleepily before his gaze locked on the cooking food, and Shiv held his shoulders to keep him from the fire.

Enka leaned forward, her eyes wide as she studied Lyshus. "Is... he is..."

"A queen," Shiv said. "I am a queen's daughter with her own tree, and every tribemate I seek to take becomes a queen or dies, and the swamp does not care!" She sucked her teeth, frustrated and confused. "There must be another story that tells what really happens."

Enka took a deep breath. "All tales have a heart root of truth. Every child like you has been killed." She gestured to Lyshus. "This...he is likely why, though no one like him is mentioned in the tales. Perhaps we remember the outcome but not the reason, so we use..."

"Madness," Shiv whispered. She sat again and held Lyshus close. "But I will not let us be killed, young or aged." She jerked her head back at the trees. "We leave the swamp tomorrow. You may go back to your tribe. If we return here, Lyshus will no longer be a queen, or perhaps I will not, but either way, our troubles will be settled, and we will not be a tale to teach others."

Enka was silent a long time, and Shiv wished she would frown or fidget, but when not shocked into expression, she was as still as a tree. "How?" she finally asked.

"Human power. Simon Lazlo can change other humans. Perhaps in time, he could have changed us, but we could not stay with him." She would not say why, that Lyshus could and would attack other queens' trees. She did not know what Enka would do with such information.

And she could not bring herself to say it aloud.

"So," Shiv said, "I go toward a greater power than even Simon Lazlo's. She lives in the mountains now, and she will help us."

"The fire in the sky? Did this human cause it?"

"She flew in what the humans call a ship."

Enka frowned. "You trust her?"

Shiv laughed. Sa would have laughed, too. "Ahwa, no! Not with the way humans lie. But she has need of us somehow, so I will bargain with her. And I will have surprises ready in case of attack." She was a little unsure about what those surprises would be, but she could dream some up.

Enka frowned harder. "Queen…"

Shiv wanted to prompt her, but she waited. Someone with nearly one hundred summers had to have something interesting to say.

Enka's mouth opened and closed several times as if she kept weighing her words and finding them uneven. "Allow me to come with you," she said at last. "I know you can care for yourself, but you are a queen." She swallowed and nodded at Lyshus. "And so is he, and I would protect you. Let me be one of your surprises."

Shiv's core warmed, and she ached to ask Enka into her branches, but she fought the urge, knowing it would mean death. Still, she had to lean around the fire and take Enka's hand, gratitude and affection bright inside her. Simon Lazlo would say that Enka was simply responding to drushkan instinct, but Shiv did not care. No other drushka had said as much.

Enka returned Shiv's smile and squeezed her hand. "You will allow it?"

"Ahya," Shiv said, feeling another pang that they could not communicate mind-to-mind without the aid of Enka's queen. Enka would never feel her gratitude. It hurt to have to treat her like a human, but there was one difference: humans could lie.

So, Shiv would have to show her gratitude. She allowed Enka first pick of the meat, then allowed her to touch Lyshus when he moved to sit on her knee. At least he could feel what Shiv felt, and she was certain they would have more to be thankful for in the future. Someone so old had to know a few surprises for potential enemies.

CHAPTER NINETEEN

L ydia hadn't known what to say as she and Fajir went back to their tent. Her temper was up, and she had to keep biting her tongue to stop a flow of recriminations, both about Fajir's gods and Fajir herself.

She knew she shouldn't be hasty. Fajir had gone through a lot of changes in a short amount of time. It was unreasonable to expect her to stand up to her gods, but she'd already admitted that they'd abandoned her in her hour of need. How much harder was it to tell them to leave her alone?

And she hadn't stood up for Lydia, either.

After their fiery kissing session, no less.

"You're angry," Fajir said when they reached the tent. The camp was calming down a little, the night noises returning to normal.

Lydia ducked inside without answering and fought the urge to cross her arms and face the wall. She straightened the blankets instead, separating them into two very distinct piles. It would be best if she could get some sleep. She'd be less angry in the morning.

Maybe.

Fajir followed her. "If you're angry because we didn't escape, there wasn't time with—"

"Why didn't you stick up for me?" Lydia blurted. "They didn't believe me when I said I had nothing to do with those yafanai, and you didn't say anything when the Sun-Moon scrambled their brains." She shivered at the memory but repressed it quickly. Anger would serve her better now. "And before, you let them threaten me with whatever they want to do with my power." She took a deep breath so she wouldn't yell and tell the whole camp their business. "And you didn't argue when they called you *their Fajir.*" Those words had given her the same acidy stomach as when Fajir had redonned a widow's robe.

Fajir stared, expression neutral. Lydia worried that she might have overtaxed Fajir's newfound sense of introspection, but at last, she sighed.

"You do not know the Lords, Nem...Lydia. They can't be lied to. They take the answer from your mind when they're not using their power in other ways. And Nem...Lydia—"

"Oh, for fuck's sake, just call me Nemesis if you have to!"

Fajir began to smile, then ducked her head as if she feared the expression would piss Lydia off more. "Lydia," she said firmly, "outright rebellion would not serve us here. We must be cautious and take advantage of the Lords' distraction in order to *escape*, not argue with them and make them watch us closer." She took Lydia's hand. "You know my feelings better than they. Am I their Fajir?"

"No," Lydia said softly, her anger melting.

"Do you fear I will become so?"

Lydia's cheeks burned as she met Fajir's soft, determined gaze. "I can't read minds."

"You don't have to," Fajir said. "I'm terrible at disguising my feelings, especially from you."

Lydia chuckled. "You can go pretty blank when you want to."

Fajir tucked a strand of hair behind her ear and shrugged. "Most of those times, I'm not feeling anything."

"Yes, you are," Lydia said, scooting closer. "That's your 'I'm confused about what to do and am covering it up for pride's sake' face."

Fajir grinned as she leaned close. "See? You know my thoughts better than anyone, even the Lords with all their power." The last words were barely spoken, a whisper of breath across Lydia's lips.

Maybe there was time for a little more kissing after all.

Voices outside the tent interrupted them again. Lydia ground her teeth and thought the Sun-Moon must be spying in order to ruin the possibility of sex.

The voices were quieter this time, and Fajir only had to poke her head out to ask what was going on. When Lydia heard Nico's voice, and Fajir's response was an angry growl, Lydia looked out, too.

Nico turned a glare on her, and his lip curled into a sneer. "Back inside," he said in the plains language, his accent heavier than Fajir's.

Fajir made a retort in the Sun-Moon language. Nico's sneer increased, and he rolled his eyes. Fajir's brows lifted, and she said something else, the tone slightly disbelieving but also low, dangerous. Nico swallowed and said something else, including "Seren," which Lydia knew meant captain or leader, Fajir's old title.

Fajir ducked back in the tent, pulling Lydia with her.

"What's going on?" Lydia whispered.

"More intruders. Nico said his orders were to keep us in the tent."

Lydia sighed. "They know we want to escape."

"Possible," Fajir said, but her tone was doubtful.

"Did he say who the intruders are?"

"Only that we must stay here."

"And you took exception to that?" Lydia asked. "You sounded angry, and he backed down quick."

"I warned him not to speak to you disrespectfully, and when he rolled his eyes, I asked if he needed a lesson in courtesy."

It was all Lydia could do not to jump on her. When had the threat of violence become a turn-on? Lydia restrained herself to kissing her cheek. "So, we overpower him and run into the night?"

Fajir gave her a slightly condescending smile. "There are more widows waiting, and I…" Her face turned down as if she was embarrassed.

"You don't want to hurt them or risk killing anyone, no matter your threats." Lydia took her hand and wanted to jump on her again. "I don't want you to do that either."

Tears hovered in Fajir's eyes as she cupped Lydia's face. "Because you care about people and don't want to see anyone get hurt," she said, quoting Lydia's earlier words to the Sun-Moon. "Another reason I call you Nemesis."

"There's more to you than violence," Lydia said, leaning into Fajir's touch. "And I'll admit that I found your threat to teach Nico some manners gave me…warm feelings."

Fajir's brows lifted again, but before she could say anything, Lydia kissed her soundly, then sat back before the kiss could deepen. No matter how she felt, she was not going to have sex with Nico standing right outside.

"What's the plan?" Lydia asked.

Fajir sat back, and her sigh was so frustrated, Lydia nearly laughed. "The front of the tent is guarded. They'll watch the back as well, in case we make a bolt hole. We must wait."

That was the hardest part, especially when they heard the occasional noise, and tingles passed over Lydia's skull. Someone was using a lot of power. She also heard a muted crack that she remembered from the boggin invasion of Gale: a gunshot. Paladins.

Fajir demanded updates from Nico, but he kept repeating that he knew nothing. He said it in a very respectful tone, though.

It felt as if they were stuck in the tent for hours, but it couldn't have been that long before Nico called, and Fajir hurried out, Lydia with her. He eyed both of them, and Lydia could have sworn that a wave of jealousy passed over his face. After a few curt words, he strode away.

"We are to pack the tent and blankets," Fajir said with a frown. "The camp moves tonight."

"In the dark?"

Fajir shrugged. "Someone will bring our ossors, and we're to load them."

Lydia blinked, struggling to understand. "I heard a gunshot. That means paladins, not yafanai, and unless a group of soldiers has taken to worshiping the Storm Lord again, it has to be Captain Ross and the drushka." She clutched Fajir's arm. "The people we've been trying to find were here, and now the Sun-Moon are taking us away from them!"

"I know, Lydia, I know, but think." She grabbed Lydia's shoulders. "A ride through the dark with all we need for survival. What better time to slip away?"

Lydia nodded and fought down her own frustration as she packed. When the army set out, it was slow going, their path carefully picked out by lanterns until they reached the foothills, and the sky lightened with the coming dawn. Lydia tried to watch for the opportunity to escape, but even that prospect couldn't keep her from nodding off in the saddle again and again. Each time she looked, Fajir was awake, eyes scanning the surrounding party, but if she saw an opportunity, she didn't say. The Sun-Moon had them thoroughly guarded.

As dawn broke, the army halted. Lydia stretched and wondered if they were finally going to get some sleep. Maybe Fajir could sneak the two of them away while everyone slumbered.

Lydia stifled a yawn. At this rate, Fajir would have to carry her.

A ripple of murmurs passed through the army, and everyone turned to face south. Lydia spotted the Sun-Moon's geaver plodding in that direction until it reached the army's rear. Everyone paused, waiting. When Fajir barked a question at Nico, his quick answer only made her frown.

Lydia's stomach clenched, and her power rose inside her again. She could simply skip ahead, find out what was coming, though it couldn't be anything good, and after she saw it, she'd have to watch it happen in real time.

Still, her power argued, she could be prepared.

She clenched her fists, resisting the urge, though her breathing sped, and her sense of doom reached such heights that she wanted to scream.

An insect buzzed past her nose. She froze. She'd seen that before.

Sure, she tried to tell herself. She'd seen hundreds of insects in her lifetime, thousands. Some had to have buzzed right by her face.

No, she'd seen that very one with the blue cast to its wings and the long white body.

Lydia gripped Fajir's arm. "It's happening."

Fajir peered at her with concern. "You've gone pale."

"This is it." Lydia heard her voice from far away as if in a dream.

Or a nightmare.

Or a vision.

Fajir frowned before realization seemed to dawn, and she looked at her Lords with her mouth open.

The Sun-Moon put their hands to their heads as if concentrating, and a hot, acrid breeze blew past, ruffling Lydia's hair and filling her nostrils with the scent of char.

"No," she whispered. But she'd seen it, and it couldn't be stopped.

An orange-white flash erupted on the plains below, causing more than one person to cry out. Lydia couldn't do more than gasp as a wall of fire burst to life on the plains, separating the Sun-Moon army and the mountains from the rest of the world.

Including, in the distance, the great drushkan tree.

"Nemesis," Fajir breathed. The flames reflected in her wide eyes, just as they had in Lydia's vision.

And Lydia felt like a nemesis now: the ultimate adversary who'd put Fajir's feet on the path to killing her gods.

Cordelia came awake with a start just as Nettle jerked upright beside her. "What's going on?" Cordelia asked with a slur. They were together in one of Pool's cubbies, and Cordelia could have sworn she'd just dropped off to sleep after their long night.

Nettle practically leapt outside and ran into a morning that seemed pretty under-baked to Cordelia's eye. She tried to blink the sleep from her brain and followed. She sensed Pool's alarm but couldn't pinpoint the source. After she'd stumbled outside and stretched, she got a hazy answer.

Fire.

Aboard the tree? But no one was running around like she'd expect with a fire. Indeed, she didn't see any drushka. She followed the murmur of human voices to the north side of the tree, then realized they were moving, the long roots undulating over the ground far beneath them.

She joined Simon and Samira and gawked at a wall of fire in the north. Even though it seemed far away, lighting the horizon with an orange glow, she could feel the heat with every gust of wind. "What in the Storm Lord's name?" she whispered, forgetting in her wonder that he wasn't her god anymore.

"We'll be lucky if it doesn't consume every inch of the plains," Simon said.

And Gale.

And the world.

As they watched, the fire calmed some, though it still burned brightly; now it had the look of a normal fire rather than one as tall as a dust storm. "What the fuck happened?" Cordelia asked.

"It's Lydia's vision," Samira said; the words had hatred behind them. "It's come true, and I'm not there to help her like I said I'd be." She didn't turn her glare on Cordelia, even though there was no doubt who the words were for.

Cordelia couldn't acknowledge her anger, couldn't stop watching the flames. Maybe she hadn't woken up, and this was a nightmare. Simon was certainly paler than usual. He kept muttering about Horace. Cordelia took a deep breath and tried to calm her racing heart.

"Patricia or Naos has him," Cordelia said quietly, hoping it was true. "If anyone can defend against a raging inferno, it's those two."

Simon's breathing stayed shallow, but he wiped his lips and said, "Especially if they started it. Though I'm certain if we sought out the Sun-Moon again, we'd find them on the opposite side of that inferno."

The power of the Sun. Well, Cordelia knew he and the Moon weren't done being pains in her ass. Now they'd managed to put everyone in danger as well as block the path to the mountains unless they swung way to the west.

Where the wind was blowing from, pushing the blaze eastward.

"Pool!" Samira shouted. Cordelia jumped. Simon rocked forward at the noise, and Cordelia grabbed his elbow, hoping to cover her own nerves. "You have to put me and my scouts down!"

The tree didn't stop, and no drushka appeared, not even Nettle or Reach. Cordelia was getting vague impressions from Pool. All the drushka were clustered around their queen, leery of fire, their greatest enemy.

No, this was more than wariness. She couldn't get a coherent thought at all.

"She has to put us down!" Samira said. "We have to ride hard and warn the other plains dwellers. Simon, the Engali are to the east, and if the fire catches them unaware…"

The fire *was* gusting that way. Cordelia wasn't as close to Mamet and her people as Samira was, but Cordelia didn't want them to be wiped out.

"Stay here." Cordelia's continued queries to Pool went unanswered, so she climbed. Pool's bark provided plenty of hand and footholds. She supposed it was too much to ask for the wind to change direction, to come from the south and blow the fire back at the Sun-Moon and Naos. They could have batted it between them and left everyone else the fuck alone.

With a grunt, Cordelia hauled herself onto a branch amid a host of drushka. No one reached to help. They stood as still as statues, eyes locked on the blaze. Cordelia stepped carefully between them, only knowing they were alive by the gentle movement of their chests.

Pool stood in the middle, head and shoulders above the rest. Strange to see her steer the tree without riding in her cupola of bark, and she almost always faced whatever direction the tree was traveling in. Like the rest of the drushka, she watched the fire, barely moving, not blinking, like a human in shock. Even Nettle, who stood by Pool's side, didn't acknowledge Cordelia's arrival, though her hands twitched as if aching to be held.

Cordelia took one of her hands, gave it a squeeze, then turned to Pool. "Pool?" It was hard not to whisper amongst the silent company. "Pool?"

Pool's head tilted. Cordelia looked down her body to see that she carried a human infant in her large hands. Where had that come from? She suddenly recalled that Pool had killed one of the pregnant yafanai in a horrific show of strength. Was this that child?

Now, like then, Pool seemed too alien, far beyond understanding.

Cordelia took a deep breath and tried to hang on to another memory: Pool saying how dear Cordelia was to her. "Pool, Samira needs to go. She has to warn the plains dwellers."

When Pool didn't respond, Cordelia reached to take the baby. If the drushka were stuck like this, Cordelia couldn't leave the child here.

Pool's eyes focused on her so quickly, Cordelia jumped again. "So much destruction, Sa," Pool said, her voice hollow. "So much death and cruelty."

Cordelia swallowed. "I know."

"They must be stopped."

That was more like it. "They will be, but—"

"They must be stopped," the drushka said together, even those who didn't speak Galean, all united by Pool's horror. Cordelia's skin crawled; it was too much like something Naos would do.

"Pool." Cordelia put a hand over Pool's long fingers and kept the other underneath to catch the child if Pool dropped it. "You need to stop."

Pool shuddered, and Cordelia froze, worried Pool would fling her away or have the tree remove her from the drushkan communion, but Pool blinked. "Ahya." The drushka around her began to move independently. "Ahya, Sa." She lifted the infant and held it tighter.

"We'll stop it, Pool," Cordelia said, relieved beyond words to feel Nettle take her hand.

"We *will* stop them, Sa," Pool said. "Someone must pay for this with their life."

"Okay," Cordelia said quietly, happy they were talking. Nettle squeezed her hand tighter, and Cordelia glanced at her sorrowful face.

"You journeyed with me to fight the Shi inside the drushkan homeland," Pool said, "and now I shall do the same for you, but the tree?" She stared at the fire again. "The tree shall return to the swamp."

As if comforted by her words, the tree slowed to a stop.

Cordelia thought that a good idea, but Pool was as important as the tree. "Pool, you can't—"

"Go, Sa. Gather your people and prepare."

A branch lifted her, brooking no argument, and took her back to Simon and Samira. More of the humans had joined them, paladins, yafanai, and the plains dweller scouts. Cordelia glanced through the branches at the surrounding landscape. The tree hadn't gone due south but had strayed southwest, closer to the swamp. The tree had been running, covering a lot a ground.

After gathering everyone, Cordelia explained what had happened, then lost herself in barking orders. There'd be time enough to speak with Pool again and convince her to stay behind.

Under Cordelia's orders, the humans scrambled to get equipment and provisions together. Cordelia put off all the questions she could. The yafanai who hadn't yet given birth would stay aboard the tree, as would those with newborns. The non-pregnant yafanai would continue the journey north. Miriam and Victoria wanted to go as well, leaving their children with Mila and the drushka who'd remain with the tree.

Cordelia looked them up and down, but they returned her stare calmly as they reported for duty. "Why?" she asked, letting their answer determine her final decision.

"It's only temporary," Miriam said, her tone indicating that of course she would succeed in vanquishing her enemies. Failure was not on the agenda; Cordelia could admire that.

"Someone needs to kick the Storm Lord's ass on behalf of all the women and children he left behind," Victoria said.

Cordelia chuckled even as her stomach was still in knots. "Good. We can use all the vengeance we can get."

CHAPTER TWENTY

Horace had never been so bored. He'd only been in the tunnel for part of a day and a night, but it felt as if he'd been there for years, sitting, checking on an unconscious Jon, and looking for a way out.

But the Storm Lord hadn't taken his eyes off Horace. Even when Horace woke up through the night, the sharp stones of the tunnel digging into his back, the Storm Lord sat there watching him like a pissy statue.

Patricia had done more than make him uncommunicative; she'd taken away his need to sleep, maybe even to eat. Sickening. Both the Storm Lord and Patricia liked to tinker with what should have been left alone: him with boggins and yafanai and her with regular people.

They deserved each other.

And he would have gladly left them *to* each other, but they seemed determined to involve him in their plans.

After only sleeping for a few hours, they meandered down the tunnel, carrying Jon's body with them. It was the slightly less boring part of the journey. Horace had been able to figure out that most of Patricia's guards were miners, with two others being from one of the human clans in the hills. Another tidbit of information Horace intended to pass on if he ever escaped.

Up ahead, Patricia gasped so loudly, it echoed. Horace left off ruminating and trying to keep his footing on the uneven ground. He stood on tiptoe, trying to see around Liam, who kept well back from his ally whenever she made a strange noise.

In the lantern light, Patricia leaned on her knees, breathing hard. She straightened and turned a slow circle, eyes bulging as if the tunnel walls held a scene she couldn't believe.

"They couldn't..." she said. "They..." She gasped as if hyperventilating.

Horace could aid her if she'd let him. And if she let his power go...

"Let me help you," Horace said around Liam. The Storm Lord breathed down on him, no doubt ready to pull him back in line.

Patricia muttered something like, "No one can help this." She looked back with horror on her face. "We have to run."

She tottered a few steps down the tunnel, picking up speed as she went. Liam gawked after her until the Storm Lord's meaty hand gave him a push.

Liam turned with a glare that could have melted glass. "Keep your fucking hands to yourself."

The hair on Horace's arms stood up, and the tunnel filled with the scent of ozone, harbingers of the Storm Lord's power.

"Maybe we should go," Horace said. "I can feel his power."

"His power?" Liam said with a sneer. "For fuck's sake." He rolled his eyes and began to jog after Patricia.

Horace started to run, then yelped as the Storm Lord picked him up. The world went sideways as he flopped across the Storm Lord's shoulders.

"Put me down, you asshole!" Horace cried, forgetting his caution about power. Every running step drove the Storm Lord's shoulders into Horace's ribs and pelvis, and his head bounced around, guaranteeing a horrid neckache to come. He had to shut his eyes to block the nauseating scene of the lanterns bobbing ahead.

"Liam!" Horace cried out of desperation. "Please tell him to put me down!"

"Don't want to tackle that *power*, sorry."

What he had to be grouchy about, Horace didn't know, but now was not the time to ask. "Patricia, I can run on my own!"

Either she was too far away or she didn't care, but Horace had to endure the painful, undignified mode of travel for what seemed like an eternity. When they finally stopped and the Storm Lord dumped him on the ground, every inch of him hurt. His legs had gone numb, and he had to fight to get to his feet. He turned to yell at Patricia, at the Storm Lord, at Liam and everyone else, but the scent of fresh air stopped him in his tracks.

They'd reached the end of the tunnel.

Horace let himself be prodded into the light of early morning and looked at a mountain towering above. The slope was covered with dark green grass and spindly trees. Off to the right, another mountain dwarfed the first one, the high peak coated with snow like icing on a fancy cake.

"Beautiful," Horace said, awed in spite of his anger. He glanced left to get Liam's opinion, but Liam was staring at the plains behind them. Without a word, he reached for Horace's shoulders and turned him.

Horace fought his irritation but went along. "I'm getting tired of being gr—"

A line of fire scurried across the plains, getting wider by the moment and devouring everything in its path.

A trick of the light, reflecting off the mountains? Horace closed his eyes and opened them, but the fire still burned. And now he could smell it, the musky scent of burnt grass and the acrid sting of smoke. Two senses engaged meant it wasn't a trick. A hallucination? Not by the wide eyes of everyone else.

If that fire kept spreading, all of humanity and their allied drushka lay in its path, except for those already in the mountains.

He'd rather be losing his mind.

"Simon," he whispered. More names tumbled through his mind: Evan, Cordelia, Reach, Nettle, Pool, Samira, Wuran; Galeans, plains dwellers, drushka.

Everyone.

"How?" he managed.

"The Sun-Moon," Patricia said with a snarl. "I felt them getting closer. I tried to distract them." She glanced at him and put a hand to her mouth as if she hadn't meant to let that last part out.

"They were the rock in your rock and hard place metaphor?" Liam asked. He glared at her, and Horace didn't need powers to read his anger and disbelief. "You pointed them at the Galeans, and look what they did!" His finger stabbed at the flames, and Horace felt the tingle of the Storm Lord's power again. He stepped closer to Liam, but the feeling didn't dissipate.

Patricia waved the words away. "I just…alerted the Galeans to the Sun-Moon's presence, that's all. What they chose to do after that is not on me."

"That's utter shit," Liam snapped.

"You don't know anything, you selfish prick!"

They grew louder, arguing, pointing, and the Storm Lord was watching them, Liam in particular. A bit of luck at last.

Horace took a step backward, closer to where the guards had laid Jon on the ground. All the guards were watching the argument, which grew louder and louder, each movement suggesting violence. Horace tested his power, but Patricia still held it tight. He couldn't carry Jon out of there, but Jon would tell him to run for help.

If help even existed anymore.

Well, then *he'd* have to be the help instead.

He scanned the surrounding terrain. They'd catch him quickly if he fled down the tunnel. He couldn't run toward the fire, either. That left the unfamiliar territory of the mountains, but even though the mine was nearby, the territory was probably unfamiliar to Patricia, too.

Horace began to kneel as if checking on Jon. The only man who glanced at him, one of Jon's minders, looked back to the fight once Horace knelt. Horace edged around Jon slightly, then stood again and backed up another step. He continued slowly, every instinct telling him to run, but he couldn't afford to attract their attention, not yet. He reached a stand of trees and slipped inside, sliding out of sight.

He ran, never so happy to be underestimated. He zigzagged through the trees, stumbling over roots and loose rocks. He tried to listen for pursuers over his ragged breathing but heard nothing. All he had to do was get far enough away for Patricia to lose hold of him, then rescue Jon, get out of the mountains, and go save Simon.

And possibly, the world.

Patricia had to die first, Dillon decided. Then Jonah. The rest of Patricia's cronies would be on him by then, but he could survive a few blows long enough to hit them with lightning bolts of their own.

He had to put her off guard first, though. She was still howling like a banshee when he noticed the gap in their ranks. "You know your captive got away, right?" he asked when she paused for a breath.

She blinked at him, and he reached for his power, but she stepped behind one of her henchmen and looked for Horace. Dillon kept his power bottled; he had to have a clean shot to make sure she fell.

When she failed to find Horace, she yelled at Dillon, at Jonah, at all her people.

"Shouldn't have made your puppets so worshipful," Dillon said with a sneer. "They were too busy guarding you from me."

"Shut up." She stalked up and down the slope and jabbed a finger at the distant fire. "You going to do something about that or what?"

He supposed he should. He still didn't know what his plans for the future were, but it would be nice if this part of the world was still standing in case he wanted to live there.

And he had to make sure his kids survived.

Dillon closed his eyes and focused, reaching with his power. The small storm he'd called the night before had dissipated, but there had to be another one around. It was all about finding particles with the right charge.

But it had been much easier when he could see the systems from space.

He found a nice fat storm over the ocean and gave it a yank, the force making pain throb behind his eyes. He charged the particles in the air between ocean and mountains, and the storm followed along like a dog after a ball.

When he'd completed a road for it to follow, he opened his eyes. The sky to the south was already darkening, but the change in wind direction would blow the fire right at them. Dillon quickly shut his eyes again and tinkered with a pressure system he detected over the mountains, calling it southward. That would slow down his storm, but the clash of winds would also slow the fire. When he opened his eyes, the sun disappeared behind a wall of clouds.

"Happy?" he asked.

"No." She had her own eyes shut, but Jonah had taken up a spot in front of her, watching Dillon. "I can't get a fix on Horace, and if he gets too far, I'll lose my grip on his power." She smacked her fists against her hips. "I can feel Naos poking around, blanketing this area in power. She probably knows we're here, and she's fucking with my senses."

"And if you reach too far, you'll bump into her."

She barked a laugh that told of nothing but fear. Her expression said she knew she was in over her head.

Dillon waited, letting his own power fade and leaving him with his headache. If the circumstances were right, maybe he could feed Patricia to Naos as a sacrificial lamb. "Now what? Unless I miss my guess, Laz and the others are on the other side of that fire. The whole 'defeat Naos' plan isn't going to work with just the two of us."

"I can call the breachies up from the mine," she said distractedly. "They're not much, but they were aboard the *Atlas*. They're better than any of Simon's yafanai."

"My yafanai," Dillon mumbled. At least, they *had been*.

"And the Sun-Moon are no doubt on this side of the fire, too."

Dillon's gut burned. "Those assholes? No way!"

She muttered something about beggars and choosers, and he almost blasted her right then. Of all the goddamn indignities he'd had to suffer lately, working with the stuck-up former bridge officers was the absolute limit. "I'd rather side with Naos against them," he said. "Maybe if we feed them to her, she'll leave us alone."

Patricia rounded on him. "She's never satisfied; don't you get that? Even when I was with her, first she wanted this body, then followers, then Celeste. If she'd had gotten it, she would have wanted the world." She hugged herself like a little kid. "She's hungry because I was always hungry. I wanted to be a fleet admiral someday."

Dillon choked back a laugh. From copilot to top brass? Only some pretty sweet connections could move a person from the front of the bridge to the command chair. Patricia would have needed even sweeter ones to go from a ship to a big shiny office.

But with the tenacity he'd seen in Naos, maybe she could have made it.

When she sat on a boulder looking dejected, he sat beside her. "You'd have had an easier time switching over to field duty," he said. "Running logistics for ground missions, then working your way into a lower level office, planning missions behind the scenes. The office was always more willing to promote from within rather than take grunts from the ranks, whether infantry or ship."

"I didn't want to go planet-side," she said. "The idea never excited me, not until I got away from…her."

Thinking back, he chuckled. "I always got sick on missions; some parasite or another would make a meal of my insides. I'd have to pound back meds so my troops wouldn't catch me barfing my guts out."

She coughed a laugh, and he reminded himself that she could be useful when controlled. "Not anymore," she said. "That body is used to everything this planet has to throw at it."

Reminding him that he owed her. Nice. He didn't respond.

"We don't have a choice, Dillon," she said. "Standing here reminiscing or yelling won't do any good. Our best chance is to take Naos out before she pelts us with more asteroids, and the only people nearby who can help us are—"

"The goddamned celestial duo." He put his head in his hands. "I hate them so much."

"She doesn't like them either." Patricia nodded to the north when he glanced at her. "Maybe we can take out all three of them while they're trying to destroy one another."

That was an appealing thought. And unless the Sun-Moon just attacked on sight and barreled through the blocks Patricia put in his head, they wouldn't know who they were really dealing with.

He stood. She ignored the hand he offered and stood on her own. Smart but frustrating. She couldn't *know* how easily he could chuck her down the slope. No matter. He could deal with her in good time, maybe even convince Horace to come back and give his friend the mayor a hand.

❖

By the way the army began to settle, it was clear that the Sun-Moon meant to snag a few hours' rest on the slopes of the foothills. Lydia didn't know how they could possibly do so with the fire spreading below them, but no one seemed concerned.

Fajir stared at the fire one moment and her gods the next, even after the Sun-Moon dismounted their geaver and became lost in the crowd. Her brows were drawn together in sorrow. Lydia didn't know whether to comfort her or give her space, and indecision wasn't the only thing that held her back. She didn't want Fajir to blame her, couldn't bear to hear it. And she didn't think Fajir would take comfort in the fact that soon she'd sport a look of steely resolve and put her sword to the problem.

Or had it been resolve? Lydia had thought so after her vision, but it could easily have been stoic acceptance or unfeeling shock.

Lydia caught Nico's arm as he strode past. He gave her a disdainful look, then glanced at where she touched him. She pulled back, hoping he spoke enough of the plains language for her to get her point across.

"How can you sleep after that?" she asked, pointing toward the fire.

He frowned but answered slowly. "The Lords will keep the smoke and flames away."

She barked a humorless laugh. "I'm not asking how you can be comfortable. Your Lords have lit the plains on fire! What about the plains dwellers, the Galeans? It could spread to the swamp and the drushka. It could reach your own people!"

He shrugged, and she'd never wanted to hit someone so much in her life. "The Lords will stop it before Celeste, our people."

"And who cares about the rest, right?" She was yelling, attracting attention, forgetting Fajir's plan to act like good little captives until they could sneak away. And she didn't give a shit. Someone who shrugged in the face of so much death deserved to be yelled at, deserved to be punched.

Nico faced her fully now, one foot forward, elbows slightly bent. His dark eyes raked over her calculatingly, and his compact, stocky body seemed poised. He could take her down in an instant, but she'd scream at him until then.

But how to yell a conscience into someone?

A touch on her arm made her spin around, hands raised to slap or punch or gouge for all she was worth, but Fajir caught her wrists effortlessly and lowered them gently.

"Nico," Fajir said, stepping so that she faced him at Lydia's side. "This is not right."

He frowned hard and said something in the Sun-Moon language.

"No," Fajir replied. "Such faceless death shames us all."

"You didn't care so when we killed the plains vermin," Nico said after a contemptuous glance at Lydia. "Only your killing is without shame?"

"I admit to those deaths. I looked in all their eyes. Even in the grip of rage, I would never have done this."

She didn't seem as remorseful as Lydia might have hoped when talking about the people she'd killed. It turned Lydia's stomach, but this Fajir was miles away from the creature Lydia had first met. That one had pleaded to either be killed or be set loose so she could continue her murder spree. Lydia had a vision again of Fajir's hands around her throat, even while the slump in Fajir's shoulders made her want to take those same hands in a gesture of comfort.

Nico shook his head and looked around as if searching for words, his face a mask of disappointment. "Seren, are these your words or hers? This fire could cleanse all the vermin, even the killer of Halaan. It can do what you could not, and then..." He gestured as if embracing the future. "All will be well!"

"Sure," Lydia said. "Once every single one of your enemies is dead, all will be well. Except you'll never kill all of them, or the fire will kill people who had no grudge with you at all. Then those people will pledge to kill you or your people, and maybe they'll drag in others, and it will go on and on and on until we're all dead!" She shouted the last few words, her breath coming in heaving gasps. If Fajir would have grabbed her at that moment, she would have fought like a grelcat just for the chance to strike someone.

Maybe she understood this rage violence more than she thought.

Nico eyed her warily, but his look of contempt turned a bit thoughtful. Or maybe that was just her desperate imagination.

"We must go to the Lords, Nico," Fajir said calmly, "and ask them to stop."

So, Fajir wanted to ask, even though she knew that wouldn't work. She wanted to try to change the future. Lydia tried not to be hurt. Everyone did it. But Lydia knew this would only be stopped by the sword. She took a few deep breaths. It *would* stop. She could afford to be calm, but anger wouldn't leave her. If the Sun-Moon hadn't done something so utterly cruel and stupid, she would never have seen it in a vision, and her feet would never have been set on this path.

And Fajir would still be a murderer, and Lydia would still be an ex-prophet hiding from her powers on the plains.

Nico seemed to consider Fajir's words, but all too soon, he shook his head. "I thought you couldn't be found, Seren, but I was wrong to stop trying. I won't stop now. Once the plains vermin are dead, you'll feel better."

Fajir put a hand to her sword. Nico's eyes went wide, but he rested his hand on his own weapon.

A cry rose from the side of the camp. Lydia stepped away from Nico and looked in that direction, thinking someone had seen these two squaring off.

She spotted figures running through the rocks and trees of the hills, humans darting in and out of the shade, their clothing blending with the terrain. The Sun-Moon worshipers had caught sight of them, too, and were forming into ranks. Arrows began to whistle from the trees and land among the camp, several finding targets who shouted in agony.

The Sun-Moon weren't even bothering with their shield anymore, it seemed.

Leaving their power free for other things.

A great swath of the hillside heaved, rocks and trees and dirt folding over several attackers like a wave. That had to be the Moon's doing. Maybe the Sun was too busy tending the fire. More of the hillside archers fired, and several worshipers returned the shots, but most were crouching behind bundles of supplies.

"We should take cover," Lydia said, but Nico and Fajir didn't move, hadn't shifted from their threatening positions. No arrow had reached this far into the camp yet, but the fight was just getting started.

And the Sun-Moon were distracted by it, their power directed elsewhere.

"Fajir—" Lydia started.

She couldn't tell who drew first, maybe both, then their bone swords clacked together, both of them feinting and striking, ducking and weaving, two masters of a brutal dance.

They split apart for one second, and Lydia felt her power trembling, but she clamped it down. She knew who'd win this fight, would have known even without her power. Nico was weeping, and Fajir's face was still. A small advantage was all she needed.

A battle between former friends should have lasted days, maybe weeks, like something from a story, but it was over in moments. Fajir's sword rushed past Nico's guard and plunged into his chest. Lydia clapped a hand to her mouth to keep from crying out. No one else had noticed with the fight going on, but Lydia ached enough for all of them. She'd hoped Fajir would only wound him, even for all his stupidity, but he hadn't given her the chance.

Fajir caught him as he fell and lowered him to the ground. His eyes had already glazed, his life fled at once. She stood without ceremony, without whispering any final words. When she stood, her gaze caught Lydia's, and her head tilted before she smiled softly, her own eyes filling with tears.

"You care for this death, too?" Fajir asked. "Even though he would have killed you gladly?"

Lydia felt her own tears but couldn't stop them. "I can't help it."

Fajir's arms went around her, comforting her and moving them both under cover, the height of efficiency. "He is with his partner maybe and happy."

Lydia rolled her eyes. "You want to make me cry harder?"

"But…he is *happy*, so why—"

"I can't explain," Lydia said, pushing away. "And now's not the time." She brushed her tears away. Fajir's hadn't fallen, but Lydia knew they'd been for *her*, not Nico, and that made her want to cry again. "We have to get to the Sun-Moon."

"Yes."

Lydia couldn't help hoping that maybe this one time, they could change the future. Maybe Fajir could make a fantastic speech, and the Sun-Moon would be so moved, they'd put the fire out.

Then Naos would come out of the mountains with armloads of metal for everyone, and they'd sing heartwarming songs and toast one another and live in happiness forever.

She sighed. That would have been so lovely.

Chapter Twenty-one

Patricia had learned much from Dillon, including knowing when he wanted to kill her.

No doubt he thought he'd mastered the poker face, but she'd learned his tells: the way his lips twitched when he was holding back words, the way his face went completely still before he donned a placating smile. She couldn't believe she'd ever fallen for his bullshit.

She never would again. Right now, he was useful. As soon as he wasn't...well, she'd see what happened then. Unlike him, she didn't plan to kill people, not if there was another way.

That was why Horace was still alive and had been able to escape, though. That didn't piss her off so much. Her bridges were burned with Simon Lazlo anyway. Once Horace had returned to him, they could all either go their separate ways, or maybe even salvage their alliance. Simon didn't seem like the kind to hunt her to the ends of Calamity for once kidnapping his boyfriend.

Besides, Patricia could just give him Dillon. Simon would probably appreciate that more.

When she and Dillon decided to visit the Sun-Moon, they left the unconscious paladin where he lay, taking their supplies and the paladin's armor. Dillon wanted to wear it, but Patricia wasn't about to let that happen. He'd wanted to do away with the paladin as well, saying something about having an enemy at their backs, but what could a lone man do to them? He wasn't even a yafanai. He'd wake up, maybe find Horace, and the two of them could ride off into the sunset together.

Or in this case, the whopping big fire.

"You have to stay out of sight, Jonah," she said as they walked. The Sun-Moon had dropped the shield that hid them earlier, and she could have found them blindfolded with the way they were throwing power around.

"Yes, mistress." Jonah had seemed downcast ever since Horace escaped, but she couldn't be mad at him. She'd made him ultra-protective, so it wasn't a surprise that he chose to take his eyes off Horace when she seemed threatened. She wanted to take his hand but didn't want to put up with Dillon's snorts or eye rolls or pithy comments. They walked in silence up the slope of the hill and over, through evergreens and boulders. The ground was thick with bluish needles and what looked like hairy fruit. She wondered if they were edible and made a note to ask her hill dwelling allies.

Later, after the world was done burning down.

Some kind of animal call ululated through the trees, setting Patricia's spine on edge. Compared to the mine, the hills reverberated with sound that echoed off the rocks: chirping insects, a far-off throaty roar, and that trilling call that made her teeth ache the more she heard it. When the animal sounds began to die off, she was grateful. Until she heard the yells, cries of pain, and the rumble of churning earth.

Patricia hurried ahead and broke through the trees to find the Sun-Moon camp not far below them. A group of hill dwellers fired at the camp from the heights, peppering it with arrows until their hiding places turned upside down under macro-psychokinetic power. Still, they scampered away, shooting, while the Sun-Moon worshipers returned fire. Soon, the Moon would have to stop her attacks or risk bringing a landslide down on her people.

"Great," Dillon said. "Which side do you want to join?"

The answer seemed obvious. The hill dwellers could do nothing against Naos, and they weren't the clan Patricia had already claimed. "If we stop the ones closest to us, we'll look like heroes coming to help."

"Or someone joining in the attack," he said, rubbing his chin. "Maybe you should send a telepathic signal and tell them we're coming."

A tingle passed over Patricia's scalp, and she had just enough time to yelp before the ground bucked underneath her. Jonah grabbed hold of her arm as two of her followers tumbled down the slope. She watched in horror as the ground lifted over her like a thrown blanket, the earth torn from the hillside in order to bury them.

Patricia flung up a macro-psychokinetic net and caught the dirt, shifting it away. Dillon ducked, as did her remaining four guards.

Patricia turned, fighting Jonah's grasp as she searched for the two who'd fallen.

One lay on the rocks below, his legs twisted. He howled piteously. The other had fallen out of sight. Patricia brought her micropsychokinetic powers to bear and focused, healing the fractured legs as quickly as she could. He yelped once, then went still.

"Motherfuckers!" Dillon cried. "Not even giving us time to say why we're here?" He reached for the pack that held the paladin's armor and drew forth the sidearm. Kneeling, he sighted into the camp.

"Wait!" Patricia sent out a telepathic signal, trying to tell the Sun-Moon she meant no harm, but they didn't seem to be taking chances. Her signal was soundly rebuffed as they shielded themselves against telepathic intrusions.

"I can't see them," Dillon said, the barrel of the gun moving around the camp. "Any ideas?"

"They're shielded. If I could get their attention, I could get them to listen!" She couldn't just walk away from this opportunity. The Sun-Moon had to know they couldn't take on Naos alone.

"I'll get their fucking attention," Dillon said.

She felt another tingle as he accessed his power. His eyes fluttered, and his body relaxed. She grabbed the gun and handed it to Jonah. The wind shifted, and the storm Dillon had called that morning surged closer, the clouds billowing like cream through coffee.

The fire billowed north in a rush, and great gouts of smoke roiled through the trees like fog. Patricia used her power to keep the smoke away, noticing the same happening in the camp. The macro attacks on the hill dwellers ceased; Dillon had distracted the Moon, at least, and the Sun would be working to keep the fire from coming up the hillside.

"Climb down and get Rian," she said to two of her guards while Dillon worked. "And look for Vaun." They obeyed and helped Rian up the slope. They'd seen no sign of Vaun, and when Patricia searched, she sensed nothing. Already dead. Her temples burned, but she had to forget grief and anger if she was going to work with the Sun-Moon. She wouldn't say that to Dillon, not wanting to hear his snarky commentary.

"Try them now," Dillon said finally, his breathing hard and his face flushed. "They should be distracted enough for you to get through."

Patricia didn't bother to soothe his fatigue. Better for everyone if he stayed tired. She tried another telepathic signal but found the shield still up. No matter what their other powers, telepathy was their meat and milk. She didn't even know if one could survive the death of the other, they were so linked. Or if one did live, it wouldn't be for long. "Nothing. Can't get through."

"Fuck it then," Dillon said as he stood. He glanced at his empty hands, then frowned at the gun tucked in Jonah's belt. "Whatever. Let him blow his balls off, see if I care."

Patricia ignored that. "We can't just leave empty-handed."

He pointed to the arrows bristling across the camp. "Do you want to walk in there and become a pincushion? Or maybe you're thinking to kick the Sun-Moon's followers' asses until they listen to you. That makes people very receptive, from what I hear."

"Oh, shut up," she mumbled, hating when he was right. Maybe the Sun-Moon would listen if she gave them the Storm Lord trussed up like a holiday dinner. Too many people wanted a piece of him, that was the problem. Better to save him for Simon Lazlo, she supposed. At least he might hesitate before killing her when their partnership was at an end. She couldn't be certain of the same treatment from the Sun-Moon.

"Let's head for Naos," Patricia said with a sigh, fighting down the fear that roared inside her at the thought. She took a few deep breaths and kept her voice level. "We can see who else makes it. Maybe whoever does will be so beaten up and desperate for allies, they'll listen before attacking."

He laughed. "That's the worst plan I've ever heard, but since I don't have a better one..." He gestured for her to lead the way.

She gave him a look but did as he suggested, putting Jonah and another of her guards between them. She noticed the way Dillon's face had gone blank before he'd asked her to lead; he was thinking of another way to get rid of her. She thought again of putting him under a yoke of power, but lately, when she'd tried such things, she found it extremely difficult, as if trying to jog through a swamp. She'd stopped the Moon's attacks and healed Rian just fine, but when it came to altering someone's mind...she had to do it the old-fashioned way. By talking. What a pain.

No doubt it was Naos. But when Patricia felt for any telepathic signals, she got pulled in the direction of the Sun-Moon or the sense of her breachie followers currently headed into the hills or some yafanai on the plains. Maybe there was just too much goddamned power flying around in too small a space.

❖

No matter her words to Lydia, Fajir kept seeing Nico's face as she walked through the camp, headed for the center, for her Lords. It might never leave her.

She deserved that.

No one paid her any mind; no one looked at widows at the best of times. Now, even with Lydia behind her, no one noticed. They wouldn't notice Nico's body either; his death would be laid at the attackers' feet.

Should she admit what she'd done? Claim she'd only sent him to his beloved partner? If her fellow widows accepted such a reason, they'd be likely to kill one another and return them all to partners long dead.

No, Fajir killed him for Lydia, for the future, for unseen people she didn't know who'd never see the faces of those who'd killed them. She'd never realized how important it was to look her targets in the eye. She'd thought she wanted to see their fear, but killing had never made her happy, not really. It was a task that needed doing. Maybe that was why she hadn't struck down Halaan's killer. After he was dead, people would have expected her to be happy.

She hadn't wanted that, not until she'd begun to see Lydia, her nemesis, in her dreams.

"I'm sorry, Fajir," Lydia said. She clung to Fajir's left hand, keeping Fajir's sword arm free.

"I know." Fajir didn't doubt her sincerity. Lydia wept at Nico's death, and she'd claimed to care for him, but she'd been weeping for Fajir, too. She wept for her enemies, mourned those she barely knew, and her heart bled for those she cared about. She made love into something as epic as war.

"Stay here," Fajir said as she caught sight of the Lords. They were turning back and forth from the attack to the fire, which was gusting this way, tendrils of it winking out before they could reach the foothills.

"No fucking way," Lydia said.

Fajir had to laugh. She pulled Lydia close, kissing her. "I won't be able to focus if you put yourself in danger."

Lydia bit her lip, standing so close that her features blurred. "I can't..."

"You will. In your vision, you saw me walk away."

With a sob, Lydia looked at the blaze again, tears flooding the cheeks of her beautiful face. Fajir followed her gaze. A herd of ossors rushed from a ravine as the fire flushed them out; they keened and ran, but the fire overtook one, and Lydia turned away. The way she'd described her power, she followed the line of one person's future, but if that target met another person in her vision, then she could follow that one.

Fajir wondered if Lydia had started this vision by seeing her own future, then hopped among the army, maybe even the plains dwellers; groups of them could be dying just out of sight, the fire stretched so far.

Fajir waited a heartbeat, wishing she could say what she was feeling. Halaan would have wanted her to admit her love, but she couldn't, not in this place of violence and death, not with her own death in front of her. And she had no doubt her death was near; no one should survive killing their gods.

Slowly, Fajir leaned in and whispered in Lydia's ear. "When we meet again, in a world made of starlight, I will kiss you and Halaan and your Freddie, and we will all live in peace." She tore away before Lydia could respond or weep or undo Fajir's determination as only a true nemesis could.

The wind gusted, and a blade of grass seemed to hover near Fajir's shoulder, the strand half eaten by embers. Fajir caught it in one hand and snuffed it out before the wind carried it away. A small fire burned between her and the Lords, as if they'd thought to cook something before the attack had begun. Such a mundane thought on such a day.

It masked her approach nicely.

She leapt the flames, and a pair of worshipers guarding the Sun-Moon moved to intercept her before pausing, surely wondering what a widow was doing approaching the Lords with her blade drawn. Fajir darted right, slicing one of their legs, then brought her sword up and gouged the arm of the other before nicking his head. Both fell, their cries lost in the sound of the blaze coming closer.

If the Sun had only extinguished it, Fajir would have left him alone, but it seemed as if he kept trying to turn the fire back to the south, unable to let go of a plan once it was in motion. He wouldn't be reasoned with, not in the future Lydia had seen. She saw her gods now for who they were: two-hundred-year-olds who really should have known better than to start new circles of violence.

She'd learned the same lesson in less than a year.

The thought made her smile as she stepped over the wounded worshipers. Her Lords had their eyes half-open as they watched north and south. One of the other pairs that guarded them turned, paused to stare at Fajir and the wounded, then shouted, getting more attention.

Now or never.

Fajir dashed, keeping low, hoping that if the Lords opened their eyes, she'd stay out of sight long enough. One step brought her close enough to see the sweat on their faces, but she could only reach one before the guards were upon her.

The Sun had to die first. To stop the flames.

His skin parted easily. Strange, she'd thought killing him would feel different than ending normal people, but the blood that poured from his throat was every bit as red. The disbelief in his eyes was the same as everyone else's. Not even a god could believe their life was at an end.

Fajir heard a shriek and began to turn. Her feet lifted off the ground, and she flew into the air, wondering if she'd died, if this was her spirit escaping. But her hair fluttered around her, and she rose high above the flames but could still see the smoke, could fill the chill of the wind. She arced over the flames, and the ground rushed toward her. Terror filled her mind as she dropped like a stone, and her chest seized as she screamed.

Darkness clawed at her, overruling her thoughts, and she gladly gave in to the panic, her last thought one of relief that she wouldn't feel the pain of impact.

Cordelia saw Samira off to warn the plains dwellers, then looked at her motley army. She'd be happy to go into battle with any of them, but they weren't nearly as impressive as they'd been with a giant tree behind them.

They were, however, much closer to the swamp than they'd been before. Cordelia wondered if Pool had been unconsciously running for water. Or maybe it wasn't unconscious at all. They could still see the smoke in the distance, but the wind had sprung up from the south, and a huge storm gathered on the horizon. Maybe the Storm Lord was doing something good for a change.

Cordelia wasn't prepared to give him any credit, though.

Pool approached where Cordelia stood with one foot up on a boulder as she scanned the plains and the nearby trees. "My drushka and the humans who will remain aboard my tree are ready, Sa."

"Good. I want to scout first in my astral form." Cordelia didn't need to turn to know Nettle was frowning; she could almost feel two holes burning into her neck.

"You did not listen when I told you to stay in your body before," Nettle said as Cordelia turned. "And you suffered for it."

"I know."

"Simon did not listen when I tried to hurry him from the Sun-Moon camp, and he suffered for it."

"Yes, but—"

Nettle raised a hand, her lichen-colored eyes so narrow Cordelia could barely see the color. "Samira did not listen when I told her we must escape rather than argue, and do you know what happened?"

"Everything worked out fine?"

Nettle's stare had not an ounce of humor. "You will listen now and not repeat that suffering."

Pool turned away, an illusion of privacy for her human allies.

"I have to look," Cordelia said, "to find a way around the fire. Simon will be with me. Pool will be with me, and so will Miriam, and she's a telepath. We'll be ready for anything."

"Including Naos? This Miriam is a match for her? Then we shall rejoice and let her go into the mountains alone!"

"One peep from Naos, and I'll rush back to you, I swear!" Cordelia took her hands. "You've seen me throw myself into danger plenty of times. Why is astral projecting so different?"

Nettle's stony expression melted into one of sadness. "I had to carry your soulless body once before, Sa. It is a memory to make the night cold."

Cordelia pulled her close, even with the armor. "When Naos snapped my tether, it wasn't fun for anyone. And I'm sorry. But Simon wasn't with me then. Neither was Pool. We weren't prepared. Not even Naos can sever the connection I have to the drushka."

"Nor to me," Nettle said as she kissed Cordelia's brow. When they parted, Nettle lifted her chin. "You have but minutes, Sa. If you do not return to your body, I will run for the mountains to kill Naos myself."

Cordelia started in surprise. "Even if I'm okay? You'd be throwing your life away."

Nettle gave her a flat look. "Minutes, Sa. Fifteen of them. Then I leave you with Simon and start for Naos."

When Pool gave Cordelia a serious look instead of a teasing one, Cordelia knew Nettle was telling the truth. "Right." She sat on the ground, and Nettle knelt beside her, but the firm set of her lips said that if fifteen minutes went by, she wouldn't be there when Cordelia woke up.

Best to get started, then. She slipped free of her body and felt Pool and Simon with her. The tree still stood nearby, waiting for Pool to command it to leave, but Cordelia liked having all the drushka behind her at the moment.

She floated north, noting the fire still blazing. They were lucky they'd swung as westerly as they had. The fire didn't extend all the way to the swamp yet; they'd have to skirt the edge of that mass of trees and water in order to escape the heat.

Cordelia felt her tether tightening behind her, but she stretched it, trying to see farther. "A moment, Sa," Pool said in her mind. The tether gave a little, flaring with light, and Cordelia imagined it as an extension of Pool's limbs as she stretched to increase her reach.

She couldn't venture as far as the foothills, not to mention the mountains, but she spotted movement here and there, both in the mountains and on the plains, but she couldn't get close enough to tell what it was. Probably people or animals desperate to escape the flames.

"That's a shame, isn't it?" a voice asked. If it had been possible, Cordelia would have said it whispered in her ear.

Fear tingled like ice rubbing over Cordelia's spirit. Pool yanked on her tether, and she raced for the tree. Simon's power roared through her, but there was nothing to strike. She could faintly hear him yelling at Miriam to find him a signal.

"Oh, this is nothing!" Naos's voice said, following along as if she drifted by Cordelia's side. "Barely a wisp of power, nothing to find, only here to talk. Don't be so bloody paranoid!"

"What do you want?" Cordelia asked, not stopping. Pool's protective instincts flowed around her like a wall, pushing back her fear.

"Just saying hello, that I'm looking forward to your visit…that sounds like a message someone would leave on a vid, doesn't it?"

Cordelia ignored her rambling and watched the countryside go by. She spotted something at the edge of her senses, something large moving north of the swamp. She tried to slow, but Pool was pulling too hard. It was too large to be a person or any animal except a geaver, and they didn't range that far west. A tree? A queen's tree?

But it was too small for that.

Unless it was Shiv.

"It's all so exciting!" Naos said. "All the flittering about, all the goings-on. Can I tell you a secret?"

"No." Cordelia hurried even faster, feeding images to Pool: Shiv, headed to the mountains like everyone else.

"I've been keeping a little lid on everyone's power, just to even the playing field, and hardly anyone's noticed!" She laughed like a delighted child. "And I may have given a few emotions the odd nudge, too, just to hurry everyone up a bit. Seriously, you're all so *slow*."

Cordelia knew she shouldn't engage, but she couldn't help it. "You're lying. Simon would have known."

"Oh yes, all hail the mighty Dr. Lazlo. He's *so* powerful. It's not as if you can take him out just by hitting him on the head or anything." She cackled. "He bumped his noggin, and I just creeped on in. Of course," she added with a sigh, "he got rid of me soon enough, even if he didn't know what he was doing. His power is always fixing him, and I was like a virus. A fabulous virus, but still."

Cordelia thought through everyone's behavior the past few days, then dismissed the idea. If Naos couldn't fuck with them with power, she'd spread paranoia. "You can take anyone out if you hit them hard enough. Even you."

"Grr," Naos said. "I love it when you talk tough!"

Cordelia felt another emotion fill her, Simon's satisfaction. His power flared again, mixed with something else, Miriam's telepathy. He swirled their abilities with Pool's, and Cordelia felt their anticipation as if she was face-to-face with an enemy, and someone handed her a railgun.

She caught a flicker of power like a sparkle in her far periphery. She used herself as a targeting system, directing the power and heard a mental howl in response before Naos's presence quickly withdrew.

Cordelia wanted to crow, but she was so close to her body that she dove inside and came awake with a happy cry.

Nettle leaned over her, blocking the light. "Just in time, Sa."

Cordelia sat up and kissed her. "We drove her off!"

"Ahya, Sa, just," Pool said as she helped Nettle and Cordelia to their feet. Behind her, Simon was beaming, and Miriam looked smug. Every non-drushka seemed mystified, but Cordelia was certain word would spread, and morale would greatly improve. They'd driven Naos away even if she had just been using a wisp of her power.

And that wasn't the only important fact.

Cordelia shook off her fear and worry as Pool commanded the tree's roots to dig long tunnels through the soil, as far as the tendrils could reach. Cordelia braced herself, taking deep breaths before the roots pulled her under and sent her careening through the soil as they had in the swamp, when she'd gone to confront the Shi. This time, though, when she popped back up to the surface, far from the tree, she had more than Pool, Nettle, and Reach. Surrounded by paladins, drushka, yafanai, and one former god, Cordelia led the way north of the swamp and west of the fire. Soon, they'd have Shiv in their party as well. And if one queen could help drive away Naos, she ached to find out what three could do.

Chapter Twenty-two

L ydia couldn't breathe, and it had nothing to do with the smoke
blowing over her. The last few moments had felt like a vision.
Indeed, she'd seen some of it before: Fajir walking away, shoulders
back, stride confident. She'd caught a fire-eaten blade of grass. She'd
leapt some flames, though in her vision, Lydia thought they'd been
some of the flames Fajir was helping to stop.

When Fajir's sword sank into the Sun's throat, time seemed to
slow, and Lydia heard nothing but ringing in her ears. He'd died so
quickly, one minute moving his arms in the air as if directing musicians,
the next clutching his ruined throat and trying to hold his life inside.
She'd expected a dramatic showdown, something out of an epic, with
recriminations and speeches and tears. Killing a god should have taken
longer than a fraction of a second.

But this was Fajir, wise enough to know that time could only be
used against her. She'd wounded her fellow countrymen, then did what
she came to do.

Lydia hadn't even had time to weep for her before she was lost to
the flames.

The Moon shrieked once the Sun was cut down, a noise of such
pure anguish that it sliced through Lydia's shock. Fajir flew into the
smoke, her lean body lost to where the flames were licking the side
of the hill. The Moon collapsed at the Sun's side; her grief felt almost
tangible, like a half-formed ghost rising off of her, and Lydia stumbled
a few steps toward her to offer comfort before she remembered where
she was.

Escape.

She turned, trying to see through tears and smoke. Fajir was dead,
and Lydia had to escape, but her legs felt like lumps of clay. Run, she

told them, but they couldn't obey, ready to mourn Fajir even if she wasn't. At least her vision was over, but even that didn't cheer her. Losing something that had driven her for weeks was still a loss, and her body wanted to grieve for that, too.

"Go, go," she told herself, hating the breathless sound of her voice. Fajir wouldn't be weak right now. She'd slip out of this camp and find her friends and do what had to be done.

Her friends? Nico had been Fajir's friend, and she'd killed him for Lydia's sake. This whole shitty quest had been for Lydia's sake, or at least for the sake of her power. She squeezed her hands into fists until the pain brought her back to reality. Her stupid power and its stupid visions weren't her fault. This future was always going to happen. The fire, the deaths, all of it! And if she didn't get away now, she would be one of them.

Maybe that would be for the best.

"No," she said with a growl. She wouldn't be ruled by her stupid power or her stupid fucking feelings! She had to move.

She saw people ahead, heard cries and the thud of weapons. Some of the attackers had made it into camp. Lydia turned and stayed low, using the smoke to hide. She couldn't go that way. Picking another direction, she tried again. Her bearings had deserted her. She could barely tell which way was up, and the smoke was beginning to thin.

Lydia's right foot slipped out from under her, and she cried out as she fell back. She'd reached a ledge off the flat area the Sun-Moon had chosen for a camp. The wind gusted over her, stinging her eyes with smoke but clearing the way enough that she could see that the fire was dying, almost out. Whether the Sun had been feeding it or if in his death, he'd extinguished most of it, she couldn't know.

Fajir had done it. She'd saved them all.

A crack of thunder made her jump, and she jerked to her feet as the sky opened. She gasped at the shock of cold water pouring on her head. It muted her grief even as it killed what was left of the fire.

Lydia turned, fighting the urge to search for shelter. The rain would help her get away. She squinted against the sting of the raindrops and put a hand up to shield her eyes as she stumbled through quickly forming mud. No one else wandered around this edge of the camp, so if she could find some trees—

Lydia pitched forward, the fall so sudden she couldn't cry out before the air rushed from her lungs as she hit the ground. Her face stung as she curled around her breathless chest and sought to keep her face out of the mud. She hadn't even had time to put up her hands as she fell. Not a fall. A push.

And no one had touched her.

Her breath came back slowly as she was lifted in the air, hovering amidst the raindrops. She rotated slowly and saw blood dripping onto her hands. She tried to touch the harsh sting on her forehead but couldn't move, stuck in a fetal position, dripping with mud and blood.

The Moon's shoulders heaved up and down as she breathed. The rain left steam drifting around her head—more ghosts—and those of the worshipers gathered behind her. The air felt heavier as she stalked closer, murder making her eyes shine in the gloom.

"I want to rip you apart," she said, a whisper more frightening than a shout. Maybe rage had clogged her throat. "And I will, as soon as I get what I want. Until then…" She put her hands to Lydia's head.

Lydia gasped as a buzzing sound filled her mind, louder than the rain, than her own breathing in her ears. Her vision filled with swirling motes that winked as they flew, almost beautiful.

"I have to use my power."

She heard her own voice, but the words made no sense. She hated to use her power. That was why…

Something…had happened.

"I have to use my power *now*."

It rose within her, and she embraced it, imagining time as a skein of yarn. She saw herself and the Moon, but she couldn't focus on the absurdity of her body floating in midair. She had a future to follow.

The Moon's time skein unwound, and Lydia watched, urging it to speed through the Sun-Moon camp collecting itself and moving on, mopping up the rest of their attackers on their way up the hill. They left their animals in a guarded camp, and the Moon herself led the way toward a mountain in the distance.

"That's enough."

Her own voice again and not to be denied. She let the skein rewind, then gasped as the Moon's power released her, and she fell with another painful thud.

"I could scramble your brain," the Moon said, still far quieter than she should be. "But I want you aware so you can anticipate your death."

Lydia barely had time to process those words before the Moon walked away, and her worshipers rushed forward, binding Lydia's arms tightly behind her back. The Moon was done taking chances, it seemed.

Lydia couldn't even cry out as they hauled her upright and shoved her after the Moon. She never thought she'd lament her fate and stubbornly feel she deserved it at the same time.

❖

Even without the tree around, Simon could feel Pool's anxiety as she tried to contact Shiv. He knew their method of communication revolved around the trees—he meant to really study them one day—but Pool kept trying to reach her daughter with her mind alone. She let out a whoop of victory just as the heavens turned on the faucet.

"Since I do not have my tree, she has agreed to come for us," Pool said, raising her voice above the rain.

Simon nodded. If they'd still had the tree, Pool would have been hesitant to contact Shiv at all, not with Lyshus and his power to sap other queens' trees of energy. "Fantastic," he yelled. "Because this ground is quickly turning to sludge."

The plains had been getting soggier even before the rain. Runoff from the swamp transformed the whole area into a treeless mire.

"Keep slogging," Cordelia said. "The more time we save, the better." She squinted eastward, and Simon turned to look, too. Through the rain and the lingering smoke, they couldn't see the glow of the fire any longer. Maybe the pouring rain had finally conquered it.

"Do you think this is him?" Victoria asked as she walked behind Simon, Miriam at her side. She'd been prepared to fight any fires that came near them, but Simon had doubted she could overcome the Sun's power. "This rain?"

"The Storm Lord?" Miriam asked before Simon could respond. "If it is, he's only doing it to save his own skin."

Simon snorted a laugh. "Or it was a happy accident."

They both smiled, and he fell back to walk beside them. It was always nice to talk shit about the asshole he'd once had feelings for with people who felt the same. When Victoria slid in the mud, Simon helped catch her while Miriam said, "Watch your feet, graceless."

"Look who's talking. You walk like a drunken hoshpi."

As they fell into comfortable bickering, Simon recalled why he hadn't been walking with them in the first place and moved toward the center of the group. Reach and Nettle walked on either side of Pool, who craned her neck trying to catch a glimpse of her daughter. Cordelia marched in front of them, the water spattering her armor with a succession of sharp pings. The sound reverberated off every suit of armor nearby, a paladin symphony.

Simon stepped up beside Cordelia, who threatened to outpace him even with her heavy armor. "When you attacked the Shi in the swamp," Simon said. "Did you have a plan, or was it more like this?"

"We had a loose plan: run, don't get killed, keep running, deliver Pool, run some more, don't get killed."

He chuckled. "I like the part where you made sure not to get killed."

"It's part of my everyday plan," she said with a smile, dark eyes sparkling.

He couldn't ask if she was enjoying herself. He wouldn't be able to resist a few sarcastic comments if the answer was yes. "Do you think Horace is up there?" He nodded in the direction of the mountains that had all but disappeared in the driving rain.

"Probably. Everyone else is."

Her voice held a note of false cheer, and he shook his head. "And with the way he's been spoiling for a fight, he won't miss the action if he's able."

Cordelia cleared her throat, and he felt her discomfort. Her normal advice to people with too many feelings was probably something along the lines of: get drunk, get laid, or get in a fight. Before she could say anything, though, he felt her mood shift to something brighter.

"You know, Naos said she's been tinkering with people's powers and emotions. I thought she was lying, of course, but maybe that's part of his problem. She claimed that she's so subtle no one would notice, even said she'd done it to you after you'd been hit on the head, but your body healed itself. Maybe Horace doesn't quite have that instinct down yet."

Simon frowned and tried to recall the fight with Naos. He hadn't really been listening to what anyone said. He'd been too busy badgering Miriam to find a telepathic signal that was barely there so he could attack. He'd thought Miriam didn't have the strength, but what if Naos had been using a subtler hand? That would explain so much.

And he wouldn't have to face the idea that maybe Horace was dissatisfied with his entire life.

Neither thought mattered, really. He couldn't consider either until he got Horace back.

Cordelia was spared more outpouring of feelings by the appearance of Shiv's tree through the rain. Simon had to fight to keep his jaw from dropping. When he'd last seen it, it was barely taller than her, and she could still lift it from the ground. Now, it was at least thirty feet tall. Shiv rode near the top where the branches fitted together as tightly as a bench. She lifted a hand as if to wave, then quickly dropped it.

Simon stared again when another drushka dropped from the lower branches and eyed them curiously. With a gray cast to her skin and clothing and her silver hair, he hadn't seen her amongst the limbs.

Pool strode forward, a happy yet cautious smile on her face as the limbs lowered Shiv to the ground. Lyshus wasn't with her, but Simon had no doubt he rode aboard the tree.

"Daughter." Pool held out her arms, and Shiv's face shuddered. So much had passed between them. Lyshus had attacked Pool's tree; Shiv had attacked her own mother, yet there were Pool's arms, ready for an embrace. With a cry that was half moan, Shiv threw herself into her mother's arms.

"Shi'a'na, I am so sorry!" The water running down her face looked like tears, making her seem more human. "I could not stop it, could not stop myself."

"I know, daughter."

Shiv pulled back, her face lighting up. "Lyshus's powers can be wondrous as well as painful, Shi'a'na. He can use human telepathy and has contacted Naos, who has offered to help us."

Everyone went still. Simon's mind whirled. A drushka who could use human telepathy? Who reached all the way from the swamp to the mountains and talked to *Naos*?

Who offered to *help*?

Everyone began speaking at once. Pool suggested caution; Cordelia said they couldn't trust Naos to offer them a drink, let alone help them; and Nettle asked who the strange drushka was.

"I am Enka," the drushka said, stepping forward. "Here to aid the young queen."

"How?" Simon asked in the lull. He waved at Enka before she could respond. "Not you. How did Naos propose to help you, Shiv?"

She grabbed his shoulder as if welcoming him, then straightened and looked at her tree. "Is it not wondrous, shawness?"

Simon knew delaying tactics when he saw them. "You don't know how she plans to help you. She just offered, and you jumped at it?"

Everyone began speaking again, but Shiv slashed a hand through the air, cutting them off. Simon saw a spark of the same desperation and anger he'd seen before. "I had to act! Do you wish to come with me, or will you remain here?"

"We go to defeat Naos, not to speak with her," Pool said.

Shiv lifted her chin. "Defeat her after she helps Lyshus and me." Her tree reached for her, and when she was seated back on her limb bench, she called, "Well?"

Pool seemed as if she might speak again, but Cordelia grabbed her arm. "We're coming."

Simon tried to argue, too, but Cordelia's eyes widened, and she nodded at the tree as if hurrying him aboard so she could say what she wanted in private.

The tree lifted them all and seemed very crowded indeed as it began to move north. Shiv stayed near the top, and Enka moved to be closer to her, eyeing the humans and other drushka with curious caution. Cordelia sat in the crook of two branches, and Pool stood beside her, leaning close. Simon clambered as close as he could to them, but the motion of Shiv's tree was a lot more jarring than Pool's. He grabbed hold of several branches until Reach braced herself against his back, and he could lean close to Cordelia.

"Let her believe what she wants for now," Cordelia said softly. "If she distracts Naos, it's better for us."

Pool sucked her teeth. "I cannot lie to my daughter, Sa."

"Don't say anything at all."

"What if she can help?" Reach asked over Simon's shoulder. "Should we not let her?"

"Help do what?" Simon asked, fighting to keep his voice low. "Strip Lyshus of his…queen-hood? Sever their connection? That still isn't going to solve the problem of Shiv not being able to have a tribe."

Pool's eyes turned down, and Simon felt her sorrow. It had been her decision to have a child of her own body. "Something must be done," she said softly.

Simon sighed. "I need time to study the problem. I've never trusted anyone who offered quick, easy answers."

Cordelia snorted. "Naos might be quick, but whatever she has in mind, it won't be easy. That's why we stay quiet and let Shiv believe what she wants. If Naos actually wants to help Shiv, Simon can spy on what she does, and we can hit her afterward. If, as I suspect, she's fucking with Shiv for some purpose of her own, maybe she won't be expecting the rest of us to come in with Shiv, and we can surprise her."

Pool's mouth set into a thin line as if she didn't approve of the plan, but she didn't object. When Cordelia looked to Simon, he nodded. He wouldn't have any problem holding back the information, but Shiv was another piece of this ever-shifting plan, and he didn't know how they could ever be ready for so many contingencies.

Keep running, he reminded himself, and don't get killed.

❖

Fajir heard voices. She lay still, trying to piece the last few moments together. She'd been lying beside Lydia in a hammock overlooking the sea, a jug of beer beside them, and an entire afternoon to do nothing at all.

One of the voices muttered something about rain.

"Real rain I can handle," a closer voice said. "I'm just hoping no more murderous assholes fall from the sky."

Samira. Was she still bound by Samira, Mamet, and Nemesis? Had Lydia been a dream?

No, she'd kissed Lydia, killed one of her gods, and had flown through the air. Instead of a hammock, the ground was her bed.

"I know you're alive," Samira said.

Fajir cracked one eye open. She shouldn't be alive. The Moon had thrown her over the huge fire. She should have landed hard enough to break her body apart. She sat up slowly, eyeing Samira, who stood over her with arms crossed.

"In case you're wondering," Samira said, "I caught you. Barely. It's my bad luck that I just happened to be riding by on my way to warn the Engali about the fire started by your fucked-up gods. If I'd known it was you, I'd have let you fall."

Fajir blinked at her. She didn't know what to say, hadn't really planned to be alive past Lydia's vision.

"Where's Lydia?" Samira asked.

Fajir turned around, looking for the flames.

"The fire's out," Samira said. "Where's Lydia?"

Fajir hadn't had time to look at her before the Moon's power had thrown her away. She saw again the river of blood cascading from the Sun's neck. An unnamed feeling tried to rise within her, but she pushed it down. "Was I the only one?"

"You mean the only person pretending to be a bird? Yes. One more time, Fajir, where's Lydia?"

If the Moon hadn't thrown Lydia, what did that mean? "There was a camp." She pointed past where smoke still swirled on the plains. "On the slope there." But Lydia wouldn't be there. She'd been standing on the other side of the campfire. The Moon couldn't have missed her. And if Lydia hadn't been thrown *with* Fajir, then she'd been thrown in another direction, one where no one waited to catch her.

Nemesis, Lydia, was dead.

Samira didn't seem to consider this; she took the plains dwellers with her and rode to the north, toward the smoke. Fajir struggled to her feet. She was alive. Nico was dead, the Sun was dead, Lydia was dead, and Fajir was supposed to be with them. In the afterlife made of starlight, they could've had peace.

Fajir found her sword a few feet away. All she had to do was fall upon it and die. As she readied herself, she heard the keen of ossors above the pounding rain. Plains dwellers, even better. She walked toward the sound, and a group of them slowed as they neared her.

"We saw the flames," one called. "What's happened?" He nudged his ossor closer then pulled up short as Fajir wiped her hair from her face. His eyes went wide as he stared at her tattoos, her warrior's robe.

"You're a Sun-Moon widow," he said.

"Yes." She kept walking toward him. He looked to the others, and they dismounted, glancing at each other in curious fear. They were young, but she didn't want to wait for someone older.

"Do you need help?" another asked. She stepped around her fellows. "I'm Kai, we're Engali, from—"

"Perfect," Fajir said. A full circle at last. "My gods started this fire. They no doubt killed some of your people and hoped to kill more."

Now the Engali youngsters frowned. "Why?" one asked, outrage and horror in his voice.

"Because they wanted to." She held out her sword, grip first. "They're not here, but I am. Take your vengeance."

Kai frowned at the sword and made no move to take it.

Fajir sighed. Nothing ever came easy. She flipped the sword, caught the grip, and struck Kai in the face with the flat of the blade. Kai fell back, one hand to her unmarred cheek, eyes wide. The others cried out in protest, and two drew their weapons.

Fajir flipped her sword around again and held it out. "Kill me before I kill you. It's simple."

"She's crazy!" one of the youngsters called. He hauled Kai backward and pushed her toward her ossor while the others mounted. Kai stared at her in shock as they rode away.

"Get back here!" Fajir yelled, anger sharp inside her. "Don't you know anything about destiny?"

Clearly, they did not. They called out to someone who answered back. Fajir marched in that direction, still a little unsteady but hopeful again that she'd see Halaan and Lydia soon. Many dark forms moved through the gloom, plains dwellers enough for anyone determined to die.

"Who's there?" Fajir said, trying to get anyone's attention.

Another plains dweller rode out of the rain. "Engali." A man's voice. Older. Good; maybe he'd know what to do with a sword. "Are you the insane woman those children were babbling about?"

He was smiling, a look that faded as his eyes flicked to her sword.

Fajir's heart froze, but she made her feet keep moving. She had to see him more clearly; her eyes had to be seeing what couldn't be there: the eyes, the scar on his chin, the shape of his face. This was the very Engali who'd killed Halaan, the man she'd hunted with Cordelia Ross. His bit of the Engali clan roved farther west than the rest of them. She should have known they'd come here first, should have known the circle had to be entirely complete.

She laughed, and he rode closer, frowning before his eyes widened, too.

"I know you," he whispered.

She waited for him to recognize her from when she shot his daughter, but he nearly fell from the saddle before he clasped his hands together. "I...killed your partner almost a year ago. I've never forgotten your face."

Fajir blinked. She hadn't expected him to remember, didn't know she'd haunted his dreams as he'd haunted hers.

"It was an accident," he said, straightening. "I'm sorry. I always wanted to tell you."

"I shot your daughter," she said. "I don't want your apologies."

His mouth dropped open before his brow darkened. "That day on the ridge?"

"I meant to kill her, but my shot was spoiled." She held her sword out. "Here. Or would you rather use your own?"

"Why?" he asked, not even looking at the weapon. His hands became bloodless fists. "Why?"

"I wanted you to suffer as I had suffered." She shook the sword. "I deserve to die."

For a moment, he stared at the sword as a starving man might look upon a feast. His hand twitched toward it before he lowered his arm to his side. He reached for his own blade. Maybe that was more fitting, to be killed by his sword. She wondered if he was seeing his daughter's wounded hand; maybe she'd been maimed, and he'd had to nurse her for days. That needed vengeance.

When he looked at her again, he spat at her feet. "I will not let myself become you." He turned quickly and mounted his ossor.

Fajir's stomach dropped. "What?"

He rode away. Fajir ran after him as she had so many years ago when Halaan's body had been cooling on the ground behind her. But just like then, the Engali outpaced her quickly. This time, instead of looking back at her with a horrified expression, he didn't even turn.

Fajir pulled up quickly. There'd be no Nico to find her this time if she exhausted herself in the chase, no Samira to catch her if she fell. She turned a circle and screamed for all she was worth, denied a good death yet again. Nemesis's curse was still with her.

Fajir sat in the wet grass and breathed hard. She still had her sword, could still end herself, but the idea had lost its appeal. And if she truly believed that her nemesis was not letting her die, that meant Lydia might yet be alive.

It was the hope of a fool, but why not be a fool for a little while?

Fajir stood again, put her sword through her belt, and followed in Samira's footsteps.

CHAPTER TWENTY-THREE

"Can you feel anyone nearby?" Dillon asked again.

Patricia gave him a dark look, but he felt her power. While she searched, he looked around but couldn't see anyone through the trees. They'd been heading steadily upward, and the day was wearing on. The storm had thinned out and spread, but he couldn't see if the fire was out yet or not; the trees were too thick.

As they'd climbed, the green of the needles gave way to a darker blue, and the temperature continued to drop. They were all wet, and the only reason they weren't shivering was because they kept moving.

"I can't feel anyone past our group," Patricia said, heavy irritation in her voice. "Just like the last time you asked."

"Just checking."

When he turned back to her, she eyed him critically. "Can you keep the wind off of us?"

"No, my power's not working right, either." A total lie, but he didn't reach, so she couldn't check to see if it was true. They both suspected Naos of fucking with her, but as always, the mad goddess's motives remained a secret.

Patricia started off again, two of her cronies in front of her and Jonah behind. Three more of them brought up the rear. If Patricia couldn't use her power anymore, Dillon didn't see any use for her except as a Naos lure. He was trying to figure out a way to knock her unconscious and kill the rest of them when he felt a tingle.

He made himself keep walking. The voice was faint, all he could get through Patricia's telepathic blocks.

"Liam? Can you hear me?"

Horace. Dillon fought a smile. He supposed it could also be Naos fucking with him, but he decided to play along and thought back a positive response.

"If you can hear me, nod," Horace said. "I can't hear your thoughts past the blocks I sense in your mind."

Dillon nodded, glancing around, trying to spot Horace in the trees. "Is Jon Lea alive?"

Dillon nodded again, wondering if Horace would have kept talking had the answer been no. Of course, Dillon wouldn't have admitted that if it was true.

"Do you want to get away from her? I can't sense her using her power, so now would be the time."

Fan-fucking-tastic. Dillon coughed to hide a grin and nodded again, wondering if the cronies behind him saw and what they thought of all his nodding. Maybe they'd think he had a song stuck in his head.

"I can knock out Patricia and the Storm Lord, but I might have to fight their power. Can you handle some of the others?"

Another nod and a barely avoided eye roll about Jonah's "powers."

"Ready? You're about to pass by me…now!"

Patricia and Jonah staggered. Dillon whirled around and sank his fist into Rian's stomach. He hid a lightning bolt in the contact, hoping Horace wouldn't notice the burnt smell. If he did, he'd probably chalk it up to the "Storm Lord."

Rian fell, and Dillon ducked under a punch from the next man. He delivered a shot to the guy's gut and another to the face, hiding another surprise inside. The last one tackled him from the side, sending them both sprawling in the leaves and needles. Dillon brought his elbow down on the man's head, and he let go with a grunt. Dillon scooted away and kicked the man in the face, flattening his nose and nearly caving in his skull.

Dillon scrambled to his feet. Jonah was down. Patricia was on her knees, breathing hard. Her unfocused eyes settled on Dillon, and her mouth twisted in hatred. Dillon ducked behind a tree, not certain what she could still do but unwilling to wait for it. He circled around to the two cronies who were trying to help her and came at them from behind. Locking his elbow around one of their necks, Dillon hauled backward, lifting the man and choking him. When the other rose, Dillon swung his captive and knocked the last one back. He fell over Patricia, and she cried out before going limp.

The last man got to his feet, cast a despairing glance down at his mistress before his eyes rolled back in his head, and he collapsed. Horace emerged from the trees and nodded at Dillon's captive.

"You can let him go now."

"Right." Dillon pumped a few volts into the man, just enough to stop his heart, then he laid him down as one might an unconscious foe.

Horace knelt next to Jonah and Patricia and felt for their pulses. "They're alive."

"What're you going to do with them?" Dillon asked quietly. There were plenty of rocks and broken logs about. If his answer was anything other than, "Give them to Naos," Dillon was going to flatten the man while his back was turned.

Horace straightened and put his hands on his hips. "I think we should offer them to Naos and hope that convinces her to leave everyone else alone."

Dillon froze before he could bend and pick up a rock. He really hadn't been expecting that.

"I'm not normally bloodthirsty," Horace said. "Well, I wasn't before all this god stuff started, but I think if anyone deserves to get gobbled up by the monster, it's these two. Right?"

"You know," Dillon said. "I couldn't agree more." He strode to the three dead cronies in the rear and started piecing together the paladin armor from their packs.

"Where's Jon?" Horace asked.

"After you escaped, they left him on the hillside," Dillon said. "The rain probably woke him up already." Dillon donned the armor, only wishing the paladin had thought to bring the battery so he could have charged it, but without power, the battery was too much dead weight.

Still, any armor was good armor. He took the gun back from Jonah and slipped the helmet on. "Ready when you are."

Horace smiled and looked him up and down. "I keep forgetting you were a paladin before you were the mayor."

Dillon smiled back. "True."

Shiv's tree moved fast, much more than Cordelia expected, maybe even faster than Pool's tree, though the ride was far less smooth. Just as when she'd ridden a running geaver, Cordelia's stomach threatened to turn over, and only Simon's power washing over her kept her breakfast inside.

When the tree reached the first slopes, Cordelia expected it to slow. Pool's tree would have risked slipping on the rocks. Shiv's tree moved easily between the spindly hill trees and scurried up the slope, going ever higher in the direction Naos had given her.

Cordelia tried not to fidget as she scanned the growing darkness. The rain had stolen their ability to see all afternoon, and now night was almost upon them again. It seemed as if only moments ago she'd been stumbling aboard Pool's tree, but all the traveling had eaten up the day and put her on edge. She didn't dare scout outside her body, not so close to Naos's lair.

She chuckled at that thought. They'd made Naos into a fairytale monster desperate to rip out their hearts and eat their souls. Her brief laughter died. It'd be more amusing if Cordelia didn't think Naos had exactly that in store. What else could they call it when one person carved out another person's mind and attached it to their own, leaving the body a husk?

Trying not to dwell on it, she drummed her fingers on the bark. Nettle rode just above her, and she was surrounded by people she cared about. She should take this opportunity to tell them how she felt in case the worst happened, but the hillside was so quiet. Even the animals and insects seemed to think it'd be safer not to be noticed.

They crested the hill, the ground leveling. Cordelia worried they might have to go down another then up again, but a steep, rocky slope abutted the top of this hill, reaching toward the darkening sky. Piles of rocks lay scattered along the bottom, their color bright as if recently broken, and the tops of the nearby trees were scorched, the tips missing.

They were close.

Shiv's tree climbed up the slope without difficulty, but several of its riders cried out as they slipped, just managing to hang on. Cordelia grabbed a limb with one hand and Nettle with the other as she tightened her legs around the branch she sat on. Simon grabbed one of her armor plates. He had an arm curled around a branch and was holding Reach with that hand. Pool's large hand was fisted in his shirt, and her other hand held on to Nettle, who grabbed hold of Cordelia with one arm, her queen with the other, and had her legs wrapped around a branch.

Cordelia barked a laugh. "Well, if we fall, we're all going together."

"My daughter will not let us fall." Pool sounded confident, but her grip didn't slacken. Cordelia was certain Shiv didn't *want* them to fall, but she was new to this moving tree thing. It had to take practice to hold people in the branches.

Finally, the tree rounded the edge of the steep slope. Cordelia looked back and found it much more cliff-like from this angle. When her stomach threatened her again, she faced forward and gasped at the sight before her.

The *Atlas* had made a crater where it landed, a blackened hole of rock and ruin. Pieces of the ship were strewn around the dented boulders along with bits of trees and a few burnt animal carcasses. No light came from the great machine, no hum. It shone in the last bits of daylight filtering under the cloud cover, but even with its long nose and with broken pieces jutting from its sleek hull, it seemed more like some great animal carcass than anything worth fighting over.

"Shiv," Cordelia said as loudly as she dared. "Take us to that stand of trees."

The order passed up through various murmurs, and the tree moved cautiously around the edge of the crater. The trees to this side of the *Atlas*'s nose still stood, though they were covered by dust and debris kicked up during the crash. Once under cover, Cordelia climbed down with the rest of the humans and Pool's drushka.

Shiv came, too, her face shining with hope. "I will go ahead while you remain here," she said to Cordelia and Pool. "Naos expects me."

Cordelia only hoped Naos didn't know they were all there, but what now? If Shiv had to go into that behemoth, how would they know when to strike? She was about to say so when she spotted movement on the other side of the crater, two forms half walking, half sliding down the slope and dragging two others.

And one was wearing armor.

Simon grabbed her arm. "It's Horace and Lea!"

Cordelia breathed a sigh of relief. Leave it to those two to get away from their abductors before they had a chance to be rescued.

"I can reach them with my power," Simon said.

"No," Cordelia said. "Naos will sense it."

"I will tell them to withdraw," Shiv said.

"Wait," Cordelia said, but Shiv was already underway, her tree carrying her down the slope into the valley. Horace and Lea froze when they saw her, and she made her way to them swiftly.

"Fuck!" Cordelia said.

"Now what?" Simon asked. She could practically feel him vibrating with the need to run to Horace.

"Where's the door to the *Atlas*?" she asked.

"Um." He thought for a moment and rattled off something about airlocks and the Chrysalis bay and escape pods.

Cordelia held up a hand. "Where can we approach without Naos seeing us or popping out a door?"

He thought for another moment before saying, "The nose, probably. There aren't any windows on the bridge."

That didn't make any sense to her, but she supposed they had vids and computers to tell them where they were going. Maybe if they could have looked out a window, they wouldn't have crashed.

She glanced at the setting sun. "Wait until it gets a little darker, then we go. Hopefully, Shiv will have sent Horace and Lea away, and we can sneak inside after Shiv goes in."

Simon frowned hard but settled in. Cordelia drew her sidearm and waited next to him, their allies arrayed around them, and night falling fast. If Cordelia still prayed to the Storm Lord, she would have asked him to keep everyone safe. Instead, she took another look at Nettle, Pool, Reach, Simon, all her troops, and the drushka and silently told them that they'd better stay the fuck alive.

"Fuck," Liam whispered.

Horace looked up, wondering what Liam had seen. He dropped Patricia's arm where he'd been dragging her and stared in wonder at the tree walking toward them. Not as large as Pool's tree, it was still quite a sight. He'd have appreciated seeing it sooner. Then he and Liam wouldn't have had to drag Patricia and the Storm Lord, though Horace had given himself and Liam plenty of boosts to keep their muscles going.

Liam hung back as Horace went forward, peering into the branches. When Shiv dropped to the ground, his mouth fell open in happy surprise. "You're back! How did your tree get so big?"

She smiled, then glanced at the *Atlas* as if doubting that they should have this conversation now. Horace recalled the stories that Shiv had attacked Pool, but she seemed normal, not flying at anyone in a rage.

She squeezed his arm. "Sa and shawness Simon wait behind me, and you must go to them."

"Simon is here?" The need to see him burned inside Horace, but shame filled him, too. He'd been such an ass, and he didn't think he'd see Simon so soon. He didn't have an apology speech prepared, didn't know how to make things right.

"What are you doing down here alone?" he had to ask.

"I will see Naos first, then you may do as you please." Her mouth set in a line as if she expected an argument.

And she was going to get one. "You can't go in there alone, Shiv."

"I will not be." She gestured above, and Horace spotted Lyshus high in the tree and another drushka he didn't know.

"Three isn't enough. I don't know what you want in there, but—"

"Please, shawness," she said, her fists clenching and releasing, the claw prominent. "Go."

"Come with me." He turned, wondering why Liam hung so far back. He and Shiv had broken up or something, so was he feeling shy? "Liam, talk her out of this."

"Liam?" Shiv said softly. She looked around Horace as if just now noticing someone else was there. Liam came forward slowly, clearing his throat as if he didn't know what to say.

Shiv's face seemed to wobble, and she threw herself forward, leaping to wrap her legs around Liam's waist. He staggered but held on as she kissed him wildly.

"Go now, kiss later," Horace said. He glanced at the *Atlas*, wondering if Naos was listening. "We're giving Patricia and the Storm Lord to Naos, and that should satisfy her."

If it did, she made no answer.

Shiv dropped to the ground and hissed, backing away from where Liam stood looking stunned. "You are not Liam," she said, a growl in her voice.

"What?" Horace took a step toward them just as a hatch on the *Atlas* lurched open in a screech of twisted metal.

Lydia regretted every single time she'd tied up Fajir. Having her arms bound behind her not only hurt like anything, she couldn't keep her footing either. And every time she'd slid around the mountain, one of the worshipers jerked her upright, wrenching her shoulders again and again until she lost all feeling in her arms.

No wonder Fajir had wanted to kill her at the time.

But any pain was better than the Moon forcing her to look into the future over and over again. She'd never used her power so much in one day, and her head pounded. The blood had finally dried on her face from her cut to the forehead, leaving her itching, and the skin pulled around the dried blood every time she moved her face. Her throat was dry as dust, but for some reason, her nose ran freely. She hoped she looked enough of a mess that it made the Moon sick to touch her.

They'd finally reached a crater that held the *Atlas*, but the Moon simply stared at it as if waiting for it to come to life. She was probably lost in the past, thinking of all her times with the Sun and how they'd never come again. Lydia would have pitied her anew, but she was too tired.

Death would come at any time now. The Moon had the ship she wanted; she had no more use for Lydia. At least that would mean an end to pain and maybe even the chance to see Fajir and Freddie again. It had stopped raining, too. For some reason, that cheered her. She didn't want to die in the rain, didn't want to feel as if the whole sky wept for her. Too poetic by far.

The Moon continued to stare until someone moved down the slope along the way. Then she stood, peering. When a tree walked down the opposite slope, Lydia almost laughed. It was too ludicrous. It wasn't Pool's tree, either. The Moon watched them, muttering to herself before she stepped toward Lydia, hands out.

Lydia wrenched away. "Just kill me!" she said, rebellion rising within her if she wasn't going to get an end to the pain. "I'm not looking into the future again."

The worshipers wouldn't let her scramble away. She jerked her head from side to side and kicked, but one of the worshipers knocked her legs out from under her, and she fell to the ground, jarring her hip and setting her head to pounding harder.

A screech of metal made everyone freeze. The Moon looked over the edge of the crater. Lydia peeked between her feet and saw that a hatch on the *Atlas* had opened.

"No!" The Moon launched herself down the slope. "It's mine." Her power flowed ahead of her and knocked several bits off the *Atlas*. Then the worshipers were running around Lydia, blocking her view. She kept her back against a tree and closed her eyes, waiting to be trampled, but in a moment, they were all gone, running down the slope.

Lydia pushed to a standing position, not believing her eyes as another group sprang out of hiding on the other side of the crater and rushed the *Atlas* as well. The light was failing, but she could just make out the glint of armor: the army from Gale. Lydia tried to walk, but her foot slipped and she fell back against the tree. She had to get someone's attention, let them know she needed help.

When they were done fighting for their lives.

"Shit." She glanced around, searching for a miracle. When she spotted a broken branch, snapped in the haste of the worshipers' rush, she fell to her knees and squirmed until it was behind her, then rubbed the rope against the jagged sides.

She wondered how everyone could continue to fight in the dark, and as if summoned by her thought, the *Atlas* made a *whoomping* sound before lights shot from small points all around it, bathing the crater in a bright white glow that made Lydia squint. All the people milling around the outside froze as one light shone toward the sky, illuminating a lone figure standing atop a shard of rock.

The figure laughed, the hideous sound filling the crater from end to end. Everyone standing inside stiffened like wooden toys before they dropped and lay as still as the dead.

Chapter Twenty-four

S imon stood in the halls of the *Atlas*, the caution lights bathing the sloping walls in an amber glow. He shut his eyes, knowing this had to be a nightmare.

But when had he fallen asleep?

"Laz?" a voice behind him said.

Simon squeezed his eyes shut tighter, but when he opened them, the *Atlas* still surrounded him, and Dillon Tracey stood behind him in his old body, surprise and just a hint of malicious pleasure on his face.

Simon reached for his power but found nothing. The sensation was enough to stop him dead. He'd only been without his power for eight months of the past two hundred and fifty years, and he didn't enjoy the return to helplessness.

Dillon spread his arms as if welcoming Simon home. "No powers, eh? If you're gonna kill me again, you're gonna have to use your own two hands, you little shit."

Simon sneered. "I don't know why that man killed you the first time, but I'm sure you deserved it." He turned away and scanned the hall, trying to pinpoint his location. If he could do that, he could find a way out.

Dillon stayed on his heels, and Simon resisted the urge to say go away. He'd only refuse or laugh, and Simon didn't want to be drawn into a physical confrontation with him unless he had…

"Cordelia," he shouted as she walked across an adjoining hallway ahead.

She backed up. "Simon, what the fuck are—" She looked past him and stopped speaking, face falling into a murderous frown. She gestured Simon forward, and he hurried to stand behind her.

"Hiding like a baby again?" Dillon asked.

"I can't beat you in a fight, not without my power, and we both know it," Simon said. "Why don't you try kicking her around?"

Cordelia cracked her knuckles. "Yeah, *God*. No power is no problem for me."

He rolled his eyes. "I think our time would be better spent trying to find a way out of here, don't you?"

"Out of where?" Simon asked. "Do either of you remember going inside the *Atlas*?"

They shook their heads. A banging sound came from behind, and Simon glanced in that direction, seeing nothing, but the sound continued. When he looked back, Cordelia had looked toward the sound, too, and Dillon was gone.

"Cowardly fuck," Cordelia said.

"Forget him. We have friends here, and he doesn't."

"I didn't see him with the Sun-Moon worshipers, and Patricia was on the ground." She sighed. "That must have been him in the armor, not Lea. Horace probably thought he was Liam."

"We can work that out later," Simon said as he headed toward the banging. He stopped when he saw Pool and a few of her drushka standing together, hammering on the cover to a set of ducts.

"Pool!" Cordelia called.

The drushka turned as one, faces confused. "What is this place, Sa?" they asked together.

Cordelia stopped, pulling Simon to a halt as she looked from one drushkan face to another. "What the fuck?"

The drushka looked to her as one. "Sa?" Even their confused expressions were exactly the same.

Simon's mind raced. They hadn't gone into the *Atlas*; they weren't asleep. He cast around for a door, any door, and one hissed open for him. He found a bed and a desk, standard crew quarters, but the monitor was what interested him. It switched on without difficulty even though the *Atlas* was a wreck. When it showed the ship as being in orbit around Calamity, he wasn't even surprised.

"We're in Naos's mind."

Lydia had given up on ever feeling her hands again when the rope snapped. Her arms dropped as if they had weights attached to the ends, and she wanted to sag to the ground and rub them together, but she forced herself to stand.

She walked to the edge of the crater. The *Atlas* still glowed, and the people were still scattered like grain and unmoving. She hesitated to go to them. Maybe whatever Naos had done only affected those she could see. Lydia ducked behind a tree and looked to where Naos was still standing. She'd gone as still as a statue, staring down at her victims, her laughter done, though she still smiled.

Lydia glanced around, but just as before, no thoughtful worshiper had left her a weapon. Well, if a weapon was needed, Fajir would make one, so Lydia picked up the largest rock she could find that would still fit in her palm. She crept through the trees, trying to be quiet and straining to see with only the glow of the *Atlas* below to guide her.

As she came closer to Naos, she stepped in a shallow hole, and the sound of crackling leaves and snapping twigs made her freeze. Naos didn't move. Did she think she had everyone? That seemed like the height of overconfidence. Lydia crept closer, studying her: the unkempt hair, the tattered blue clothing, the one empty eye socket. She was taller than Lydia and as thin as a sapling. Her hands twitched, the nails ragged and splintered.

Lydia hated the idea of hurting people, but as Fajir would say, this one definitely deserved it, and Lydia had a field of people to wake up.

The sickening thump of stone against skull made Lydia's stomach turn. As Naos crumpled, Lydia cried out and staggered back, the rock falling from her hands. She scurried forward again instantly, ready to shout that everyone should quit fighting, that she'd done what no one else could.

The bodies lay as still as Naos.

"Oh shit." Lydia knelt at Naos's side and turned her over. She still breathed, still smiled, and whatever she'd done was still happening.

"Did you think you could beat a god with a rock?" someone asked.

Lydia whirled around, scrambling to find her rock again, but Samira stepped out of the shadows, and Lydia nearly wept. She stumbled toward her friend and hugged her tightly. "What are you doing here?"

"I might ask you the same thing," Samira muttered into her hair. "I'm not alone."

Lydia looked past her to several plains dwellers. They nodded, and she lifted a hand to wave, then stopped, seeing another person step from the shadows, her face half hidden by tattoos.

Lydia's breath shuddered out, and she was out of Samira's arms and into Fajir's in a second. All of Samira's sighing and groaning couldn't have stopped her from kissing Fajir over and over.

"Save the questions," Samira said before Lydia could even ask. "And let's answer, what are we going to do?"

Lydia stepped out of Fajir's embrace. "I really thought the rock would do it."

"Why don't we try a sword?" Fajir asked.

"As much as I hate you, you might be right," Samira said, though she had the grace to grimace.

"If it's just power," Lydia said, "knocking her unconscious should have helped. Killing her might make this"—she gestured to the crater—"permanent."

"We need a macro or a telepath," Samira said.

Fajir held a hand toward the crater. "After you."

"Listen, jerk—"

"Enough," Lydia said. "I always knew I was going to have to sepa-rate you two. Whatever Naos did might be restricted to this area, like the Sun-Moon's telepathic shield. We need to get someone out, not go in."

"Throw a rope over someone?" Fajir said.

Lydia shook her head. "Don't have one."

"Perhaps we could shove one free with a tree branch."

"Before you go poking holes in people," Samira said as she walked past them, "let's see who's close enough for me to grab with my power."

Lydia grinned at her back as she followed. "I'm so happy you're here, Samira. And so is Fajir."

"Speak for yourself," Fajir mumbled.

Lyshus lay in Shiv's arms like a wooden doll, lifeless eyes staring at the ceiling. He lived; she could feel him, but he would not rouse no matter her words.

"If this is your help," she called, "I do not want it."

No one answered. She should have known the help would be naught but a ruse. Despair choked her, but she clawed through it. She had to find a way out of this cold metal place.

Turning a corner brought her to a group of her mother's drushka. She sighed in relief, though she did not know how they could help her.

She opened her mouth to speak when she saw how strangely they acted, bending or reaching as one and running into the backs of one another.

When they spoke, saying, "What is this place, Sa?" Shiv jumped. She cast around for Sa but saw no one else.

"Are you well?" she asked.

They turned to her as one. "Daughter?"

Shiv leapt back from them. "Shi'a'na?" She had heard tales of how the old Shi had dominated the minds of her drushka, but no story was like this. Shiv turned and fled, carrying Lyshus. When she heard a sound from ahead, she ducked back, staying out of sight.

A woman marched down the hall, dark hair fluttering around her shoulders as she strode. "Naos?" she shouted. "Patricia Dué, I know you're here! Show yourself." A blue circle sewn in glittery thread adorned her back, and Shiv waited until she had passed to continue on.

Shiv walked for what felt like miles, and the shining hallways did not change except that some had doors, and some did not. Shiv avoided the doors, not wanting to see what was within. At last she reached something different, a hole cut in the wall. She looked through it and saw a world of starlight above and below. She was in the sky; space, as the humans called it. Before Lyshus, before she had become a queen, the idea would have excited her. Now, though, she wanted to go home and make Naos keep her promise.

"It's beautiful, isn't it?" Horace's voice said, and only the fact that she recognized the sound kept her from clawing his face off as she turned.

"Shawness."

"Not here," he said with a shake of his head. "Here, I'm the same as everyone else."

She did not know whether the thought comforted or pained him, so she tried to pull him away. "Come. There are many strange people about."

"Tell me about it." He stepped past her and led the way to one of the rooms. The door hissed open on its own. A host of drushka waited inside, all making the same gestures and saying the same words. "I've been collecting them." He raised his voice. "Pool?"

The drushka turned as one, and Shiv was horrified to see Nettle and Reach among them. "Shawness? You have found another?"

"It's Shiv."

"Wait for us there, shawness, daughter. We shall find you." The drushka began to walk until they bunched up against the wall and walked in place.

Horace pulled Shiv from the room. "So far, the ones I put in haven't gotten out, but they'll run right over you if you stay inside."

"What is happening?" Shiv said, her mind turning in too many directions at once.

"I've been talking to Simon through Pool and…them," he said, nodding at the door. "Simon said Lyshus can use human telepathy?"

"Yes, but he is…" She lifted him and held him close.

Horace studied him a moment. "Simon thinks we're in Naos's mind. I think she pulled in you and Pool through Lyshus, but since all of Pool's drushka are connected to her…" Again, he nodded at the door.

"As Sa would say, creepy," Shiv said.

Horace smiled. "Very. But maybe keeping you in here is keeping Lyshus unconscious."

"So, if we free ourselves, he should awaken?"

"Won't know until we try." He sighed and leaned against the hall. "This is all so strange that it's hard to be irritated by it."

"Not all feel as such." She told him of the angry woman.

"Sounds like the Moon. We should avoid everyone we don't know. Powers don't work here, and I don't know if we can be hurt."

Shiv blinked, then kicked his ankle.

He sprang back, eyes wide. "Ow!"

"Now we know."

He sputtered a laugh. "Why kick me and not the wall?"

"That is not smart, shawness," she said slowly. "The wall cannot feel."

He gave her a wry look. "Right."

She wondered if they should collect more drushka, but when she turned to ask, Horace was gone. "Shawness?" Shiv walked forward a few steps and peered around the hall. Nothing. "Shawness?" she called softly.

Still nothing. He had not gone inside the door as she had not heard the hiss. She went a few halls over, tearing tiny strips off her leather shirt to mark the way, but saw nothing.

Horace had vanished.

The cold hallways of the *Atlas* became the cold ground of the mountainside in a snap that left Horace gasping. He sat up, coughing and flailing. He'd gotten used to one uniquely strange situation just to be pulled into another.

"Are you all right?"

Samira was bending down and peering into his face, and Lydia the ex-prophet was behind her along with Fajir.

"What?" he managed.

Samira knelt in front of him and smiled. She'd always had a comforting smile, but how could she be so calm when they were...

"You were down there," Samira said, nodding to the side.

Horace looked and saw nearly everyone he cared about sprawled on the ground inside the crater. "How?"

"Naos did something," Samira said. "When I...rolled you out of the crater, you woke up." She reached up, and he felt a tug on his hair as she pulled a sprig of greenery free. "Sorry about that."

Horace looked down to find himself filthy, but he couldn't be bothered. "Naos did something." He frowned, trying to remember. Shiv had accused Liam of not being Liam, then the hatch had opened. He'd barely had time to wonder what to do when a screaming horde of people raced down the crater's side, and Cordelia led her group to fight the horde. He'd run for the side of the crater and then...

"The lights of the *Atlas* came on," Horace said, "and then I was in there."

"On the *Atlas*?" Samira asked.

"That's what it looked like, but...it felt like a nightmare." The drushka acting as one, all of them without their power, and the halls that just went on and on. He shook his head and reached for his power again, comforted when it answered his call. He healed himself and those around them with the barest thought.

"I hit her with a rock," Lydia said suddenly. "Naos, I mean, because I thought it would wake everyone up, but it didn't."

Movement to the side drew his attention. A group of plains dwellers hauled a body through the trees and laid it next to him. It was the woman who'd been laughing from the heights: Naos.

She didn't seem very threatening now. Her face was slack, one eye closed, and the other a divot where an eye should be. Simon had always described her empty socket as a black hole or a well of blue light, but without her power to fool people, it was just an empty space.

"Can you figure out what she's done?" Samira asked.

Horace touched her face. As harmless as she looked now, he really didn't want to go back inside her mind. But everyone else was stuck there, and he wasn't just going to leave them.

He took a deep breath. He'd been wanting to be a hero for a long time. Now was his chance. "Get your rock ready," he said. "If I start acting like a mad god, give me a few hard hits."

Samira seemed pained by the idea. "I really don't think—"

"I'll do it if you don't have the stomach for it," Fajir said.

"Oh, fuck off, you."

Horace tuned them out and touched Naos's forehead again. With another deep breath, he immersed himself in his telepathic power and opened his mind to hers.

"Oh God, oh God, oh God," Patricia said over and over. She knew a few things: she was back in the hellscape of her *Atlas* memories, she didn't have her power, and there was nowhere to run.

Soft singing echoed in her ears. She put her hands over them and rocked back and forth in the *Atlas*'s gleaming hallways. "No, not again." She screamed, trying to drown out the singing, but as always, it was in her head.

"Why?" she shouted, the sound echoing crazily through the halls. "We were free of each other! Why?"

At least she had company. She'd seen Sun-Moon worshipers and paladins as well as pockets of strange-acting drushka. Real people or more nightmares? It hardly mattered. She ignored them all. A few had tried to grab her, but she slid through the wall away from them. They didn't understand how this place worked. You could change it, move through it, or interact with it.

You just couldn't leave.

Patricia had caught a glimpse of herself in the shiny black plastic of a toolkit locker. Her old face, her old eyes, the old hair she could never quite tame. She wore her blue flight suit with Dué stitched on the breast. At least Naos hadn't made her live with the empty socket. She no doubt reserved that honor for herself.

Patricia sobbed and curled herself tighter into a ball. "Why, why, why?" she kept asking. She tried to tell herself to get the fuck up, to do something before it was too late, but time was meaningless here. Naos hadn't even visited her, probably too busy watching all her new friends with glee. She couldn't possess people anymore, so she'd dragged them all into her instead, but Patricia bet that no one else would get a turn to drive the body.

"Patricia?" a voice asked softly.

Patricia laughed and squeezed herself tighter. "You don't need to whisper. You can shout, and it won't make any difference."

A hand touched her arm. She jerked away, prepared to glide through the wall again, but a soothing wave of power made her sit up and gape at Horace.

"How did you…" She scooted away from him, panic choking her. "You're her wearing his face. Get away from me!" She slid through the wall into one of the ubiquitous rooms that always lined these hallways. Gasping, she reached for the controls and locked the door. Maybe he wouldn't know how to work it, but if he was just her, then—

"Patricia," he said from behind her. "It's all right."

He had his hands out, placating, but that was how *she* always looked before she struck. "Leave me alone, Naos," she said, sobbing around the words. "Please."

Begging now. Patricia had never hated herself so much.

Again, those soothing waves washed over her. "It's all right. It's really me. Horace." He glanced around as if the walls could hear them. Which they could. "I'm outside the crater now. I went into Naos's mind."

She laughed and knew it sounded crazy for all his calming power. "You were out, and you came back in?" She laughed and laughed until she sobbed once more. "Please, let me trade places with you. I won't waste my time outside again, I swear it, I swear." She grabbed his hands, but he felt brittle, as if he might dissolve like smoke if she squeezed. "Get me out."

"I've tried," he said with a sigh. "It's as if you're all tied together. Her mind is your mind and…" He sighed again. "The only thing I've thought to do is…bring some of you closer together."

Patricia tried to think about his words, but the meaning escaped her. "Bring us? Out of the crater?"

"No, Samira can't reach any more of you." He waved vaguely. "It's a long story, but if I heal you and Naos together again—"

Patricia fled. "I knew it was you," she shouted as she ran, phasing through the walls, willing them to change, but she couldn't bend them like she used to, couldn't transform them into the park on Earth where she'd met her fiancé Jack, couldn't have the restaurant where they'd dined together so many times, couldn't have her parents' house, or the first ship she'd ever flown. It was all *Atlas, Atlas, Atlas!*

"Think of something else!" she roared at a group of people as she passed. "Something besides this stupid fucking hallway!" But this place took time to learn.

"Patricia!" Horace's voice said. "I'm not *here* like the others. I'm using a telepathic signal, so running from me is useless."

"I will not go back!"

"Neither will I," another voice said, and oh, she knew this one: her inner darkness given form.

"Where are you?" Patricia asked as she stopped. "It's about time you showed your real face. My face."

Horace appeared beside her, and Patricia pointed to him. "Not that one. Show me you!"

Naos appeared in Patricia's form with Patricia's hair flowing around her head as if she walked along the ocean floor. Her missing eye was a blaze of light, and she wore a black satin evening gown better than Patricia had ever worn anything in her life.

And she continued with this Horace façade, too. That was new.

"He wants to put Humpty Dumpty back together again," Naos said, turning her glare on Horace.

"He?" Patricia shrieked. "It's you! Everything here is you!"

"Patricia, please," Horace said.

"Don't talk to me, talk to her, talk to yourself!" Patricia laughed again because what else could she do.

"See?" Naos said to Horace. "I don't want this crazy person back. I'd let her go if I didn't think she'd ruin everything."

"What everything?" Horace asked as if he wasn't part of a whole. "What is your plan? You can't take over all these bodies. Your own body is lying out cold on the side of a mountain."

"I need them!" Naos said, curling one hand into a fist. "I need purpose, and she took it, so I'm getting something new."

Horace drew back. "That doesn't make any sense."

"Welcome to the fucking club," Patricia said.

"Let me heal you," Horace said, his hands out. "Let me make you whole."

"I won't go back to being her!" she and Naos shouted at the same time.

"Neither of you is going to be the other one," he said, and it sounded as if he was getting angry at last. "You'll be like two united flames, and you won't know where one ends and the other begins."

"No," they said again. Patricia looked at Naos just as Naos looked at her. They'd never been so in sync, and it seemed as if they were closer together in the hall, though Patricia didn't remember moving.

"Snake!" Patricia shouted at Horace. "You're already doing it!"

His eyes went wide, and he blinked out of sight.

"We have to find him," Naos said. "Before he does any more damage."

Patricia whirled on her, seeing her movement mirrored by her counterpart so that she was talking to Naos's back. "Let me go, and I'll kill him outside."

"You'll just run from me."

"Not before I take care of him, I swear!"

Naos turned slowly, and it took everything in Patricia not to turn as well. "I don't believe you."

Patricia started from the pain in Naos's left eye, the pain of loneliness, purposelessness. When Patricia had gone, she'd taken her own sense of direction in life, her ambition, and what was left of her inside Naos had acted out in the only way it knew how: by trying to claim everything because it didn't know what it wanted.

"I'm sorry," Patricia said. She didn't think she'd ever say those words to Naos, but she'd been capable of self-pity since she was a child.

The two of them laughed together.

"Split up," they said. "We'll find him."

Sometimes, being split in two came in handy.

Chapter Twenty-five

Dillon sighed and ran his hands along the walls of the *Atlas* just like he used to when he'd wandered this ship. He'd been as bored then as he was now, but at least then, Lazlo had been his friend. Now, he had no one.

He was just wondering when Naos was going to show herself when Horace popped into view in front of him and blinked at him before he frowned. "Of course I ran into you before anyone else."

"How are you blinking around like that?" Dillon asked, ignoring the scorn.

"I just reach for the nearest mind."

"You have your powers?" Now that was interesting.

Horace frowned. "You're much more talkative than you were in the real world. I guess being in here freed you from Patricia's thumb."

Dillon sighed, not really caring anymore about who knew what. "I wasn't in my own body out there, jackass. Patricia hollowed out my old body and made herself a sex puppet she named Jonah. She made the mistake of keeping my personality in her head, and I bugged her until she put me in the mayor's body."

"The mayor's...Liam? You were controlling Liam the entire time?"

"Surprise," Dillon said flatly. "How did you keep your powers?"

Horace backed up a step. "Is Liam here, too?"

Dillon cracked his neck and tried not to lose his patience. They were all going to be here for a while, so he didn't want to pick a fight, especially with someone who still had power. "Patricia killed him. I had nothing to do with it. I just went where she put me."

Horace sneered. "Oh yes, I'm sure you wept at the loss of life." He shook his head. "You *Atlas* people are unbelievable."

"Yeah, we're a terrible lot. So, your powers?"

Horace glared at him, at their surroundings. "If it wasn't for all the innocent people caught in here, I'd leave you all to rot except for Simon."

"Like he's so innocent." But Horace would find out one day just how nasty Simon could be. Dillon remembered the feel of the knife going in his neck as Simon had looked him in the eye.

"Shut up," Horace said. "I need to heal Naos and Patricia back together. When she's sane again, she should release you."

So, there was a way out. Dillon licked his lips and tried not to appear too eager. "Need some help?"

"Oh, so you're more interested in getting out than in reclaiming your power?"

Dillon's teeth clenched together. "Yeah, I want out, and not just for the reasons you think. Two of the mothers of my children are in here, too." He'd avoided them like the plague, but still. "And I'd like to make sure my kids grow up safe. I'm the one who asked you about them, remember?"

Well, Horace had reminded him first, but he wasn't going to point that out.

Horace frowned but seemed as if he might be listening. "Naos and Patricia don't want to go back together, that's the trouble. And with the amount of power they have, I'm not sure it would work anyway. Natalya didn't seem to be doing good on her own without Naos."

Dillon nodded as he thought about it. "They evened each other out. You need a third person willing to be part of the crazy." When Horace stared, Dillon put up his hands. "Not me. A telepath would be best, someone who needs a stabilizer of their own."

As Horace asked who that might be, Dillon's mind raced through the people he'd seen in here, one in particular: Lieutenant Marlowe, otherwise known as the Moon. She'd been without her Sun, shouting and stalking the halls like a lunatic. When her worshipers tried to follow in her footsteps, she'd screamed at them to go away, and he'd heard one of them call her a widow. At least in Naos's mind, they could all understand one another.

A widow to them meant a partner had died, and the Moon only had one of importance.

"The Sun's dead," he said quietly. When Horace looked at him, he added, "I knew the Moon as Lieutenant Meredith Marlowe. The Sun was Lieutenant Charles Christian. They were telepathically tied together ever since the accident. I'm surprised she survived his death. It's probably just rage keeping her going."

"The Sun-Moon," Horace said, brow furrowed as if thinking. "I wonder…"

Horace reached telepathically for the Moon, and she seized him like a drowning person would clutch a life raft.

"Charles?" she asked.

"No," he said sadly. He'd been coaxing the telepathic signals of Naos and Patricia together, trying to knit them as he'd sew a wound, but they were resisting, one half stubbornly holding on to all of the others. "But I've got a new partner if you're willing."

He expected her to recoil, but she seemed reluctant to let go of his signal, clinging to a remnant of power she still had that no one could take from her, her ability to telepathically connect to just one person. She'd depended on that connection, he saw. She thrived on it, so different from Patricia and Naos. Of course, the Sun-Moon were two become one, and Naos and Patricia were one split into two. Strange that the latter pair resisted the most.

He showed the telepathic signal he was trying to create to the Moon, and she grabbed it as she'd latched on to him, further drawing Patricia's two halves together. A mind scream echoed through the halls of the *Atlas*, and Horace knew that if he opened his real eyes on the mountainside, Naos's body would be screaming, too. He couldn't hold them together and reached out, searching for more power, anything.

"Horace?" Simon's voice, though Horace couldn't see him.

"Simon!" Horace grunted as he tried to hold on to the three telepathic threads. The Moon was helping, but the other two fought like thrashing geavers. "I'm trying to get Naos and Patricia back together." One thread pulled hard, and Horace ached as if it tried to yank part of him away with it. "I don't know if I can."

"Breathe," Simon said, his mind radiating love and confidence. "I never thought it was possible, but if anyone can do it, it's you."

Horace pulled himself back together under the strain, wondering if his mind could be torn apart like his body. Simon murmured to him, words of encouragement and hope.

"I love you, Simon," Horace muttered. "I'm so sorry I was such an ass."

"I should have tried to understand you better. I'm sorry, too. I love you, and you can do this. Bring me back to you."

Pain gripped Horace, but he kept pushing, even though he could hear Patricia and Naos yelling that they'd never go back, never be subsumed, but neither was going anywhere, just blending into the whole. He kept pushing, tying their signals together, bolstered by the Moon until the two voices finally became one.

Shiv awoke to screaming coming from the top of the crater. She had been gathering drushka for Shi'a'na and searching for Horace when Lyshus began to writhe in her arms, his breathing growing frantic. She had cast about for a cause, had called for help, but her mother had no answers, nor did Simon or Sa or anyone in the world. Shiv had screamed for Naos to let them go, that killing Lyshus was unacceptable if that was all the "help" she offered.

Then her eyes had snapped open, and she heard screaming along the crater's edge.

She sat up and saw drushka sitting up all around her. The humans stayed down. Her tree stood nearby, and someone knelt at its base, but the screaming was not coming from there.

By the light of the human ship, she saw a tiny hand sticking out from beyond the kneeling figure. Lyshus. He had fallen from the tree.

Shiv leapt to her feet and ran over, expecting to see a shawness helping him, but Enka bent over his body, one hand holding his mouth shut while the other pinched his nose. Rage blinded Shiv, and she charged. Enka stumbled as Shiv grappled with her, but she got a foot under Shiv's body and heaved, throwing Shiv to the side.

"Liar!" Shiv spat. "Eater of words. You said you would protect us."

"I said I would protect you, queen," Enka said. "He had trapped you."

"Naos trapped us!" Shiv dashed forward, striking with a claw, but Enka batted her hand away. She had not drawn her spear, but she would not simply let herself be killed, either.

"He lives, queen." Reach's voice. Shiv wanted to hug her, but she would deal with this deceiver first.

Enka drew her spear at last, and Shiv snarled at the thought that Enka would harm another queen, but Shi'a'na's drushka had gathered around, advancing upon her.

"Come away, daughter," Shi'a'na said. "And let the warriors do warrior business."

Shiv listened to her mother's wisdom and stepped away as the warriors closed over Enka like a fist.

The humans were stirring, and Reach was singing over Lyshus. Shiv tried not to give in to despair as she knelt at his side. He lived, but he was still a queen, and they would never have a tribe, and all hope was lost. She tried to take comfort in the fact that she would at least see Naos's defeat.

She heard arguing. Sa and Simon were kneeling over three people, two of them bound. Her Liam who was not Liam had been made to strip his armor, and the one Shiv knew to be the Storm Lord was bound next to him. Simon leaned over a woman who still lay on the ground.

"She's dead," Simon said before he closed the woman's mismatched eyes.

"Fuck." Sa grabbed the shirt of Liam-who-was-not. "Don't think you're safe, asshole. We're going to get you out of Liam however we can and put you back where you belong."

"I'm afraid not," a voice said, and Shiv recognized her as the woman who had laughed before everyone had fallen. Naos. She walked into the crater with shawness Horace and a few others by her side. "The mayor, Liam, he's dead."

Sa went completely still, and Shiv wanted to cry out, wanted to leap to Sa so they could all keen in mourning, but she could not move.

"That's a load of shit," Sa said, her voice quavering. "His body's right there!"

"She...I destroyed his mind. I'm sorry."

"She is." A woman at Naos's side linked hands with her. Shiv recognized her from the ship. The one they called the Moon. "Our minds are linked now."

Cordelia raised her arms and lifted them. "What the... How did..."

Anger dimmed Shiv's vision, but still she hoped, even with the news that Liam was dead. She stood. "Will you help me now? Or must I kill you?"

Naos's one eye turned toward her. "She...I never really intended to help you, though she was curious to see if she could."

Shiv stalked toward her, claws at the ready. The warriors had claimed vengeance over Enka, but Shiv would take her own vengeance now.

Horace stepped in front of her. "Wait, there might be something we can do if we work together."

Shiv paused. She had been about to warn him to stay out of her way, but the promise of help stayed her lips. Would she always be chasing it? Would she always be swayed? "Do you speak the truth, shawness?" she whispered. "I am tired of human lies."

Simon approached her other side and took Horace's hand. "Let us try," he said. "I'll keep an eye on them." He nodded toward Naos and the Moon.

Shiv supposed she had to trust yet again. She led them to Lyshus's side.

"You fail," she said to Naos, "you die."

The Moon frowned at Shiv, but Naos only sighed. "Seems fair."

Cordelia was getting sick of not knowing what the fuck was going on. She'd been floundering in someone's mind one minute and had come awake in the next, and now Patricia was dead, Liam was dead, the Storm Lord was maybe stuck in Liam's old body—but they still had the Storm Lord's body, too—and Naos and the Moon were acting like the Sun-Moon, and they'd joined forces with Simon and Horace to heal Shiv's fucking kid.

And Fajir was here, too, and she wasn't trying to kill anyone.

Cordelia went to Nettle. "Who am I supposed to punch here?"

"No one, Sa. It seemed the fight happened without punching, somehow."

"Fucking mind shit."

"Indeed."

Cordelia turned in a circle. Liam was dead. If what Naos said was true, he'd been dead for a while. She'd been running around as if everything was normal—as normal as her life got—and he'd been dead.

Every drink they'd ever had, every time they'd cried on each other's shoulders, every secret they'd shared. Dead like him. She'd never see his smile, hear his voice.

No, that wasn't true. Those had been stolen.

She marched to Liam's old body, the fucking Storm Lord's body and punched him in the face so hard, he nearly did a backward somersault.

He sat up as quickly as someone could with their hands tied behind their back and sneered at her with bloody teeth. "Untie my hands and try that again."

"I should fucking kill you," Cordelia said as Nettle grabbed her shoulders. "Fucking asshole, let his body be as dead as the rest of him." Her voice broke, and she let Nettle turn her away, not wanting to give that motherfucker the satisfaction of seeing her cry.

"Sa," Nettle said as her arms went around Cordelia's shoulders.

Cordelia leaned in for a moment, wanting so much to let go, but she pulled away. "No time for tears right now." She cleared her throat harshly and nodded at Lyshus and tried to distract herself. "So, what's happening here?"

Pool's sigh answered them. Her mouth was open, sharp teeth showing as her lips turned down in grief. "What I knew would happen, Sa, the only thing that could."

Cordelia looked back and forth, confused. "They're killing him?"

"Ahwa, no," Nettle said. "They change his blood, his and the young queen's. With the separation, perhaps the power will be different, too." She took Cordelia's hand, and her own head hung as she shared in everyone's sorrow.

Cordelia put an arm around both of them. Everyone had some serious grief in their future.

"Shiv will no longer be my daughter," Pool said softly. "And Lyshus will no longer be her tribe."

"Won't he still be a queen?" Cordelia asked.

"Only time will know." Pool moved toward Shiv. If she was right, Shiv would be alone in the world after the "healing," but maybe she'd be able to have a tribe of her own.

It would have made Cordelia happy if everything else wasn't so fucked up. She looked to where the Sun-Moon worshipers were still milling around in one corner, then to where the two Storm Lords sat, body and mind. The world wouldn't miss any of them, and her grief was giving way to anger again.

"I know that look," Fajir called.

Cordelia pointed to her. "I don't need any lip from you. What the fuck are you even doing here?"

"You want to hurt someone."

"What did I just say?" Cordelia stepped closer.

Fajir shrugged and shook her head. "Don't do it; do not start this fight again. You know that if I'm saying that, it must be true."

That was a personality shift as dramatic as any Cordelia had seen that day. "What the fuck happened to you?"

Fajir smiled, and Lydia slipped an arm around her waist.

"Never mind," Cordelia said as she turned away. "I guess love really does change everything."

"Ahya," Nettle whispered as she laid her head on Cordelia's armored shoulder. "Did you ever think you would say so?"

"Not until I met you." Cordelia watched the bizarre happenings around them and wondered at all the strange things that had swiftly become commonplace, love being the least strange among them.

They camped in the crater, everyone curious to crawl over the *Atlas*. Horace explained that he'd tied the two halves of Patricia back together along with the Moon, who seemed happy enough, smiling as she glided along at Patricia's side.

Patricia had abandoned her new body for her old one. Horace insisted they bury that body on the hillside with a marker bearing the name "Kora," what she'd been called before being pulled into a journey that had nothing to do with her.

It was one among many crimes to place at Naos's feet, though she seemed contrite now, sane as long as she was tied to someone else. When the Moon had seen Fajir, she'd snarled and threatened, but Cordelia pointed out that if they started swinging at one another for everyone who had been killed, it was never going to stop.

No one argued that she'd already gotten a hit in.

Fajir had smiled at Cordelia's words, and it took everything in Cordelia's willpower and Nettle's restraining hand not to knock her teeth in.

Patricia, who winced anytime someone called her Naos, donned an eye patch and claimed she'd make up to the world for all the damage she'd caused, including giving up the *Atlas* for the humans to split among them. After that, she planned to return to Celeste with the Moon, who didn't want to rob her people of two gods at once. When the now Moon worshipers had recovered from the death of one of their gods, Patricia said she and the Moon would travel around their area of the world, trying to fix some of the destruction that still lingered after the last battle.

Best of all, they were taking Dillon-fucking-Tracey with them, the man who used to be the Storm Lord and who now lived in Liam's body. Cordelia was all for killing him, but as she'd said, once someone began down that road, they'd all end up dead. Instead, she watched in satisfaction as Patricia and the Moon bound him with a mental shackle that still let him complain and lament his fate while not letting him use his power or get too far away.

It seemed a fitting punishment. And with Patricia's macro-psychokinetic powers healing him, Dillon would remain their prisoner for a long time. He didn't grouse as much as Cordelia expected, but she didn't think that was because he knew he deserved his fate. No doubt he'd try to escape as soon as possible.

Simon pledged to look after the Storm Lord's children, and the Moon said she'd give back the captives she'd taken, the rebellious yafanai left in her camp. Even if they deserved to be punished, any unborn children among the mix only deserved a clean start.

Miriam and Victoria thought the Storm Lord's punishment fitting, too, though they got in a few snarky barbs now and again that Dillon seemed to ignore, but Cordelia noted the angry flush creeping up his collar.

Patricia introduced everyone to Jonah, the personality she'd created in the Storm Lord's old body. He seemed as confused as the rest of them, and Cordelia pitied him. He'd been created to worship one person, and she didn't really exist anymore. The new Patricia even seemed ashamed of him. Cordelia wondered if she should make Patricia take him anyway as a reminder of what she'd done.

Then she had a better idea.

"Come to Gale, Jonah," Cordelia said. "I could use your help, then you'll be free to do whatever."

He looked to Patricia. "Mistress?"

She winced. "It's up to you, but I'd like it if you did what she said."

It seemed as good as an order as far as he was concerned.

The next day, Patricia and the Moon left first, their worshipers loaded down with metal pieces. Shiv carried out the rest along with quite a bit of metal herself. They collected the yafanai rebels from the abandoned Sun-Moon camp and picked up Jon Lea, who'd been wandering around the mountains, looking for anyone.

Once out on the plains, Shiv stopped, declaring that now she'd take her tree into the swamp.

She and Pool stared at each other, and Cordelia bet it felt weird not feeling that familial connection. They pressed their foreheads together as two queens might. Lyshus stood to the side, looking between them, but Shiv didn't seem as drawn to him as before. He *really* had no one, and Cordelia didn't know if he'd ever have a drushkan connection again. Horace said he seemed to have lost the power to connect to queens' trees, but as a drushka, he'd miss that fundamental bond the rest of them shared.

Her heart went out to him and she knelt, waving him over. "You're coming home with us, kiddo."

He grinned and gripped her hand. Nettle laid long fingers across Cordelia's unarmored neck. "You never cease to be a wonder, Sa."

Shiv was watching them with a bittersweet smile. "Will I ever have a tribe?"

"You are no longer a queen's daughter," Pool said sadly. "You should be able."

"There is one way to find out," Reach said as she stepped forward. "Queen," she said to Pool, "long have I been in your branches, but you chose me as your ambassador to the humans for a reason. I enjoy stepping into the unknown."

Shiv's mouth fell open as Reach bowed her head. "Queen, may I enter the safety of your hands and branches?"

Shiv looked to Pool, her mouth working. "Shawness, are you sure?"

"It could mean your death," Pool said.

Cordelia recalled the story of Lyshus's parents, who died trying to take Shiv as their queen. But if the connection to Pool was truly severed…

Shiv reached a shaky hand behind her and rubbed her thumb against a sharp piece of bark until golden blood flowed. Reach took it with a smile and placed it in her mouth, drinking the blood, making a connection, before she pressed her forehead to Shiv's.

The whole camp held its breath. Cordelia looked to Simon, who nodded. If Reach began to die, he was ready to help.

After a moment, both Shiv and Reach opened their eyes and smiled. "My queen," Reach said softly.

Shiv threw her arms around Reach's shoulders and pulled her close. "My shawness!"

Cordelia breathed out, relieved beyond words. Nettle lifted Lyshus in her arms and kissed his cheek. Cordelia wondered if she was thinking of her long-departed son. Lyshus wouldn't be alone at all.

Shiv agreed to come with them as far as Pool's tree so Reach could collect Little Paul. Then they'd venture together into the swamp to live for a time with the old drushka.

"So that we may sing a new story," Shiv said when Cordelia asked why.

All that was left was to return to Gale and plan Liam's funeral, someone who'd given his life in service to Gale. Cordelia invited everyone to get drunk with her, but even before that, she talked with Simon, Horace, Miriam, and Victoria about her plans for Jonah.

Miriam had been glaring at him since they'd met him. He might not have the Storm Lord's brain, but that didn't stop her from hating his face. Still, she agreed to Cordelia's plan. If they couldn't kick the Storm Lord's ass, they could at least get rid of him for good in the eyes of their people.

All of Gale, including the rebel yafanai who'd been healed by Simon and Horace, watched as the "Storm Lord" told his people he'd been called back to heaven, and that they should go back to doing things the way they'd done before he'd arrived, with everyone working together and relying on one another.

Then he vanished in a puff of fire, much to the delight of the crowd.

Under a telepathic shield, Cordelia sneaked him out of the city and loaded him with supplies. Simon changed his appearance, darkening his hair, eyes, and skin. In the garb of a plains dweller, he walked wonderingly toward Wuran's camp, and from there, who knew?

"Is Pool going back into the swamp?" Cordelia asked as she watched Jonah walk into the plains. Everyone else had faded back inside the city, gearing up for a massive party to celebrate Liam's life. There'd be plenty of time for tears then, but for now, Cordelia wrapped herself in hope.

"Perhaps, Sa, but whether she does or not, I will stay with you." She nuzzled Cordelia's cheek.

Cordelia turned to her, heart lifting in her chest. "Won't you miss them?"

"I would miss you more. Besides, Horace will need a new drushkan ambassador when he runs for mayor."

Cordelia barked a laugh. "Well, he won't be bored then!"

"Ahya. I love you, my paladin captain."

"I love you, too, my drushkan ambassador."

They kissed for a long time, and if anyone saw, they didn't interrupt, much to Cordelia's happiness. No one wanted to get in the way of human-drushkan diplomacy, after all.

EPILOGUE

L ydia looked back at Gale and heard the sounds of celebration in the dying light. People were laughing and singing, all of them celebrating the mayor's life. It seemed a world away from the small campfire she lay in front of with her head resting on Fajir's taut stomach.

"Do you wish you were there?" Fajir asked.

"Not even a little." Lydia turned her head to the side and nuzzled Fajir's bare skin. Their tent lay just behind them, but with no one else around and the evening pleasantly cool, Lydia saw no reason to hurry inside, enjoying the heat of the fire.

"No regrets?"

Lydia frowned. "Are you going to keep asking me if I'm happy until I have to show you with more sex?"

Fajir paused for a moment. "Yes."

With a laugh, Lydia tickled her. "I got what I needed from them." It had been simpler than she thought. When she'd told Simon that she didn't want her power, he'd taken it within moments, and it hadn't even hurt. She knew it was silly, but she felt lighter after it was gone, never to tempt or trap her again.

"That seems a very selfish thought from someone who cares as much as you," Fajir said.

Lydia surged upward, pinning Fajir back. Her black hair spread over the blanket, and she smiled, eyes sparkling in the light. She could get loose in a moment, but the fact that she didn't and the feel of their bodies pressed together made Lydia warm with desire. She kissed Fajir soundly, all thoughts of visions or grief departing.

"Where shall we go tomorrow?" Fajir asked.

"Wherever you like. I only have one errand to run."

Fajir quirked an eyebrow.

"I have to convince Samira to find Mamet and either give her a proper good-bye or a proper apology."

Fajir groaned.

Lydia kissed her again. "You don't have to come. And I don't have to see her until tomorrow, so…" She glanced at the tent as the wind picked up. "It's getting a little chilly."

With a grin, Fajir rolled them into the tent, making Lydia laugh, and she didn't need a special power to look forward to the future.

Selected Cast

Caroline Gerard—Deceased telepathic yafanai, Dillon Tracey's lover, and Evan Tracey's mother. Killed by Simon Lazlo.

Cordelia Sa Ross—Former lieutenant in the paladins, Paul Ross's niece, Liam Carmichael's best friend, and Nettle's lover. Has the ability to astral project and can speak to Pool and Simon Lazlo in spirit form.

Dillon Tracey, aka the Storm Lord—Colonel from the *Atlas*, god of Gale, electrokinetic, and father of Evan Tracey and many other children. Thought to have been killed by Simon Lazlo and a worshiper of Marie Martin's. Now living in the body of Liam Carmichael.

Enka—A drushkan hunt leader for the Shi and the poisoner of Gale.

Evan Tracey—Dillon Tracey's firstborn with Caroline Gerard.

Fajir—A Sun-Moon worshiper, widow, and seren (captain) of the palace guard. Formerly bonded with the deceased Halaan.

Freddie—Deceased lover of Lydia Bauer. Killed by a prog in the siege of Gale.

Halaan—Deceased Sun-Moon worshiper, Fajir's lover and partner.

Horace Adair—Telepathic and micro-psychokinetic yafanai, Simon Lazlo's lover.

Jacobs—Private in the paladins.

Jon Lea—Lieutenant in the paladins.

Jonah—The personality created by Patricia Dué to reside in the former body of Dillon Tracey.

Kora—Deceased plains dweller who was a vessel for Naos. After her mind was destroyed, her body was taken over by Patricia Dué.

Liam Carmichael—Former lieutenant in the paladins, now mayor of Gale. Linda Carmichael's son, Shiv's lover, and Cordelia Ross's best friend. Dillon Tracey now resides in his body.

Little Paul—Reach's adopted human son, an orphan from Gale.

Lydia Bauer—Prophetic yafanai. Fled Gale after the death of her lover, Freddie.

Lyshus—A drushkan child with a unique bond to Shiv.

Mamet—Plains dweller, Engali, and Samira Zaidi's lover.

The Moon, aka Meredith Marlowe—Former lieutenant on the *Atlas*, god of the Sun-Moon worshipers along with the Sun, telepathic, macro-psychokinetic, and permanently bonded telepathically with the Sun.

Natalya Conti—Deceased macro- and micro-psychokinetic yafanai. Killed when Patricia Dué took up residence in the body of Kora.

Naos—Entity who took over Patricia Dué's body during the *Atlas* accident. Macro- and micro-psychokinetic, telepathic, prophetic, and pyrokinetic. Was living in space. Crashed the *Atlas*.

Nettle—A drushkan hunt leader, Cordelia Ross's lover.

Nico—A Sun-Moon worshiper, widow, and was second in command to Fajir.

Pakesh—Former plains dweller, telepath, and macro-psychokinetic. Living in Gale.

Patricia Dué—Former copilot on the *Atlas*, macro- and micro-psychokinetic, and telepathic. Fled her former body which had been taken over by Naos and now resides in the body of Kora. She revived Dillon Tracey's old body, turning him into her servant Jonah. She also put Dillon's mind in Liam's body.

Pool—The Anushi (first) queen of the drushka, Shiv's mother, and bonded with the youngest tree of the original nine drushkan queens. She has a special bond with Cordelia Ross and Simon Lazlo.

Reach—Former drushkan ambassador to Gale, a shawness (healer), Little Paul's mother.

Samira Zaidi—Macro-psychokinetic yafanai, Simon Lazlo's best friend, and Mamet's lover.

Shiv—A young drushkan queen with a young sapling, Pool's daughter, and Liam Carmichael's lover. Has a unique bond with the child, Lyshus.

Simon Lazlo—Former botanist and biologist aboard the *Atlas*, micro-psychokinetic, Horace Adair's lover, and Samira Zaidi's best friend.

The Sun, aka Charles Christian—Former lieutenant on the *Atlas*, god of the Sun-Moon worshipers along with the Moon, telepathic, pyrokinetic, and permanently bonded telepathically with the Moon.

Wuran—Chafa (chief) of the plains dwelling Uri.

CREATURES AND TERMS

Ahya/Ahwa—Drushkan terms meaning emphatic affirmative/negative.

Boggins—Squat, swamp dwelling creatures that nearly destroyed Gale.

Breachie—a member of the satellite pantheon who wasn't part of the bridge crew.

Geavers—Very large, long-necked pack animals used by the plains dwellers.

Grelcat—Furred predators that stalk the plains.

Joora—a wading bird.

Hoshpis—Large beetle-like creatures that the Galeans use for meat, leather, and mead.

Ossors—Large, two-legged insects that the Sun-Moon worshipers and plains dwellers ride.

Pross Co.—The company that originally sent the *Atlas* into deep space.

Progs—Large, long swamp predators that nearly destroyed Gale.

Shawness(i)—Drushkan healers.

Shi—leader of all drushka.

Shi'a'na—Drushkan word for mother.

About the Author

Barbara Ann Wright writes fantasy and science fiction novels and short stories when not ranting on her blog. *The Pyramid Waltz* was one of Tor.com's Reviewer's Choice books of 2012, was a *Foreword Review* BOTYA Finalist, a Goldie finalist, and made Book Riot's 100 Must-Read Sci-Fi Fantasy Novels By Female Authors. It also won the 2013 Rainbow Award for Best Lesbian Fantasy. She's won four other Rainbow Awards and has been a Lambda Award finalist.

Books Available from Bold Strokes Books

Comrade Cowgirl by Yolanda Wallace. When cattle rancher Laramie Bowman accepts a lucrative job offer far from home, will her heart end up getting lost in translation? (978-1-63555-375-8)

Double Vision by Ellie Hart. When her cell phone rings, Giselle Cutler answers it—and finds herself speaking to a dead woman. (978-1-63555-385-7)

Inheritors of Chaos by Barbara Ann Wright. As factions splinter and reunite, will anyone survive the final showdown between gods and mortals on an alien world? (978-1-63555-294-2)

Love on Lavender Lane by Karis Walsh. Accompanied by the buzz of honeybees and the scent of lavender, Paige and Kassidy must find a way to compromise on their approach to business if they want to save Lavender Lane Farm—and find a way to make room for love along the way. (978-1-63555-286-7)

Spinning Tales by Brey Willows. When the fairy tale begins to unravel and villains are on the loose, will Maggie and Kody be able to spin a new tale? (978-1-63555-314-7)

The Do-Over by Georgia Beers. Bella Hunt has made a good life for herself and put the past behind her. But when the bane of her high school existence shows up for Bella's class on conflict resolution, the last thing they expect is to fall in love. (978-1-63555-393-2)

What Happens When by Samantha Boyette. For Molly Kennan, senior year is already an epic disaster, and falling for mysterious waitress Zia is about to make life a whole lot worse. (978-1-63555-408-3)

Wooing the Farmer by Jenny Frame. When fiercely independent modern socialite Penelope Huntingdon-Stewart and traditional country farmer Sam McQuade meet, trusting their hearts is harder than it looks. (978-1-63555-381-9)

A Chapter on Love by Laney Webber. When Jannika and Lee reunite, their instant connection feels like a gift, but neither is ready for a second chance at love. Will they finally get on the same page when it comes to love? (978-1-63555-366-6)

Drawing Down the Mist by Sheri Lewis Wohl. Everyone thinks Grand Duchess Maria Romanova died in 1918. They were almost right. (978-1-63555-341-3)

Listen by Kris Bryant. Lily Croft is inexplicably drawn to Hope D'Marco but will she have the courage to confront the consequences of her past and present colliding? (978-1-63555-318-5)

Perfect Partners by Maggie Cummings. Elite police dog trainer Sara Wright has no intention of falling in love with a coworker, until Isabel Marquez arrives at Homeland Security's Northeast Regional Training facility and Sara's good intentions start to falter. (978-1-63555-363-5)

Shut Up and Kiss Me by Julie Cannon. What better way to spend two weeks of hell in paradise than in the company of a hot, sexy woman? (978-1-63555-343-7)

Spencer's Cove by Missouri Vaun. When Foster Owen and Abigail Spencer meet they uncover a story of lives adrift, loves lost, and true love found. (978-1-63555-171-6)

Without Pretense by TJ Thomas. After living for decades hiding from the truth, can Ava learn to trust Bianca with her secrets and her heart? (978-1-63555-173-0)

Unexpected Lightning by Cass Sellars. Lightning strikes once more when Sydney and Parker fight a dangerous stranger who threatens the peace they both desperately want. (978-1-163555-276-8)

Emily's Art and Soul by Joy Argento. When Emily meets Andi Marino she thinks she's found a new best friend but Emily doesn't know that Andi is fast falling in love with her. Caught up in exploring her sexuality, will Emily see the only woman she needs is right in front of her? (978-1-63555-355-0)

Escape to Pleasure: Lesbian Travel Erotica edited by Sandy Lowe and Victoria Villasenor. Join these award-winning authors as they explore the sensual side of erotic lesbian travel. (978-1-63555-339-0)

Music City Dreamers by Robyn Nyx. Music can bring lovers together. In Music City, it can tear them apart. (978-1-63555-207-2)

Ordinary is Perfect by D. Jackson Leigh. Atlanta marketing superstar Autumn Swan's life derails when she inherits a country home, a child, and a very interesting neighbor. (978-1-63555-280-5)

Royal Court by Jenny Frame. When royal dresser Holly Weaver's passionate personality begins to melt Royal Marine Captain Quincy's icy heart, will Holly be ready for what she exposes beneath? (978-1-63555-290-4)

Strings Attached by Holly Stratimore. Success. Riches. Music. Passion. It's a life most can only dream of, but stardom comes at a cost. (978-1-63555-347-5)

The Ashford Place by Jean Copeland. When Isabelle Ashford inherits an old house in small-town Connecticut, family secrets, a shocking discovery, and an unexpected romance complicate her plan for a fast profit and a temporary stay. (978-1-63555-316-1)

Treason by Gun Brooke. Zoem Malderyn's existence is a deadly threat to everyone on Gemocon and Commander Neenja KahSandra must find a way to save the woman she loves from having to commit the ultimate sacrifice. (978-1-63555-244-7)

A Wish Upon a Star by Jeannie Levig. Erica Cooper has learned to depend on only herself, but when her new neighbor, Leslie Raymond, befriends Erica's special needs daughter, the walls protecting her heart threaten to crumble. (978-1-63555-274-4)

Answering the Call by Ali Vali. Detective Sept Savoie returns to the streets of New Orleans, as do the dead bodies from ritualistic killings, and she does everything in her power to bring them to justice while trying to keep her partner, Keegan Blanchard, safe. (978-1-63555-050-4)

Breaking Down Her Walls by Erin Zak. Could a love worth staying for be the key to breaking down Julia Finch's walls? (978-1-63555-369-7)

Exit Plans for Teenage Freaks by 'Nathan Burgoine. Cole always has a plan—especially for escaping his small-town reputation as "that kid who was kidnapped when he was four"—but when he teleports to a museum, it's time to face facts: it's possible he's a total freak after all. (978-1-63555-098-6)

Friends Without Benefits by Dena Blake. When Dex Putman gets the woman she thought she always wanted, she soon wonders if it's really love after all. (978-1-63555-349-9)

Invalid Evidence by Stevie Mikayne. Private Investigator Jil Kidd is called away to investigate a possible killer whale, just when her partner Jess needs her most. (978-1-63555-307-9)

Pursuit of Happiness by Carsen Taite. When attorney Stevie Palmer's client reveals a scandal that could derail Senator Meredith Mitchell's presidential bid, their chance at love may be collateral damage. (978-1-63555-044-3)

Seascape by Karis Walsh. Marine biologist Tess Hansen returns to Washington's isolated northern coast where she struggles to adjust to small-town living while courting an endowment for her orca research center from Brittany James. (978-1-63555-079-5)

Second in Command by VK Powell. Jazz Perry's life is disrupted and her career jeopardized when she becomes personally involved with the case of an abandoned child and the child's competent but strict social worker, Emory Blake. (978-1-63555-185-3)

Taking Chances by Erin McKenzie. When Valerie Cruz and Paige Wellington clash over what's in the best interest of the children in Valerie's care, the children may be the ones who teach them it's worth taking chances for love. (978-1-63555-209-6)

All of Me by Emily Smith. When chief surgical resident Galen Burgess meets her new intern, Rowan Duncan, she may finally discover that doing what you've always done will only give you what you've always had. (978-1-63555-321-5)

As the Crow Flies by Karen F. Williams. Romance seems to be blooming all around, but problems arise when a restless ghost emerges from the ether to roam the dark corners of this haunting tale. (978-1-63555-285-0)

Both Ways by Ileandra Young. SPEAR agent Danika Karson races to protect the city from a supernatural threat and must rely on the woman she's trained to despise: Rayne, an achingly beautiful vampire. (978-1-63555-298-0)

Calendar Girl by Georgia Beers. Forced to work together, Addison Fairchild and Kate Cooper discover that opposites really do attract. (978-1-63555-333-8)

Lovebirds by Lisa Moreau. Two women from different worlds collide in a small California mountain town, each with a mission that doesn't include falling in love. (978-1-63555-213-3)

Media Darling by Fiona Riley. Can Hollywood bad girl Emerson and reluctant celebrity gossip reporter Hayley work together to make each other's dreams come true? Or will Emerson's secrets ruin not one career, but two? (978-1-63555-278-2)

Stroke of Fate by Renee Roman. Can Sean Moore live up to her reputation and save Jade Rivers from the stalker determined to end Jade's career and, ultimately, her life? (978-1-63555-62-4)

The Rise of the Resistance by Jackie D. The soul of America has been lost for almost a century. A few people may be the difference between a phoenix rising to save the masses or permanent destruction. (978-1-63555-259-1)

The Sex Therapist Next Door by Meghan O'Brien. At the intersection of sex and intimacy, anything is possible. Even love. (978-1-63555-296-6)

Unforgettable by Elle Spencer. When one night changes a lifetime… Two romance novellas from best-selling author Elle Spencer. (978-1-63555-429-8)

www.ingramcontent.com/pod-product-compliance
Lightning Source LLC
Chambersburg PA
CBHW021950010726
47494CB00003B/676